FLASHPOINT

Also by Lynn S. Hightower

Satan's Lambs

FLASHPOINT

LYNN S. HIGHTOWER

HarperCollins*Publishers*

HarperCollins books may be purchased for educational, business, or sales promotional use. For information please write: Special Markets Department, HarperCollins Publishers, Inc., 10 East 53rd Street, New York, NY 10022.

FIRST EDITION

Designed by Caitlin Daniels

Library of Congress Cataloging-in-Publication Data

Hightower, Lynn S.
    Flashpoint / Lynn S. Hightower. — 1st ed.
        p.   cm.
    ISBN 0-06-017648-2
    I. Title.
PS3558.I372F58   1995
813'.54—dc20   95-498

95 96 97 98 99 ❖/RRD 10 9 8 7 6 5 4 3 2 1

For Matt Bialer, world's best agent.

ACKNOWLEDGMENTS

I had a lot of help on this one.

My thanks to Michael Miller, primary school teacher, for sharing insight and experience, and whose perception and wit made for an entertaining interview.

I was made very welcome by the Homicide and Crime Scene Units of the Cincinnati Police Department. My thanks to Police Specialist Mike O'Brien, who went out of his way to help and answer my questions, and to Police Specialist Jim Murray, Police Specialist Diane Arnold, Community Services Police Specialist Kim Moreno, and Police Chief Michael Snowden.

My sincere thanks to Detective Maria Neal, of the Lexington Police Department's Bureau of Investigation. She went out of her way to answer my questions and share insight and expertise.

My thanks to Dr. George Nichols, of the Louisville coroner's office, for putting up with my fascination with and questions about his work. I did appreciate your time and trouble.

To Detective David A. Green, of the Jefferson County Police Department's Arson Unit, even if you did say you'd be keeping an eye on me. And to Arson Investigator Gary Nolan.

To my favorite lawyer, Jim Lyon, who never tires of my constant questions, scenarios, and what-ifs.

To another favorite lawyer, C. William Swinford, who was kind to me, and represented me well.

To talented artist and good pal Steve Sawyer, for insight, discussions, and good coffee.

To Anthony Smallwood, world's best dancer, who helped Sonora with her two-step.

To Ron Balcom, of Balcom Investigative Services, for early research and last-minute questions.

To my good buddy and fellow mystery writer, Taylor McCafferty, who is always up for forensic "girltalk," and a trip to the morgue on our way to lunch. My phone bills are your fault.

To Carolyn Marino, my terrific editor, whose judgment and instinct are always dead-on, and who is a pleasure to work with.

My thanks to Allstate agent Rebecca Turner, Jonathan Edwards, Jonathan Amherst, and Physician's Assistant Lynn Hanna, who always wants to know if I'm mad at anybody before she gives me technical details on anything medical and violent.

And to my agent Matt Bialer, who told me to write this book, and didn't let up till I got it right.

FLASHPOINT

FLASH POINT: the temperature at which vapor from a
flammable substance will ignite.
                    —*World Book Dictionary*, Volume One

Sonora was not asleep when the call came in. She was curled
sideways, a blanket over her head, vaguely aware of the wind
blowing the phone cables in tandem against the back wall of the
house. She caught the bedside phone on the second ring, thinking
it was going to be a bad one. This time of night, people meant
business.

"Homicide. Blair."

"Blair, you always answer your phone like you're at work?"

"Only when it's you, Sergeant. Anyway, Sam's on call, not me."
She rubbed the back of her neck. Her head ached.

There was a pause. "You're catching it together. It's a nasty one,
Sonora. Guy burned up in his car."

Sonora turned on the bedside lamp. The bulb flared and went
out. "Sounds like insurance fraud getting out of hand. Why not let
arson catch it?"

"Arson called us. Vic, name of Daniels, Mark, handcuffed to the
steering wheel of his car, and doused with accelerant."

Sonora winced. "Sounds pointed. Where?"

"Mount Airy Forest. Couple miles in, be a uniform there to
direct. Delarosa's headed out to the scene now, E.A.T. four-fifty."

Sonora looked at her watch. Four-twenty A.M.

"Vic's still alive, unconscious, but he may come to, and if so, it
might not be for long. He's over at University, which is where I
want you. See if he comes around any, maybe even get a deathbed
statement. Could be a gay thing, you know? Those are the usual

ones in the park, weeknights this time of year. Get him to spill who done it. Any luck, we can clear the books by morning."

"It is morning."

"Do it right, Blair."

Sonora dressed quickly—sliding on a pair of black cotton trousers that satisfied the dress code, barely. She ran a pick through the tangles of her hair, took a glance in the mirror, and gave up. Too curly, too slept on. Definitely a bad hair day. She gathered the ends back and slipped them through a black velvet band. Her eyes were dark shadowed and red rimmed. She wished she had a moment for the miracle of makeup, but if Daniels was just hanging on, she didn't have time. And he wasn't likely to complain.

She turned on the hall light and peeped in at the kids. Both sleeping soundly. She maneuvered through the maze of laundry, clean and dirty, filed on the floor in an obscure system only her son understood. He was sleeping at the wrong end of the bed, a booklet on *Advanced Dungeons and Dragons* splayed on the pillow.

"Tim?"

His eyes flickered open, then closed. Asleep, he looked younger than thirteen, fine black hair cropped short.

"Come on, Tim, wake up."

He sat up suddenly, eyes wide and confused.

"Got to go to work, hon, sorry. I'll leave you locked up, but keep an ear out for your sister, okay?"

He nodded, blinking painfully, too young and too tired to be wakened in the middle of the night.

"What time is it?" he said.

"After four. You got a while to sleep. Be sure and get up with the alarm. You'll have to get Heather off to school."

"'Kay. Be careful, Mom. Load your gun." He slumped back down on the bed, turning his back on the bright shaft of light from the hallway.

Sonora left his door open and went to her daughter's bedroom. An explosion of nude Barbie dolls, some of them headless, littered the dingy yellow carpet. Sonora made her way to the bed, noting the neat pile of clothes and shoes carefully laid out in the stuffed animal bin. It was September, just a few weeks into the school year, and the excitement of first grade had yet to wear off.

A reddish blond dog groaned and lifted his head from the pillow where he'd been sleeping next to the tiny, black-haired girl. He was a big dog, three legged, thick fur coat, wise brown eyes.

Sonora patted his head. "Guard, Clampett."

The dog wagged his tail. Sonora noticed three cotton hair holders beside her daughter's lavender tennis shoes. That meant braids, only Mommy wouldn't be around to fix them.

Sonora grimaced. "Thank you, I *will* have some guilt with my homicide."

She kissed her daughter's soft plump cheek, double-checked the house locks and alarms, and left.

It was raining again, softly now, the windshield wipers doing a second-rate job. Sonora squinted through the fogged windshield and winced at the glare of headlights on the rain-slick road. Her night vision wasn't what it should be.

University Hospital was nestled amid scaffolding, piles of dirt, stacks of lumber. Health care, at least, was booming. Sonora passed a sign that said MESNER CONSTRUCTION.

The emergency entrance was brightly lit, two ambulances parked under the overhang, a smattering of patrol cars in the circle drive. The parking structure was dark. Sonora scraped by the ambulances and parked on the side of the road. She reached into the glove compartment for a flowered tie that didn't exactly match her shirt, but at least didn't clash, slid the loosely knotted loop over her head, and tucked the back band under the collar of her tailored shirt. The blazer lying on the backseat was wrinkled, but Sonora decided it would pass. She locked her car.

Inside, the air was thick with the smell of hospital and damp cops, both overlaid with a tangible odor of smoke. The muted crackle and mutter of too many police radios was punctuated by the ding of very slow elevators. An ambulance crew was bringing a stretcher through, and Sonora stepped sideways, moving away from the path of a medic holding an IV packet. A trail of blood droplets marked their route.

Sonora's vision blurred, and she stopped for a minute to rub her eyes.

"Specialist Blair?"

The patrolman at her elbow couldn't have been more than twenty-two or twenty-three. His uniform was stained with sweat and soot.

"I'm Finch. Captain Burke said I should check in with you. I responded to the scene right after Kyle. He's burned pretty bad."

"Kyle?"

"Kyle Minner, Officer Minner. He got there just before I did."

Sonora put a hand on his arm. "You see anybody? Hear a car pull away?"

The patrolman swallowed. "Don't know. It was . . . the guy was screaming and his hair was burning. I didn't see anything but him."

"Okay, you did good. You hurt?"

"No ma'am."

"How bad's Minner?"

Finch swallowed. "I don't know."

"I'll ask after him and let you know. What can you tell me about the vic? Daniels, right?"

"Car's registered to a Keaton Daniels, victim is his brother, Mark. College student, twenty-two years old, lives in Kentucky. Up for a visit. Evidently borrowed his brother's car."

"So what happened?"

"Dispatch got an anonymous call from somebody in the park. Said something funny was going on. I thought it was teenagers parking or something. By the time I got there it was burning good. The guy was screaming, sounding, God, unreal. Minner was working at that park station, typing up a report, so he's like a minute away. So he's there ahead of me, grabbing the door handle of the car. He jerks his hands back and the skin comes right off 'em. Then he reaches in through the driver's window and grabs the guy, and starts pulling him out. But it . . . he . . . Minner yells something about handcuffs. He told me before the ambulance came, this guy Daniels was handcuffed to the steering wheel. Anyway, Officer Minner disengages Daniels from the cuffs—"

"*Disengages* Daniels from the cuffs?"

Finch's eyes seemed glittery. "Guy's hands are almost burned off. It's like he snagged for a minute, then slid right on through."

Sonora squinted her eyes.

"It was the only way, the only chance of getting him out of there. So he's burning, Minner's burning, they're rolling. I've got my jacket on, so I throw it over the both of them and smother the flames."

"You sure you're okay?"

"Just singed my eyebrows a little. Minner's really hurt. And the vic, Daniels, he's charred."

"Did you ride over with them in the ambulance?"

"Yes ma'am."

"He say anything?"

"He was out. But he was screaming when I got there. Sounded like 'key' or something."

"Key?"

Finch shrugged.

"That's all?"

The patrolman nodded.

"You did good," Sonora told him. "You want to go home?"

"I'd like to stay around and see how Kyle's doing. I'm also supposed to tell you that O'Connor brought in Daniels's next of kin. The brother." Finch inclined his head toward a man who stood in the shadows of the hallway, watching them.

Sonora had an impression of height, solid presence, a face pale under heavy five-o'clock shadow.

"Anybody talked to a doctor?"

"Guy came out of emergency and talked to the brother."

"Hear what he said?"

"Just that they were very concerned with Mark's condition, and were doing all they could."

"Shit. Daniels won't make it then. They're already hanging the crepe."

"Ma'am?"

"Never mind. Get somebody to take the brother a cup of coffee, looks like he could use it. Have one yourself." Sonora headed past the plastic couches and went through the swing doors into emergency.

2

Inside the ER, the lights were bright enough to be energizing. Sonora spotted a black woman in blue cotton pants and top, hospital issue, her hair back in a cap, feet encased in plastic booties.

"Gracie! Just the woman I want."

"You here about the burn guy?" Gracie took Sonora's arm and pulled her out of the way of a technician rolling an IV pole.

"How's he doing?"

Gracie pointed to a cubicle, white curtains billowing. "They called Farrow over from Shriners. Should be here any minute, but even that may be too late. ET gave him thiosulfate to detox, but his blood gases are the worst. He's on the respirator—he won't be talking to you."

"Yes or no questions?"

Gracie narrowed her eyes. "He's conscious. Give it a try."

She led Sonora past a man pushing a steel cart that seemed to be extraordinarily heavy. They went in from the side where the curtains split. Sonora frowned. The ER doctor was Malden. Malden didn't like her.

"Okay?" she asked.

He gave her barely a glance but didn't say no. She hung over Gracie's shoulder.

Mark Daniels was conscious, which, Sonora thought as they worked him over, was her good luck and his bad. She saw death in his eyes. She was vaguely aware of the doctors and technicians, hands busy as they invaded Daniels with the nightmare of medical technology. The air was thick with the smell of smoke and the sound of jargon—hypovolemic shock, Ringer's solution, central venous pressure. Someone was gauging the extent of the burns— 18 percent, anterior trunk—the tally continued. Hypothermia, body temp seventy-eight degrees. Cardiac arrhythmia. Auscultate the lungs.

Daniels's scalp was white and hairless, with a look of pliability that contrasted with the charred and inelastic surface of his chest, arms, and neck. His face was ravaged, the lips melted and smeared. One eye was black socketed, and the right ear had the crumpled look of charred foil.

Nothing left of the right hand. Sonora saw the whiteness of bone. The left hand had a blackened lump of flesh at the end, like an infant's curled fist.

Sonora turned on her recorder. "Mr. Daniels, I'm Specialist Sonora Blair, Cincinnati Police."

He moved his head. She said it again and connected suddenly with the good eye. He focused on her face, and Sonora had the odd sensation that she and Daniels were worlds away from the doctors, the technicians, the bright, intrusive lights.

"I'm going to ask you some questions about your assailant. Mr. Daniels? Shake your head yes or no. Okay? You with me here?"

He nodded his head, smearing stickiness on the white sheet. The thick tube of the respirator parted the melted lips, expanded and deflated the scorched lungs.

"Did . . . do you know your assailant?"

Daniels did not respond, but his eyes were locked with hers. He was thinking. He nodded, finally.

"Had you known him long?"

Daniels shook his head.

"Not long?"

He shook his head. Kept shaking it.

"Met him tonight?"

Nodded his head, then turned it from side to side. Sonora wondered if he was connecting. But the awareness was there, in the eyes. Something he was trying to tell her. She frowned, thought about it.

Ground zero, she thought. "Man or woman. Mr. Daniels, was your assailant a man?"

The head shake. Vigorous. Not a man.

Wife, Sonora thought. Ex-wife. Girlfriend.

"Your assailant was a woman?"

Sonora stepped to one side, out of the doctor's way. But she caught his response. "Witness indicates the assailant was a woman," she said for the benefit of the recorder. "Someone you know?"

Back to that again. No.

"Wife?" No. "Girlfriend?" No. "Just pick her up tonight?"

That was it. A stranger.

He was fading on her. "Young?" she asked. "Under thirty?"

He focused again, aware and intent, in spite of the chaos of the ER, the sensory overload. Sonora had a sudden strong feeling that he wanted her to touch him.

She was afraid to. Afraid she would cause pain, infection, the wrath of the doctors.

Sonora tried to remember the rest of her questions. Daniels watched her, his eyes large and lidless. The fire had stripped him to almost embryonic form.

Sonora laid two fingers on the blackened flesh of his arm and thought she saw some kind of acknowledgment in his eyes. Likely her imagination.

Questions, she thought. Get this man's killer.

"Young?" she asked again. "Under thirty?"

He hesitated. Nodded.

"Black?"

No.

"White?"

Yes.

"Prostitute?"

Hesitation. No.

Young. White. Not a prostitute. Maybe.

"Black hair?"

No.

"Blond?"

Yes. Definite.

"Eyes," Sonora said. "Blue?"

He was going on her.

"Brown?"

Something about him changed. An alarm went off, the doctor shouted clear. Sonora stepped away from the table and ducked out from under the white curtains. She knew without looking that the EKG monitor would be flat.

3

Officer Finch stood in a hushed circle of uniformed cops, telling and retelling his story, answering questions. Sonora paused but kept walking. Talking would be therapeutic, at least, and Finch was young to be racking up nightmares. They seemed to be hiring them right out of the nursery.

There'd be no playing it close on this one. The cops wouldn't talk to civilians, but the hospital people would. They were the worst, even ahead of lawyers. Putting something in a medical record was worse than telling Oprah and Phil, though not as bad as faxing Geraldo.

"Specialist Blair!"

Sonora glanced sideways. Channel 81's Tracy Vandemeer moved close, trailed by cameras. No other press around. At the crime scene, Sonora thought. It was where she wanted to be. She waved a repressive hand at the camera. "Tracy, you're way too early here. Not before makeup, please."

Tracy Vandemeer blinked. She herself had had ample time, though less reason, to do her own makeup. She wore a crisp red blouse, silk, and a high-waisted Lycra skirt that could be worn only by a woman who was a stranger to childbirth and chocolate.

"Specialist Blair, can you give us the identity of the—"

"Come on, Tracy, you know better. We'll have the release out in a few hours. Any questions have to go through my sergeant."

Vandemeer smiled. "Come on, Sonora. I've got deadlines."

"Going to interrupt the farm report with a special bulletin?"

Vandemeer's smile faded, and Sonora remembered a beat too

late that Tracy had started out on the 6 A.M. broadcast, covering burley and corn crops.

"For that remark, Sonora, we'll be filming you from your bad side."

"What? Me walking in and out of the ER is news?"

"It is if you don't give me anything else."

"Homicide cop forgets to brush hair. Don't forget to call CNN."

Tracy Vandemeer let the microphone relax, eyes roving, surveying the huddle of cops in the corner. Sonora took advantage of the lapse of attention to move away. Vandemeer would have no luck with the boy's club.

Sonora scanned the room, looking for hospital security. Saw the brother, shoulder against the wall in the hallway. It struck her that hers was the last face Mark Daniels had seen.

Daniels took a sip from a cup of coffee, his free hand jammed deeply into the pocket of his coat. Moisture glistened on the navy blue raincoat that hung open and unbuttoned, the cloth belt trailing the floor. Behind him, a door stood open. The sign on the door said FAMILY CONSULTATION/CHAPLAIN.

Sonora looked him over carefully as she drew close, checking for tears in the white dress shirt, soot on the shoes and beige khakis. She took a breath, wondering if he'd reek of smoke. He didn't. But she wished he'd lose the raincoat. No telling what might be under it.

Sonora smiled and put on the mom-voice. "Your coat's wet. Probably ought to get it off."

The man's eyes were glazed, but they focused on her suddenly, intensely. He had a raw, pained look she knew only too well. It was a look that begged for a miracle, for peace of heart. It was a look she saw in her dreams.

"Your coat?"

He took it off slowly and draped it over his arm. The white cotton shirt was wrinkled but clean. If this guy was involved with the killing, he'd had time to change clothes.

No stone unturned, Sonora thought. She held out a hand.

"Specialist Sonora Blair, Cincinnati Police Department."

He met her eyes steadily and took her hand, holding tightly. He had brown eyes, and he looked intelligent, younger than she had first supposed. He had black hair, thick and curly.

"Keaton Daniels."

Keaton, Sonora thought. Key? Mark had been screaming "key" when Officer Minner had pulled him from the burning car.

"How is Mark?"

His voice was deep, shadowed with fear. He still had her hand, though she didn't think he realized it. The automatic doors swooshed open, and Sonora glanced over her shoulder.

Another news team, idling in the restricted lane out front, a guy in blue jeans and an old army jacket arguing with a uniform.

Sonora guided Daniels into the consultation room.

Inside was an oasis of worn green carpet, a brown vinyl love seat, and a well-padded easy chair. Sonora steered Daniels into the chair, for her money, the best seat in the house for comfort and a moment of peace.

"Sit down, Mr. Daniels. Be back in a minute."

She slipped into the hallway and motioned to a uniform, checking his name tag.

"O'Connor? Looks like you got plenty of help out here." She waved a hand toward the lobby. "Channel Twenty-six just arrived in their action Pinto, and there's never just one ant at the picnic. Keep them *in* the waiting room. I don't want anybody sneaking into the ER. Tracy and her bunch are okay, but watch the cameraman from Twenty-six. See that guy over there in the suit? Norris Weber, hospital security. Used to be one of us, retired. Coordinate with him. Victim's brother is in the consultation room—I don't want him bothered. Got all that?"

"Yes ma'am."

"Thank God for you."

Sonora headed back toward the ER to double-check with Gracie. It would be unkind to break the bad news to Keaton Daniels if his brother had been revived.

The door to the consultation room was shut. Sonora paused to put a fresh tape in her recorder, then pushed the door open gently.

Keaton Daniels sat on the edge of the easy chair. He'd put the raincoat back on, though it was hot in the tiny room.

"Mr. Daniels?"

"Yes?" His look managed to be both wary and stunned.

"Sorry, didn't mean to leave you quite so long."

"How's Mark? Any chance of me getting to see him?"

The vinyl love seat made squeaking noises as Sonora sat down. Her knees touched Daniels's, and she moved to one side. She checked his left hand. Wedding band.

"Is there someone I can call to be with you? Your wife?"

Keaton Daniels looked away suddenly, his eyes on the floor. "No, thank you."

"A friend maybe?"

Keaton looked at her. "My wife and I are separated. I can call a friend later."

Sonora nodded and leaned toward him.

"Are you a detective?" he asked suddenly.

"Yes."

"I thought my brother was in a car accident. You—when you introduced yourself, you said specialist."

"Specialist is the current jargon—a union thing. I'm a homicide detective, Mr. Daniels. They call me for any suspicious dea—circumstances."

He swallowed. "Suspicious—"

"I'm very sorry to have to tell you that your brother Mark is dead."

He had known it was coming, but still he was stunned. His shoulders sagged, and he cleared his throat. He fought it, but the tears would come. Sonora knew it. He knew it.

"Tell me." The words were an effort. He caught his lip between his teeth. "Tell me what happened."

"We're still trying to piece it together. The police and the fire department were dispatched to a burning vehicle. Your brother was inside. We think the fire was deliberately set."

Keaton Daniels looked at her. A peculiar, puzzled look. The tears came, coursing down his rough, unshaven cheeks, his eyes going puffy and red.

Sonora touched his hand. "Would you like some time? Can I call that friend?"

He shook his head slowly, and Sonora was reminded of Mark Daniels's white sluglike head trailing fluid across the sheet. She wondered what he'd looked like before—if he'd been handsome, like his brother.

"I need to ask you a few quick questions, the sooner the better. But if you need—"

"Go ahead."

"You're sure?"

"Go ahead."

A moment passed. Sonora fiddled with the recorder.

"Mr. Daniels, did you talk to Mark today? See him today?"

He clutched the knees of his pants. "Yes. He's up visiting. We had supper. Then he dropped me off, and went back out."

"Any idea where he went?"

"A place called Cujo's. Cujo's Café-Bar."

"Up in the Mount Adams area?"

"Yes."

Sonora nodded. "I know it. You didn't go with him?"

"I had to get some things put together for work. A lot of cutting and pasting stuff. Not hard, but time-consuming. I offered to let Mark help me with it but he was . . . bored. And I was going to go to bed early anyway. I teach. I'm a teacher. So we had some supper and he decided to go on to Cujo's and get a beer or something."

"By himself?"

"Yes."

"In your car?"

"He came up with a friend, someone from school. He's a student at the University of Kentucky. The friend dropped him off, and I was going to drive him home on the weekend. We were going to stop and see our mother." He looked at the floor, then back up to Sonora. "I need to call her, or should I wait till morning? Let her sleep?"

"Call her tonight. Otherwise she'll feel slighted. Unless—is she unwell?"

"Not exactly."

Sonora was mildly interested, made a mental note to pursue it. "This bar, this Cujo's. Is it more a bar or more a café?"

"More bar."

"You go there yourself?"

"Sometimes. For a while I was going there a lot. Then I stopped."

"I'm not sure I follow."

Daniels grimaced. "My wife and I are separated. For a while, I was going out a lot at night. Bars and stuff. Cujo's a lot. But that gets old. Plus, I really had to buckle down to my work. Hard to face the kids with a hangover every morning. Not to mention the expense, on a teacher's salary."

"What age do you teach?"

"I teach a primary program. Grades one and two."

"Elementary school?"

Her surprise annoyed him. "That's where they teach grades one and two."

Sonora let it pass. "Where'd you go for dinner?"

"LaRosa's. We split a pizza."

"Beer at dinner?"

Daniels narrowed his eyes. "I had a Sprite. Mark had Dr. Pepper."

"Any chance Mark was meeting up with some friends?"

"I don't think so. He didn't know anybody here."

"How about the one that dropped him off?"

"On his way to Dayton, far as I know."

"His? Male?"

"Yeah. Caldwell, Carter Caldwell." He rubbed a hand over his jaw. "Look, I don't understand this. Did something happen at the bar?"

"Mr. Daniels, at this point I just don't know. I know it sounds trite, but does you brother have any enemies? Bad enemies?"

"Enemies? Mark? He's a college kid, Detective. And a nice one. No drugs, no steroids. He liked to party—"

"Drink a lot?"

He shrugged. "It's a stage. A lot of kids go through it."

Sonora nodded, keeping her face noncommittal, notching possible alcohol problem in her mind.

"He was just a kid." The tears flowed freely now. "Twenty-two. He was too young and too sweet to have enemies."

"Lot of girlfriends?"

"He has a girlfriend in Lexington. They've been steady now for two years."

"She the only one?"

"Pretty much. Lots of friend girls, if you see what I mean. But not to date."

"Popular?" Sonora asked.

Keaton Daniels nodded.

"Have you ever known him to pick up a girl in a bar?"

"No."

"Come on, think about it."

"I don't think so. Not here, in a strange town. He was twenty-two. And young for his age."

"Your brother ever talk about going to a prostitute? Maybe joke about it? Ask your advice?"

The tears dried. Daniels sat forward in his seat.

"Just what's going on here?"

Sonora leaned back. "Mr. Daniels, your brother was murdered tonight. I have to cover every angle, every possibility. Help me out on it."

"How could he burn up in the car? Did it wreck or something? Was he unconscious?"

"Like I said, Mr. Daniels, we're still—"

"For God's sake, Detective." His grip on her arm was firm to the point of being painful. He stood up and leaned over her, hands clenching the arms of the love seat. "What exactly did they . . . whoever this was. What did they do to him?"

"Mr.—"

"*Please*. Tell me something."

She stood up, forcing him backward. He stayed close, his face no more than an inch from hers. Not going to give ground.

"Mr. Daniels, sit down, okay?"

She could smell the powdery scent of his bath soap, the coffee on his breath. They stayed eye to eye for a long moment.

"Please sit down, Mr. Daniels. I'll tell you everything that I can. I have a brother, okay?"

He sat back down, coat tightening across the broad shoulders.

Sonora sat across from him, laid a hand on his arm, felt him tremble. "I don't have the details, I haven't been to the scene. Mark was found in your car in Mount Airy Forest, handcuffed to the steering wheel. He'd been deliberately doused with accelerant and set on fire."

"Sweet Jesus God."

"Put your head between your knees."

"I don't—"

"Humor me. Please."

He resisted, just for a moment, then let her guide his head down.

Good going, Blair, she thought. Please explain to the sergeant how you managed to kill off the victim's brother.

"Okay?"

"Yeah, okay."

He sat up slowly, leaned back in his seat. She looked at his face, chalk white.

"I need some time."

"Of course."

"Can I . . . Can I go home, to my wife's? For a while?"

"I'll have someone drive you."

"Thanks."

"Stay put. I'll get—"

Daniels got up slowly, hand against the wall for support.

"Steady," Sonora said, and took his arm.

4

It was daylight when Sonora left the hospital. The sky was still grimy, but the rain had stopped. She was driving too fast, and the tires on her Nissan sprayed water. She tapped the brakes as the car picked up speed moving down the steep hill. Sonora was vaguely aware she'd just squeaked through on a yellow light.

In her mind, she saw Mark Daniels under the harsh lights and torturous ministrations of the ER.

It was foggy, and Sonora snapped on the headlights. Her radio sputtered the usual comforting background of static. She was never quite alone. She glanced at her watch, thinking that the kids would be waking up now, getting ready for school.

She turned right onto Colerain. A dark wall of trees lined the left-hand side of the road—Mount Airy Forest. Sonora noted pedestrian entrances, streetlights on Colerain, none in the forest. She passed Saint Anthony's shrine. The main entrance to the forest was blocked by police cars. Sonora showed her ID and was waved past. The narrow two-lane road had dried in patches, giving the asphalt a speckled look.

Three wooden signs, the bottom one crooked, let her know that the speed limit was twenty-five, wheeled vehicles were restricted to paved roads, and park hours were from 6 A.M. to 10 P.M. She was cautioned to watch for bicycles, warned not to park off the roadway, informed that the dog leash law was enforced.

Have fun, kids, Sonora thought.

She passed a battered trailer that was labeled TOOL SHED. The trees here were black oak, birch, and beech. She saw a sign for Oak Ridge Lodge and knew she was getting close.

The Crime Scene Unit's van was half on the grass, half on the road. The guys—wearing blue jumpsuits, POLICE stenciled on the back, heavy fire boots on their feet—were giving it the once-over. She parked behind the bronze department-issue Ford Taurus that she shared with her partner, fished in the glove compartment for new cassette tapes, notebook, investigation reports.

She liked to approach the scene on foot. Move in and focus. She wandered past the fire chief's wagon, the patrol cars. She thought of Mark Daniels. Why had he come out here? It was a long way from Cujo's and trendy Mount Adams. A longer way from Kentucky.

She put a new tape in the recorder as she walked, crumpling the cellophane wrapper and stuffing it into her jacket pocket.

How had the killer left the scene? On foot? Had she planned it well enough to have a car waiting? Did she have an accomplice? Where did she get the accelerant? What kind of woman handcuffed a twenty-two-year-old boy to a steering wheel and lit a match?

The CS technicians were well into the work, and Sonora, usually an hour ahead of the van, had the depressed feeling of someone who's missed the party.

She counted heads. Sergeant. Coroner. A lot of uniforms.

"Sonora?"

She climbed indelicately over the band of yellow tape and headed for a broad-shouldered, solidly built man with dark, fine brown hair, side-parted, that fell into his eyes. The eyes were blue, with crinkles around the edges, caused in equal parts by laughter and worry. His complexion was swarthy, and he had a boyish look about him. People always thought he was younger than he was, and women tried to feed him.

He was the kind of guy who watched football games, the kind of guy you'd call if you heard a noise late at night—breathtakingly normal in a world full of nuts. He and Sonora had been partners for five years.

"Hey, Sam."

"'Bout time you got out here, girl."

"You smell like smoke."

"You look like hell. How is he?"

Sonora grimaced.

"Dead, huh?"

She nodded. "Twenty-two-year-old college kid from Kentucky. Your neck of the woods. Probably one of your cousins. You're all related down there, aren't you?"

"He talk to you?"

"Had to do it around a respirator. Yes or no questions."

Sam nodded. Looking grim.

"Killer was a woman," Sonora said.

"*No* shit?"

"Blond, I think brown eyes, but he died on me there, so I'm not sure. Young, between twenty-five and thirty."

"Prostitute?"

"Said not. If I got this straight, he met her last night. Probably in a bar. The brother said he was on his way to Cujo's when they split."

Sam frowned. "Why'd they separate?"

"Brother had to go to work early."

"Cujo's, huh?"

"Place in Mount Adams."

"La-di-da."

"Hey. Not every bar has to be full of cowboys."

"Don't let your brother hear you say that."

Sonora gave him a half smile.

"Here, Mickey, give her the grand tour."

A short man, arms thickly muscled, came out from under the blackened hood of the car. Sonora looked in the side window at the gutted interior of what used to be a Cutlass.

"Rolling firetrap, otherwise known as an automobile." Mickey wore a blue jacket that said ARSON on the back, heavy fire boots on his feet.

Sonora took a speculative sniff. "Know what the accelerant was?"

"Gasoline. We'll test it again in the lab. I got a sample." He pointed to a charred piece of fabric under the gas pedal that had been peeled up, exposing ridges in the metal of the floorboard. "Had some liquid accumulate, in the grooves there, so we can back it in court. Fire burned hot, and the explosion busted the windshield front and back."

"Explosion?"

"Sure. Gasoline, right? Fire melted the glass. But everything inside's plastic, which means petroleum, which means inferno. Pretty good roast."

"God. Is that what I smell?"

Sam said, "Burnt flesh. Pretty distinctive."

Sonora thought of the frozen sirloin tip in her freezer at home. Maybe it would stay there awhile.

Mickey moved to the front of the car, walking like it hurt. He'd been a fireman on the hose until he'd fallen in a hole fighting a fire after dark, slipping a disk in his back. Most of the firemen Sonora knew didn't get hurt fighting the fires; they just creamed their backs lugging equipment, or falling down in the dark.

Mickey pointed under the hood. His gloves were thick, soot stained.

"I double-checked the fuel pump, carburetor, wiring. Pretty clear."

Sonora wondered what was clear.

"Fan belt's burned, we got melted lead from the radiator." He looked up at her. "I see under the hood fascinates you not."

"It all fascinates me," Sonora said.

"Don't take it personal. She looks grumpy because her tummy hurts," Sam said.

Mickey rubbed his eye with the back of his arm. "Still plenty of gas in the tank."

"Didn't it burn in the fire?" Sonora said.

Sam grinned. "I said the same thing."

"Gasoline isn't all that flammable," Mickey said. "It's a stupid thing to set fires with. Volatile. Got to get the oxygen mix right or it can blow up in your face. Most of the arsonists I've seen who use gasoline usually blow themselves to pieces. On the other hand, you can throw a match in a puddle of gasoline and get nothing. There's better things to use."

"Thanks for the tip," Sonora said.

"Fire didn't really get to the tank. And unlike what you see on TV, the tank isn't necessarily going to explode. 'Less you're driving a Pinto or being filmed by NBC."

"You think the killer could have used the gas in the tank to start the fire?"

"I'm saying it's a good possibility. Plenty of gas there. And thing is, we got melted plastic on the ground right by the gas tank. I'm thinking tubing for a siphon." Sonora looked at Sam.

Mickey waved a hand. "Tell you what else. We got residue inside and ash outside of some kind of rope or clothesline."

"Tell me you've got a knot."

Sam shook his head. "We don't got a knot."

"Looks like he used it as a wick, lit it from outside the car, had it tied somewhere on the driver's side—"

"Tied to Daniels," Sam said.

Mickey nodded. "Makes sense." He pointed to the melted steering wheel. "Fire started there. See the bulb in the overhead light?"

Sonora looked up. The bulb was miraculously intact. The bottom had melted to a point that aimed toward the driver's side. She stared at it a long moment, but Mickey was impatient, directing her attention to the mangled springs on the driver's side of the car.

"Point of origin. Burned the longest and hottest right there. See that?"

Two gnarled, fused loops of metal hung from the wadded steering wheel.

"Handcuffs, carbonized now."

Sonora bit her lip. Thought of Mark Daniels's hands turned to ash, the gnarled infant fist, the white of bone.

"You sure enough to prove it to a jury?"

"Easy. You come to the scene and see what is. I see what was."

"Everything on video?"

"SOP."

Sonora looked at the mess of ash and foam in the front of the car. "Too bad you guys always fuck up the scene."

"Yeah, firefighters are such bastards. Think their job is to put the fire out."

Sam put a cigarette in his mouth, studying the inside of the car with a quiet focus that worked wonders in the interrogation room as well as on women.

Sonora folded her arms, faced Mickey. "By the way. You've been saying he. It's she."

Mickey looked at her. "A *woman* did this?"

"Surprised, huh?"

He shrugged. "As I think about it, no. I been married long enough."

Sam took the unlit cigarette from his mouth and rolled it between thick, callused fingers.

"Don't smoke in my crime scene," Sonora said.

"*Your* crime scene? I haven't lit it, Sonora, I'm just tasting the tobacco. There's the sergeant. Looks like you're wanted, girl."

"Wait a second. Terry?"

A woman in a jumpsuit came out of the brush, about a hundred yards from the car. She had long black hair, carelessly tied back, broad cheekbones that bespoke American Indian descent. She wore black-rimmed cat glasses and moved in the kind of preoccupied, absentminded fog that Sonora associated with college professors with research grants.

She looked at Sonora and blinked. "Footprint."

Sonora felt a twinge of excitement at the base of her spine. "You have a footprint?"

Terry pushed her glasses up on her nose, leaving a streak of dirt on her forehead. "Small though. A woman in high heels. Which is odd, out here in the woods. Was there anybody with this guy?"

"His killer," Sonora said.

5

Around the department they called Sergeant Crick the bull-dog.

He crooked his finger at Sonora, crossed hamlike arms across a barrel chest—a Buddha with attitude. He leaned against his dark blue Dodge Aries, department issue, and he didn't look happy. He was built like a boxer gone to fat, his face seamy, red, and unpleasant enough that there was speculation that early in his career he'd been hit full in the face with a shovel. Rumor had it he worked in his church nursery whenever he had a Sunday free. People were known to wonder if he scared the babies.

Loosen your tie, Sonora thought. Your disposition will improve.

"Tell me you got a deathbed ID, Blair." Crick's voice was deep, as expected from the look of him, surprisingly pleasant when he made the effort. In his off time, he sang in a barbershop quartet.

Sonora leaned against Sam. "Killer was a woman, Caucasian, blond hair, maybe brown eyes. Young, twenty-five to thirty. Someone Daniels met tonight. He was last seen heading to a bar called Cujo's, according to his brother. The brother owns the car, by the way."

"Has the brother's car, but the brother doesn't go with him? I don't like that."

Sam stepped backward in mock surprise. "Come on now, Sergeant. I've known guys that would kill their brother, but not if it meant trashing their car."

Sonora continued, "Terry has a footprint. Setting it in moulage as we speak."

"Good." Crick scratched the end of his nose. "Cujo's, huh? Stupid name for a bar."

"Yes sir."

"Delarosa?"

Sam straightened. "Victim was handcuffed, naked, to the steering wheel of the car."

"You sure he was naked?"

"The guys that pulled him out thought so. And I asked Mickey. No sign of burned fabric stuck to the seat. No belt buckle, grommets, or burned rubber from shoes. I don't know where this guy's clothes are, but it doesn't look like they're in the car."

"Interesting. Go on."

"Fragments of rope or clothesline outside the car. Mickey thinks she tied him up, looped the rope or whatever through the steering wheel and around Daniels, then stood outside the car and got it going. Looks like the accelerant was gasoline—it's possible she got it from the tank of the car. He also said he found a small melted lump he thinks is a key. A small key."

"Safe-deposit box? Locker?"

Sam shrugged. "Anything's possible."

"Find the car keys?" Crick asked.

"Nothing yet. But the car is still full of hot spots and slush. So they may be there, just not in the obvious place."

Sonora looked at Sam. "She's not going to leave the keys in the ignition with him in the driver's seat. Even handcuffed, he might be able to get the engine going or something."

Sam nodded. "Anyway, she cuffs him to the wheel, ties the rope around his waist. Douses him with gasoline. The rope is about six feet out of the car, which is where she is, otherwise she's going to blow herself up. Windows are open, plenty of oxygen. She lights the end of the rope, so Daniels gets to sit in there and watch that fire coming at him. Then, boom, the car bursts into flame."

Sonora scratched her chin. "The footprint is small. Woman wearing high heels. So where did she go, in shoes like that? How fast could she move?"

"Maybe she changed them," Sam said.

Sonora nodded. "I wonder if her car was parked here. We need to search the park, do a neighborhood canvass."

Crick was nodding. "I've got uniforms in the woods and officers coming in."

"Any witnesses?"

"Not a one. The call that came in was anonymous, guy used the pay phone at the front entrance."

"Man or woman?" Sonora asked.

"Man." Crick looked at her, then at Sam, and pulled the lobe of his ear. "We'll get you manpower on this. I'll cover the canvass here. Get out to that bar, the two of you. Likely Daniels picked her up there."

Sonora pursed her lips. "Yeah, right. Next you'll be telling me he wore his jeans too tight and had his shirt unbuttoned to his waist."

"What's that supposed to mean?"

"Who picked up who, Sergeant? She's got handcuffs, rope, and, for my money, a getaway car. We're not talking date rape and revenge, are we? This woman was looking for trouble. This woman was hunting *him*."

Sonora winced. The ulcer said hello with a pain that was a little like hunger pangs, with an overlay of just pangs.

She looked at Sam. "Leave my car here and you drive."

Sam reached into his jacket pocket, pulled out an envelope of Red Man, and stuffed a wad of loose tobacco into his cheek.

"You look deformed when you do that. Like there's a tumor on your cheek."

Sam shifted sideways in the driver's seat, dove back into the jacket pocket, and came up with a crumpled cylinder of paper and cellophane that had pictures of tiny strawberries on the front. He pitched the packet into Sonora's lap.

"Feed your ulcer."

"The less I eat the worse I feel, but the worse I feel the less I want."

"You lost me there." Sam started the car, did a U-turn, headed out of the park.

Sonora unpeeled the wrapper, stripped the dried fruit off the plastic, and rolled it into a tube. "Since when did you start eating fruit roll-ups?"

"I keep them for Annie, she loves 'em. Trying to see if I can get her to pick up a little weight."

"I thought she'd added a pound or two, last time I saw her. That was what, two weeks ago?"

Sam didn't smile, but there was warmth in his eyes, as if he appreciated the effort. Annie at seven was small for her age, and thin enough to break her daddy's heart. She'd been diagnosed with leukemia a month after she'd started kindergarten, about the time Sam had been headfirst in a special investigation he only told Sonora about on stakeouts, or after several drinks. He hadn't played ball with somebody special, and he was going to have to like his rating exactly where it was. He'd never see another promotion. If Crick hadn't gone to bat for him, he'd have lost his job.

"So how is Annie?"

"Tires too easily. Shel's worried and so am I. She's dropping weight she can't afford, and her white blood count is up." Sam spit tobacco out the window. "No little girl should have circles under her eyes like Annie does."

Sonora studied her partner, seeing new lines on the tired face. The last two years had been rough ones—trying to hold on to his job and his little girl.

"She's cranky as hell."

"Annie? Or Shel?"

"Both. Eat your roll-up."

Sonora wadded what was left of fruit, corn syrup, and mysterious chemicals into a chewy red ball. Sam eased the car to a stop, waiting at a red light, staring moodily out the window.

"Killer's a woman, huh?"

"Yeah, and it isn't her first time," Sonora said.

Sam spit tobacco out the window, a stream of dirty brown juice. "The patrol car must have just missed her. I wonder if they saw anything."

"I talked to the guy who got there second. He didn't see anything but the fire. And the first guy—Minner. He was trying to pull Mark Daniels out of the car. But it's worth checking. He was still unconscious when I left the hospital."

Sam looked at her. "What do you mean, this isn't her first time? The killer?"

"Well planned, perfectly executed."

"We just haven't poked in the holes."

"So far so good, okay? Pretty bold, pretty efficient. We're not talking virgin killer, we're talking pro."

"Like a hit?"

"Idiot. No, not like a hit. Like loving care. Like somebody who's enjoying what they do."

"Like some kind of psychopathic serial killer."

"Gosh, no, I think some normal person burned Daniels up."

"You said a woman."

"Women can be serial killers."

"Why sure, Sonora, I bet your mama raised you up to be any-thing you want. There are still about as many women serial killers as there are women CEOs."

"You think there's some kind of glass ceiling for murderers? I'm putting it out on the system, Sam. See if there's been something similar, another jurisdiction."

"I say we look at the brother and the wife."

"No wife, but a girlfriend. The brother, no. I don't think so."

"Okay, Sonora, consider the girlfriend. Or a prostitute. Think S and M, going a little too far."

"I'll say. You know what worries me?"

"I know three things that worry you. Car repairs, college tuition, and orthodontists."

"Those terrify me, I'm talking worry. About the case. I'd like it if Mickey found some melted lump and said car keys."

"He might."

"She took the clothes, she'd probably take the keys. Which means Keaton Daniels's keys. Car keys. Probably house keys."

"What can she tell from a key?"

"She could have grabbed the car registration."

"You might let the brother know."

"I might at that. While I'm at it, I can warn him to leave the tight jeans at home and keep his shirt buttoned up."

"I'm trying to remember if you were this bitchy before the ulcer."

6

They were halfway to Mount Adams when Sonora's cellular phone rang. "Bet Heather missed the bus," she muttered. "Hello? Hi, Shelly. You, Sam, your wife."

He held his hand out.

Sonora glanced out the window. Wondered why two teenagers were walking so close behind an old man with a briefcase, and not in school. The man turned, suddenly, and told the kids to catch up.

Sam tromped the accelerator jerkily, then hit the brakes, barely pausing at a stop sign. "No, Shelly, I wish I could, but we caught ourselves a hot one. Can you put her on?" His shoulders were tense, his voice tired. Someone honked; he didn't seem to notice. "I see. I'm sorry. Tell her I love her and do what you can. She'll get through it."

Sam handed Sonora the phone, and she pressed the end button because he always forgot to.

"What is it?" Sonora said.

"Doctor wants Annie back in for some tests and she's having hysterics. Blood work, needles, et cetera."

"Sorry, Sam."

"Shoot, last week when we drove by the hospital on the way to take her to see a movie? Honest to God, she threw up in the truck, just from the bad associations."

Sonora looked out the window. "You better go."

"No chance."

"I'll cover, Sam."

"You've covered enough. We don't be careful, girl, we'll both be out of a job."

Sonora chewed her lip. They'd been walking a fine line the last eighteen months.

"Look, Sam, I want to talk to the brother before I go to the bar anyway. Get a picture of Mark, get a line on the girlfriend. You go to the hospital with Annie and get her settled in. She calms down the minute you walk in the room, you know that. Even if you have to leave her later, you go with her through that door."

"I don't know."

He did know, and she resented, just a little, having to do the old familiar nurture talk, but only just a little.

"Come on, Sam, Mark Daniels is dead, he'll keep. I'll drop you off at the house, and you can meet me later at Cujo's."

"Thanks, Sonora."

"Yeah, yeah."

Keaton Daniels hadn't answered his door when Sonora tried the Mount Adams address, which was when she remembered he'd said something about his wife. She flipped through her notes. The other side of town, naturally.

She checked her machine on the way, got a message from Tim that Heather had gotten off to school okay and he was on his way. She worried about him, walking alone so early in the morning. Part of the daily ritual, that worry. In the afternoon, she would worry until the two of them made it home.

The mailbox said Mr. & Mrs. K. Daniels, and there was a For Sale sign out front. Getting serious about the divorce, Sonora thought, if their house was on the block. There was no swing set in the backyard, no toys on the porch, no Halloween decorations in the window. No children. Just as well, if things weren't working out.

The house was small, a tiny three-bedroom ranch on a postage-stamp yard, much like her own house and not without charm. A lush fern hung in a basket by the front door, and a white wicker rocker sat on the tiny concrete porch. Sonora figured the rocker and the fern had a pre–stolen/vandalized life span of about six weeks.

The living room curtains were a gossamer film of fine white lace—lovely, but giving no privacy at all. The blinds in the bedrooms were tightly closed, and the porch light was on.

Sonora rang the doorbell.

For a lonely moment nothing happened. She was debating ringing it again when she heard the snap of a deadbolt being released.
The door made a cracking noise and swung open.

Sonora was surprised more often than not at how little outward
change there was in people in trouble. You had to look carefully,
sometimes, to see the signs. Keaton Daniels was showing the signs.

His shirttail was out, and he still wore the khakis—wrinkled now,
like he'd slept in them. Thick white socks sagged and bunched
around his ankles. He hadn't shaved. The slight childish fullness in
his cheeks, which Sonora had found rather sweet, had somehow
hollowed and sagged, making him seem older. All of thirty, perhaps.

He ran a hand through thick black hair, the kind of hair that
looked good, even messy. Men were often lucky that way.

"I woke you up," Sonora said.

"No, no." He rubbed the back of his neck.

Sonora did not envy him the months ahead. She'd been there
herself, when Zack died, dealing with the grief of her children.
Heather had been just a toddler, and Tim had turned very quiet,
asking, from time to time, why she did not cry, and if she really
missed his daddy.

Sonora touched Keaton Daniels's shoulder. "I'm sorry, sleep's
the best thing for you right now, and I hate to disturb you. But it's
pretty urgent that we talk."

"Come in, please. Sit down."

He moved a rumpled blanket to one side of the couch and sat
while she took the rattan rocking chair. He clasped his hands, letting them hang heavily between his knees. He seemed dulled,
somehow. Muted.

"Mr. Daniels, I'm very sorry about the death of your brother."
She always said the words, and they always seemed inadequate.
People appreciated it more often than not.

Daniels nodded, and his eyes reddened. Sonora wondered what
he was like in real life, regretting, more than usual, that she had to
meet him under harsh circumstances. It was the way she always met
people.

Once in a while someone kept in touch, cards and such. Usually
the parents of murdered children, grateful if they'd been shown
tact, more grateful if the killer had been caught.

Daniels rubbed his face. "Look, I bet you could use a cup of
coffee."

Sonora studied him. Not from Ohio, then, but somewhere farther south, though it didn't show up in his speech patterns.
Otherwise he'd have said *I* need a cup of coffee. She had a sense of
time slipping away, but knew from experience it was better not to
hurry these interviews.

Daniels kicked over one of his shoes—tennis shoes, high-tops,
white with a gray swoosh. It knocked into a pile of other shoes—
one more with a gray swoosh, a pair with red, and an odd one out,
solid white. Sonora was reminded that Heather's shoes were getting tight and that Tim would fight for Nikes, and promptly ruin
them on the first muddy day. She saw Daniels watching her.

"Got enough tennies?" she asked.

He stretched. "You have kids?"

"Two."

"So you know that even in elementary school, they're very
brand conscious. If Mr. Daniels wears Reeboks, everybody wants
Reeboks, and the kid with Nikes feels bad. Last year I taught at a
different school, one in the city. A lot of my kids didn't get breakfast in the morning, their moms couldn't go out and buy brand-
name stuff. One kid in particular was catching hell from the others
because his were from Kmart, so I went out and got a pair from
Kmart. Next thing you know, half the class has shoes from Kmart.
From then on, I started wearing about every brand there is. But I
always start with Kmart."

"I think you're very kind. And I wish you taught my son."

Daniels smiled. "Let me get you that coffee."

Sonora leaned back in the rocking chair and closed her eyes.
The bubble of a coffeemaker starting up drifted comfortably in
from the kitchen, the warm smell of coffee a comfort. Sonora let
her head roll sideways, thinking how peaceful the Daniels house-
hold was—no ringing phones, no arguing children, no hair-
pulling chorus of video-game theme songs playing over and over
again.

She wondered if Tim had helped Heather get the tangles out of
her hair, and if her daughter had felt bad about not having Mom
there to plait her hair into braids.

She caught herself just before she drifted off to sleep and was
properly wide-eyed and alert when Keaton Daniels came back in
the room. The flowered porcelain coffee cups looked delicate in his
large hands.

"You look tired, Detective."

"Not at all," she said. He surprised her. Crime victims rarely noticed much beyond their own pain. She took a sip from her cup and gave him a second look.

He had gathered himself together, there in the kitchen. She was aware of a physical self-confidence, a maleness that made her wish it wasn't a bad hair day. And he was looking back at her in a steady way that made her nervous. She had the sudden urge to go sit beside him on the couch. She knew certain male cops who would do exactly that if the witness was attractive and female.

Sonora scooted to the edge of the rocking chair. "Mr. Daniels—"

"Keaton."

"Keaton. Let's get this over with."

His voice went dull. "What do you want to know?"

"The last time you saw your brother. He dropped you off at your apartment and headed for Cujo's Café-Bar."

"Right."

"What time was that?"

"About eight-thirty. Quarter to nine."

"You never saw Mark after he left for Cujo's? He didn't call or anything?"

"No. The phone rang once, but whoever it was hung up."

Sonora frowned. "You hear any background noises?"

"Yeah, there was some noise. People talking, like at a mall or—"

"Or a bar?"

He frowned. "Could be. But if it had been Mark he would have said something. He wouldn't just call and listen."

"You think he got cut off? Think back now, give me the whole thing. What were you doing?"

"I was on the floor in the living room, doing some cutouts and stuff. Catching the tail end of somebody or other on the comedy channel." He squinted his eyes and looked up at the ceiling. "So the phone rang and I said hello. And got nothing. But there were background noises from the line, so I thought maybe I didn't hear what they said. I turned the television down and said hello again. Then whoever it was hung up. Not Mark, because he wouldn't just breathe at me. Besides, I've been getting calls like this awhile now, where they listen and hang up."

"How often?"

"Every few days. Two or three times a month. Depends."

"How long's this been going on?"

He glanced toward the bedrooms, where his wife was likely still asleep. "Last few months, mainly at the town house. I'm subletting it from a friend who's in Germany on business. I figured it was kids or something."

"Any reason to think your brother might have gone somewhere else after Cujo's? Pub crawl kind of thing?"

"It's possible. Mark was restless and outgoing. He talked to people, made friends."

"Girlfriends?"

Daniels narrowed his eyes. "You keep going back to that. You really think he picked up some girl?"

"His killer was a woman, Mr. Daniels. She had to come from somewhere."

"That was why you asked me about prostitutes? Look, Mark wasn't some kind of sleazy jerk, Specialist Blair. He had a girlfriend in Lexington and they were committed. They were thinking about moving in together. Talking about getting married."

"Were they engaged?"

"Nothing official. Mark talked about it, but he was only twenty-two. And her parents wanted her to wait till she was out of school."

"Wise," Sonora said absently. "Okay, look, I'm going to ask you a question that's going to seem a little offensive. Get over it fast, think hard, and be very honest."

Daniels pulled his bottom lip and frowned at her.

"Was your brother into any kind of unusual sexual practices? He have a lot of bruises, you know, more often than would seem average?"

"You have a nasty turn of mind, don't you?"

"Hazard of the profession, and I do have to ask. Your brother is still the victim here, I haven't forgotten that."

He leaned back on the couch. "It's not like I know everything about my brother's sex life. You have a brother, you know what I mean. But I never saw any sign of anything . . . anything like what you're saying. He didn't go to tough bars. He didn't date girls who wore lots of mascara and black leather and a leash around their neck. He read *Gentlemen's Quarterly* and *Playboy*."

"For the articles."

"For the foldouts. And he always bought the swimsuit issue of *Sports Illustrated*. I'd say my brother's reading material was pretty much normal, for a healthy American male."

"American as apple pie."

Daniels smiled at her, just a little one.

"What's as American as apple pie?"

Sonora hadn't heard the woman come in—the carpet had muted the sound of her high, spiky heels. She was the kind of female Sonora had always envied—naturally thin, brown eyes, thick, shiny auburn hair. The kind of woman for whom makeup was optional, who got the part in the school play.

Daniels stood up. "Ashley. This is Police Specialist Sonora Blair. She's investigating Mark's . . . Mark's death."

Sonora stood up and offered a hand. Ashley Daniels was dressed up—soft rose business suit, white stockings, high heels that Sonora knew she herself wouldn't last in for more than an hour.

She shook Sonora's hand firmly, then bent close to Keaton, trailing perfume and kissing him gently on the cheek. "You all right, Keat?"

He patted her shoulder. "Yeah."

"I need to go down to the booth just a few minutes. I have to pick up a couple of files, make one or two calls, and then I'll be right back. Will you be okay?"

"I'm headed home anyway."

"You sure?"

He nodded.

Sonora felt their awkwardness. Sort of married. Sort of not.

Ashley Daniels's voice turned cool. "There's that car again. I hope it's somebody interested in the house." She walked across the room, shifted the curtains to one side.

Sonora set her coffee cup on the end table and went to the window. "What car?"

Ashley Daniels looked at her over one shoulder. "Gone. Why?"

Sonora looked out at the street. Pavement, new sidewalk, baby grass on vulnerable, emerging lawns. No cars.

Ashley looked at Keaton. "You want the rental car delivered here or at your place?"

"Here, I guess. Can you get it for me this morning?"

"Done. And I'll have your check in three days. There are some advantages to having an Allstate agent in the family." Ashley smiled at Sonora, pulled a business card from her blazer pocket. "I work out of a booth at Tri-County Mall. If you ever want a rate estimate, give me a call. Mostly I handle property and casualty—car insurance, homeowners. Life when I'm lucky."

Sonora nodded, pocketed the card, watched Ashley Daniels go into the kitchen, heels clacking. She heard a garage door.

"Where were we?" Keaton said.

"You were telling me what kind of magazines your brother read."

"More interesting than the ones I get. *Weekly Reader. Highlights for Children.*"

"For the foldout."

"They have some great ones where you connect the dots."

Sonora tilted her head to one side. "Mr. Daniels, one thing I want to bring up. Our arson investigator couldn't find your brother's keys."

"The car keys?"

"Yeah. What keys were on the ring?"

"Keys to this house. Keys to my apartment. My car and Ashley's car, and my desk at school. They must have burned up."

"Even so, he should have been able to find them. Melted, carbonized, they'd still be there."

"And he'd be able to tell?"

"Reads fires scenes like you read *Highlights for Children*. It's possible the killer kept them."

"You think it's something to worry about?"

She opened her arms. "I'm not saying go overboard, but I don't like the killer having keys to your house. Just to be on the safe side, why don't you change your locks?"

"She won't know where I live, anyway."

"Was there a registration in your car?"

"Yeah, sure."

"There you go."

"You really think—"

"I think it's a good precaution. Do it, why don't you? Getting robbed is no fun."

"You think she'd rob my apartment?"

She thought robbery might be the least of his worries, but she didn't point it out. "It's best to take precautions. Change your locks, Mr. Daniels."

7

The only picture of Mark that Keaton Daniels had handy was a wedding picture he'd removed from a gilt-edged frame. Sonora had been reluctant to take it. The pose showed Keaton, sturdy and serious, with Mark on one side and Ashley, radiant and beautiful, on the other. Mark looked young and smug, his elbow on Keaton's shoulder.

They did not look particularly alike, these brothers. Mark had light brown hair, fine and straight. His face was thin, chin pointed. He build was wiry in contrast to his brother's more solid mass. His eyes were blue.

Not a case of mistaken identity.

A Closed sign hung in the window of Cujo's Café-Bar, but the front door was unlocked. Sonora saw no sign of Sam, and didn't feel like waiting on the doorstep. She thought of Annie, tiny in a hospital bed. She would try to take Heather over for a visit.

The café was warm inside, divided into two main sections. The first was a bar, the second a small dining room with a Nonsmoking sign over the frame.

The bar itself was beautiful but battered, the rich teakwood scuffed and gouged. The brass plate along the bottom needed polishing. The barstools were high, but they had backs and armrests. Comfortable, Sonora thought, settling in. She studied the array of bottles grouped under the mirror that ran along the back.

The sight of so much alcohol so early in the morning offended the ulcer, and Sonora checked her jacket pocket for a Mylanta tablet. She was frowning at an empty foil packet when she heard soft footsteps and looked up to see a woman, short and stout like a fireplug, walk in from the dining room.

"Ma'am, I'm sorry, we don't open till noon."

"Yeah, I figured there might be a reason the chairs were stacked up on the tables. Plus the Closed sign was kind of a tip-off." Sonora opened the leather case that housed her ID, waited patiently while the woman looked the badge over carefully. The days when you could flash ID and not break stride were long gone.

"Detective Bear?"

"Blair," Sonora said.

"Sorry, I don't have my reading glasses. What can I help you with?" The woman moved behind the counter, heading for a coffeepot. She'd have to stand on a stool to tend bar. "Get you a cup?"

The ulcer had segued neatly from ache to nausea, and Sonora grimaced. "No, thanks." She heard a car engine and spotted a pickup pulling up by the curb out front. Sam. She took the recorder out of her purse and laid it on the bartop.

"You work here, Ms. . . . ?"

"Anders. Celia Anders. I'm day manager."

The bell over the front door jingled, and Sam came into the bar. Sonora waved.

"Ms. Anders, this is my partner, Detective Delarosa."

He nodded. Celia Anders smiled at him. She liked him, Sonora could tell, though all he'd done was walk through the door. Sonora looked at Sam in mild irritation.

"Ms. Anders, did you work last night?" Sonora asked.

Celia Anders looked at the recorder. "No, I'm *day* manager. I go home at seven."

"Who was here?"

"Let's see. Usually Ronnie seats people in the restaurant part. And Chita tends bar. They own the place. Ronnie Knapp and Chita Childers."

"Either of them around?" Sam asked.

"They're in the kitchen. At least, Chita was."

"We'd like to talk to them," Sonora said.

"What's this all about?"

Sonora smiled.

"Okay then," Celia Anders said. "I'll get 'em."

Sonora glanced at her watch. Both Tim and Heather should be snug in school. Provided, of course, Heather's bus hadn't wrecked or been hijacked by terrorists, and some middle-aged man in a raincoat hadn't forced Tim into his nondescript brown car. Sonora sighed, and Sam looked at her. He had an air of distraction that let her know he was upset. Annie was no doubt having a rough morning.

"Okay?"

He put a hand on her shoulder and squeezed. "We got her settled."

Sonora heard muted female voices, then a tall woman with a pure vanilla complexion and frizzy red-gold hair walked in, followed by Celia Anders. They looked remarkable, walking together, one tall, thin, and confident, the other short and squat, shoulders hunched together as if she expected to be hit.

"Hi, I'm Chita Childers."

Her voice was thin and she'd sing soprano. Her eyes were blue and her hair was long, pulled up on the sides with a silver-and-turquoise barrette. She wore jeans and a Bengals T-shirt.

"I'm Sonora Blair, this is Sam Delarosa, Cincinnati Police."

"What did you want to see me about?" She looked over her shoulder. "Ronnie!"

"I'm in the bathroom." The voice was muted, male, irritable.

Sonora put the wedding picture on the counter.

"Do you recognize this man?"

Chita Childers squinted and stared down at the picture. "Yeah, this one. He's here all the time."

She stabbed a long skinny finger at Keaton Daniels. Her nails were long and coated with maroon polish. Glued in the corner of each squared-off nail was a tiny zircon, glinting like a diamond.

"*This* guy?"

"Yeah."

"Was he in last night?"

Childers squeezed her eyes shut and tilted her head upward to aid her memory. So all the thoughts in the top of her head could slide into her brain, Sonora thought.

"No, I don't think so. He hasn't been in that much lately. For a while, he was here two or three nights a week. But"—she opened her eyes—"not last night."

"Who about the other one?"

"The woman?"

"Either."

"The woman, I don't know. She's a type. Ronnie might remember."

"And the guy?" Sonora pointed to Mark Daniels.

From somewhere close came the sound of a flushing toilet, the noise of running water, a door opening, closing. A man in his mid- to late thirties, slender, thinning brown hair and a mustache, came in from the dining room. He stopped in the doorway.

"Oh."

"Police Specialists Blair and Delarosa," Sonora said. "Didn't mean to catch you at a bad time."

Knapp's cheeks went dusky red. Sam coughed and cleared his throat.

Knapp extended a hand to Sonora and gave her a firm, damp handshake. He glanced at Celia. "We're out of paper towels in the bathroom, by the way." Sonora wiped her hands on the back of her jacket and settled back down on the stool.

Sam scooted the picture across the bar. "Mr. Knapp, did any of these people come in last night?"

Knapp picked up the picture and studied it. "Last night, hmmm. That one didn't."

Sonora rubbed her stomach. "Which one?"

Knapp flipped the picture around and pointed to Keaton Daniels. "This one. He used to come in a lot, but I haven't seen him lately. The other guy was here, though."

"You sure?"

"Yeah. Talking to the blonde."

Sonora felt rather than saw Sam tensing. She kept her voice casual. "What blonde?"

"Just some girl."

"She a regular?"

"Been in a few times."

"What blonde is this?" Chita Childers asked.

"You've seen her. Kind of little. Delicate, sort of. Never smiles."

"How long did she talk to this guy?" Sonora pointed to Mark's picture.

"Awhile."

"Do you remember how long?"

"Not really."

"An hour?"

"Maybe not that long."

"Just a few minutes? Half an hour?"

"Longer than half an hour. Like maybe forty-five minutes. Like that. They had a drink together. She drinks Bud from the bottle."

"What was he drinking?"

"Draft beer. Bourbon chaser."

"Did they leave together?"

"No."

"Who left first?"

"Don't know."

"About what time?"

"Jeez, I really don't know. Before eleven."

Chita Childers edged forward, and Celia Anders had to step backward. "She must have left before he did, then. 'Cause this guy stayed late."

"How late?" Sam said.

"Almost midnight. I thought he'd be around to close us down."

Sam smiled at Celia Anders, then turned his attention to Chita Childers. Sonora leaned into the back of the stool.

"And the blonde had left by then?" Sam asked.

"Yeah."

"He talk to anyone else?"

Chita shrugged. "He talked to lots of people. He talked to me. How come? He in some kind of trouble?"

"He's dead."

"Dead? Killed?"

"Burned to death in his car."

"*That* guy? I heard that on the news this morning." She gripped the edge of the bar, eyes wide. "Oh, God, and I just talked to him. He was so young, too. I actually carded him. The news said somebody burned him *alive*."

Ronnie Knapp sat down on a stool, turning it so he faced Sonora. "You think maybe this blonde saw the killer?"

Sonora kept her voice careful. "It's possible. Right now we're trying to reconstruct Daniels's last hours. This blond woman—you didn't overhear a name, by any chance?"

Ronnie and Chita both frowned. Chita's tongue came out—more help with concentration. Then she shook her head.

Sonora looked at Ronnie. "You?"

"No."

"How'd she pay? Cash? Credit card?"

He shook his head. "I don't remember."

"She tip?"

"Uh, yeah."

"Stingy? Generous?"

"Kind of in the middle."

"Cash or on credit?"

"Cash."

"All right. Gather up all your credit receipts for last night, and make copies. In fact, we'll need copies of everything that's come in over the last, say, six weeks."

Ronnie nodded glumly.

Sonora smiled. "We appreciate your cooperation, Mr. Knapp. It would help us a lot if you'd bring the receipts down to our office today and make a formal statement. We'll make an appointment for you to get with our artist on a sketch of this blonde. We're on the fifth floor of the Board of Elections building, 825 Broadway. Public parking lot a block away. Just tell the man in the booth out front what you're there for, and he'll tell you where to go."

Ronnie and Chita acquired the glazed and wary look of people who suddenly found themselves in the middle of a murder investigation.

"As soon as possible," Sonora said.

"What if she comes back in?" Celia Anders had been left out and didn't like it.

Sonora took a card from her jacket pocket.

"She comes back in, call me, anytime. If I'm not there, be sure and explain to the detective who answers the phone, don't just leave a message. Here, this is my home number." Sonora scrawled on the back of the card with a pen. "Any of you see her again, don't approach her, just give me a call."

"Out of earshot," Celia said.

Sam grinned at her.

"There a pay phone here?" Sonora asked.

Celia pointed down a dark hallway to the left of the bar. "Right between the bathrooms."

"Works okay?"

Ronnie nodded.

"Get pretty noisy in here last night? You have a crowd?"

"Not bad for a weeknight. We offer twofers from four to seven and that brings people in on their way home from work."

Sonora looked at Ronnie. "Tell me everything you remember about the blonde."

Ronnie closed his eyes and his brow furrowed. "She was real blond."

"Real blond? Like me?"

He opened his eyes. "Lighter."

Sonora sighed. "Look dyed?"

"Not really, but it's hard to tell sometimes. It didn't have that fakey, cotton candy look to it. It was very light. Kind of collar length and turned under. Very . . . kind of . . . ethereal."

Chita Childers made a rude noise. "Ethereal? It was dyed, if it's the one I'm thinking of."

"Eyes?" Sonora asked.

"Brown. Big brown eyes. Kind of . . . funny."

"How could she have funny eyes?" Chita said.

Sonora clenched her fist, let it go. Smiled at Chita Childers and looked back at Ronnie.

"Brown eyes," Ronnie said.

"Blue," Chita chimed in. They glared at each other.

"Maybe she changed them. With contacts." Celia Anders looked pleased.

Sonora glanced at Sam. The old witness shuffle.

Ronnie scratched his chin and looked at Sonora. "She's very small. Shorter even than you."

"Wow," Sam said. "Pretty short, huh?"

Ronnie grinned. "She looked kind of, I don't know, fragile? But she never smiled. Oh, and her lips were scarred. Like she bit them a lot."

"She talk to a lot of guys? Flirt a lot?"

"Not with me. I thought she seemed kind of shy. I remember being surprised she was talking to that guy. In the picture."

"She was dressed to kill," Chita said. "Short black jean skirt, and cowboy boots, and a bodysuit. Lots of makeup and long earrings."

Ronnie nodded. "Yeah. She had on a short skirt. I noticed that."

Chita sounded deceptively sweet. "She's come in before, dressed like that. I've seen her talking to the other one."

Sonora turned the picture around, her fingertips grazing the features of Keaton Daniels. "The other one? This one?"

"Yeah, him."

"The woman in the picture. The bride here. You ever see her come in?"

Chita frowned and shook her head. "Not that I remember."

Sonora passed the picture to Ronnie.

"No. Her I would remember."

"I just bet you would," Chita muttered, and was politely

ignored. Ronnie handed the picture to Sonora, but Celia Anders intercepted it and gave it a good look. Sonora thought of sticky fingerprints. It was high time for copies.

Sam pulled his ear. "Did Mark Daniels or the blonde use the phone? Ask for change, maybe?"

Negative. Blank looks. The witness fairy wasn't going to come.

Sonora climbed down from the stool, took her purse with her, found a quarter to call her answering machine and check out the phone. She listened. No emergencies. And the pay phone worked. She pulled out her notebook and jotted down the number. They could pull records from the phone company. She wanted to know if Keaton Daniels had been called from the bar.

8

Sonora went into the Board of Elections building and took the elevator to the fifth floor, to Homicide. There were Non-smoking signs in three places, one of them over a metal ashtray. Crimestoppers wanted-posters were pinned neatly on a bulletin board. There were no coats in the coatrack out front. There never were.

A woman sat in the glass booth doing a crossword puzzle, and Sonora waved. The door on the left led to the Crime Scene Unit, the other to Homicide. Both warned against entry without proper police escort.

Sonora veered right, walked past the worn-down interview rooms, smelling fresh coffee. The box outside the door of the brass's office was full of soda cans. Homicide recycled. As always, she glanced at the poster board that listed homicides for the year, solved and unsolved. Most of the unsolved were drug drive-bys. Hard as hell to track and prove, and the only satisfaction was in knowing that the shooter had a good chance of showing up on the board as a victim sometime in the next few months.

Mark Daniels was the latest entry.

Everyone was in, and the energy level was high. A lot of people on the phones, and Sonora getting speculative looks. Daniels was a real whodunit, and the other detectives were being pulled off their cases to run down leads.

This one would be a headliner.

The message light on her phone was lit and blinking. Her desk, piled with forms, files, a Rolodex, an evidence bag, and a half-filled can of Coke, was placed in the center of the room, butted up to Sam's. Every desk had a plastic-wrapped teddy bear on top—some new program or other. A grant for every cop to carry a stuffed animal to give to children trapped in the crossfire of adults who screwed up. Sonora tossed her purse underneath the desk and kicked it where it would be out of range of the wheels of her chair.

Her phone rang just as she settled into her chair. "Homicide, Sonora Blair."

"Can I please speak to one of the detectives?"

"You're speaking to one."

"You're not the secretary?"

"No, I'm not the secretary."

Sonora heard a laugh, looked over her shoulder at Gruber.

He grinned. "They want a real cop, I'm available."

Sonora put a hand over the phone. "Make yourself useful, honey, and get me a cup of coffee."

Gruber looked her up and down in a way guaranteed to annoy. He had bedroom eyes, a perpetual slump to his shoulders, a swarthy complexion, and New Jersey manners that offended some people and attracted young women.

Sonora focused on the voice on the other end of the phone. "I'm sorry?"

"You know that guy that burned up?"

Sonora frowned and picked up a pen. "What guy is that?"

"The one in the news. They didn't give his name. But I think I better explain to you the situation with my brother-in-law, make of it what you will."

Not much, Sonora thought. She made a face, took useless notes. No stone unturned.

"Another nut," she said, hanging up the phone.

"You attract 'em," Gruber said. "'Member when we took you out trawling? You pulled in the weirdest nutcases, even for a hooker detail."

Sonora nodded. She'd hated and resented the prostitution detail and had been unable to refrain from giving prospective johns the copper's eyefuck. Only one or two had been inexperienced or desperate or intrigued enough to try and do business. Sonora had been pulled off the streets after two weeks.

"I always wondered if you screwed up on purpose, you know? To get off that detail."

Sonora smiled. "Keep wondering, Gruber."

"Molliter didn't think so, but I figured maybe you did."

"Where is old Molliter these days? He quit and become a television evangelist?"

"Working personal crime since last Christmas."

"*Molliter?*"

Gruber folded his arms and cocked his head sideways. "Can't you just hear him lecturing the rape victims on provocative clothing and those jiggly walks?"

Sonora bit her lip. Actually, she could.

Gruber shrugged. "Yeah, well. Bad choice. They had to pull him out of vice, he was trying to save souls. Didn't really fit in down there, if you know what I mean."

Sonora draped her jacket over the back of her chair. Thought about coffee, thought about ulcers, decided against the one she had some choice about. The message light on her machine was still blinking. She settled into her chair and pushed the button.

One informant looking for a handout, a terse one from Chas, who was feeling neglected, a coroner's assistant about the suicide she hadn't liked. There was a message from one of the mothers from Heather's class reminding her to send cupcakes for day after tomorrow (shit, Sonora thought) and the one from Tim, letting her know that Heather had gotten on the bus okay, he was on his way, and *yes* he had his keys.

Sonora took out a scratch pad, roughing out the description she would put out on the NCIC. Early days yet, but this one looked like a repeater, and she wasn't asking permission. Under key points, she put homicide involving white female, victim white male, burned to death in car. She chewed the end of her pen.

She felt a large hand on her shoulder and a familiar presence by her side. "Sonora, girl, that pen taste good, or you didn't get any breakfast?"

Gruber waved a hand. "It's an oral thing. What she needs . . . " He caught the expression on Sonora's face. Trailed off.

"Wise," she told him.

She swiveled her chair and looked at her partner, and flashed back to a night four years ago, before she really knew Sam's wife, Shelly, and, hell, she'd decided not to feel guilty about that anymore. Sometimes she looked at Sam and still felt the urge. Something about Gruber put thoughts like that in her head.

"Crick wants us," Sam said.

The brass had their own office, more desks butted together,

phones, files. Crick was at the computer when Sam and Sonora walked in, and he looked irritable. He did not get along with the department terminals, which were inferior to the setup he had at home. He was often overheard making rude comments about archaic software.

Loosen your tie, Sonora thought. Your disposition will improve. Someday she would say it out loud.

"Sit down, Blair. Delarosa." Crick rolled his chair backward. Sam took two chairs from behind empty desks, straddled one, aimed the other at Sonora. She stopped it with her foot. "God, the two of you. Just sit."

Sonora glanced at Sam and wondered if he was thinking what she was thinking. Were they caught? Were they going to get fired?"

"How are you doing on that suicide?" Crick said.

Slow, Sonora thought. Way behind. She cleared her throat. "Family went squirrelly over the autopsy, Sergeant. We're moving them along easy, trying to keep things from boiling over."

Crick stuck a finger under his collar and scratched his neck. "Drop the bullshit, Blair."

She crossed her legs, resting a foot on her knee. "I don't like it. There's a large insurance policy involved, just barely past the two-year limit on suicide. Coroner can't find anything definite, but we're waiting for test results. We can fly by the grand jury, but if we go to trial, their forensic whores will take us apart."

"How'd the coroner sign it off?"

"I'm pressuring, but he's probably going to rule it suicide."

"Drop it, then."

"Lot of money at stake."

"Let the insurance company worry about it. I can tell you now or the DA can tell you later."

"Yes sir."

"What else you working on?"

"Crenshaw baby. Stabbing on Ryker Street, looks like a drug burn. And we got that burning bed, Meredith."

"You sure the wife did it?"

"No doubt in my mind," Sam said.

"No doubt the husband deserved it."

Sam wagged a finger. "You got to get off this 'I hate men' kick, Sonora. Not all guys are like your dead husband."

They had this conversation two or three times a month, and Sonora went on with her lines. "Yeah, *they're* breathing. So why is it, Sam, if a woman calls a spade a spade, or a jerk a jerk, she gets labeled a man-hater?"

Crick waved a hand. "Enough already, you guys are worse than my kids. Give your files to Nelson, and sit up and pay attention here. Coffee?"

"Sure," Sam said. Sonora nodded and looked at Sam. He winked, but he was worried. There were budget cutbacks again this year. They'd seen some pretty good people get screwed.

Maybe they were being transferred somewhere awful.

Crick poured them both a cup from a pot that sat amid stacks of computer printouts. Sonora was aware of a tiny, annoying buzz coming from the timer that turned the pot on every morning at 7:50. It was the wrong kind of timer, not made to handle the load, and had melted down twice. Fire hazard, Sonora thought. She was seeing them everywhere all of a sudden.

Sonora took a big sip of coffee, tasting nothing. Crick sat back down. His chair squeaked. He squinted his eyes.

"You feeling okay, Blair? You don't look too good."

"What am I, Miss America? I been up all night looking for a killer who set a twenty-two-year-old kid on fire. How would you look?"

"My wife says I always look the same, no matter what."

Can't argue with that, Sonora thought.

Crick leaned back in his chair. "This Daniels thing is going to be a big deal. Heinous crime, innocent kid. It's all over the news, we been getting calls like you wouldn't believe. There's a lot of leads to follow and a lot of coordinating to do with the arson guys." He pointed a thick finger. "You caught it, you're the lead detectives. You got to know everything that goes down. Every witness statement, every tiny piece of evidence, you know the drill. We're going to task-force this thing. We'll pull in twelve detectives from district, plus our own people. You're even going to get your own computer."

Sam whistled.

"We'll meet every morning to hand out lead cards, then everybody goes out. We meet up again the end of the day. Couple of guys from arson will be in on this, Lieutenant Abalone and I will handle the press. Any information we hand out, we'll clear through the task force. Kick it around first. We can use the media on this, maybe push a few buttons with this headcase we got here. Run a description, if we get a good one.

"Nobody's taking anything away from you, you understand? I'm just pulling in some help, organizing everything all around you, so you two supercops can bring me this bitch's head on a stick."

Sonora took a breath. They weren't being fired. She could still pay the mortgage. Her children were safe.

Crick's phone rang. "Yeah. She's here." He looked at Sonora. "You got a call. Keaton Daniels. Wants to talk specifically to you."

"I'll take it at my desk."

The light on line four was blinking red when Sonora sat down. She picked up the stuffed bear and tossed it on Sam's desk.

"Specialist Blair," she said, propping her chin on the shoulder piece. "Mr. Daniels?"

"Yeah, hi. I thought I should let you know. I've had an odd phone call."

He sounded confident. A woman, Sonora thought, would have been defensive, would have apologized for bothering her, and would have made five disclaimers about how it was probably nothing. At least men didn't have to be coaxed and reassured.

"Tell me about it."

Sam had come out of Crick's office and was examining the bear on his desk. He glanced at Sonora out of the corner of his eye.

"She said—"

"She?" Sonora asked.

"It was a woman. She asked me about Mark."

Sonora sat forward in her chair and picked up a pen. "Start at the beginning, Keaton, and tell me the exact words, as well as you can remember."

He paused. Sonora pictured him, concentrating, gathering his thoughts.

"She called me . . . I guess an hour ago."

Sonora checked her watch. Made a note on the scratch pad.

"I said hello. And there was a long silence. I was about to hang up, then she said she wanted to check on me, and see how I was doing. I thought at first it might be Ashley, my wife. I even thought for a minute it might be you. So I said I was shaky, and kind of numb. And she made a noise, you know, a sympathy thing."

"Sarcastic?" Sonora asked.

"It didn't strike me that way."

"Go on."

Sonora saw that Sam was watching her, intent on her end of the conversation, waiting her out with a patience that always amazed her. Mr. Stakeout.

Daniels cleared his throat. "She said . . . how did she put it? She said, it's a terrible thing, to lose a brother. Were you . . . no. She said you'uns. 'Were you'uns real close?' "

"You'uns," Sonora muttered.

"And I said . . . I didn't answer her. It dawned on me that I didn't know who this was. But I still had the feeling that it was a friend or something, because she knew about Mark. So I said, I'm sorry, who is this?

"And she said someone who's interested. Then she asked if I was thinking much about how he died. Was it terrible for me? Was I missing him, had I thought about the funeral? So then I thought maybe she was a reporter or something. I was going to hang up, but it made me mad. I thought she was out of line, and that I should get her name and her newspaper, or whatever, so I asked her again who it was."

Sonora gave him a moment. "What did she say?"

"She said . . . she said Mark was brave."

The nib of Sonora's pen tore through the paper on the notepad. She listened to Keaton Daniels's breathing on the other end of the line. She flipped the notepaper up, exposing a clean sheet.

What is it? Sam mouthed. Gruber had picked up on the tension. Sonora could feel him edging close behind her.

"Mr. Daniels, I don't guess you've had a chance to change the locks on your doors?"

"No."

"Why don't you get on to that right away?"

"It was her, then, wasn't it?"

Sonora pursed her lips, measuring her words. "It's a possibility. It's also possible, likely even, that it was some crank, some sick puppy out there getting a nasty little vicarious thrill."

Sam raised an eyebrow at her.

"We haven't released your brother's name to the press," Sonora continued. "But something like this—the gossip mill churns pretty fast. The hospital people will talk. The reporters know the ID from the car license. Forgive me, but your wife may have talked about it to the wrong person at work." How well are the two of you getting along? Sonora wondered.

"I don't think it was a reporter. And it wasn't my wife, I'd know it."

Jumped right on that one, Sonora thought. She'd seen divorcing parties do worse.

Keaton's voice thickened. "There's something else."

"Yes?"

"After she said that about Mark. That he was brave. She said . . . will you be?"

9

Mark Daniels's roommate had said the apartment was in the Chevy Chase area, next to the University of Kentucky campus. The Taurus inched down Rose Street, and Sam squinted as he strained to avoid the knots of university students who seemed oddly oblivious to traffic. Sonora glanced at the sheet of directions.

"Take a right at the intersection. I can't read your writing here, Sam. Eunice?" She glanced at a street sign. "Euclid. Turn here." She noticed a Hardee's and a Baskin-Robbins and decided she was hungry. "Here," she said, looking up. "No. Casa Galvan, that's the Mex restaurant he mentioned. Turn around, we've gone too far."

It was a part of the city that mixed campus, old residential, and commercial. Mark's apartment was in a pinkish red brick building with a black, wrought-iron fire escape down one side. Sam parked the car a long block away, tucking the Taurus between a pickup and an ancient Karmann Ghia.

Sonora shut the passenger door softly. "Well, Sam, Lexington is one town where your pickup would blend."

Sam gave her a look. "Yeah, and who do you call when you need a load of firewood?"

Sonora grinned and Sam waved her ahead, always the gentleman. The pebbled sidewalk in front of Mark Daniels's apartment building had cracked and buckled. The lawn was sparse, equal parts crab, dandelion, and bluegrass.

Sonora paused on the front walk and looked at the windows. No one was stirring. The mix of sagging venetian blinds, cheap threadbare curtains, and woven shades—one open, one closed—

gave the building a bedraggled look of neglect. People slept here. They didn't stay long.

Sonora checked her watch. Just after seven. Sam caught her look.

"Yeah, well. Be sure to find people home, this time of day. Plus the roommate has an eight-o'clock class."

Sonora thought of her own university days. "Doesn't mean he actually goes. I can't believe you got me up at five to drive down here."

She wondered if the killer had stalked Mark Daniels, if she'd known him from Adam. Was this a random hit? A well-planned hit, random victim? Why did Keaton Daniels come up every time she looked for Mark?

The linoleum in the apartment hallway was peeling up in the corner and overlaid with muddy footprints. The mud was reddish brown—most of the prints showed the webwork of rubber soles. Big feet, too. A lot of size tens and elevens, one that looked bigger. Mostly guys, Sonora decided. Lexington had evidently had its share of rain. Their footsteps were muffled by a hideous, raisin-colored runner.

"Sam, what color was the mud in the park?"

"Gray-black, Sherlock."

Sonora was out of breath by the time they passed the second floor. "What's the kid's name?"

"Brian Winthrop. Age twenty-three."

"Ever notice we never talk to people who live on the first floor?"

"It's a well-known phenomenon. Always the third-floor people who get into trouble."

"Is he going to say you'uns too?"

Sam gave her a sour look.

"Hey, I only meant to be offensive."

Sonora scooted to the door ahead of him and knocked, thinking how much time she spent on doorsteps, wishing she could some-how convert it to time spent with her kids, or better still, sleeping. She crooked her finger at Sam, and he dipped his head to listen.

"The guy *I* want to talk to is the one who called it in. You think there's any chance he'll get back to us?"

"Shit, no. He's in Mount Airy Forest on a weeknight, after dark, in the rain. Who do you know who goes to the park under those circumstances?"

"Gays."

"Closet gays. He did his civic duty and called nine-one-one. I don't look for him to buy any more trouble."

A dead bolt clicked, and the door cracked open just slightly, then stuck. The thin wood bowed inward, and Sonora heard a muted mutter.

"Yes?"

Mark's roommate was a tall boy, and thin; shoulders bumpy, hip-bones jutting, Adam's apple prominent. His head seemed overlarge for his body. His hair was dark brown and wavy, and a bad barber had given him a poor haircut too long ago. His skin showed blemishes here and there, nothing major, and he was of an age to shave daily, though he hadn't. Sonora wondered if he was into the stubble look or trying to grow a beard.

Sam showed his ID. "Specialists Delarosa and Blair, Cincinnati Police Department, about Mark Daniels. We talked last night?"

Sonora tried not to yawn. "Can we come in?"

"Inside. That would . . . yeah, in the room, that would be to say, for the best." Winthrop nodded vigorously and stepped back.

Sonora scratched her cheek and looked at Sam. He raised one eyebrow and motioned her ahead.

The room smelled like fried fish and tartar sauce. The rug was worn, mustard colored, with a rusty-looking stain under the window.

Bloodstain? Sonora wondered. Always a copper.

A card table sagged under the clutter of books, papers, and pizza cartons. A set of barbells and weights sat in the corner. Along the wall behind the couch was an IBM PS/2, a modem beneath a phone, and a Hewlett-Packard laser printer. The computer screen was lit, the background a searing blue. A miniature cartoon man in a green suit with an orange vest did backflips to the tune of a ditty that set Sonora's teeth on edge.

Winthrop flung an arm toward the living room. "Place to sit. Here. If you'd like. Of course, you might not, but probably you would."

Sam sat in the middle of the couch and reached into his coat pocket for his recorder. Sonora took a worn armchair that had a Salvation Army look. The chair sank beneath her, a wayward spring the only thing keeping her off the floor. She scooted forward, balanced on the edge, and studied Winthrop.

"Brian, how long were you and Mark roommates?"

"You . . . we were friends a lot of, well, knowing. I could tell you but remembering is one thing, but it is more than years."

Sonora wondered if Winthrop was sincerely unable to communicate, playing it smart, or terrified of police. Sam met her gaze, raised his right shoulder slightly. Big help.

It could never be easy.

Sonora tried again. "So you've known Mark several years?"

Winthrop made an obvious effort. "Three. That would be as roommates. Ten as known friends. Longer really."

For the first time in her life, Sonora missed the sneering streetwise punks who were sometimes irritating, sometimes chilling, but at least able to communicate, often in lyrical, if obscene, rap.

"So you've roomed with Mark for the last three years?"

Winthrop nodded vigorously.

He seemed bright enough. She detected a working mind behind the intelligence of the gaze, and a look of panic to go with the sheen of sweat on the forehead. He could have had something to do with Mark's killing, but she didn't think so. Her instinct told her the panic was due to sheer social nervousness, and she supposed that if she talked the way Winthrop did, she'd be nervous too.

She thought of her brother, going through school with his speech impediment, teased, imitated, retreating every afternoon to his room.

Winthrop cleared his throat loudly. Impossible not to root for him in his intense effort to organize his thoughts into speech. And that was the problem, she decided. Some kind of mental stuttering.

She grimaced, turning it into a smile. "Did Mark date around a lot? Was he pretty popular with girls?"

"No, but they all, to say, that's because you know Sandra. But they would if he wouldn't."

"Sandra's his girlfriend, right?"

Winthrop nodded.

"Did he date anyone else?"

"Well I don't. Not to my . . . my own understanding, I couldn't say always know ever. But he, as far as I would know, and I didn't ever see it."

"He didn't as far as you know?"

She was beginning to get the hang of talking to this guy—very like communicating with a two-year-old. Grab the gist, double-check the results, and resist the urge to drop to your knees and beg him to just *say* it.

She led him through the routine patiently, getting a lead on Mark's favorite bars (three or four, Lynagh's in particular); favorite restaurants (the Mex place, Casa Galvan, and Jozo's Cajun); what he studied (social work); and what bothered him (the job market, AIDS, final exams). There were no surprises—an average male college student in his early twenties.

He loved Sandra, he partied on Friday and Saturday, spent Sunday afternoons playing pickup basketball, and studied weeknights after work. He worked evenings, but had recently been "let go" by new management. Nothing major there, just something of a personality clash with the new guy. Winthrop suspected Mark had been fired because the new owners didn't want to pay more than minimum wage. They were letting a lot of the regulars go and putting in new people. Mark hadn't been the only one out the door.

Sonora shifted on the uncomfortable rim of the armchair, wishing she'd beaten Sam to the couch.

"Okay, Brian, there's something I want you to think about. Did Mark get any odd phone calls—anything unusual, maybe someone calling and hanging up?"

"The phone now that's a . . . its . . . I might not. Because you never know if he'd say in particular, though he might, you know. He might." Spittle spewed from lips that were thick, chapped, and dry. Sonora shifted to one side so that Sam was in the direct line of fire.

"Anything you're sure about? Any calls you took, any calls Mark mentioned?"

"I don't. No. Usually, Mark would—"

"Mark answered the phone?"

Winthrop nodded. Sonora nodded too. Made perfect sense.

"Did he seem upset over anything? Ever mention he thought somebody might be watching him?"

Winthrop's blank look answered that one.

Sonora's back was aching, and the computer-generated song made her grind her teeth. She wondered what sin she had committed to deserve this witness.

"Brian, Specialist Delarosa and I need to take a look at Mark's room, go through his things. Any objection? Good. While we're looking, I'd like you to write down everything you remember that happened the last day you saw Mark. I'm interested in everything, all the routine stuff, and of course, anything unusual."

Winthrop nodded.

Sonora stood up. She had more questions, but not in a chair with a spring coming up, and not with a computer game chanting in the background.

10

Sonora looked at Mark Daniels's bedroom, thinking that she wouldn't call him neat.

Likely he'd left for Cincinnati in a hurry, but the signs were there of someone always in a hurry on the way to somewhere else. A large mound in the corner would probably prove to be a chair. Clothes were piled on the floor, and the bed had an ingrained unmade look Sonora recognized. Likely it was pulled together on special occasions only.

A Gameboy sat on the edge of a cheap metal desk. Sam picked it up, and Sonora took it away from him.

"Gosh, Mom."

They gravitated to their "own" parts of the room, a pattern and rhythm set by countless shared homicide investigations. Sonora gathered a stack of CDs.

"New Age shit and rap." Sonora stacked them in a dust-grimed corner. The desk drawers were crammed to the limit, and she had to work to get them open. "Just once, I'd like the DB to be a neat freak. Like those victims you always see on TV? Bank statements neatly filed, a journal with—"

Sam looked up. "You found a journal?"

"No, I'm talking about TV."

He coughed. "At least on TV they change the sheets."

"I hope I never get murdered. I wouldn't want you and Gruber tossing my house."

"Better clean it up, Sonora, you're just the kind of female who does get murdered. Which reminds me, Chas called me up last night."

"Chas called *you*?" Sonora sorted carefully through the top middle drawer, finding it touchingly similar to her own son's clutter. A collection of bottle caps—she wondered why guys collected bottle caps—several Superballs of various colors, baseball cards, a half-eaten Butterfinger candy bar that had gone white around the edges. "This chocolate actually tempts me, Sam. I must be further gone than I thought."

"I've seen you pick M and Ms up off the floor."

She started on another drawer, sorting through an eclectic collection of tiny screwdrivers, wrenches, stray nuts and bolts. "What did Chas want? Ah. A bank statement. Looks depressingly like mine."

"No money?"

"When he gets it, he spends it."

"Barhopping is expensive."

"I vaguely remember, back from the days when my life was fun."

Sam looked at her and smiled. "That would be before children?"

"Like everything else pleasant." She looked at him covertly, saw the shadow that crossed his face, realized he was wondering if his daughter would get a chance to grow up. Time to quit making stupid parent jokes.

Sam finished with the mattress and under the bed and was methodically going through the pockets of Daniels's discarded clothing.

"Anything?" she asked.

"Trojans be the brand of choice. At least two in every pocket."

"I like Ramses myself. I wonder if Sandra's on the pill."

Sam nodded. "That would let you know if he was looking."

"Or if it's a true like a commitment of a—"

"Shhh, Winthrop'll hear you." Sam moved across the room and closed the door. He picked a shirt up off the floor.

"You going through the underwear, too?"

"I'm not that dedicated."

Sonora opened another drawer. "Jesus, this guy's still reading comic books. What a baby."

"I read comic books. Hey, the X-Men. And by the way, Chas wanted to know why you weren't returning his calls. Playing hard to get, girl?"

Sonora found a packet of pictures. The negatives fell to the floor, and she bent over and picked them up.

"I never get the reason for these stupid strips of negatives. Nobody ever really uses them. They're just there to fall out and be irritating."

"I use them."

"You do not either." Sonora began sorting. The pictures had been developed on the twofer plan, so she got to see everything twice.

"I thought you liked Chas," Sam said.

"He's okay for Friday nights, but now he's talking marriage."

"Let me be the first to congratulate you, girl."

Sonora scooted backward in her chair. "Marriage, Sam, is for men and sweet young things in their twenties. I'm happy as I go."

"You have an ulcer."

"I'm happy all around this ulcer."

"So live with him."

"My washing machine won't take another person."

Sam looked at her over his shoulder. "You know, Sonora, just because your dear departed was a son of a bitch—"

"I know, I know. Doesn't mean all men are sons of bitches. I'd marry you, Sam, if you changed your socks more often."

Sam tossed a shirt onto a pile and sat on the edge of the bed. "Last year you said you were lonely."

"Last year I didn't know I had it so good."

"No, now, something happened. Three months ago you were over the moon about this guy."

"Yeah, well. He did a funny thing with the car."

"What kind of funny thing?"

"It . . . I'm embarrassed, okay?"

"No it's not okay. This is me, remember? You got me worried here, girl. What thing?"

"It just made me realize. I mean, if I didn't know better, I'd think I was dating my dead husband all over again."

"Run, girl," Sam said, giving her a look.

Sonora grinned. "Run screaming."

A toilet flushed in the apartment next door, and a door slammed in the hallway. Sonora opened another envelope of pictures. "So this is Sandra."

"You're changing the subject on me."

"Can't get anything past you, can I, Sam?"

He stood by Sonora's elbow. "She doesn't look old enough to have a boyfriend."

"My six-year-old has a boyfriend."

Sandra looked impossibly young, plumpish, brown hair over-permed. She stood next to Mark, giving him a look of intense adoration that could only be mustered by a very young woman.

Sam took the picture and squinted. "There goes our number one suspect. You can't tell me *she* handcuffed him to a steering wheel and set him on fire."

"Glued him to a pedestal, maybe."

"What?"

"I'm agreeing with you."

Sam turned the picture sideways. "You ever look at Chas like that?"

"I don't have to, he does it with mirrors."

"Is it police work, Sonora, or were you born mean? I mean, this thing with the car, whatever it was, maybe you're making too much of it. Maybe Chas was under pressure or something."

"Shut up, Sam, before you annoy me."

Sonora turned her back on him, flipped through another stack of pictures. Lots of friends, lots of parties, a few of the same faces again and again. One of Winthrop straining at the barbells. A lot of the three of them—Daniels, Sandra, and Winthrop. Winthrop looked happy in these, Mark, tolerant, Sandra, enduring. If Winthrop had been murdered, Sandra would be up at the top of the list of suspects.

Sonora selected two or three shots, set them aside, and opened an old cigar-style school box. MARK DANIELS had been printed across the top in purple Magic Marker by a childish, sloppy hand. Inside were more bottle caps, fantasy miniatures, gum-ball-machine playing cards, and more pictures.

These were older, various sizes and camera types, a collection from the past. Sonora picked them up and thumbed through.

The brothers had been close—at least when they were younger. Mark was the mug, making faces and devil horns behind his big brother's head; never serious, but somehow never quite comfortable in the eye of the camera. Keaton self-confident, solid masculine build contrasting with his brother's gangly boy's body.

A number of shots caught Keaton behind a fishing pole, looking relaxed and happy. Mark was always pictured displaying a nice-sized, dripping fish, Keaton ever without a trophy. How was it she knew that Keaton had caught those fish?

Keaton Daniels was very much on her mind. His footprints were everywhere—natural, perhaps, he was Mark's brother. Sonora wondered if Keaton would go back to his wife in the midst of his crisis.

As the thought occurred, she ran across a picture of Keaton Daniels asleep, his back to a tree, muscles slack, fishing pole loose in his hands. The shot was recent, likely taken by Mark. She placed it on top of the pile she had set aside, then changed her mind and slipped it into her jacket pocket.

Sam stretched, then scratched the back of his neck. "What do you think?"

"I think he was a typical kid, young for his age, and on the verge of getting engaged before he had any business being married. I don't see him inspiring a killing like this. I don't see him stirring that mature kind of rage."

"Just one of those random, drive-by, handcuff-'em-and-douse-'em-with-gasoline killings."

"No, Sam, this killer stalked her victim. She just took advantage of a small and unexpected opportunity."

"Such as?"

"Such as Mark. The little brother."

"The little brother? So you're saying—"

"Yeah. Of her intended victim. Keaton Daniels."

11

It was late when Sonora and Sam made it into Lynagh's to ask about Mark Daniels and a mysterious blonde. The Metropolitan Blues Allstars were playing, and the air was thick with cigarette smoke and the smell of beer. The music was dark and bluesy—beautifully executed and way too loud for conversation.

Sam staked out a tiny table for two in the back left corner, the only empty seats left in the house. The Allstars packed 'em in, even on weeknights.

Sonora watched the crowd—a mix, spanning the college and thirty-something generation. A noisy group of men and women in chinos and plaid shirts sat at a long table in the middle of the room, generating enormous activity at the bar. The women watched the dance floor wistfully; the men pretended not to notice.

". . . no, she said put on your clothes and go home."

". . . burned the canoe, instead of the . . . "

". . . pounding him till he pays . . . "

". . . oh, no, the judge is a total nutcase."

Lawyers, Sonora decided.

"Sonora, you want a Coke or something?" Sam was shouting in her ear.

She shook her head, then focused on the kids at the tables in front, wondering if any of them knew Mark. One of the girls looked familiar—long brown hair past her waist. Sonora pulled the snapshots she'd taken from Mark Daniels's desk. This girl was in one.

Sonora tracked her, watching to see who she talked to, eyeing the kids she hung out with. Mark was supposedly a regular—maybe this was his crowd. She nudged Sam, and he saluted her with his Dr. Pepper. She took the glass out of his hands, drank deeply, and winced. Her children drank Dr. Pepper too. She wondered why.

Sonora showed Sam the picture, then nodded her head toward the girl on the dance floor. Sam nodded and stuck a wad of tobacco in his cheek. Sonora suddenly remembered that she was supposed to deliver thirty cupcakes to her daughter's primary class the next morning.

She crooked her finger and Sam leaned close. She pointed to her watch. "*Time.* I'll go talk to the girlfriend. You stay here and see what you can get with that bunch up front, particularly the girl. I'll pick you up on my way back."

"Which girl again? The redhead?"

"In your dreams. That one over there. Hair to her feet and fingernails."

"Figures."

Sonora stopped in the ladies' room—cramped, dark, and overheated; gouged linoleum and paper towels lining the floor. There was a pay phone, and she checked on the kids—safe at Grandma's—and the machine at the office.

Two messages—one from Chas and one odd one. Sonora frowned, dialed the work number again, fast-forwarded through Chas, and listened hard.

"Hello there, girlfriend, recognize my voice? I bet not. You'uns get around, don't you? Don't worry, I'll call back."

Sonora ran a thumb up and down the coin slot. You'uns. The woman who had called Keaton had said you'uns. This was no blast from the past, no playful old college buddy blowing through town. No threats, no challenges, a friendly woman in a good mood.

This was the killer calling in.

12

Sandra Corliss lived with her parents on Trevillian Street in a small trilevel house that would have been new about the year Mark Daniels was born. Trees were few and far between, and the street had an unadorned look of bitter age. The cars parked in the driveways were old V-8s that had good pickup, touched-up paint jobs, and the solid build of tanks. Good safe family cars. There was the usual sprinkling of pickups, par for Kentucky.

The hazy glow from the streetlights showed the Corliss house backed up to a park, the backyard sloping toward a wide expanse of open meadow. A large, above-ground pool squatted at the end of the driveway. The front porch light was on.

Sonora parked the Taurus in front of the house, locked the doors, and walked up the asphalt drive. She cut sideways across the lawn and bumped a ceramic "yard boy." The paint was peeling away from the statue's right eye, giving him an aura that was both shabby and grotesque.

Sonora rang the doorbell twice. The television noises stopped abruptly, and the front curtain, heavy and blue, twitched at the edge. The front door was pulled open, creating a momentary suction that rattled the storm door.

Sandra Corliss's father was a large man, with broad stooped shoulders. His brown corduroy shirt strained at the belly. His hair was sparse, still fair, blond eyebrows thick. He held the sports section of the newspaper loose by his side. He looked tired.

"Mr. Corliss? I'm Specialist Blair, Cincinnati Police. Excuse me for disturbing you so late. I spoke with Mrs. Corliss yesterday?" She held out her ID.

"Sure, come in." He took a furtive glance at the identification, as if he felt the inspection was impolite. Sonora saw that he was wearing worn brown slippers.

A collection of shoes, various sizes, was lined neatly on a mat near the front door. The wall-to-wall carpet was pale blue, very thick, and in mint condition.

Sonora wondered if this was one of those households where everyone took off their shoes to preserve the carpet. She was uncomfortably aware that the heel had worn through in her left sock, and she pretended not to notice when Corliss glanced at her feet. Police officers did not take off their shoes on duty. No doubt there was a regulation.

"Sandra's in her room," Corliss said.

Sonora wondered if he expected her to fetch the child herself.

"Perry, who's this?" A woman in an emerald green sweat suit came in from the kitchen. She was carefully made up with frosty blue eye shadow and heavy eyebrow pencil, and her hair had been securely sprayed in place. The woman's knuckles were coarse and red.

Sonora extended a hand. "I'm Sonora Blair, Cincinnati Police Department. We talked yesterday?"

Mrs. Corliss nodded firmly. "Yes, of course." Her voice dropped to a whisper. "Sandra is very upset. She's in her room."

"Sit down, Detective." Sandra's father led her to the couch.

Sonora's ears were still ringing from the music in the bar, and she knew she reeked of cigarette smoke. She felt bad suddenly, one of the inexplicable waves of illness she was getting lately. It felt good to sit down.

Corliss settled in a gold velveteen recliner. A picture of a Spanish galleon in storm-tossed seas hung from the wall over his head. An open jar of peanuts sat on a floor lamp that also had a built-in table, imitation marble. The lampshade still wore the plastic slip-cover put on at the factory. Corliss sat on the edge of the recliner, tucked the newspaper on the seat behind him, and let his heavy, coarse hands hang between his knees. Sonora wondered what he did for a living.

"Sandra's been real upset," he told her. "We all have."

Sonora nodded. "How long had your daughter been dating Mark Daniels?"

"Two . . . no, three years. We were expecting them to get engaged sometime down the road." He noted the look on her face.

"Me and Sandra made an agreement when I took on extra time to pay for her college. She's not even supposed to think about getting married till after she graduates. Sandra's real smart. Her mama and I agreed she's got to finish school, not quit and put somebody else's boy through."

"I think you are very wise, Mr. Corliss."

He nodded. He agreed.

"What's her major?"

"Computer science, though her mom's got her taking secretarial courses. That way she'll always have something to fall back on."

"You could get her a couch," Sonora muttered.

Corliss frowned. "A couch?"

To fall back on, Sonora thought. A door opened and closed, and she heard the soft tread of slippered feet on thick carpet.

The girl was heavy hipped and fleshy in blue jeans and a pink sweatshirt with kittens on the front. Her hair was neatly flipped under, and she wore no makeup. Sonora had seen junior high school girls with a more worldly air. Sandra was like Mark, who had baseball cards and bottle caps in his desk drawer. She probably had stuffed animals on her bed and would live at home till she graduated.

Sandra kept her eyes downcast, her mother a force at her back. She took soft tiny steps and came all the way to the couch to shake Sonora's hand.

Mrs. Corliss stood at the edge of the kitchen. "Unless you need us, her daddy and I will be in here."

Mr. Corliss looked startled to find himself relegated to the kitchen, but obediently stood up.

"That will be fine," Sonora said, well aware they would be listening in. She took out her notebook and inserted a blank tape in the recorder. She could see that Sandra had been doing a lot of crying and was likely on the verge again. True love, she told her cynical self.

"How long have you and Mark been dating?" Sonora asked. Always start with something easy.

"Two years and two months."

"Two years and two months," Sonora repeated softly. She had the feeling that Sandra would be able to reel off hours, days, and minutes.

Sandra swallowed heavily and tucked her chin to her chest, reminding Sonora of her own little girl. Remember the cupcakes, she thought.

Sandra lifted her head and gave Sonora a look of pain-laced eagerness she often got from victims. Still new with their grief, still in denial, they looked to her to bring order to the chaotic abyss of violent crime.

What I bring, Sonora thought, is more pain. She looked at Sandra steadily, knowing the question would bring tears. She was used to tears.

"Talk to me about Mark, Sandra. Tell me all about him." She hit the button on her recorder. Sandra would be inhibited at first, but in a few minutes she would forget it was there.

Sandra cleared her throat. "Mark was smart. He was nice. He was fun."

Sonora liked the look of intelligence in the girl's eyes. She leaned sideways against the couch and braced herself for a sanitized description of a boy Sandra would mold into the kind of sainthood engendered by sudden, bitter death.

"He liked animals, and basketball, and walking in the rain."

Sonora's smile was friendly. "He *liked* walking in the rain?"

Sandra squinched her eyes together. "Sort of." She twisted the ends of her sweatshirt. "Mainly, I guess he didn't like fooling with umbrellas."

Here we go, Sonora thought. The terrible truth.

"What else can you tell me about him?"

"Well, I guess Mark thought Keat hung the moon. Their dad died when Mark was in high school. He had a heart attack. And Mark is very . . . he really looked up to Keaton. Keaton's the kind of brother you look up to. Not like mine." She grimaced.

"Were Mark and Keaton competitive?"

Sandra pulled her bottom lip. "Only a little. Keaton always tried to build Mark up, you know? Make him look good, talk guy stuff, go to basketball games. But Keaton is always good at everything, and people just like him. Women like him." She seemed puzzled by women who would prefer Keaton over Mark. "So sometimes I think Mark was a little . . . oh, I don't know."

"Out to prove himself?"

"Yeah, like that. But it wasn't tense or anything. Not like they were rivals."

"Mark have a lot of friends?"

"Gosh, yes. He liked goofing. Like he liked going out, and playing jokes on his friends. He'd talk to just anybody."

Talked to one body too many, Sonora thought.

"Was he in a fraternity?" she asked.

Sandra shook her head. "He really had a thing against them. See, he's got this friend, this roommate, they've known each other from junior high school. And the roommate is one of those, you know, he—"

"Brian Winthrop? I've met him."

"Oh, so you know. They both went out for rush, but nobody wanted Brian, so Mark said the heck with the whole thing. Keaton hadn't been in a fraternity either, because he worked all the time, to make sure there would be money for Mark too. I mean, Mark's the kind of guy you imagine in a frat house, he fits in with the guys and likes all the company and goings on. But he wouldn't, because of Brian."

It showed character, Sonora thought. Mark was taking shape. Keaton's admiring little brother, Sandra's courteous fun-loving boyfriend, Brian's staunch friend.

He was brave, the mystery woman had said over the phone. Had Keaton been talking to the killer?

Sandra's mother leaned into the room, feet still in the kitchen, not *officially* interrupting, but ever mindful of being the hostess.

"Can I get you something to drink, Detective Blair? Some coffee, or maybe a pop? I got Diet Sprite, Diet Orange, and Coke Classic."

"A Coke sounds really nice," Sonora said.

Mrs. Corliss looked at her daughter. "Sandra, you want a Diet Sprite?"

"No, Mama."

The sound of ice being dropped into glasses was distracting. The small rapport between Sonora and Sandra faded.

The drinks came on a tray with a plate of cookies—homemade and high in fat. Sonora took a sip of Coke. It did not sit well.

Sandra ignored the cookies and took a tiny sip of the Sprite that had been delivered with the attitude that Mama knows best. She grimaced and set her glass down with a gesture that dripped rejection.

Grief indeed, Sonora thought.

"Everything tastes like sawdust. Mama's been on me to eat since it happened, but food makes me choke."

Sonora had been much the same when Zack was killed—food like ashes in her mouth. She'd also wanted to make passionate love to all of the men that she liked. She decided not to share this with Sandra.

"She's just worried about you. Mothers look after their children by feeding them."

Sandra nodded, eyes glazing over.

"What did your mother think of Mark?" Sonora asked.

"She was crazy about him, she was always inviting him to dinner. He ate like a field hand, and she liked that. He could eat and eat and not gain an ounce."

"How irritating." Sonora picked up a cookie.

Sandra nodded vigorously. She picked up a cookie. A tear spilled down her cheek. Sonora could not help but think of her own daughter, of Heather's steady intelligent eyes behind round lenses, the way she would blink if you looked her eye to eye and push the glasses back on her nose. She hoped never to have to talk a child of hers through something like this. Mr. and Mrs. Corliss were not going to have an easy year.

Mark had been a practical joker, never cruel, but constant, always up for a laugh. And never at the expense of Brian, who made an easy target. Sonora listened closely, head bent, hearing the edge that hardened Sandra's voice whenever Winthrop's name came up.

Sonora probed gently but got no hint of jealousy, other than of Winthrop. If Mark had been looking past her, Sandra hadn't known. Sonora wondered what kind of story Sam was getting from the brunette at the bar.

"Sandra, did Mark say anything about strange phone calls? Or maybe someone he met who was . . . peculiar?"

Sandra frowned. "No, not that I know of. And he would have told me, I'm sure."

"Did he seem worried or subdued?"

"He was upset about losing his job. He thought they were unfair, and it hurt his feelings."

Sonora nodded.

"But he was pretty much over it. I think Keaton gave him some money to kind of tide him over, and he had some saved. He was doing okay. He has . . . he had a real heavy load this semester, so Keaton told him to wait on another job till after finals, then put in a lot of hours as Christmas help. So he was okay. He had more time even, and it took a lot off him. That was why he was up seeing Keaton. 'Cause Keat was kind of down, and Mark wasn't tied to work, so he could go."

Sonora leaned back against the couch. "What was his brother down about?"

"Him and his wife are having problems. They've been separated for a while, and Keaton was trying to make up his mind if he should go back to her."

"What did Mark think he should do?"

"There was some kind of problem about the schools where Keaton taught. He took the inner-city ones, by request, and she pushed him into going to a nice one in the suburbs, and he wasn't happy. But he didn't seem so happy *without* her. He was lonely, going to bars a lot. I know Mark was worried. He'd have to be to cut class to go up there."

"Do you know Keaton's wife?"

"Ashley? I've met her a few times. She works a lot."

"Mark make any new friends lately? Say in the last month or two?"

"A couple new guys he was playing basketball with. Mainly pickup games."

Sonora reached into her briefcase. "I want you to look at this sketch, and tell me if this woman looks at all familiar."

Sandra took the sketch, turned it to one side, studied it carefully. Sonora watched her and felt disappointed. The blank look on the girl's face seemed genuine.

"It's just a sketch, it's not dead-on," Sonora said. "Does it remind you of anyone at all?"

Sandra shook her head. "Nope. Who is she?"

Sonora was aware of irony. "Could be a witness. We just want to talk to her."

13

The parking lot at Lynagh's had emptied by the time Sonora got back to pick up Sam. She noticed a Minimart next door, remembered she needed mix for Heather's cupcakes. Her ears were still ringing from earlier in the bar, so she didn't hear the pickup truck pull up.

A young guy with longish hair and a sun-bronzed neck leaned out the window and grinned. Sonora did not catch what he said, but the sexual hostility was thick, and the three men in the front seat laughed.

Sonora went into the grocery. Instinct led her to the aisle where chocolate was sold brazenly out on a shelf like any other uncontrolled and unregulated substance. She heard a masculine snicker and saw, from the corner of her eye, that the three guys from the pickup had followed her in. She was aware of pain in her stomach—the ulcer was dependable, if nothing else. Her face felt hot. She was tired and not in a good frame of mind for this kind of stuff.

The one who had shouted at her, Bronze Neck, ripped into a carton of cigarettes and extracted two cellophane-wrapped packets. His fingers were thick, oil-stained. He nudged the guy next to him—overalls and a red neckerchief tied around the top of his head.

The third one had a crew cut and a space between his front teeth. He stuck the tip of his tongue through the gap. "*My*, oh, *my*."

Sonora moved away, thinking she would not be sorry to see

these three handcuffed to their pickup and set on fire. She found an aisle that looked promising, passed Apple Jacks, pancake syrup—Aunt Jemima, juice boxes. She heard laughter, saw the men huddled at the end of the aisle. They headed toward her, balancing potato chips, snack cakes, beer, and cigarettes.

The diet alone would kill them, Sonora thought. Just not soon enough.

Neckerchief walked close, jeans almost but not quite grazing her legs.

Sonora stayed put. Wondered what they'd do next. Her heart was pounding, which annoyed her. She did not give ground. They turned and went by again, shark passes.

Boys will be boys. Sonora paid for the cake mix, hands unsteady while she dug for change.

They were out front when Sonora left the store—short attention spans focused on a fresh victim.

She supposed that to certain Neanderthal-thinking juries, the girl could be dismissed as looking for trouble. She was anywhere from fourteen to twenty-four. Makeup was like that.

Hers had been put on with a heavy hand, black eyeliner making the face look pale and harsh. The line of blemishes across the forehead and clustered on the chin were caked with foundation and pressed powder. Her hips were slim, jeans tiny, fashionably torn at the knee. The hair was carefully volumized with scoops of gel, and the small pointed breasts were loose under the T-shirt.

The girl was smiling, but it was an embarrassed smile, ingratiating, please-just-leave-me-alone.

One of the men had her arm.

"Come on, jailbait."

Sonora winced. It was a term that always put a bad taste in her mouth.

". . . not safe for a girl looks like you do." It was Neckerchief talking. "Hop on in the truck, honey, and we'll take you home."

The girl pulled away. "No thanks. My mom's coming."

"Your mom?" Crew Cut swished a toothpick to the other side of his mouth with a tobacco-stained tongue. "Let's ride around a while 'fore she gets here. How 'bout that? That sound good?"

"Please," the girl said. Neckerchief still had her arm, and she tried to pull away. Her laugh was nervous but polite. "Really, don't."

"Don't, stop, don't, stop." Bronze Neck talking. The men laughed, circled in closer.

"I got to go now," the girl said softly.

Sonora wondered if her mom was really coming, if there was a mom, what this kid was doing out so late on a school night, how old she really was.

Neckerchief's grip tightened, and the girl winced. "Where you want to go, now, honey? We'll see you get home right and tight."

This last brought the laughter out from all of them, and Neckerchief pulled the girl toward the truck.

Sonora unzipped her purse, hand resting on the Baretta with a light but joyous touch. The threat was tangible, and she gave herself permission to get involved.

"I really don't like you guys." It was the first thing that came to mind. The girl looked up, startled, still smiling. Sonora was not smiling.

Bronze Neck laughed, but Crew Cut was frowning. Something about her seemed to disturb him. One mark for intelligence.

"I think I want an apology." Sounded good, Sonora thought, wondering what she should do with these guys. Arresting them would be incredibly time-consuming, and on what charge? Menacing? They'd be back on the streets before the paperwork was done. And this wasn't her town.

"What you give me if I do?"

Sonora looked over her shoulder. It was late. That was always the way—nobody around.

"Looking for help, honey?"

Sonora took the gun out of her purse, took careful aim.

Crew Cut took a step backward. "Aw, shit. We were just fooling around."

"Say you're sorry," Sonora said.

"No way."

"Okay, fine. But get in your truck, and get out of my face. You too, Neckerchief Head."

"Bitch."

Later, when she went over the incident in her mind, she could not remember making the conscious decision to shoot. But the gun went off in her hand, and the man's face went dead white, and Sonora was sure for a minute that she'd hit him.

The bar door opened and closed. Sam. His look of bewilderment hardened as he turned from her to the men.

They were already scrambling into the truck. Sonora saw no blood, no sign anybody was hurt. Her luck had held, she was still a terrible shot.

The pickup's engine caught on the second crank. Tires screeched as the truck pulled away.

"We'll be back, bitch."

"Yeah, and this time there'll be two of us," Sam yelled.

Sonora looked for the girl, saw she was gone. Ten points for brains, if not manners.

Sam opened the passenger door of the Taurus. Gave Sonora a look. "Accidental discharge tomorrow morning while you're getting ready for work. Get *in*."

She got in. He started the car, slammed the gears into reverse, pulled out of the parking lot.

"When the hell did you decide you were Clint-fucking-Eastwood?"

Sonora looked at her feet. "Why don't you calm down and hear my side of it?"

He wasn't listening. "Those are probably the only three rednecks in Kentucky without a gun in their truck. You're lucky one of them didn't come up shooting. What would you have done then?"

Sonora shrugged.

"What *is* it with you these days, girl?"

"What is it with *me*? What is it with them? I got no patience for this stuff anymore, Sam."

"No patience for what, Sonora, real life?"

"Hey, it was a rape in progress. Didn't you see the kid? They were trying to force her into the pickup."

"Oh, well, then just blow their heads off, you got cause."

"I think so, and you would've too, if you'd been there."

"Maybe. And maybe we're feeling a little bit pissy these days, how about that?"

"Sam, you know me—"

"Your point?"

"I've seen you do worse."

"You have not."

"Fine, just shut up about it."

"*Sonora*—"

"*Drop* it, okay?"

"What you going to do if I don't? Shoot me? What's so funny, girl, nothing here funny."

Sonora closed her eyes and folded her arms. "Interesting, isn't it, Sam? Women live with the implied threat of violence from men, and that's all right. Turn the tables and you don't like it much."

"That's got nothing to do with this, Sonora. Don't put me in that pig category just because I'm male. You're a police officer and you're on duty, and you've got procedures."

"It felt good, Sam. For a minute or so, it felt really good."

"Let me know when you get fantasies about handcuffing men and setting them on fire."

"If you think you're funny, you're not."

14

It was 3:30 A.M. when Sonora and Sam parted company in the parking lot on Broadway. The downtown streetlights cast a blurred yellow glow on the rain-slick pavement. Some of the office buildings were lit, all of them empty.

Sonora got into her car and rolled the window down.

Sam leaned an elbow on the open sill. "Going home, Sonora? Not strapping on a six-shooter and ridding the city of vermin?"

"Home to *bake,* how's that for innocent?"

"I'm going to grab a few hours' sleep, then go in early. You don't make it in on time, I'll give out the informant story."

"Thanks, Sam."

It was usually the other way around. His daughter's illness did not always coordinate with the murder rate. Sonora worked double time and lied liberally to cover for him when Annie was having a bad spell.

Sonora grabbed Sam's sleeve before he could get away.

He looked at her. "What?"

"I didn't tell you this 'cause I was mad. I had a weird message on my answering machine. The office machine."

"I get weird messages all the time, Sonora. Usually it's my wife."

"This was a woman—"

"So's my wife."

"Quit playing and pay attention. She didn't say much, but she did say 'you'uns.'"

That caught him. He leaned into the window. "You think it was her?"

"Yeah."

"What'd she say?"

"Just hello, you don't know who this is, but I'll call back."

He thought for a minute. "I wonder why she's calling you."

Sonora shrugged.

"If it is her, Sonora, then she likes the chase. She may be one of those nutcases looking for a police playmate."

"It's not like we thought she was normal."

"Good point. Watch your back, kiddo."

Sonora watched him get into the car, turn, and wave. She glanced up to the fifth floor of the dingy brick building, looking at the lit offices of Homicide. Fluorescent light poured through bent, yellowed venetian blinds. In spite of the chill, someone had opened a window.

She was glad to be going home.

Her car made the usual straining noises as it ascended the hill. Her engine would not last much longer on the streets of Cincinnati.

The rain had stopped, but the garbage piled up and down the sidewalk was sodden, raindrops glistening on dark plastic under the glare of headlights. A woman leaned out of a two-story window, tattered yellow curtains thrust to one side. In the light from the apartment, Sonora could see that the woman had coarse blond hair and a hard look. She smoked a cigarette, gazing listlessly at the wet, garbage-filled streets.

Cincinnati was depressing after dark. Sonora rolled up the windows and settled in for the drive to the suburbs. She felt out of sync, equally pulled by the squad room and the home fires. Fires, she thought. Home fires. Car fires. Mark Daniels up in flame. Keaton Daniels . . .

A horn honked and she jerked herself upright. She was in the wrong lane. She swerved to the right, hands trembling on the wheel. Sonora rolled the car window down, breathed chilled air, and leaned forward in her seat, driving slowly.

God, it was so easy. One minute you were driving, the next you were asleep. Was that what it had been like for Zack? Had he woken up before the collision? Felt pain?

There had been no alcohol or drugs in her husband's bloodstream. Sonora hadn't needed the coroner's confirmation. Zack had fallen asleep behind the wheel because he was exhausted. It tired a man out, juggling a wife, two kids, a full-time job, and the blonde of the week.

Sonora turned down her street and pulled to the side of the driveway, careful not to block the black Blazer parked in front of the garage. Clampett met her at the door, eyes bleary, tail wagging. The children, Heather most likely, had brushed out his fur and tied a ribbon around his collar.

Sonora gave Clampett a gentle nudge with her knee to make him move away from his ever ecstatic perusal of the garage. The house had the hushed peacefulness it acquired when the children were finally, deeply asleep. Sonora heard the hazy burr of static coming from the television in the living room. She went through the kitchen, set her purse in a chair, saw that there were dishes in the kitchen sink. Popcorn kernels littered the floor. Smears of chocolate syrup and rings of melted ice cream glazed the table and cabinets. Sonora wondered if they'd eaten the ice cream or spread it around with a brush.

She grabbed a blank pad of stickup notes and scrounged for a pencil in the small tin of odds and ends on the microwave.

I am not the maid, she wrote in large block letters. *No TV or video games tomorrow to help your memory. Next time clean up your mess. Love, Mom.*

She stuck the note on the refrigerator.

Sonora walked into the living room, where her brother was asleep on the couch. The sports section of the newspaper was fully open and draped over his head and shoulders. His cowboy boots were on the floor. *He* did not have holes in his socks.

Sonora turned the television off. Her brother sat up, shoulders hunched forward, and rubbed a hand across his face. He reached for the round-lensed glasses that sat on the arm of the couch, slid them on his nose, and blinked. He looked very much like Heather, except that his hair was blond.

Sonora sat in the rocking chair and closed her eyes.

"How many drinks of water do you give Heather when she goes to bed?" His lisp was very faint—only noticeable when you listened for it.

"One. How many did you give her?"

"Sixteen."

Sonora shook her head. "Idiot."

He yawned and stretched. "About dinner."

"Yeah?"

"The deal was a home-cooked meal for baby-sitting. Hungry Man TV dinners—"

"You didn't read the fine print. I *owe* you a home-cooked meal."

"That's six in the hole."

"You hear about that guy burned up in the car?"

He pushed his glasses back on his nose. "That *yours*?"

Sonora nodded, closed her eyes. "Man, I'm tired, and I still have to bake cupcakes."

"You don't want to go in the kitchen."

"Too late. You look exhausted, too. Did you play with the kids all night?"

"Horsey rides and piggyback for Heather. Monopoly with both of them. It's very energetic, the way they play. I can never figure out why you have to run around the table *twice* when you land on a railroad."

"You could stick them in front of the TV."

"Always the devoted mother. What time is it?"

"Four A.M. Like in the middle of the night."

He shook his head at her. "Why are you making cupcakes? Bakeries, dork. You've heard of them?"

"These have to be mommy-baked."

"Lie."

"Heather would know. Mine are always misshapen. They plump out."

"Remember the night I was here and you grilled chicken?"

"Thank God you carry a fire extinguisher in your car."

"Come on, get moving, I want to see how you charcoal-broil your cupcakes. Can I use your phone?" He picked up the cordless mounted on the kitchen wall, punched in his code, and listened for messages. "By the way, Sonora, you had a pretty strange call right around dinnertime."

"Leave a message?" Sonora got a mixing bowl from the cabinet and studied the box of cake mix. Duncan Hines. Eggs, water.

"No. It was a woman. I go 'hello' and she starts singing."

Sonora looked up from the back of the box of cake mix, trying to keep the oven temperature in her head. Bake 375. "She what?"

"*Sang.* An old Elvis song. 'Love Me Tender.' "

"That's not an Elvis song."

"He sang it, he made it his."

Sonora scratched her cheek. "Wait a minute, I don't get this. She sang 'Love Me Tender' to you over the phone?"

"Yeah."

"Sing good?"

"So so." He hung up. Grimaced.

"What?" Sonora asked.

"Big crowd at the saloon tonight. A lot of people there for line-dancing lessons."

"That's good."

"Yeah, but the girl who teaches went home sick and it looks like the flu, which leaves me with problems tomorrow. I can't cover for the kids, unless you want them at the club."

"Not on a school night."

"Oh, and Chas called. Wanted to know where you were, didn't believe me when I said you were working, and wants you to call no matter how late you get in."

"Damn. Fine."

"So don't call him."

Sonora picked up the phone, punched in a number, rolled her eyes. Stuart looked at her.

"Not home. At"—she looked at her watch—"four-sixteen A.M. He did this on purpose."

"Had you call and then doesn't answer?"

"If he's there."

"Not all guys are like Zack," Stuart said. Sonora looked at him and he grinned. "Some are worse."

"Boggles the mind, don't it?" Sonora got a large spoon out of the silverware drawer and pretended not to notice that her brother was peeling her stickup note off the refrigerator. He rinsed ice cream out of the bowls and loaded them into the dishwasher. Sonora could not remember ever seeing him do one dish the entire time they were growing up. She started to say something, then closed her mouth. In all the years they had fought over the bathroom, insulted each other, and been rude to one another's friends, she had never pictured her brother baby-sitting her children and cleaning her kitchen.

"Oh, my God," Stuart said.

"What?"

"Chocolate syrup on my polo shirt."

"I'm going to an autopsy first thing tomorrow. Guess what kind of stuff I get on my shirt?"

Stuart cringed. "Aren't you going to use a mixer?"

"I can't find it."

"It's in Tim's room."

"I'll just use a spoon. The lumps will probably bake out."

"Do you think you should fill the little cup things so full? That's probably why they stick out like that. Sonora, didn't Mom teach you any of this stuff?"

"Yeah, I'm Donna-fucking-Reed."

The phone rang as she was finally getting to bed. She picked it up on the third ring.

"What's so important you have to talk now, Chas, or don't you know it's the middle of the night?"

Silence. A giggle. Sonora frowned.

"Don't tell me you'uns got man trouble in the middle of everything else."

You'uns. Sonora caught her breath. "Who is this?"

"Don't play games with me, Detective, that kind of crapola is for men friends, not girl friends."

Sonora sat up in bed, hand sweaty on the receiver. "Girl friends, huh? So how about we get together and have a good talk?"

"Shop till we drop and go get some fancy desert?" The voice had a wistful twinge. "You and I both know we'd wind up in one of your little interrogation rooms."

"We like to call them interview rooms. Be nice to have someone to talk to, don't you think? I bet you have a lot on your mind."

"If you're tracing this call, Detective, won't do you no good. I'm at a pay phone, and it ain't my usual place."

Sonora listened for bar noises. Nothing.

"He's cute, isn't he?"

Sonora frowned. "Who?"

"Keaton Daniels. Don't pretend, I can tell you like him."

"You going to kill him?"

Dead silence. "You take the direct approach, don't you? Acting like a three here."

Sonora frowned. A three?

"How about this? I stay off him, if you'uns do the same. You won't believe me, I know, but I don't want to kill this one. He reminds me of somebody."

"Who?"

"Just . . . a guy I used to know."

Keep her talking, Sonora thought. "Look alike?"

"It's more than that, Detective. It's a certain kind of thing, an energy, a feel about him. Like he really sees me. It's the way he makes me feel. He puts me in the place I want to be."

"You know him, then?"

"I know him. He don't know me."

Sonora cocked her head. "What do you want from him? Why do you want to hurt him?"

"I don't want to *hurt* him. I want to be important. In his life."

You got that, Sonora thought. "You telling me you kill men to be important?"

Laughter. "You got to admit, it's a surefire way to get their attention."

"Surefire? Cute."

"And they deserve what they get. You be honest, Ms. Detective girl, you'uns would see my point. These men deserve it. This can't be a whole new concept, or you always been good?"

"Always," Sonora said, thinking of the men in the pickup.

"One of those good girls who do what they're told. Don't you see how that sets you up? Be miserable for the sake of everybody else. Never get what you want, 'cause that's bad. Build your life around some man, or you're nothing."

Sonora took a breath, wondered if she was out of her mind. "What makes you think I'm so good? I shot at three men in a pickup tonight."

Silence. Keeping her off balance a little, Sonora thought. Hoped.

"You did not. Not a good girl like you."

Sonora frowned. Was that a train in the background? "Believe it or not, suit yourself."

Silence. Then, "Why would you do that? Police work?"

"I had my reasons, like you have yours. You do have reasons, right?"

"Nice try. It's funny, I didn't expect to like you."

A click, and the connection went. Sonora grabbed a pencil and wrote on the back of a box of Kleenex, trying to get the conversation down verbatim, wondering in the back of her mind if she'd stirred the pot a little too hard.

15

The blade would hit the skin at 9:00 A.M. Sonora made it to the coffeepot in the lounge by 8:40. She poured herself a cup and wandered down the brightly lit hallway in search of the pathologist.

A sign taped to the green tile wall said BODIES MUST BE TAGGED AND BAGGED. At the bottom was a handwritten scrawl that said, *Please don't tie the pull tags on the bag together!*

"Sonora."

She turned. "Eversley, yo. I was looking for you."

"You wandered right past like a zombie. These early-morning chop sessions must be hell on a girl with a social life."

"I don't have a social life, I have children."

"You must have had one sometime or other." Eversley sat on the edge of the desk, smiling smugly. His eyes were gray, his face round and ravaged by old acne scars. His hair was dark and wiry, and if he carried a bit more weight than would be advised by the American Heart Association, it made him look cuddly in a sweater. Something in his attitude suggested perpetual exasperation.

He glanced at a clipboard on the desk. "You would be here for the crispy critter?"

"I would."

"At least it's recognizably human. We got one in last week that would fit in your microwave."

"Homicide?"

"Down girl. Somebody smoking in bed in their mobile home— otherwise known as an invitation to Infernoland."

"Who's up this morning?"

"Dr. Bellair."

"Ah, well," Sonora said. It meant everything by the book—goggles, apron, shoe covers, and gloves.

"This one did not go gently into that good night. Talk about your date from hell."

Sonora leaned against the edge of the desk, close enough to Eversley to smell his shaving lotion. She wished he wouldn't wear scent in the autopsy room, where one more smell, in the cacophony of other odors, was nothing short of an assault on the senses.

She yawned. "This guy wasn't a date, he was a victim."

"I heard about this one, Sonora. He was handcuffed, right? S and M."

"It's not a sex thing, Eversley. If it was a sex thing, it's going to be like this, don't you think?" Sonora raised her arms in the air, holding them out to the sides. "Or this." She moved her hands over her head. "He'd be cuffed to the headrest, or the door handles."

"He'd have to have a hell of a wingspan to catch both door handles."

Sonora pulled her hands forward, wrists together, waist level. "Instead, he's cuffed to the steering wheel, like this. You could call it the prisoner position."

"You could, but I wouldn't."

The soft tread of rubber-soled shoes caught their attention.

Even in dark blue scrubs, Stella Bellair had an air of dignity and elegance that managed to be distancing. Her posture was erect, her air of professionalism and courtesy rarely breached. She wore her hair in a chignon, tiny coral earrings adorned her ears, and her ebony skin, perfectly made up, glowed with health and well-being.

Sonora wondered how she managed. Bellair's schedule was as demanding as her own, and she was the mother of three. Why did Sonora know the woman's home was immaculate? Why didn't she wonder such things about men?

Eversley bowed. "Good morning, Stella."

"Morning, all. Is the DB out of X ray?"

Eversley nodded. "I saw Marty wheeling him out about fifteen minutes ago."

"Coffee," Bellair said, heading back down the hall to the lounge.

Eversley slid forward on the desk. "Okay, picture this. Guy meets Girl. Guy gives Girl a ride. Guy gets the wrong idea. Girl—"

Sonora felt the vibration of the pager that hung from an empty belt loop at her waist. "Hang on, Eversley." She pulled the beige phone across the desk. "Dial nine to get out?"

"What a good guesser. Nine is exactly the number you want. How'd you hit on it, are you some kind of psychic genius?"

"Can't deal with the living, so they handle the dead."

"That is *so* offensive."

Sonora chewed her bottom lip as she dialed. "Tell me this. *Why* is it always nine? And why is it nine-one-one for emergency? What is this nine thing? Why . . . yeah, hello, Blair here."

Sam's voice was thick with exhaustion. "The brother called."

"Keaton Daniels called in?"

"Yeah, that's what I said, he called in."

"So what's up?"

"Thing is, Sonora, he wouldn't tell *me*. Said he wants to see you right away, and it's got to be you."

Dr. Bellair walked by, heading for the autopsy room. Sonora realized that Eversley was gone. They'd be starting any minute.

"Will he keep?"

"I told him you'd be a couple hours. He said he was at his apartment. Number is—"

"The Mount Adams address? I got that."

"Wait. Your son's algebra teacher called too."

"Who?"

"A Miss Cole. She said you should call her. Want the number?"

Sonora swiped a coupon for a buy-one-get-one-free chicken dinner off the desk and flipped it over. The price of a two-piece dinner had gone up again. "Yeah, Sam. Oh-two-six. Okay. Jesus. Anything else?"

"You hear back from your new buddy? Sonora?"

"Yeah, I did, and it's not so funny, Sam."

"What'd she say?"

"We'll talk later, gotta go." She hung up, listening to sputters.

Sonora headed down the hallway, nodding once to a surgical resident working off his bout of indentured servitude.

She went past the viewing window, where families could look through meshed glass to identify their loved ones, provided features were intact. She passed a sign warning of biohazard, wondered what was up in algebra, and paused outside the green swing doors by a metal cart that held, among other odds and ends, goggles, shoe covers, and plastic aprons. She skipped the apron but took time for shoe covers and goggles. The gloves, coated with something powdery to make them go on smoothly, were way too big, leaving an inch of latex hanging loose from her fingers. She double-checked her camera awkwardly through the gloves, made sure it did, indeed, have film and working batteries, then went through the double swing doors.

There were several autopsies in progress, the sound of running water, large gray trash cans overflowing with waste. The smell of blood was strong but overpowered by the cloying scent of Calgon Vestal Lotion soap.

Dr. Bellair, hands on her hips, was studying a set of X rays illuminated on the wall. Eversley was looking over her shoulder. Bellair pointed.

"Right there."

Eversley nodded.

"What you got?" Sonora asked.

"Bullet frag."

Sonora scratched the back of her head. "You mean he was shot too?"

"Talk about your overkill."

The gurney carrying Mark Daniels's body was moving, as if by magic, toward the table. Sonora craned her neck, saw that Marty was at the other end, blocked by the rise of Mark Daniels's head. She took a cautious step backward to avoid being run over. Marty always swore he could see where he was going, and no one liked to argue and lay themselves open to a charge of political incorrectness toward dwarves, but a month ago he'd given one of the pathologists a solid thump, and last week he'd knocked over one of the technicians. With Marty, of course, it might have been intentional.

He eased the gurney beside the examining table—stainless steel, raised edges, water hoses, and drains.

"Nothing about it in the hospital report," Eversley said.

Bellair turned away. "They had other things to deal with. Let's get him on board."

Marty shoved his stool up under the head of the table and climbed to his perch. Like most dwarves, he was solidly built and broad featured. Sonora noticed that his gloves fit snugly, but his hands were larger than hers. His hair was brown, coarse, and curly, his thick handlebar mustache going gray.

Two women, both senior medical students, took their places beside the table. The brunette, Annette something or other, Sonora recognized, the redhead she did not. Annette, as usual, was unfathomably hostile, her dippity-do hair flipping up neatly all the way around. She had disliked Sonora on first sight, and Sonora saw no reason not to return the favor.

The bag was unzipped, and everyone except Sonora took a hand in lifting Mark Daniels from the gurney. They rolled him facedown on the table. Sonora rubbed the bridge of her nose, thinking how uncomfortable he looked. The backs of his thighs and his buttocks had not been burned. Blood had pooled there after death, giving the skin a dark, bruised-looking lividity. A small trickle of blood ran from Mark Daniels's nose and trailed to the table.

"No clothes, right?" Sonora said.

Eversley sounded exasperated. "Hospital says they're at the morgue, morgue says the hospital has them, EMT won't be available—"

Bellair was shaking her head. "From the look of these burns, Detective, there aren't going to be any clothes to speak of. The ER doctor could tell you for sure, but with burns like these, the clothes would have been embedded in the skin, unless it was a belt buckle or something."

"The arson guys didn't find a thing. I'm just double-checking. Actually, we think the killer took them, so if you find a fragment or something, let me know."

They all nodded thoughtfully. Everyone in the room liked being in on the whodunit stuff.

The body was turned, supports positioned. The neck sagged, the eyes wide. Nobody home.

Eversley picked up a hose and began to rinse the body. Marty worked his fingers along the back of the white, sluglike head.

The redhead was touching Mark Daniels's belly. "Is this a knife wound?"

Sonora grimaced. "Come on. Not a gun and a knife."

Eversley touched the split in the skin. "I'd guess it's a fissure from the burns. Let me grab a magnifying glass."

Bellair pushed the recording pedal with the slip-covered toe of her shoe and began her external examination of the body. The others, Sonora included, stood poised at the edges of the table, waiting to take the puzzle apart.

"Subject is white male, age twenty-two, sustaining several . . . "

It was long and tedious, the burned skin carefully examined with a five-power magnifying glass. Sonora yawned and stood on one foot, and wondered if Tim had been turning in his algebra homework.

She studied Mark Daniels's concave belly, the flattened buttocks, the hairless blistered scalp, and tried to connect what was left to the snapshots she'd seen. He would not get the chance to follow in his big brother's footsteps.

Eversley held up his camera. "Another Kodak moment."

They took turns shooting the blistered scalp, the charred stump of ear, the second- and third-degree burns, the blackened stubs of the hands. Bellair probed the bullet wound, and Sonora made notations in her notebook. The gloves were hot, and her fingers and palms were sweating inside the latex. Bellair wrestled the ventilator tube from Daniels's open mouth. The plastic popped and buckled.

Eversley put his camera back in the cabinet. He arched his back and stretched. "Get your scoopers, people. Time to make a canoe."

Sonora heard the whir of the small circular saw, the blade cleaving a Y shape at the top of Daniels's chest. The thick layer of skin pulled away like a heavy apron, exposing a butcher-shop panoply of meat and fat and fouling the air with the dark, human smell of an open body cavity. As always, the yellow globs of fat made Sonora promise herself that she would begin regular exercise. Tomorrow. First thing.

"I don't feel so good," Sonora said mildly.

Eversley and Bellair looked up sharply, always in expectation that anyone outside the closed circle of death specialists would give way and hit the floor. It was considered bad form to go from the morgue to the emergency room—even worse to make the complete circle and come back dead from the ER with a fractured skull.

"Just kidding," she said.

Bellair's expression was tolerant. Eversley stuck out his tongue. He took a large pair of lopping shears and cut through Mark Daniels's ribcage, and the orchestrated mayhem began. The intestines were scooped out, the internal organs removed, weighed, then set on a cutting board where a med student took slices and chunks and put them in specimen bottles.

Bellair took a cup of blood from the chest cavity, and the redhead used a syringe to extract urine from the bladder.

"No gallstones," said the brunette. She wrestled a knife across the tough yellow-opaque membrane of the gall bladder. Bellair slit the stomach, and Sonora suddenly smelled the loud odor of bourbon.

"Bourbon. Undigested popcorn. Some other stuff here, eaten a few hours earlier. Eversley can figure it out in the lab."

Sonora made a note. Mark Daniels's last meal. Bourbon and popcorn—Cujo's?

Sonora looked up in time to see Marty peeling the scalp over the top of the head. It pulled away like skin from a chicken, looking like a thick Halloween mask, and exposing the blood-reddened skull beneath the skin. Marty took a circular saw and cut through the back of the skull, a fine grind of bone clouding the air like chalk dust.

He took the carefully cut pieces of skull away, and Sonora thought of removing the shell from a horseshoe crab. Marty was precise and orderly, and instead of crabmeat, his reward was Mark Daniels's brain.

"Epidural hemorrhage," Marty said.

Sonora looked up. "A blow to the head?"

Bellair raised a hand. "Maybe." She examined the tough membrane covering the skull and cut the back section. "I'd say this is from the heat."

Sonora picked her camera up and took a picture of the skull and membrane Bellair had exposed, then stepped back out of the way.

The sounds that came from the med students' cutting boards made Sonora think of boning chicken. It was all much too much like what one found in the meat department at Winn-Dixie, which, Sonora thought, at least provided a small insight into cannibalism. She hadn't eaten meat for several weeks after her first autopsy.

Bellair was frowning. "Soot in the air passages. Pulmonary edema."

Sonora made notes on the details of Mark Daniels's agonizing death. And it was over at last, Bellair pulling off her gloves, intestines and various odds and ends belonging to Mark Daniels packed into a plastic bag, tied off, and left to rest between his legs.

Even dead people had stuff to keep up with.

Eversley wadded his soiled gloves into a ball, tossed them underhand into an overflowing trash can. "You know the accelerant?"

"Gasoline."

"I'll get back to you on the carbon monoxide levels, and the levels of hydrogen cyanide or sulfide nitrous oxide."

"What's the cyanide from?" Sonora asked.

"Died in a car, right? All that stuff is petroleum-based plastic. Which means it burns like hell and gives off toxic gas. Likely he's dead from a combination of carbon monoxide and cyanide."

"Not the burns?"

"They didn't help. But if it was just burns, he would have hung on for about three days, probably even lived. We'll see what the carboxyhemoglobin levels are, but cyanide disappears from the blood and tissue at a rate that in no way relates to the concentration."

"Tell me what you're saying, Eversley."

"He likely died of a combination of carbon monoxide and hydrogen cyanide poisoning. The cyanide levels will be hard to pinpoint, especially if the EMT was smart and gave him thiosulfate." He looked at Bellair. "They do that?"

"Wouldn't cyanide have killed him in a matter of minutes?" Sonora asked.

"Nope. Even with a hefty dose. Don't opt for the cyanide capsules if you ever hit death row."

"Thank you, Eversley. I'll write that down."

"It isn't a fun way to die. DA could make something of it in court."

"Eversley, he was handcuffed, doused with gasoline, shot in the leg, and set on fire. DA should be home free."

"Plus you got pictures. Because the defense attorney—"

"Eversley, you got to quit watching so much TV."

16

Sonora had always liked the Mount Adams area—the town houses crowded cheek by jowl, teetering over the hillside, overlooking the river and the city proper. The gears of her car made whirring sounds as the street rose at a twenty-five-degree angle.

A man stopped on the sidewalk and paused to look at the window display in the kind of jewelry store where they didn't bother to show prices. Something about the man, the set of his shoulders, the very shape of him, made Sonora hit the brakes and look back over her shoulder.

He did not notice, did not even look up, and it took no more than a quick second glance for Sonora to know that this was not Zack, didn't even look all that much like him.

She pulled the car back into traffic, feeling the sag in her shoulders, an ache in her back. She hadn't done this in ages, and she hated herself for it, that quick moment of recognition—yes, there he is—paths of logic in her mind setting off warning bells—no, Sonora, this can't be right.

For months after Zack's death she had unconsciously looked for his face in every crowd—mall, movie, grocery store—expecting, God knew why, to run across him at the Dairy Mart buying Shredded Wheat. Some part of her held those everyday mundane images, some part of her refused to believe that she would not walk into the bathroom and see him shaving.

The nightmare really was over.

She realized that the man reminded her of Zack because he looked angry—angry because she worked long hours, or because the kids were noisy, or because he was unhappy and any unhappiness was her fault, and life was unjust, and no one ever treated him right. Angry just because.

Sonora inched the car up the steep hillside, moving into the residential part of Mount Adams.

Years ago the area had been favored by university students, but the Volkswagons and Karmann Ghias had given way to four-wheel-drive Jeeps, Audis, and Saabs. Every other town home had been gentrified, and everything, from the facade of a bar called Longworth's to the Buckeye Security signs in a sprinkling of front yards and the trimmed and beribboned sheepdog prancing down the sidewalk, said *yuppie* loud and clear.

For Sale signs were common.

Sonora passed Rookwood Pottery, all wooden beams and English Tudor attitude, maneuvered around a blue truck that said H. JOHNSON MOVING AND STORAGE, and smiled to herself when she spotted a town home that was in bad need of paint, with a yard gone to weeds and an old church pew on the front porch. Rebel heart.

The church pew proved to be too much of a distraction, and she barely missed a brown metal Dumpster that said RUMPKE on the side.

If she did not have children, Sonora thought, she would live here. Provided a bag of money fell on her head.

Daniels lived in one of the better ones—a renovated, slender, three-story building of reddish pink brick trimmed in the shade of dark blue that the paint stores called Early American. The tiny patch of lawn was neatly landscaped and lovingly groomed.

Keaton Daniels had the front door open by the time she was parked and halfway down the walk. He was unshaven and did not look well, beard stubble against chalk white skin. He wore khakis again, a white T-shirt, thick cotton socks.

In Sonora's mind came the image of the brother, violated on the metal gurney, Marty massaging the scalp before peeling the face away and baring the skull beneath. Sonora pushed hair out of her eyes, trying to shed the image, focusing on Keaton. I do not want to see this man on an autopsy table, she thought.

"Mr. Daniels?"

He nodded and opened the door, mouthing polite words that ran together and sounded absent and empty.

He bypassed the living room and headed into the kitchen. Light streamed into the breakfast nook. Daniels led her to a round oak table covered with white terry cloth, a half-filled coffee cup at one place, along with a brittle-looking piece of buttered whole-wheat toast, one large bite off a corner.

A red dishcloth was thrown across the middle of the table. A rolled-up newspaper was thrust to one side, the red rubber band peeled off, the paper uncurling. A stack of mail sat next to the plate, two or three envelopes ripped open. Sonora saw a water bill. Visa.

She took out her notepad and sat down across from the interrupted breakfast and waited, chin in hand, elbows on the tablecloth.

Daniels did not sit. He rested a knee in his chair and shoved a thick finger toward a cheap white envelope with an Elvis stamp, canceled.

"I didn't go out yesterday, I didn't even get my mail. But this morning, I tried to at least get back in some kind of routine, so I made breakfast, got the paper and stuff."

Sonora checked the tape recorder, saw it was working, then resumed eye contact. Daniels leaned his weight on the knee.

"All that time, this was sitting in the mailbox."

He picked up the red dishcloth and uncovered a Polaroid snapshot. The picture was upside down from Sonora's point of view. She moved Keaton Daniels gently to one side.

Mark Daniels looked through the open window of the car, shirtless, hair wildly mussed. His hands were cuffed, stretched to the limits of their rings as he tried to pull them free. Sonora could see something wrapped through the steering wheel and looped around his waist. His hair looked wet, like he was sweating. No, she realized. Gasoline. He'd been doused with gasoline.

Just before ignition, Sonora thought. The look on his face was one she hoped never to see on someone she loved.

Sonora had gone through some nasty little caches before, but she had never known a killer to send one of the pictures to the victim's family. She sat down slowly in the hardbacked Windsor chair.

Her first impulse was to throw the dishtowel back over the picture, but the cop took over and she let it be. Keaton Daniels was beside her, pointedly looking away.

She took his arm. "Come on."

She had liked the look of the living room when she'd come in, the honey beige love seat nestled between two worn bookcases filled with paperbacks, a few hardcovers, children's books and games. An old walnut desk sat perpendicular to the couch, making a corner of comfort amidst the black-leather-and-chrome furniture tastefully grouped on the other side of the room.

Sonora looked from one side to the other.

"The good stuff belongs to the guy who owns this place," Keaton told her. "His company sent him to Germany for nine months. The junky stuff is mine."

"By all means, the junky stuff." Sonora sat on the love seat, and Keaton sat on the edge of the cushion beside her.

"There's more," he told her. "I called my mother after the picture came. I was afraid *she'd* gotten something."

"And?" Sonora had her notebook out again, the recorder going.

"No. But she had an odd visitor. She's . . . she's in a sort of convalescent home. She's young but . . . it's complicated."

"What kind of visitor?"

"A young lady. My mother's words. Who wanted to talk about Mark, and about me."

"About you? Did your mother describe this young lady?"

"Small and blond. Kind of fragile."

Sonora ran a hand through her hair. "Name?"

"Wouldn't give one."

"What did your mother think of her?"

"She was puzzled. She didn't like the woman's questions, she was too *familiar,* that's how she put it. She means—"

"I know what she means. So what happened then?"

Keaton clutched the arm of the couch. "That's pretty much all I could get out of her. I told her I'd come and see her, I'd see that it was all right. That made her happy. She likes her sons to come running."

The bitterness came and went quickly, but Sonora wondered if the role of big brother and elder son wore thin.

"I'll go with you," Sonora said.

He inclined his head toward the kitchen. "What about that?"

"We'll have a technician look at it. See if we can pick something up."

"Fingerprints?"

"Prints, saliva on the seal of the envelope, hair. Whatever."

"That would be something," he said woodenly.

It would also be unlikely, Sonora thought. This killer was too intelligent to lick the envelope.

The papers were calling Mark Daniels's killer the Flashpoint killer, a term culled from a quote by an arson investigator who had been discussing the flash point of the fire. Around the department they were calling her Flash.

Sonora wondered if there would be more pictures. It could get a whole lot worse. She studied Keaton Daniels, wondering how he'd hold up.

He caught her eye, held her gaze. Something changed, and she realized she was breathing a little too hard. She felt high-strung, suddenly, and nervous.

"Did you change your locks?" she asked abruptly.

"Yeah."

"No, you didn't."

"What?"

"I'm a cop, remember? I know when people lie to me."

"Must be hell on your kids."

"It is, and don't change the subject. If your problem is the expense, I know somebody who will do a good job for a cut rate. Look, I'm not trying to be a pest about this. But this killer may have your house keys. She's called you, sent you a picture, maybe even gone to see your mother. I'm worried about you."

It was true, but she hadn't meant it to sound so personal.

He moved away from her on the couch. Shrugged. "I had some idea that if she came here, I could take her on."

"Pictures change your mind?"

He nodded.

"Good." Sonora glanced back at the front door. Glass panels lined both sides, which meant locks would not keep the killer out. "You might want to think about an alarm system."

"I'm subletting. I can't do something like that without permission."

Sonora leaned against the desk, faced him. "I've got something I want you to take a look at." She dug into the briefcase, maroon vinyl, a gift of love from her children who had spent some time saving up for it. She took the sketch and set it on the couch beside Daniels, then stood in front of the desk.

The artist had worked with Ronnie Knapp for two solid hours, and Ronnie had been happy with the results. Sonora had made a point of asking him later, in private. People often said the sketch was good when the artist was in the room—afraid of hurting his feelings.

The woman in the profile was blond and unsmiling, though she did not look ethereal to Sonora. That kind of quality would be hard to catch.

Keaton Daniels frowned, but his eyes held the light of recognition.

"I don't know," he said.

"Keep looking. She says she knows you, but you don't know her."

"She *says?*"

"She calls me too."

He looked ill. Went back to the picture, chewed his lip. "I can't be sure, but she's familiar. Like I've seen her around, or something, but I can't place her."

"Anything comes to mind on it, let me know. Look, I need to make a call, can I use your phone?"

"Sure. One right there, and one in the kitchen."

"Let me take care of things in the kitchen. You get ready, and we'll go pay a call on your mom."

"Do you think she's in danger?"

"I wouldn't think so, but I'd like to hear what she has to say."

Sonora went into the kitchen, took the red cordless phone off the wall mount, looked at the picture of Mark Daniels while she dialed. Eversley's words from the morning autopsy echoed in her ears.

Another Kodak moment.

17

Keaton Daniels's mother lived in a convalescent home in Lawrenceburg, located between Cincinnati and Lexington on the Kentucky side. The "home" was several miles down a two-lane rural road. Sonora followed Keaton's rental, a navy blue Chrysler LeBaron. He turned left into a dirt and gravel drive—more dirt than gravel—and stopped beside a wood-and-brick ranch house that had been built sometime in the sixties or seventies.

Keaton led Sonora to the side of the house and up three steps to a concrete patio. A rusty grill, red paint flaking off, sat next to a wet mop. The grill was full of water. Lumps of white, burned charcoal floated in soot-streaked sludge. Old lawn furniture, black wrought iron, floral-print vinyl, was stacked in the corner. The cushions were torn, the chairs missing legs.

Daniels knocked at a screen door that opened into a dark cluttered kitchen.

"They expecting us?" Sonora asked.

"I like to drop in unexpectedly."

Sonora glanced over her shoulder. The house was surrounded by tobacco fields, stubbled with the withered brown stalks of stripped burley. The lawn was patchy and full of clover.

"Well, Keaton, oh, my word." The voice was loud and hard edged, and a woman opened the screen door in obvious invitation. "Keaton, honey, I'd thought you'd come sooner. Come in, come in, bring your little girl in."

Keaton stepped up into the kitchen and was gathered into an awkward hug that neither he nor the woman seemed to find palatable.

"This is Police Specialist Blair," Keaton said.

"Police?"

"She's a homicide detective, Kaylene. About Mark."

The woman's mouth opened wide, exposing stubbles of yellowed teeth, one going black, several missing. She was a hefty woman, solidly built, and encased in a loose tentlike print dress, gaping armholes exposing a grimy beige slip. The woman was braless, and her breasts sagged onto the expansive soft belly. Her hair was gray, sparse, pinned into a bun. Her eyes were pale blue, the whites yellowed, like wax buildup on a kitchen floor. She had a faint but noticeable mustache on her upper lip.

Sonora wondered if Keaton Daniels hated his mother.

"Honey, this whole thing is jest awful, jest awful." She led them through the dark kitchen to a dining room and den that had obviously been added on. The family pictures on the walls perpetuated every nasty rural stereotype Sonora had ever heard.

"All my people were upset about your brother, Keaton. We're all family here. And honey, your mama. Your mama like to die. I wished you could of come up just that night."

Keaton looked stricken.

"I'm afraid Mr. Daniels was with the police all night," Sonora said.

Kaylene opened her mouth, then closed it. "Oh, well. Well then."

The den wasn't dirty exactly. In fact, Sonora decided, it was clean. But the furniture was old, the flowered orange-and-yellow couch worn through on the armrests. An avocado green easy chair with a footstool had newspapers in the seat and a soiled lace doily on the headrest. A space heater glowed orange in the corner of the room. The fireplace was boarded up, and a black wood-burning stove sat in front of the hearth. There were baby pictures of toothless infants with unusually large heads, and a bronze pair of baby shoes sat atop a stack of *Reader's Digest*s on the mantle.

Keaton glanced around the room and over his shoulder. "Is my mother in her room, Kaylene?"

"That's where she is, hon. You go on, go on, I know she's wanting to see you."

Keaton looked uncertainly at Sonora.

"Take a few minutes alone," she said.

He nodded and moved down a corridor to the left. Sonora wondered if that was where Kaylene's "people" were. If so, they were a quiet bunch.

"Come on and sit down, honey. I guess I should say Detective." Kaylene settled onto the green easy chair and patted the footstool in front.

Sonora wondered if she was expected to sit at the woman's knees. She settled on the edge of the couch and hoped Keaton would get a move on. She'd felt safer working undercover narcotics.

Sonora put a tape in the recorder. "How long have you run this home, Mrs.—"

"Oh, you can call me Kaylene. But if you need it for your records, my married name is Barton, and my maiden name is Wheatly."

"Kaylene Wheatly Barton."

The woman gave her a royal nod. "Honey, you want some ice tea, or a pop?"

"No thanks."

Kaylene picked up a Popsicle-stick fan that had a romantic picture of Jesus on the front—brown curly hair, soulful eyes, white skin. Angelic sheep and storybook children clustered around his knees.

"I don't know about you, but I'm burning up. I got to keep it warm for my people, because they get cold. Blood thins, I guess, when you get old. Mr. Barton says the blood will thin."

Sonora began to feel fascinated by this woman with bad teeth who called her husband *Mister* Barton.

"How long has Keaton's mother been here?"

"'Long about four years."

"What's wrong with her?"

"I guess, you know, it's her laigs."

Must mean legs, Sonora decided. She heard the deep male mumble of Keaton Daniels's voice.

"I understand she had a visitor."

"You must mean that little girl come by yesterday."

"What was her name again?"

"Well, Lordy, Detective, you know she never did say. Just told me she was a friend come to call. Mr. Barton told me this morning I ought not to have let her in, but *I* didn't know. She didn't hurt nobody. But, oh, Miz Daniels, she was awful upset after. Awful."

"What did she say when she came to the door?"

"She come to the front door. Most of my people's family come to the side door there by the kitchen, we hardly use the front. And she says she's here to see Miz Daniels. Well, she's a pretty little thing. Tiny, you know, and that blond blond hair, not quite down to her shoulders, and wavy like. Brown eyes, and pale skin, but her cheeks was bright red. Scarlet, like she'd got a fever. I thought she might be sick even, and she seemed kind of shy. So I let her in, and took her to see Miz Daniels. I was expecting to see family and such, with Mark kilt like that."

Sonora nodded.

"She's in there, and I was in the kitchen, making up some corn pudding for supper. My people love that corn pudding. It's sweet and they like that. I got the recipe from my cousin. She wrote a cookbook once, self-publish by my brother-in-law."

Sonora nodded again. Patient, always.

"And then I hear crying. I might not have heard much in the kitchen, but I was going through the den to check on Mr. Remus, 'cause he needed his Haley's flavored M-O. My people have schedules, you know, and they don't want to miss. It upsets them."

Sonora was unclear on exactly what was scheduled, and had no intention of asking.

"So I pass by Miz Daniels's room on the way to give the Haley's flavored M-O to Mr. Remus, and I see her door's closed. Now that's odd, I'm thinking, because I like my people to keep the doors open, so I can just check on them and such. But it's closed, and I think I hear something, kind of a bird noise almost, then voices. So I go on and get Mr. Remus his Haley's, and I'm there awhile, 'cause he don't like that mint flavor, he likes the regular, and he can't make up his mind to take it. So finally, finally, I just say, well, now, Mr. Remus, I'll just leave it here while you make up your own mind."

Something about the way she said "make up your own mind" made Sonora think of Sam, and she smiled, and Kaylene smiled back and kept on talking, and everything felt friendly in the room.

"So I just leave the little plastic cup on the dresser. I put it in little plastic cups just like they do at the hospital, because I don't cut corners, you know, like they do at some places. I do things right, though what they charge for them little cups is just nasty." She nodded her head and blinked.

"Everything's gone up." Sonora leaned back on the couch and uncurled her fist. Patience. Patience.

"Now when I go on out of Mr. Remus's room, I see Miz Daniels's door is open, and Miz Daniels is up on her walker, though you can see her laigs is bad and hurting her something nasty. And that little girl is leaving, but they don't hug or nothing. Now you would think, if she was a niece or something, she might give Miz Daniels a hug, and might check with me to see if Miz Daniels needed anything. But I tell you I saw right off something funny was up. Because Miz Daniels looks mad as can be, and her eyes are red, like, and the tears is just a-running down her cheeks." Kaylene pressed her fingertips to her own cheeks, then cocked her head to one side and frowned.

Sonora waited expectantly.

"Sorry, I just thought I heard one of my people."

"Was the girl upset?"

"No, she seemed kind of excited, like. Really, she seemed sort of like my dog when he's got that cat down the road in a corner."

"Smiling?"

"No, don't think so, but smug, that's what I'd call it. That shyness was kind of gone, and she seemed pretty pleased. And I didn't get a nice feeling, looking at this girl. The feeling I got was nasty."

Sonora made notes. She dug in the vinyl case and took out the sketch of Mark Daniels's killer. "Is this anything like her?"

Kaylene took the picture with eager hands.

"Well, I just don't know, it could be. My reading glasses are in the kitchen. Let me get those, so to get a better look."

Sonora followed Keaton Daniels down the thinly carpeted corridor to an add-on that had obviously been built to accommodate Kaylene's "people." The ceiling was low, and Keaton dwarfed the hallway. His footsteps were quiet, the whole house was oddly hushed, and Sonora realized that Daniels had different tennis shoes on—Nikes this time.

Kaylene Wheatly Barton had not been sure that the woman in the sketch was the same girl who had visited, but her description—tiny, shy, unsmiling—dovetailed with the impression Sonora had from the bar owner of Cujo's. Sonora did not like the feeling she got from this killer, as if Mark Daniels's death was just the starting point for what she had in mind.

Keaton stopped suddenly, and Sonora bumped into him.

"Sorry." He put a hand on her arm, and Sonora was aware of the weight of it. He leaned down and spoke softly. "She's being difficult. I told her she has to talk to you, but I don't know." He scratched the back of his head. "She used to be very normal, your all-American mom."

Sonora touched his shoulder. "It'll be all right." She moved around him and went into the tiny cubicle. "Mrs. Daniels?"

Aretha Daniels was on the tall side and had likely been slender most of her life. Her waistline had thickened, and her shoulders slumped forward, back rising in a hump that meant advanced osteoporosis. Her hair was dyed jet black, and she wore black-rimmed cat glasses with an old-lady chain.

She sat on the edge of a single bed that was made up with a worn green bedspread of cheap ridged cotton. There was a chair near the bed, plastic with a walnut veneer, harvest yellow padding, a waiting-room kind of chair. The walls were paneled with fake walnut, there was no window. A small table sat beside the bed, the surface overwhelmed by a stack of magazines—*Good Housekeeping, Ladies' Home Journal, Mature Health*. A box of Puffs blue tissues was half full, and a glass of water with lipstick stains on the rim sat on top of a magazine that featured the fresh, intelligent features of Hillary Rodham Clinton.

Three gray cartridges had been tucked into the tissue box for safekeeping. Gameboy cartridges. A book of crossword puzzles lay open on the bed, a dull-pointed pencil wedged in the gutter between the pages. Sonora smelled perfume—White Shoulders—and mentholyptus.

Aretha Daniels was hunched over a Gameboy, feet propped on the bottom rail of the bed. She sucked enthusiastically on a cough drop; Sonora saw it glisten on the edge of her tongue. Aretha Daniels's thumbs moved quickly.

"Fireball," she muttered, her face mirroring the dull intensity that Sonora thought of as the video-game look.

Sonora recognized the recurrent bar of music that rolled forth from the handheld console. Super Mario.

"Mrs. Daniels, I'm Police Specialist Sonora Blair. I work homicide for the Cincinnati Police Department. I'm handling Mark's case."

The woman glanced up. "Sonora? That's unusual." She went back to the game.

Keaton sat on the bed beside his mother. Tension was apparent in the controlled way he put an arm around her shoulders. Very close to ignition, Sonora thought.

"Mother. Put the game on pause and talk to Detective Blair."

Sonora winked at him, turned the chair backward, and straddled it, resting her chin on top. Aretha Daniels watched her out of the corner of one eye, and Sonora got the feeling she was annoyed by imagined disrespect. Good.

"Keaton tells me you're a schoolteacher."

The woman rose slightly on the edge of the bed. "I *was* a schoolteacher. I haven't taught since my husband's death. My legs gave out on me." She patted her knees and winced.

"Are you in pain? Should I ask Kaylene to get you something?"

"Young lady, I am in pain every minute of my life. I wish there *was* something you could get me."

Keaton Daniels winced, but Sonora ignored him. As did his mother, who put the Gameboy down on the bed and gave Sonora a sideways suspicious look.

"All right, young lady, you want to discuss Mark. Very well. When are you going to catch his killer?"

"If I don't track her down this week, then we're talking months, years, or never."

Mrs. Daniels's hand hovered over the Gameboy. She pulled it away and pursed her lips. "*Never* is not acceptable."

"I don't like it either, so help me out. Because I think you talked to your son's murderer yesterday, and I want to know everything she said."

Aretha Daniels made a choking noise. "That horrible little girl that came yesterday? It was her?"

The irritable mom-voice was gone. Aretha Daniels sounded cowed and old. Sonora turned her chair sideways and leaned toward her. Keaton moved close to her on the bed, and she put her hand over his.

Sonora's voice was gentle. "Tell me everything you remember."

Aretha Daniels rubbed the top of Keaton's hand and took a breath. "She was Keaton's friend. That's what she said."

Keaton's look was intense, guarded.

"She talked about Mark. No, that's not exactly right. She wanted to know how I felt about Mark's death. She actually asked me that. At the time I thought she was simply . . . awkward. Socially. But she kept at it, kept questioning me."

"What kind of questions?"

"Well, like, wasn't it awful, how he died? Did I think he was in a lot of pain?" Aretha Daniels swallowed and clutched Keaton's arm. "Did I think about it, imagine it? Did I think he . . . think he . . . " The tears came suddenly, and Aretha Daniels sobbed.

Keaton pulled his mother close and slipped a wad of Puffs tissues out from under the Gameboy cartridges.

She blew her nose. "She wanted to know if I thought he had cried. If I thought he had *called* for me."

Sonora felt the heat rise in her cheeks, felt the ulcer acknowledge the call to arms, her jaw clench as the anger flooded her senses with an intensity that seemed dangerous, at the very least to her stomach.

"And the whole time she was watching me. It's hard to explain. It was like she was hungry for what I had to say, but her eyes were . . . odd, somehow, the expression. And she never smiled. Not even at first when I said hello."

Sonora knew that Aretha Daniels had been afraid and that the fear had shaken her, and hurt her, and that she would never admit it.

"Then what happened?"

"I told her to leave."

Keaton's jaw was clenched. "I want you to come and stay with me awhile, Mom."

"Keaton, no, I won't. I will never be a burden on you."

"You aren't a burden and I want you to come."

But he didn't, and all three of them knew it.

"Did she say anything else?"

Aretha Daniels shrugged, lifted a hand, let it fall.

"Did she ask you about Keaton?"

"At first, Keaton was all she talked about. I thought maybe she . . . " She turned to her son. "I thought she was some kind of a girlfriend. That maybe she was the reason you and Ashley—"

"No, Mother." Repressively.

Aretha Daniels looked across the room at Sonora, her gaze an accusation of a sort. "You have children."

"Two," Sonora said.

"Ages?"

"Six, my daughter. A son thirteen."

"Thirteen? No wonder you look tired. Up late worrying, I suppose. Keep him in hand, it will pass."

Sonora smiled but felt oddly comforted. "I hope so. There seems to be a problem with algebra."

"At that age, it will be a lack of organization and study. Likely as not he hasn't been turning in homework. Be firm with him, Detective."

"Yes ma'am."

Aretha Daniels looked at her sharply, as if sniffing for sarcasm. She patted Keaton's cheek, then pushed him away gently.

"You should go, it's a long drive home for you."

"Mom, come on. Come home with me awhile."

Aretha Daniels picked up the Gameboy and stared at the tiny screen. She patted Keaton's knee. "Be careful, son."

18

Sonora went from the porch steps into the muddy yard and took a deep breath. Keaton Daniels walked beside her, steps quick, hands deep in his pockets.

"Is there any place to eat around here?" Sonora asked.

"Probably something in town. Dairy Queen at the next exit."

"I've got to feed my ulcer. Meet me at the Dairy Queen, we need to talk."

He nodded, started to say something. Sonora waved him on. She wanted out and away. She did not like leaving Aretha Daniels behind in this farm-hell. She got her engine started first, gravel sputtering beneath the wheels of the Taurus. Keaton wasn't behind her when she turned onto the narrow two-lane road, and she looked back over her shoulder. Daniels was hunched forward over the steering wheel of his car, head bowed. Sonora grimaced and hit the accelerator, heading down the winding road toward the blessed interstate. She kept an eye on the rearview mirror until Keaton's blue LeBaron showed up behind.

By the time Sonora pulled into the crumbling asphalt parking lot of the Dairy Queen, she was queasy and tired of the car smell. She parked next to the inevitable pickup, and Keaton pulled up beside her. She dug her cellular phone out of her purse.

Yes, the kids were home. Yes, the kids were safe. Yes, their grandmother, Baba, was coming to pick them up. Heather asked when she was coming home, sounding wistful. Tim asked if she had her gun and if it was loaded, and told her to be careful.

Sonora tucked the phone into her purse next to the gun and went into the Dairy Queen. Keaton was inside, studying the menu. He moved close to the cash register. Ordered fries, a barbecue, a Sprite.

"For here," Sonora told the girl behind the counter. "Chili dog, onion rings, and a Coke. Yeah, I want chili on it. That's usually implied with a chili dog, right?"

Keaton looked at her. "Be nice, Detective, this is a small town."

The food came on red plastic trays. It was late afternoon, well past the lunchtime crush, and they had their pick of sticky tables.

"Over here." Keaton took a wad of napkins and wiped a frosting of salt from a corner table.

A fern in a basket over Sonora's head dropped a leaf on the seat beside her.

Keaton Daniels stabbed a french fry into a white paper cup full of catsup. "Nice place to leave your mother, isn't it?"

"Why is she there?"

"Her choice. Kaylene is supposedly a cousin of some cousin two hundred times removed. And my mother . . . my mother is nuts."

"I take it you weren't consulted?"

"My mother made the decision so she wouldn't be a burden. Pays her own way, except Kaylene calls me on the sly every month or so needing money for what she calls 'Mama's extras.' "

"Do you pay?"

Keaton looked at her.

"I'm a cop, I'm nosy."

"Sometimes." He took a large bite of barbecue. "My mother didn't used to be like this. The woman who limited my television when I was a kid now has carpal tunnel from playing video games."

Sonora looked at the chili dog, wondered how the ulcer would handle it, toyed with an onion ring.

"What was your mother like? When you were a kid?"

Keaton stacked three french fries and ate them in a wedge, sans catsup. "She was a teacher. Where I lived, most of the mothers were stay-at-homes. Not like now."

"What grade did she teach?"

"Elementary school mostly. Middle school for a while, then she was a principal."

"Not surprised."

"She was good at it. Good with the kids, but no nonsense. She would come home every day, pick me up at my grandmother's, or whoever I was staying with, and she'd be all full of energy and the things that happened during the day. Always had funny stories to tell me and Mark. She always seemed more interesting than the other moms. I work with teachers, older women, and they remind me of what she was like back then. The ideal mom time. I miss her. It's almost like—"

Sonora had the feeling he was going to say "like she's dead." He stacked up three more french fries, then leaned back, chewing.

"So. You married?"

Sonora laughed. "No. My husband's dead."

Keaton tilted his head to one side. "You're the first woman I've ever met who laughed when she said her husband was dead."

"Cop humor."

"Whatever. You're easy to talk to. Is that because you're a woman? Do you think women cops are easier to talk to?"

Sonora shrugged, ventured one bite of chili dog.

"I'm not being sexist. I know from my own work, men and women are different, have different strengths. Is it better for a cop to be male, do men get more respect?"

Sonora thought about it. "Once in a while when I worked patrol, I'd answer a call, say a prowler call, and people would ask why they sent a little thing like me."

"Is it weird being the only woman in male territory?"

"There are other women. I'm one of the boys at work. After work, no, I get left out a lot. But I see these guys all day, I have two kids, it doesn't break my heart. I don't like it when people think I get a promotion just because I'm female."

"I know exactly what you mean."

"Yeah? How's that?"

"Hey, I got hired *because* I'm a man. I get picked for committees *because* I'm a guy. See, if I advance, it's because men always get preferential treatment. They all think I have the advantage because I'm a white male."

"Do you?"

"Maybe I'm just a damn good teacher."

"How many men are there, teaching elementary school?"

"I used to be the only guy at my school, my old school."

"You were the only man there?"

"Only. Custodian, principal—all female."

"Is that good or bad?" Sonora started getting serious on the chili dog.

"Both. I liked being different, being the unusual one."

"And bad?"

"You know how women, when they work together, their periods synchronize? How'd you like to go to work in a building with forty-five women all having their period?"

Sonora coughed violently. Keaton leaned over and patted her on the back.

They were eating ice cream. Sonora had gotten to that point where the food had been in her stomach long enough to make the pain of the ulcer go away. She felt pretty good. No ulcer pain and a hot fudge sundae.

She shook her head at Keaton. "My situation *is* tougher. Look, even the little things. One assignment I had, women had to hike three floors to get to the bathroom. Men never have to put up with that stuff."

He poked the bottom of a frozen lime push-up. "At my school there *was* no men's room."

"They plant a tree in your name?"

"No, they just declared the bathroom unisex."

"So?"

"So? I go in, there's a tampon dispenser on the wall. Three women combing their hair and pulling up their panty hose. You think I feel welcome? Like I'm comfortable in there with a magazine?"

Sonora was eating french fries now, Keaton working on an order of onion rings. He pulled the streamers of onion out of the thick crunchy batter and ate them separately.

"Anytime they need a piano moved—ask Mr. Keaton. One of the teachers wants help carrying in boxes—ask Mr. Keaton. I'm the school brute."

Sonora stuck a straw in the milk shake. "The men are way over-protective. Sam's been my partner, more than five years. Even now, I know there are times he just wants me to stay in the car."

Keaton peeled a piece of chocolate topping off his ice cream cone. "Try this. The first teaching job I got offered I lost, because I wouldn't coach the basketball team. I guarantee you the women don't have to coach."

Sonora nodded. "The minute I get promoted, I get jokes about my love life. And guys that don't have half my smarts, honestly they don't, they get these great assignments."

"How'd you get homicide?"

"A lot of reasons, one of which is I write a good report. The clincher was because of a creep named McCready."

"Why, he your superior officer?"

"No. You really want to hear this?"

"Yeah, I do."

"Okay, let me back up to the beginning. I'm in uniform, and I get a call. A woman comes home and somebody has robbed the house. I'm first on the scene.

"So I'm looking around. And this woman, she's upset, you know, trying not to cry, because she's got her little boy, he's maybe two. And the house is a mess. Whoever has been in has ransacked the place, turned it upside down, pulled all the woman's underwear out of the drawer. And the whole time I'm in there, I get this weird feeling, something's not right. Just a feeling, my intuition, okay?"

Keaton nodded, leaning forward.

Sonora stared at a smudge of mustard, but she saw the house again, the woman, pale, biting her lips, holding her little boy, sleepy-eyed and slack in her arms. They had come home from the grocery store, and the trunk of their car was still open, still full of bags, when Sonora arrived alone in her patrol car. It was past the baby's nap time. Sonora remembered that he kept rubbing his eyes, laying his flushed pink cheek against his mother's shoulder. The mother had been young, blond hair tied in a ponytail, nose and cheeks pink with sunburn.

It had struck Sonora that nothing was actually missing. The TV was there. Radio. Loose cash on the dresser.

She had done it by the book. Asked the woman to wait outside, called for backup, gone through the house room by room. Endured the tolerant kindly look from the husky black patrol officer who had come at her call.

Getting the details down for the report, it had dawned on her that her best friend in elementary school had a house just like this one and that there was an obscure, little-used attic entrance in the closet ceiling of one of the bedrooms.

She'd gone to check. Sure enough, an attic entrance, but no smudgy handprints on the cover, which was wedged neatly in place. A child's stool lay on its side next to the open closet.

Sonora had stood on the stool, still barely able to reach, and had had to ask the cop, Reilly, to give her a boost. He had been good-natured but skeptical, offering to go up in her place. She knew from the glimmer of amusement in his eyes that this was going to be a "story" tomorrow at roll call.

She dislodged the attic cover, sweat staining the back of her uniform, though it was cool in the house, air-conditioning going full blast. The attic was dark, tiny slivers of light coming in from a ventilation grill up under the eaves.

The attic was hot, smelled of mildew. The air was thick and close, and her cheeks were flushed. She hesitated. If someone was there, she would be exposed. But Reilly was looking impatient. Any minute now he'd take over and send her off to the kitchen to finish taking the report.

Sweat rolled down her temples as she stuck her head up into the attic, eyes adjusting slowly.

No floor, just a bare-bones skeleton of wood supports and thick pads of pink fiberglass insulation. Something large in the corner, huddled to one side.

Sonora took her gun from the holster, thumbed the safety off. With her left hand, she took the flashlight off her belt and flipped it on.

The spread of light revealed a man with a gun aimed at her head. Their guns went off simultaneously. His misfired. Her bullet tore through the man's windpipe; he was dead before the ambulance arrived. His blood had soaked the ceiling of the hallway outside the bedrooms.

It was the only time she had fired her gun in the line of duty. She had killed one Aaron McCready, out on parole, a PFO with a history of rape, drug trafficking, and public disorderliness.

At the time, she had felt lucky. Passed over. Then two weeks later Zack had his accident and was dead.

"What's that?"

Sonora looked up.

"What's PFO," Keaton asked.

"Persistent felony offender."

He leaned back. "What if you hadn't looked? Think what if you had left him in the house with that woman and her little boy."

She shook her head. "I don't think about it. I dream about it. But I don't think about it."

*   *   *

"It's hard to explain. The guys will be all together like a football huddle, and they'll have this kind of laugh. Then they'll look at me funny, like they forgot I was there."

Keaton ate a spoonful of chili. "Listen, I know about those conversations that stop. Only mine are in the teacher's lounge. Usually, it's about M-E-N. Or childbirth. That's all they talk about, the agony of labor. I mean, God, how bad can it be?"

"You don't want to know."

"Why do you assume that?"

"What?"

"That I don't want to know? They look at me and launch into this big discussion of basketball. Like, I'm a guy, so all I can talk about is sports?"

"Let's just say they don't ask me to the poker games."

"Count your blessings. I'm the only man in America who has to go to baby showers. And they always think my gifts are funny, no matter what I buy."

"*Parties?* Do you know how many men want to see my handcuffs?"

"At least you're not some kind of male Madonna. Tell a woman at a party that you teach first grade and she gets all starry-eyed. Like you're the Mother Teresa of elementary school. Puts a real damper on any kind of intelligent conversation."

Sonora picked up a chicken finger, then laid it back on the paper box.

Keaton Daniels picked up a pork fritter and chewed halfheartedly. The glass doors of the Dairy Queen began to open and close, and people were lining up at the counters. Sonora glanced over her shoulder. Keaton looked at his watch.

Sonora thought, with a certain urgency, about the women's bathroom. And what it would be like if there were three men in there, checking their flies, jockstrap dispensers on the wall.

"What's so funny?"

"Nothing. I think I have a junk-food hangover."

Keaton started stacking trash. "You know, at home and stuff, I eat salads. Fruit and cottage cheese."

"I hear denial."

*   *   *

Outside, the temperature had dropped. The sun was going down, the sky dark blue. They walked silently to their cars, pausing by Keaton's LeBaron.

He put a hand on the door handle. "Day after tomorrow I bury my brother. Maybe I should buy a suit."

"You don't have one?"

"Just my khakis. Teacher clothes. Most of the children I teach— suits mean divorce lawyers. Makes 'em big-eyed and quiet." He cocked his head to one side. "You'll be there?"

"Unobtrusive." Sonora was aware of the roar of traffic on the interstate, the papery patter of brittle leaves blowing across the broken asphalt.

Keaton closed the car door, rolled down the window. "Too bad we're not in one car. We could drive home together."

She raised a hand and went to her car, smiling but uneasy. She had been thinking exactly the same.

19

Sonora took the elevator up to the fifth floor, where Homicide looked out over downtown Cincinnati. She leaned against the wall, tried not to think about the embarrassment of riches she had consumed at the Dairy Queen.

The front booth was empty now, after hours, though an extraordinary number of detectives were working late tonight—most of them on her case. She heard sobbing as she walked down the hall.

Sam steered an elderly woman toward the exit—she was tall, big boned, and her hair was set in an old-fashioned finger wave. She held a lace-trimmed handkerchief to her eyes.

"Hi, Mrs. Graham."

"Detective Blair, how are you, dear?"

"Surviving. You?"

"Better, now that I've gotten everything off my chest." She patted Sam on the cheek. "Are you sure I'm not under arrest?"

"No ma'am, Mrs. Graham. I need you, I know where you're at." He took a bill out of his wallet. "Now you take that, and don't be waiting at the bus stop after dark. Get you some dinner and a cab, you hear me?"

The woman patted his arm and folded the bill carefully. "Do you think I should set it aside for the legal fees?"

"No get ma'am, we have legal aid for that."

Sonora smiled sweetly and watched Mrs. Graham into the elevator. "What was she confessing to this time?"

"Daniels, third one today. Must be a full moon tonight."

Sonora stopped by her desk, saw the message light on the

answering machine said two. She pushed the button. The volume was up, and Heather's sweet voice filled the squad room.

"Mama, guess what, I learned to belch the alphabet today."

Several detectives looked up from their desks.

"Help me out here, Sam, I forget how to turn this off."

"No way, I want to hear."

At *Z* the squad room erupted in applause. Sonora grimaced, waited for the second message. A detective in the Atlanta police department. She scooted forward in her chair and dialed the number he'd left.

"Detective Bonheur." The voice was male, black, pleasant.

"This is Police Specialist Blair, Cincinnati. I have a message you called?"

"Yeah. About that NCIC report you put out on the arson murder. You file VICAP with the FBI?"

"Not yet."

"Just curious if you'd talked to them. Said your victim was a white male, age twenty-two, handcuffed to the steering wheel of his car and set on fire?"

Sonora was guarded. "Yeah, you got something similar?"

"Pretty distinctive, don't you think?" He made a groaning noise, and she pictured him settling back in his chair. She wondered if it was sunny in Atlanta. She should move south. Cincinnati was ever overcast, ever gray.

"Had one a lot like it about seven years ago, almost to the day. That's what made me wonder. But mine didn't use handcuffs."

"It was a she?"

"No question. Victim survived."

Sonora sat forward in her chair. "Tell me about it."

"Man name of James Selby. White male, he'd be about twenty-six or -seven the time it happened. He'd been in a bar drinking. Not a bad place, yuppie hangout. When he left, a woman approached him in the parking lot. Said she had car trouble. He told me at the time that he thought she looked familiar. I think he'd seen her in the bar, nodded at her or something. You know how they do."

Sonora wondered who "they" were. Yuppies, she guessed.

"He offered to look at the car. She said she'd been having transmission trouble, and she was going to ask AAMCO to come out the next day and take care of it."

"Pretty smart," Sonora said. "Nobody's going to pull out a tool belt and jury-rig a transmission."

"Yeah. So he agrees to take her home."

"His mama never told him not to pick up strangers?"

"He said it was kind of the other way around. That she seemed shy and scared to ride with him, but afraid to hang around the parking lot. He even offered her cab fare."

"Nice guy."

"Too nice. But she said no, just drive her home. She gave him directions, and they wound up way back in a subdivision that was under construction. Some houses finished, most of them frames—a lot of empty lots, earthmovers, broken sidewalks."

"They do that in Atlanta too?"

"Do what in Atlanta?"

"Build the sidewalks, then tear them up putting in houses."

"Ummm."

"This victim of yours. How does he describe her?"

"Small. Long blond hair. Brown eyes, he thinks, maybe green."

"That might be my girl. Think he'd be willing to take a look at a sketch?"

"Probably if he could, but he can't."

"I thought you said he survived."

"Blinded in the fire. Vocal cords damaged. Disfiguring facial scars, nerve damage to his hands. He was in and out of hospitals for three years."

"See any pictures of this guy before the attack?"

"Nice looking, as I recall. Big, solid build."

"Dark hair, brown eyes?"

Bonheur seemed surprised. "Sounds close enough."

"Did he say if she took pictures, after she tied him up? Use a Polaroid, maybe, or one of those Instamatics?" Sonora heard papers rustling.

"No, not that I recall, and I think I'd remember that kind of detail. On the other hand, you know how it is when people get hurt like that. He had gaps in his memory. He didn't remember getting out of the car, didn't remember the teenage couple who helped him before the ambulance came. He blocked a lot of it, so who knows?"

"Was that it? I mean afterward, did she bother him anymore? Try to get in touch with his family?"

"Not that I know of."

"Okay. If I can get my sergeant to approve it, I'd like to come down and talk to you. I'll show you my case file, if you'll show me yours."

"I'm cool."

"Any chance of me talking to the victim?"

"I could give him a call."

She paused. "How'd he get away?"

"Untied the ropes. She didn't use handcuffs, but I was thinking maybe by now she's perfected her technique. If it's the same one. You ought to talk to a Delores Reese in Charleston, West Virginia. She had something, arson murder, young white male victim. Happened about three years ago."

Sonora wrote D. Reese and Charleston on a scratch pad. She heard Sam calling her name, the background shuffle as people headed for the conference room.

"Anyways," Bonheur was saying. "My girl used a rope—laced it through the steering wheel. I guess with your guy in handcuffs, he didn't have a chance."

Sonora thought of Mark Daniels under the brilliant lights of the ER. "No. No chance at all."

The air was stale, the room thick with the odor of old coffee and tired cops. Sonora tried not to look at the powdered white dough-nuts in a grease-spotted Dunkin' Donuts box. Sam tossed a file on the table, gave Sonora a second glance.

"Look like you're going to be sick, girl."

"Dairy Queen, and don't ask details, just get those doughnuts out of my sight."

Sam moved the doughnuts, sat down, teetered backward in his chair. He pointed to a short, hefty man who drank coffee like it was a chore.

"It's Arson Guy."

"My friends call me Mickey, my kids call me Dad, my wife says you jerk. But here"—he peeled something off his tongue and examined it in the light—"here, I'm not a name or a number. Here I'm Arson Guy."

"Somebody toss that man a cape."

The door opened and Crick walked in, settled heavily into a chair. "What you got, Mickey?"

The room went quiet.

Mickey drummed a thick finger on the table, scattering crumbs. "No wallet, and no keys, except the one that we found on the floor of the car, driver's side."

"Car key?" Sonora asked.

"No, too small." Mickey made a space with two fingers. "Might fit a briefcase, security elevator, or a pair of handcuffs. We're still working on it."

Sam scratched his chin. "Why would the key to the handcuffs wind up on the driver's side, where Daniels was?"

"Maybe Flash dropped it," Gruber said. "Or maybe Daniels got it away from her."

"No sign of car or house keys?" Sonora said.

"You asked me that already. Nope."

Crick looked grim. "So she's got the keys and the wallet, the shirt and the shoes."

"Trophies," Sam said. "Hey, Sonora, you tell the brother to change his locks?"

"More than once."

A woman laughed in the hallway, and Molliter closed the door. Sonora checked her watch. A cop who sounded happy this late in the day was a cop who was going home. Sonora toyed with her coffee mug, finger smearing the lipstick stain on the rim. The smudge gave her pleasure—the mark of a woman in a room full of men. Plus it kept people from borrowing her cup.

Crick frowned. "Sanders had court and it ran over, but she pulled the phone records from that bar, Cujo's. It's a definite that somebody called Keaton Daniels's Mount Adams town house the night of the killing."

"Time?" Sonora said.

Crick stretched. "Nine-thirty, thereabouts."

"So it was her." Sonora leaned back in her chair and closed her eyes, seeing Mark Daniels on the autopsy table. She thought of Keaton, and how she had left the tape recorder off at the Dairy Queen while they talked. She opened her eyes and leaned toward Crick. "We got a problem with the brother. You see the picture Flash sent him?"

Crick looked up. "Still in the lab, but yeah, I've seen it."

"Flash has been to see this guy's mother, too."

"Mark Daniels's mother?"

"Yeah, asking about *Keaton*. No question she's after him, Sergeant. She's called him, sent him pictures. Snags Mark in the bar that Keaton goes to. Kills Mark in Keaton's car."

"Your instinct again," Molliter said.

"For Christ's sake, Molliter, look at the behavior here."

"Hey, don't jump down my throat, Sonora. Think about it. She did the dirty deed, maybe she'll move on."

"Yeah, and clap three times for Tinker Bell."

Sam scratched his chin. "But she's not moving on, Molliter, that's the whole point." He picked up a file, looked at Sonora. "What was it she said on the phone? She wanted to be important?"

"It's not just that," Sonora said. "She said there was something special about Keaton. She said she didn't want to kill him."

"You believe her?" Gruber asked.

Crick waved a hand over his head. "Sanity check, folks, *believe* her? This woman is a manipulative sociopath, she'll say anything to get what she wants."

"That's the point," Gruber said. "What's she want?"

"She wants Keaton," Sonora said.

Gruber pointed a finger. "She's calling *you*."

Crick leaned back in his chair and folded his arms. "Let's put a little extra surveillance around the town house. Get the night man to give Daniels a regular call, check up on things."

Sonora realized she'd been holding her breath. Exhaled. Knew what the answer would be, but asked anyway.

"How about real surveillance? Somebody outside the town house at night, and with Daniels during the day at work, or at least to and from the school."

Crick gave her a small smile, rubbed the back of his neck. "Sonora—"

"She's after him, Crick, you know she is. Surveil *him* and we'll catch *her*."

"Sonora—"

"You want another one? Up in flames? You seen the Daniels autopsy shots?"

"Sonora—"

"I'll put in extra hours." She waited.

"Oh, good. I get to finish a sentence." He held up a finger. "One, you're already working extra hours. You going to quit sleeping? Two, something like this, it's open-ended. She could hit him now, next week, next month. Could even be next year. We don't have that kind of manpower and you know it."

Sonora nodded. She knew the load, the budget, the economy. "This can all be traced back to George Bush."

Molliter looked up. "Excuse me?"

Sonora caught Crick's eye. "You realize she likes games. She's playing catch-me-if-you-can. That's why I'm getting the calls."

Crick gave her a cagey smile. "Glad you brought that up. Much as the camera loves my face"—he slapped his left cheek—"Lieutenant Abalone and I have talked it over, and we want you, yes, you, Sonora, to do the press conference. Which, by the way, is scheduled this evening in about one hour."

Sonora swallowed. "Very funny, sir."

"Couldn't be more serious. We like the woman-to-woman angle. She does too, obviously. Flash will be watching, and we want her watching you. Maybe she'll call you again. Have a little girl talk."

Sam grimaced. "The things you girls talk about."

"I like it," Gruber said.

Molliter looked her over. "She's got a spot on her tie."

"Look, Sergeant, I don't see what this has to do with giving Keaton protection, and I'm not feeling too good, and I'm really bad at any kind of thing where I have to get up in front of people and—"

Sam shook his head. "She'll get nervous and throw up. She's scared to death to stand up and talk in front of people. Won't even raise her hand at a PTA meeting."

Gruber shrugged. "Just make sure she throws up before they start the cameras."

Crick raised his voice. "Just look confident, Sonora. Say you're closing in, that you're going to make an arrest anytime now. Be patronizing. Make it clear that you know Flash isn't half as smart as you are."

"Gonna take some acting to pull that off." A voice from the back.

"You want her to show the sketch?" Sam asked.

"We sent it over to the television stations this morning when we set this up."

Sonora looked down at her tie, then over at Sam's. "Yours is clean. Too bad it's ugly."

He pulled the knot loose and tossed the tie across the table.

Sonora looked at Crick. "Anything else?"

"Withhold the business with the handcuffs. Hold the keys—the small one and the ones that are missing." He stood up, stretched, looked her up and down absently. "And comb your hair."

20

Sonora took a count of reporters, camera people, pretty faces with microphones. She looked down at Sam's tie. Ugly.

Mokie Barnes, Cincinnati PD's public information officer, gave her a worried look, saw she was watching, and smiled encouragingly. Sonora was not without sympathy. If she were a PR person, she would not consider herself good material either.

Barnes stepped in front of the lights and cameras, said a few words Sonora was too nervous and preoccupied to make sense of, then motioned Sonora to come forward.

The lights from the cameras warmed the room. Sonora had everyone's complete attention. She didn't want it.

She swallowed, throat dry, knees shaky, thinking of the Monday-morning quarterbacks at the department who would be watching with critical eyes. She cleared her throat, then remembered Mokie had told her not to. Strike one. She lifted her chin and began to speak.

"Sometime late last Tuesday night, Mark Daniels, age twenty-two, left a local bar with an unknown woman. Mr. Daniels was later rescued from a burning automobile in Mount Airy Forest, by Patrol Officers Kyle Minner and Gerald Finch. Mr. Daniels sustained severe burns and died early Wednesday morning at University Hospital. Officer Minner was critically injured while freeing Mr. Daniels from his car—"

"Did Daniels live long enough to identify his killer?" Tracy Vandemeer. Right on cue, cooperating, as asked.

Sonora looked sternly into the camera. "Mr. Daniels was able to give us detailed information on his assailant before he died. We expect to make an arrest very soon."

"Was the killer the woman he left with from the bar?"

"Do you have her name?"

"Can you describe her?"

"Is the killer a woman?"

Sonora nodded. "We believe so."

"How did she kill him?"

Sonora looked grave. "Mr. Daniels was tied up, doused with accelerant, then set on fire."

"Was he conscious?"

"Yes."

"Had he had sexual relations with this killer?"

"We don't believe so."

"Was this woman a prostitute?"

"How long was he in the car before the officer pulled him out?"

Sonora made a grudging show of reluctance. "We do not think the killer was a prostitute, but we do not rule that out."

"Can you describe her?"

"Was she working with a partner?"

"Was Daniels robbed?"

"Did Daniels know his killer?"

"We believe Mr. Daniels met the woman in a bar Tuesday night, a few hours before his death."

Intense faces. Furious scribbling from the print media.

"Had they known each other long?"

Sonora shook her head. "We're still working on that."

"Do you have her name?"

"We can't release that information at this time."

"Wasn't Daniels from Texas?"

"He was from Kentucky, wasn't he?"

"Mark Daniels was a student at the University of Kentucky, and was working on a bachelor's degree in social work."

"What do you know about the killer?"

"The woman last seen with Daniels is small boned and short. She has brown eyes and wavy blond hair. We have a sketch." Sonora waited for the cue from the cameraman. He nodded and she went on. "Anybody who has seen this woman, or has any information about this crime, is asked to call the police department immediately, and ask for Specialists Blair or Delarosa."

"Detective Blair, don't you consider this a rather grisly crime for a woman to commit?"

"I think it's a grisly crime for anyone to commit, and I personally intend to see the perpetrator brought to justice." God, Sonora thought. I sound like *Dragnet*. But Crick had said to make it personal.

"What kind of a person does this?"

Sonora thought of her key words. Pathetic. Dysfunctional. "We're obviously talking about a *pathetic* individual with extremely poor social skills—"

Someone in the back of the room laughed loudly. "I'll say."

"A severely dysfunctional individual." Sonora took a breath. She'd gotten it all in. She looked at them, felt relieved—let them hammer, then wind down. She nodded, did not smile, thanked them for their attention, and walked away.

Someone called her name. Tracy Vandemeer smiled maliciously. "*Love* the tie, Sonora."

21

Mark Daniels's father had been born, raised, and buried in Donner, Kentucky. In death, at least, Mark would follow in his footsteps.

Sonora drove and Sam frowned over a map. He smelled faintly of cologne, his cheeks pink and freshly shaven. He had gotten a haircut the day before, and he looked younger than ever, different in his best suit.

He refolded the map, pulled down the visor, and looked in the mirror, fingering his tie.

"I don't know, Sonora. Yellow? What do you think?"

"I kind of love it, Sam."

"I hate any tie I don't pick out my own self. That a new lipstick?" he asked.

"Yeah."

"Too dark."

Sonora looked in the rearview mirror.

"Watch *out*."

She looked up and slammed on the brakes.

"*Jeez,*" Sam said. "Your lipstick is fine."

"You'll be the visible cop," Sam was saying as they pulled up to the redbrick church. White columns gave the structure a feeling of elegance and grace. "Here, here, park here."

"I hate to parallel park."

"Come on, Sonora."

She pulled to the side of a white Lincoln Continental.

Sam shifted in his seat. "Molliter and Gruber should be here already, looking through the crowd. Flash will be tempted as hell to show up."

"I'm staying close to Keaton. He'll signal if someone looks promising, odd in any way. You watch the girls in the pews, see if they're crying like their hearts will break, or looking smug. Looking hellish at Sandra, or watching Keaton."

"Yeah."

"Love that tone, Sam. You don't think he had anything to do with it?"

"No. It was too nice a car to burn up if it was his own."

Cars were arriving in a steady stream, circling the church parking lot and cruising up and down the main drag, looking for a place to light. Sonora looked over her shoulder, turned the wheel hard to the right.

Sam pretended to wipe sweat from his brow. "I was sure that Lincoln had bought it, as least as far as the paint job."

"It's hard to see in this Taurus, Sam."

"We need teeny tiny cars for teeny tiny cops." He unbuckled his seat belt and got on the radio. "I'll bet Molliter's been here a half hour. He's usually early."

"He's anal retentive." Sonora laid her head back on the seat. They hadn't stopped for lunch, and the ulcer was saying hello. She glanced at Sam, still on the radio, coordinating, and tapped a fingernail on the steering wheel, half expecting Sam to comment on the dark nail polish.

She recognized the navy blue Chrysler LeBaron immediately, watched as it pulled up across the street, stopping in a no-parking zone. The driver's door opened and Keaton stepped out. He wore the inevitable khakis and a blue striped shirt, dark tie, sport coat. Reeboks this time, and they looked new.

Sonora laughed softly. "So he didn't get the suit. Good for you, Keaton."

He opened the passenger door and helped his mother out onto the curb. She leaned heavily on two canes, her steps slow, short, and cautious. Keaton stayed close, looking both ways before they crossed the street, stepping between his mother and oncoming traffic.

They were up onto the sidewalk when he saw Sonora. He smiled and she smiled, and they looked at each other for a long steady moment before he turned back to his mother, gave her his arm, and helped her up the concrete stairs.

Sam clicked the radio off. "What was all that about?"

"All *what* about?"

Sam looked from Sonora to Keaton, then back to Sonora. "You know better."

Sonora flipped hair over her shoulder. Opened her car door. "Butt out, Sam. There's nothing here for you to worry about."

"Tell me another one, girl."

The cemetery was on the outskirts of town and badly in need of mowing. Trees were few and far between, headstones thick across the gentle roll of hills in this community of the dead.

Sonora saw a headstone for a PFC Ronald Daniels who had died at age nineteen. She looked at the month and year of death. Tet offensive, Vietnam. A tiny American flag speared the ground beside the pinkish marble headstone.

Sonora was aware of intense activity in every direction. Frail elderly men and women being helped into chairs, Keaton Daniels moving from one group to another. His mother, seated up front, wiping her eyes with a neatly folded handkerchief. Molliter, Sam—detectives looking at license plates, faces in the crowd.

The papers had reported that Mark Daniels had lived long enough to describe his killer. Flash would know better than to come.

The temperature dropped as the wind whipped up, sending hats flying. People bowed their heads and shoulders, partly in grief, partly against the wind that tore at their clothes and rippled their hair. Sonora jammed her hands into her jacket pockets, grimacing when the wind carried her tie over her shoulder and made her skirt billow and bare her legs. The crowd shifted and settled as the graveside ceremony began, and Sonora wondered what was left to be said that hadn't already been covered inside the church.

A car from Channel WKYC-TV-Live-From-Oxton pulled presumptuously onto the lawn, and Sonora groaned, amazed that such a small town had a television station and news team. The *Cincinnati Post* had sent a photographer, who had taken a few quick shots of mourners in front of the church, then gone.

Sonora wondered if some regional opportunist was stringing for a Cincinnati station. At least if they covered the funeral, they'd show the artist's rendering of Flash. Maybe someone knew her.

The reporter was shunned as she videotaped the funeral from a discreet distance, disapproval evident in the stiffly turned backs. Only the children watched openly.

One of the funeral directors, face tensely polite, descended upon the camerawoman, smiling, gesturing, explaining the legal range. The woman went rigid, legs braced, thick blue-black hair blowing in the wind. She shrugged, moved a few yards away, and lifted the camera.

Odd for her to be working alone, Sonora thought.

The minister called for a prayer. Every head bowed, except Sonora's. She watched Keaton Daniels, sport coat whipping in the wind. And realized that she was not the only one watching.

The reporter had the vid-cam focused almost exclusively on Keaton, and Sonora turned and stared.

The woman leaned forward, arms rigid, and even from a distance, Sonora could see that her complexion was fair, despite the perfectly aligned black hair.

Everything fell into place—a strange woman in a black wig, working a camera alone, focusing on Keaton.

Flash.

Sonora started toward her, pacing herself. Keep it slow and easy; don't spook her. The woman was short, maybe five-one, fine boned and disappointingly average looking. Just as Sonora was wondering what she expected—some physical manifestation of bloodlust?—the camera swung reluctantly away from Keaton, capturing his mother and his wife, then moved again, panning the crowd, making a circle and resting at last on Sonora.

Flash let the camera drop, and for a long moment the two of them eyed one another. Sonora paused midstride, and any doubts she'd had dissolved. The wind blew hard against her chest, and her mouth went dry. The woman tucked the camera under her arm and turned away.

Got you, Sonora thought.

Flash went straight for the car, walking quickly but not running. Sonora picked up her pace, slowed by high heels that dug into the spongy ground, all the while thinking about the sensible flats in the bottom of her closet beneath the snow boots, also unused.

"Shit," she said. "Shit shit."

Flash was moving faster now, skirting the back of the car. Sonora's purse slid down her arm, and she kicked off the high heels and ran, aware that some of the mourners were beginning to turn and stare, aware that if she was wrong she was going to disrupt Mark Daniels's funeral and look like an idiot and maybe get a reprimand from her sergeant. The damp grass was a cold shock through the nylon on her feet, and it crossed her mind that if she was going to make a habit of wearing ten-dollar panty hose to work, she would have to start taking bribes.

"Hey, girlfriend, wait up!"

Flash faltered, then slid into the front seat of the car and slammed the door. Sonora thought of her gun, buried amid the rubble in her purse, which she had dropped along with the shoes. She was a homicide cop. Out of the gun habit. DBs didn't shoot back.

Loose gravel bit into Sonora's feet as she hit the pavement. The car engine caught just as she reached the side door. She snatched the handle. Locked.

Sonora made eye contact, saw Flash set her lips in a thin line. Flash jerked the car into reverse in a spurt of acceleration that ripped the metal handle out of Sonora's hand, twisting her wrist with a bruising wrench. Sonora stumbled forward and fell, skidding on her knees. She heard the shift of gears and the growl of the engine being revved, and she tried to scramble to her feet. No time.

Sonora threw herself sideways, vaguely aware that someone—Sam?—was shouting her name. She saw the left bumper of the car veer toward her, saw spots of rust on the metal. She shut her eyes, bracing for the blow.

Sonora felt a rush of air. The tires passed inches from her head. She lay still, feeling the wet ground seep through her jacket and skirt.

Too close, she thought, thinking the unthinkable—Tim and Heather, orphans in the world. She wondered if she had enough life insurance.

It was getting damn personal, this case.

22

The world was suddenly full of legs and voices, people calling her name. Someone shouted "officer down," and Sonora looked up to see Sam crouching beside her. She sat up, aware that her knees were stinging and sore.

"You hit?"

"It was Flash, Sam, get on the—"

"Done, girl, you think you're the only one around here with a brain? Called it soon as I saw you running. You okay?"

Sonora looked at her legs. Balls of nylon hung from a large hole in her panty hose, and her knees showed tiny pinpricks of blood across abraded flesh. Her kids often came inside with worse, and she'd stick a Band-Aid on them and send them right back out.

She felt mildly disappointed.

A new voice interjected. Gruber. "What'd you chase her for, Blair? She wouldn't have spooked if you'd just called it in. We could have—"

"Can the Monday-morning quarterbacking, will you?" Sam said. "You going to sit on your butt all day?"

Sonora took his hand, felt hot pain in hers. Gruber went behind her, putting his hands on her ribs, and lifted her to her feet.

They were thick around her—Sam, Gruber, Molliter. She looked over Sam's shoulder, saw Keaton Daniels three feet away, watching. He waved. She waved back with the hand that didn't hurt.

Off in the distance, there were sirens.

*   *   *

Sonora sat sideways on the passenger's side of the Taurus, trying to fill out a report with her left hand. The door was open, and her feet dangled over the side of the seat. She shivered. Her skirt was wet. It was getting cold out.

The radio crackled, the voice of the local dispatcher providing a comforting cop background. Sam sat on the hood of a Kentucky State Police car, talking amiably with a tall man in a Smokey hat.

"It was her, wasn't it?" Keaton Daniels rested an elbow on the car door, a pair of black high heels dangling from his fingers. He handed the shoes to Sonora. "It was her." Sonora turned the shoes over, studying the heels.

"Filming it. Filming my brother's funeral." Keaton spoke through clenched teeth.

"Filming *you* at your brother's funeral. There's a difference, and I don't much like it."

"I thought you were right-handed," he said, focusing on the pen in her left hand.

She showed him the wrist that was swelling and taking on a bluish cast.

"I thought she'd hit you. With the car."

"She gave it her best."

"But you're okay."

"Yeah, I'm okay."

He handed her a slip of yellow notebook paper. "I'm going back to the house. My great-aunt's house. This is the address and phone number."

"I'm sorry about all this, Keaton. As soon as I hear something, I'll be in touch."

Her mud-stained blazer was draped over the headrest of the seat. He ran a gentle finger down the torn lapel.

"Be careful, Detective."

He turned his back and walked away, and she watched him until the sound of heels on pavement caught her attention. Sam came toward the Taurus, gave Daniels a look that was not exactly friendly.

He rocked back and forth on the balls of his feet. "Word just came in over the radio."

"They got her?"

"No, she got them. Body of a security guard, over at WKYC-TV in Oxton, multiple gunshot wounds in the back. DB was found near a Dumpster that'd been set on fire. And the station car is missing."

"Flash, then."

He took a handkerchief out of his pocket, spit on it, wiped mud off her chin.

"Gross, Sam. Oxton people mind if we come take a look?"

"Said to come along. What about your hand? You want to get it looked at?"

"No. You drive, let's hit the road. Know how to get there?"

"Nah."

"God forbid you should ask directions."

The road passed through farmland in a succession of hairpin turns. Sonora admired the locals who could regularly drive the posted speed of fifty-five miles per hour and live to tell about it.

Her wrist throbbed, and she shifted to a more comfortable position, watched the By-Bee Mobile Home Park go by. The playground out front was abandoned and bedraggled—swings missing from the rusted metal A-frame, a merry-go-round listing dangerously to one side. There was only one board intact on the seesaws, red paint peeling away.

The mobile homes were old, rusting, the parking lot full of pickups, Trans Ams, and Camaros. One of the houses had window boxes, but no flowers. A yellow dog trotted under the swings, nose to the ground.

The speed limit went from fifty-five to twenty-five miles per hour. Oxton was tiny—a feed store, Farmers Food Co-op, Bruwer's Bakery, Super America. A small grocery store advertised Marlboro Lights and videos. They passed a Church of God's Disciples for the Lord. Sunlight glinted on Pabst Blue Ribbon beer cans stacked by a yellow sign warning of hazardous curves. Sam pulled over and studied the map.

"It's a small town, Sam."

"Yeah?"

"So I see flashing lights, as in emergency vehicles. Over the hill there, see? How many emergencies you think they have in one afternoon?"

"No more than one or two."

WKYC-TV was housed in a squat concrete cube, the back parking lot fenced off with twelve feet of chain link topped by barbed wire. Sonora and Sam parked alongside the street in front of an H&R Block and a Yen Yens Quick Chinese.

"I want an egg roll," Sonora said.

"Let's look at the DB first. If you seriously want to risk Chinese in a town this size."

Sam got out of the car and headed for the deputy. Sonora hung back to watch, waiting for Sam to work his good-ole-boy magic.

She put her high heels on, smoothed her skirt, which had wrinkles and mud enough to be attention getting. She straightened her tie and put on more of the dark lipstick Sam didn't like.

Sam wiggled his fingers at her. Go to work, she told herself. Dead body time.

"Deputy Clemson, this is my partner, Specialist Blair."

Sonora moved stiffly, offered her right hand without thinking. Clemson had a firm grip, and she winced, bit her lip, pulled her hand away.

"Sonora came a little too close to whoever it was stole that car out of the lot and killed your security guard."

Clemson looked her up and down and touched the brim of his hat. "That so? I'd kind of like to get close to that guy myself. Come on around back." He motioned to the orderly knot of people who stood talking by the curb. "Y'all move on back, come on now."

Another deputy appeared and made kindly shooing motions, and people backed politely away.

At least things were friendly, Sonora thought. Saw things were not so friendly around back.

The hearse was open, and the DB had already been loaded. A fire engine, OXTON VOLUNTEER FIRE DEPT stenciled on the side, sat next to a burned-out Dumpster that dripped water and foam. Sonora peered at the asphalt near the Dumpster, noting the thick oily bloodstain. She went to the hearse, glancing over her shoulder at Deputy Clemson.

"May I?"

He nodded.

She fished rubber gloves out of her purse and peeled the bloody sheet away.

The man looked like somebody's grandfather, pale blue eyes wide and vacant. Sonora ran her fingers through the thick white hair, noticed that the full mustache was yellow with tobacco stains. She probed the scalp, found an indentation on the left temple. Probably hit his head when he fell.

The body was pliant, only just beginning to cool, but it was heavy, and shifting it was awkward. Sonora was aware that the men watched her. One of them stepped close and helped her turn the body. A deputy. Young.

"Thanks," she said.

He stayed to watch up close.

The old man wore a brown uniform and a leather jacket that was drenched with stiffening blood. Sonora probed gently, saw two holes on the mid quadrant of the left side of the back. She picked up a limp, heavy hand, noted the gold wedding band, the curly white hairs on the wrist. No wounds on the palms or fingers. No blood. He hadn't fought, or had time to react, which meant the first shot likely killed him.

She pulled the sheet back over the body and looked up to find Sam watching her.

"What you think, Sonora?"

"Hey, he was shot."

Sam gave her a lazy look.

"Hard to tell with the blood, Sam, but looks like two shots with a twenty-two through the vena cava. He never knew what hit him, didn't put up a fight. Makes sense. She's a small woman, she's not going to want to go hand to hand."

Clemson opened his mouth, then closed it. "You said she?"

Sam waved a hand. "Deputy Clemson here tells me that the guard called in a fire, then went out to investigate. When he did, he left that back gate unlocked."

Clemson shifted his weight. "What I can't figure is why he, I mean she, would start that fire up in the first place. Just calling attention to herself."

Sam stuck his hands in his pockets. "Car she took was parked over on the other side of the parking lot—which is where the body was found, right? She starts the fire as a diversion while she steals the car, only instead of putting out the fire, the security guard calls the fire department, leaves the fire to burn, and starts looking around the lot. He gets too close and she kills him."

"Why here?" Clemson said.

Sonora waved a hand. "Locals in Donner wouldn't know her, wouldn't know she had no business with the car. And excuse me, but this is a small town for a television station. Seems odd to me they even have a car."

Clemson pushed his hat farther back on his head. "It belongs to the owner's son—a little prick who likes driving around with the logo on the side." He glanced at the body, turned his face away. "This guy fought in World War Two, got four grandchildren. Wife's been sick the last five years. This is like to kill her."

"What was his name?" Sonora said.

"Nickname was Shirty. Shirty Sizemore. That's her, right over there. His widow."

The woman was small, figure wide and lumpy, shoulders sagging. She had a beaten-down air about her, a wilt that took years to acquire. Sonora met her eyes, saw intelligence, shock, and, oddly, relief. The same look she'd seen in her mirror the night Zack had died.

Another grieving widow.

Sonora leaned up against the hearse. "Still got his gun holstered."

Sam gave her a look. "What's bothering you, Sonora?"

"I was thinking about Bundy."

"Ted Bundy? Theodore?"

She nodded. "Just the pattern. Plans carefully year after year, but then something changes or sets him off, and suddenly he's going on a blitz. Taking big risks. Rampaging through a sorority house in Florida, with the cops on his tail up north."

"Think she's cutting loose?"

"I'm worried, Sam, I really am. They all do it, sooner or later. If this is her blastoff, we're in for it." Sonora rubbed the back of her neck. "Any sign of the murder weapon?"

Sam shook his head. "They'll go through the Dumpster when the hot spots cool. Sheriff says the autopsy will be done in Louisville, and he'll get back to me with results. And we've been officially asked to keep our murderers up north where they come from, and unofficially asked to be in on the kill if at all possible." He yawned. "You still want an egg roll?"

23

S onora went home and took a hot shower before she picked up the kids. She put on a black T-shirt, a pair of jeans, and worn boots, then threw on an old flannel shirt to cover the bluish swelling on her wrist. If the kids asked about it, she wouldn't lie, but it was best to tone things down.

Her daughter clung to her when she picked them up, and even Tim gave her a hug. They kissed their grandmother good-bye, then climbed into the back of the car. They reeked of tobacco smoke and seemed subdued.

Sonora waved at her mother-in-law. Baba watched them from the doorway, cigarette dangling from her lips, her three little dogs jumping and scrabbling the screen.

Grandchildren were exciting.

"What's for supper?" Heather asked.

"Whatever we pass on the way home."

They rented a movie, and Heather and Tim curled up on the den floor while Sonora built a fire in the fireplace. Once the blaze was small, but steady, Sonora settled on the couch with two Advil, a Corona, and a heating pad for her wrist. Clampett put his head in her lap and licked the bottom of the beer bottle. Sonora pushed his nose away.

"You guys sure you don't want to watch *Witness* first? It's a classic."

Tim rolled his eyes. "Mom, we've seen that movie so many times, we know all the dialogue."

"Can we make popcorn?" Heather asked.

Sonora fed Clampett a mushroom. "Have to do it yourself, I'm not getting up."

The doorbell rang, three times quickly.

Tim laughed. "Yeah, right. Want me to go?"

"Not after dark."

"Probably just some lady with a gasoline can."

Sonora pushed the dog off her lap and gave her son a look. She turned the porch light on and squinted through the peephole in the arched wood door.

Chas stood on the front steps, bouncing up and down on the balls of his feet. He wore new jeans, a shirt that had likely just been removed from an L.L. Bean box, and an Outback hat with a feather in the brim.

Sonora considered not opening the door.

Chas set a shopping bag on the porch, folded his arms, and shifted his weight to one foot, mouth small and tight. Really, it was amazing how much he was reminding her of Zack.

"Mama!" Heather's voice was shrill. "Clampett's eating your pizza!"

Sonora sighed. Opened the door. "Hello, Chas."

He took off his hat, pushed back the straight black hair, silver at the temples. He had broad cheekbones, a dark complexion, blue eyes. "Hey, babe. You didn't need to dress up, just for me."

Sonora maintained silence.

"May I come in?" He said it with such meek politeness, Sonora felt guilty.

He was good at that, she thought. Giving guilt. She pushed the screen door open, and he stepped through just as Clampett came running, Heather right behind.

"Chas!" Heather wrapped her arms around his waist. Clampett pawed his leg, tail wagging, thumping the wall.

Chas stepped backward, patted Heather awkwardly on the top of her head, then nudged her away. He looked at Sonora. "We need to talk. Privately."

Heather backed away, chin sinking to her chest. She pushed her glasses up on her tiny button nose, and Clampett licked her elbow.

Sonora squatted down next to her daughter, winked, and gave her a hug. "Go watch your movie, Heather. Take Clampett with you."

"Will you come too?"

Out of the corner of her eye, Sonora saw Chas grimace. So handsome, she thought. Such a prick.

"Later, sweetie, you go ahead."

Sonora watched her daughter trudge toward the den, head bowed, dog at her heels. Any doubts she might have had were gone. Chas bent close to kiss her hello, but she turned her back and led him up the stairs into the living room.

"Sit down, if you want."

He paused by the back of the couch. Heather and Tim had been playing with Tim's miniatures, and the floor was covered with plaster-cast mountains, fake trees, painted archers and dragons. One of the pillows had bite marks, and Clampett had clearly had an accident beside the coffee table.

Sonora sat on the edge of the couch, stiff backed and regal— queen of her domain, God help her. "You want to sit down?"

Chas curled his lip. "You need to do something about your dog."

Sonora felt her cheeks turn red. "He's just old."

"Maybe it's time to put him out of his misery." Chas sat close to her on the couch and gave her a confident smile. It dawned on her that he had a habit of sitting too close, standing too close, grabbing hold of her arm. "You've been dodging me, Sonora."

Time for a dramatic pause, Sonora thought, waiting it out.

Chas frowned, leaned back against the couch, closed his eyes. "I've had a long day. Hell, I've had a long week. I'm dead tired and mega-stressed."

"Aw, gee."

He opened his eyes, folded his arms. "Okay, so you're mad. I've talked to Sam and your dad. Even your mother-in-law."

"You talked to my dad?"

"I know you don't get along, Sonora, but I wanted to let him know my intentions."

"Which are?"

He rummaged in his bag, pulled out a Dove bar, and smiled.

No, Sonora decided, a smirk, not a smile.

"Chocolate. And better than chocolate. Diamonds." Chas held a black velvet box up in the air, just out of reach. "Make me happy, Sonora."

"I'm supposed to jump for it?"

His lips tightened, and he leaned close. "Stop playing games, Sonora, and tell me what's on your mind."

She took a breath. "You remind me of my dead husband."

His mouth opened, then closed, and he swallowed. The smirk came back. He had decided to be amused. "Is that all?"

"Let's just say it's not a compliment, and I don't want to make the same mistake twice."

"Maybe he's better off dead," Chas muttered.

"Maybe I'm better off."

He shook his head slowly. "I thought you'd be happy to get married, I *know* you would. There's got to be more to this. Something's going on you're not telling me."

"Maybe I don't like the feather in your hat. Or that you whistle *Carmen* all the time. Maybe I don't like it that you play competition Frisbee."

"What's wrong with Frisbee?"

"Nothing, unless you call it *ultimate* Frisbee and get intense."

"It's that incident with the car, am I right?"

Sonora cocked her head to one side. "Reason enough, don't you think?"

"I promise, I *promise* you. Nothing like that will ever happen again."

"You're right about that, Chas."

"It wasn't that big a deal, Sonora."

She leaned forward, into his face. "It *was* a big deal. You went off. For no reason, out of the blue, you go nuts behind the wheel. You hit that Volvo on *purpose* and had the unmitigated gall to get out and tell the driver it was *my* fault for making you mad. You used the car like a weapon—"

"Oh, I can't believe I'm hearing this. So now you're abused?"

"Go home, Chas. You make me tired."

"Just like that, huh?" He stood up, walked three steps, then turned around, smoothing the thick black hair, his pride and joy. "You've got someone else, don't you?"

"This discussion is over."

He tossed the velvet box on the floor by her feet. "Don't you even want to look at it?"

"No."

"I have champagne in the bag. You want to keep it to celebrate your aloneness tonight?"

"Take it and go."

He grabbed the bag and the box, but did not notice the Dove bar wedged between the center couch cushions. Sonora followed him to the door.

He looked back at her over his shoulder. "I take back my marriage proposal, Sonora. But we could have been a dynamite couple."

She inclined her head in the direction of the den and the kids. "I'm past the couple stage, Chas. I'm a family."

"Be picky if you want, Sonora. But it's not going to be easy to find someone willing to put up with a pissy dog and two kids."

"What's difficult is finding somebody worthy of the privilege."

She closed the door in his face. Heard applause. Tim stood on the staircase next to Heather, who ran and put her arms around Sonora's waist.

Tim shook his head. "Good going, Mom. You'll never get married at this rate."

Sonora was aware of thunder, and a tiny tap on her shoulder. Lightning cracked and lit the room. Heather stood beside the couch, eyes wide, thumb in her mouth. She was neatly belted into a white bathrobe with pink rosebuds and wearing her favorite kitty slippers—two sizes too small. She had likely been roaming the house for a while, trailing her favorite blanket.

The room went dark again, dimly lit by the glow of the television and the tiny green lights on the VCR. Harrison Ford was on screen, fixing a broken birdhouse.

Sonora moved Clampett off her feet, shoved the half-eaten Dove bar out of her lap, and raised the end of the quilt to let her daughter under.

"Scared of the storm?"

Heather nodded, crawled onto the couch, and laid her head on Sonora's shoulder.

"Mommy?"

Sonora yawned, closed her eyes. "Hmmm?"

"Will you be home when I wake up in the morning?"

The phone rang, and Clampett opened his red-rimmed brown eyes. Sonora pulled her arm out of the cocoon she'd made with the heating pad and reached for the cordless, realized her hands were shaking. Flash calling? Who else, this time of night. Phone taps were in place. She swallowed.

"Sonora Blair."

"Sonora. I'm sorry, I know it's late, I've been on the road all night."

She recognized his voice immediately, as well as the cadences of panic. "Keaton? What's wrong?" She glanced at her watch, squint-ing. One-thirty A.M.

"I just got home, to the town house. And there's another one of those envelopes. Like the other one, you know?"

"I know, Keaton." Use his name. Keep him calm. She pulled Heather close.

"It feels like there's two pictures in there this time."

"You haven't opened it?"

"No."

"Don't open it, okay? Keaton?"

"Okay."

"Look, I'm coming over, just sit tight. I'll be there as soon as I can." She rang off.

Heather sucked her thumb, blue eyes stoic. "You got to go again, Mommy?"

"Yeah. But I'll get Uncle Stuart to come keep you safe in the storm."

"Mom?"

Sonora looked up. Saw Tim in the stairwell, still in blue jeans. She looked at her watch. "Why aren't you in bed?"

Clampett padded up the stairs, licked the boy's bare toes.

Tim scratched the dog's ears.

"You got to go to work, Mom?"

"Afraid so."

"Don't forget your gun."

"I won't. I'll get Stuart to come."

"I can take care of things."

"I know. But he's still coming."

Tim nodded. Seemed glad. He was young, Sonora thought. And it was the middle of the night. And Flash was out there, some-where.

24

The town house was dark, though a light glowed from the back. Sonora parked at the curb and shut the car door softly. The street was still, the houses dark and silent. In the background came the roar of the highway.

Sonora's boot heels were noisy on the sidewalk. The front door was open, the storm door shut. She rang the bell and waited—tried the handle, found it unlatched, and went inside.

Keaton Daniels had left a trail. A canvas briefcase had been dropped in the foyer, a tie unknotted and hung over the banister that curved into the living room. The kitchen light was on. Sonora could see a stack of mail on the table, a curling newspaper.

A bottle of gin was open, next to a half-filled glass.

The mail was scattered. *Men's Health, Gentlemen's Quarterly, Highlights for Children*. A MasterCard bill, good news from Ed McMahon, pizza coupons, something official from the legal firm of James D. Lyon. A bill from Hallock Construction. A cheap white envelope next to the one from the legal firm, torn across the top.

He hadn't been able to wait. Sonora glanced at her watch and saw that it was 2:40. She had left him alone too long.

The pictures were Polaroids, one sitting crooked. Sonora resisted the urge to straighten it up. She focused on the pictures, shivered, sat down slowly, and put her head in her hands. Then looked again.

In the picture on the left, Mark Daniels struggled with the handcuffs. Sonora could see the sweat rolling down his temples. She looked closely. Something odd, something in his fingers.

The second picture was the bad one, taken just as the fire licked the top of the car window and Mark Daniels faced death. His mouth was closed. He was not screaming.

Sonora went to the back door and looked out at the tiny, sloped yard that was enclosed by an eight-foot privacy fence. She flipped the porch light on. Keaton Daniels had his back to her, hands jammed in his pockets. He was looking over the fence to the city lights below.

The rain had not come, but there was thunder crowding close. Sonora walked across the yard, grass curling around her boots.

"Keaton?" she said softly.

He didn't seem to hear. She touched his shoulder with her left hand, and he laid his hand on top of hers and squeezed.

"Don't say anything." His voice was thick, as if he'd been crying.

Sonora moved in front of him.

He had changed in some subtle way that troubled her, as if once he was *there,* and now he was *here.* The funeral, just that afternoon, seemed miles and years away. She squeezed his hand, took a step toward him, her shirt just a hair's breadth from his. He did not back away. She took his face between her hands and stood on her tiptoes to kiss him.

He hesitated, and her stomach tensed and fluttered. Then he bent close. He grabbed her hard, his tongue in her mouth, and she felt the sandpaper bristles of his unshaven cheeks, the soft chill wetness of his tears.

When she pulled back he caught her shoulders. She closed her eyes. Tonight he was vulnerable. Tonight would be taking advantage.

"You shouldn't be alone, Keaton, can I drop you somewhere?"

"No," he said.

"You're sure?"

"Sure."

"I'm going back in the kitchen for a minute. Stay here."

She went through the house to her car, got a paper grocery bag from the kit of stuff in the trunk, put the pictures and envelope in. She stacked his mail, glanced out in the yard. He had his back to her. She was halfway to him when he turned.

"You're leaving?"

She nodded. She could think of no words of comfort, no words to take the pain away. "I'll call you."

"Sure."

She paused at the gate, hand on the latch, and turned to see he was watching. "I'll get her," she told him.

25

Sonora carried the paper bag up to the fifth floor of the Board of Elections building to Homicide. She saw a shaft of light beneath Crick's door, waved at Sanders, who'd pulled the 8 P.M. to 4 A.M. shift. Her favorite.

"Something up?" Sanders asked.

"More pictures."

Sanders scooted back in her chair, pushed hair out of her eyes with a hand that shook. "From Flash?"

Sonora nodded.

"Bad?" Sanders said.

"Bad. Anybody in the lab?"

Sanders shook her head.

Sonora headed for the swing door that joined Homicide and CSU. "Better here than in the trunk of my car. Let Crick know, will you?"

She left the Polaroids on Terry's desk with a note. Was leaving just as Crick and Sanders came in.

"Sonora?" Crick said.

"Over there, Sergeant." She pushed past him. She wasn't up for another look at Mark Daniels, brave, agonized. She checked her watch. After three; A.M. at that. Her message light was blinking.

One from Delores what's her name, returning her call. Another from a cop in Memphis, unsolved arson/homicide. Sonora made a note of his name and number.

"Sonora?"

She jumped, though the tone of voice was gentle. Crick looked angry, as usual. Sonora did not have the urge to tell him to loosen his tie, because he'd already taken it off. She rested her elbow on the desk, propping her chin.

"You still here?" he said.

"Such a detective. You see the pictures?"

He answered with a grimace. "Wonder how many more like that she's got."

Sonora shrugged. "Not sure Daniels can take too many more."

Crick rocked back and forth on the balls of his feet. "Not sure I can. Maybe Terry will get a print this time. And Blair, go home, you look like hell."

"Sir, I got a message here from a homicide cop in Memphis. Three years ago they had a murder pretty similar to the Mark Daniels killing."

"Think it's Flash again, huh?"

"Even better than Atlanta, except the victim didn't survive. Killer was a woman, and she used handcuffs."

"So now you want to go to Memphis."

"I'm also playing telephone tag with a Delores something or other in West Virginia."

"*Another* one?"

"Yes sir."

He rested a hand on the back of her chair, making it creak. "You file VICAP with the FBI?"

"Not yet. You think we could get some kind of voice analysis?"

"To tell us what? She's a homicidal maniac? That she's dangerous? That she's going off big time?"

Sonora bit her lip. "Point taken."

"Sorry, didn't mean to blow off on you, Sonora. Hang on." He went to his office, left the door gaping. She heard a file drawer open, a curse, the file sliding closed. Didn't quite catch, from the sound of it. Which bugged her. She got up and went to the doorway.

Crick waved a thick booklet of papers. "Here we go."

"The drawer didn't catch."

"What?"

"File drawer." Sonora crossed the room, pushed the drawer, second from the bottom, with the toe of her shoe. Heard the click. Felt better.

"You happy now?" Crick said.

She pointed to the booklet. "You know and I know the FBI

won't come in on this till we have a name, address, and signed murder warrant. Why are you giving me this at three o'clock in the morning?"

"So you'll go home and leave me alone. It's negative reinforcement. Plus it covers our ass, proves we tried everything."

"Here's everything for you, sir. She has a rural background, and probably grew up in a small town—somewhere in Kentucky where they say you'uns. My guess is she's been snagged on some kind of shoplifting charge, sometime in her life. She's been setting fires for sexual gratification since she was a teenager, maybe younger. She tortured animals for fun when she was little, and she likes to watch the families of her victims suffer. I'd bet my last penny she's stalking Keaton Daniels, and I will tell you again we should stick to this guy like glue."

"How about an address for her, Blair. You got that?"

"Will I get an address by filling out this form?"

Crick waved a hand, the gesture unenthusiastic, tired. "Never know till you try."

"Make you a deal. I fill out the form, and you clear me for Memphis and Atlanta."

"You fill out that form, and I'll get back to you."

Sonora stayed put. Looking at him. Willing him to agree.

He growled. "Anything else, Specialist Blair?"

"No sir."

"Go away."

26

The parking lot was well lit and empty. Sonora slammed the car door and checked the locks. She had a weird, unsettled feeling, and she turned and scanned the backseat. Empty. Should have looked before she got in.

She started the engine, glanced up at the foggy windshield, and saw that someone had traced a three over the driver's side.

Flash?

The cellular phone rang, as if on cue. Sonora picked it up, listened.

"Hey, girlfriend, how you doing? Keaton get my package okay?"

Sonora flicked on the headlights, checked the rearview mirror. No one, no one close. But Flash was likely around somewhere. Watching.

"Yeah, we got it." Sonora pulled the car out of the lot. She turned left, heading toward the river, trying to remember where all the pay phones were.

"We?" A pause. "Funny, isn't it, that you knew it was me right off in that graveyard today. See, I think we're connected, you and me. I think—"

"How'd you get this number?"

"Forget how I got it. Maybe you gave it to me. Maybe I am you, maybe I'm your dark half. Maybe you did the killings and don't remember. Maybe you're six and I'm three."

"What's that supposed to mean? Make some sense, why don't you?" Sonora scanned the streets. Empty.

Silence on the other end. Then, "Okay, girl, let's talk about you."

New tone of voice, Sonora thought. Change of tactics? New buttons to push?

"It wasn't no stroke now, was it? What killed your mama?"

Sonora hit the brakes, pulled the car to the curb. "What are you talking about?"

"You know, my mama died, too, when I was real little. At least you were all grown up."

"What happened to your mother?"

"We're talking about yours, Detective. Your mama. The doctor never was too sure what happened, isn't that right? Too many pills, or what. You could've said the word, but no, no autopsy for *your* mama. You think she took them pills herself, or you think your daddy give 'um to her? Or maybe he just held a pillow on her face, when she's all doped up. Think she knew? When it was happening? You should see people's faces when they know they're going to die. They get the funniest looks."

27

It was cold in the conference room, early-morning chill. The smell of new coffee was comforting. Sonora took a small bite from a plain cake doughnut, barely aware of the buzz of voices. She had not slept. She had lain in bed and closed her eyes and seen Mark Daniels, cuffed to the steering wheel, flames licking the side of the car. Saw her mother, looking grumpy and sad in the coffin.

Sonora pulled her bottom lip and watched Sam trace a thick forefinger across the map.

"Right along the Big South Fork here. And around this part of southern Kentucky, particularly near the Tennessee border. I mean, it's a joke to a lot of people, but in some of these rural areas they say you'uns like we say y'all."

There was a ripple of snickers.

"We?" Gruber was grinning.

"We'uns from farther south. And by the way, fuck all y'all, which is another thing we say in the south."

Sanders looked up. She was the rookie in the group, thin and young, hair cut short and swingy. "Do you think maybe—"

The door opened. Sergeant Crick walked into the room, black lace-ups polished and shiny, a burly tan sweater stretched over his shoulders and chest. Terry followed, looking distracted. She wore a soiled blue smock, and a strand of hair had come loose from her ponytail.

Crick settled at the head of the table and waved a hand. "Terry?"

She pushed her glasses back on her nose. "We lifted a print from one of the pictures."

Sonora looked up. "You mean Flash didn't wear gloves?"

Terry tucked the strand of hair behind her ear. "I'm pretty sure she did. Thin ones. But she has very pronounced friction ridges, and she touched the surface of one of the Polaroids, which is very porous. Plus, it's been humid with all the rain we've had, and warm for this time of year. Which helps. We got lucky."

"Is it a good print?" Sam asked.

Terry smiled, catlike.

Sonora leaned forward in her chair. "Where did she leave the print? Where on the picture?"

"On Mark Daniels's face."

Crick looked at Gruber. "Your turn."

Gruber gave them a lazy smile. "We went back to the neighborhood canvass. Had some houses we missed the day of the killing, nobody home. Sanders here found a lady who noticed a bronze Pontiac off to the side of the road, near the park. She thinks it was there that whole day before Daniels was killed. It's a little picnic area there, on Shepherd Creek.

"Anyway, this woman notices the car because she lives across the street, and you notice strange cars in your neighborhood. So we figure, okay, if Flash leaves her car so she can make her getaway that night, where does she go when she drops it off? And a ways down the road we got a Dairy Mart and a BP Oil, both with pay phones. We pull the phone records, and find somebody called a cab from BP Oil the afternoon Daniels was killed. We talk to the guys that work there, and one of them remembers seeing a blonde making a call. The hair's a little different from the sketch. He said she had real short bangs, said they looked funny. Ragged and uneven. So we got the cabdriver who picked her up. Took her to a place downtown. Shelby's Antiques."

"How far was it from the car to where Daniels was killed?" Sam asked.

Gruber opened his mouth, but Molliter held up a hand. His voice was flat.

"Maybe I should answer, since I'm the one that walked it off." He pointed a freckled finger at the map. "It takes eight minutes, walking briskly, to get from the kill spot to the area where the car was parked."

"Longer in high heels, and after dark," Gruber said.

Sonora frowned. "Provided she went by the road."

Molliter gave her a patient look. "She's not going to go crashing through the underbrush down that hill in a pair of high heels."

Terry took off her glasses and rubbed the two red spots on the bridge of her nose. "She changed her shoes."

Sonora nodded.

"Come on, girls. She's got track shoes in a tiny little purse?"

"Big purse," Sonora said. "She's got a lot of stuff to carry. Plus her feet aren't as big as yours, Molliter."

Gruber was nodding. "Remember, she's got to have her rope and camera, so why not tennies?"

Sam waved a hand. "And she gets the gasoline out of Mark Daniels's car. You found that melted plastic next to the gas tank, right, Arson Guy?"

Mickey looked up. "Absolutely. Makes more sense to siphon it than to carry it around."

"Anything on the type of rope?" Crick asked.

"Garden variety clothesline. Find it in every hardware store in town."

Sam rubbed his nose. "So how did she get to this Cujo's if her car's in the park? Taxi there too? Catch a bus?"

Gruber's eyes widened. "Good point."

"Check it out," Crick said.

A knock at the door gave him pause. Crick raised an eyebrow, and Molliter went to the door, muttered something, walked around behind Sonora's chair, and dropped a package on the table.

Sonora looked up from her notes. She shook the package, then peeled the tape back, which ripped the paper and brought all eyes to her side of the table. Mickey paused, then continued.

"Is it ticking?" Sam whispered over her shoulder.

Sonora peered inside. A note, and something small, square, covered in foil. She took the foil pack and put it in her lap, tried to open it quietly, peeling the edges slowly back.

Toast—two pieces. Whole wheat, lightly browned, delicately buttered with the crusts cut off. Sonora scratched her chin and reached into the mailer for the note—a piece of lined second-grade paper, thin and gray.

The handwriting was strong, made with a thick black felt-tip pen, slanted steeply to one side. Sonora squinted and held it close to her face.

I would have made you breakfast. K.

Sam looked over her shoulder. "What is it, girl? Your face is turning red."

Sonora snatched the note from his probing fingers and jammed it deep into her jacket pocket.

"Nothing." The room was suddenly silent. She looked up to find Crick looking at her. "Sorry, I miss something?"

"Arson Guy said the key they found goes to handcuffs, but not the cuffs used to bolt Mark Daniels to the steering wheel of his car."

Sonora settled the package in her lap. Thought a minute. "This makes no sense. You absolutely sure?"

Mickey scratched his chin. "The key we found would never fit the cuffs on Daniels. Whole different manufacturer."

"One of those pictures Keaton got, it looks like Mark is holding something. You can't quite see it, but his fingers are pinched together." Sonora held her hand up, thumb and forefinger touching. "And that patrol officer, Finch, he said Mark was screaming about a key, that he kept saying it over and over. Maybe he *wasn't* calling for his brother. Maybe he was talking about the key to the cuffs."

Sam cocked his head to one side. "So he's got a key to the cuffs, but it's the wrong one?"

"Doesn't add up." Molliter tipped his chair backward. "None of this works for me."

Sonora thought of that last picture of Mark, fire following the wick of rope wrapped around his naked, vulnerable body, the awful look of knowledge on his face.

Gruber made a noise, and Sonora looked at him, knowing the thought hit him the same time it hit her.

She cleared her throat. "Try this. Flash gives Daniels a key to the handcuffs and he thinks he's going to be able to get away, right up till the last minute, when he gets the key in the lock, and finds out it doesn't fit."

"Let me get this straight. She cuffs them to the wheel—"

"Why does Daniels let her do that?" Gruber crumbled a chunk of iced caramel doughnut.

"Could be a sex thing," Sam said. "Let me cuff you and love you."

"What kind of guy would go along with that?" Molliter's face was red, and a film of perspiration lined his upper lip.

"Nine out of ten," Gruber said.

Sonora snorted. "What do you mean what *kind* of guy, Molliter? Are you saying if he spreads his knees for some girl he just met, he got what he deserves? That what you're saying?"

"Enough of that," Crick said.

"He's made remarks like that about women victims. What do you think with the shoe on the other foot, Molliter? Is it different now?"

"Listen, Blair—"

"I said *enough*." Crick's voice was impressively authoritative. Sonora decided she would imitate it the next time she was mad at her son. A Crick voice. Something to cultivate.

Sanders bit her lip. "Aren't we forgetting that Daniels was shot? That was in the autopsy report, wasn't it?"

Sonora nodded. "Okay, she threatened him with the gun, he gave her trouble, and she shot him in the leg. Snap on those handcuffs, boy, or I'll shoot you again."

Molliter's face was bright red. "But what's the point? The key doesn't fit. Why give it to him?"

Sam waved a hand. "Somehow or other she gets this guy's wallet and his clothes and gets him handcuffed to the steering wheel. Now, face it, men aren't threatened by a little thing like Flash. They're not going to take her seriously. She probably has to shoot them just to get their attention. She's smart. She gets a gun on them and she's got the power before they even know they got a problem."

"So it's not a sex thing." Molliter sounded relieved.

"Not for the men," Sonora said.

Sanders raised her hand, chin level. "Going back to that geographic thing—"

"I think we were on the *porno*graphic thing," Gruber said. "And I don't know about the rest of you guys, but this sure takes the fun out of picking up women."

Sanders smiled. Cleared her throat. "I wonder—"

"We get anywhere on park witnesses?" Gruber asked.

Sanders's cheeks went dark red, and she raised her voice. "Sam? Aren't there several community colleges in that area of Kentucky you were talking about? The places you pointed out on the map?"

Sam gave her an encouraging nod.

"Then I was wondering. Maybe she went to school there. We might check with some of the community colleges and see if they have any history of arson, or—"

Gruber waved a hand. "She could have gone to school anywhere, Sanders, if she went at all."

Sam was shaking his head. "No, if she did go, Sanders could have something. The rural kids stick close to home those first two years. It's cheaper, for one. And they go to a school with their own, instead of heading off to a large university where people look down their nose at 'em. Then they're either happy with a two-year degree, they drop out, or transfer to a university that disallows most of their credits."

Sanders looked at Sonora. "You were talking about going back to her early years. If she went to college, there might have been some unexplained fires. We could talk to the campus police."

Crick started stacking papers. "Good idea, Sanders. Get on it today."

"Out of the mouths of babes," Gruber said.

Sonora looked at Sanders, saw the woman's red face, waited. Sanders picked up her papers, eyes downcast.

"Okay," Crick said. "Gruber. Stay with the taxi and the transport. See if you can pick Flash up after the antique store. Sonora, you and Sam take the store itself. Molliter—"

Molliter checked his watch. "I have a possible suspect due in. Late, already."

"This early and he's late?" Sam asked.

Gruber grinned. "She. Hooker, on her way home from work."

Molliter blushed. "She may pan out, as an informant. It's always possible our killer is a prostitute."

"Go to it." Crick rubbed the back of his neck. "Any more phone calls, Sonora? Hang-ups, anything?"

Sonora glanced at the floor. Did she really want to tell Crick and everyone else what Flash had said about her mother? She wondered how Flash had gotten the number to her phone, how she'd found out the things she had no business knowing.

"No sir."

It was the first lie, a gentle lie, to protect a part of herself that needed to stay private.

28

Sonora listened to her daughter sob on the other end of the phone.

"It's my tea set that Santa Claus brought me. The one I use for the ponies."

Sam walked by, mouthed "antique store," and pointed at his watch. Sonora nodded at him. Okay already. The side of her neck was aching. Too much time on the phone.

"When's the last time you had it, Heather? Maybe it's just in the closet, in all the mess." If it was, Sonora thought, it might never be seen again.

"I had it out on the back porch. Somebody's tooken it."

Taken it, Sonora thought. "That's what happens when you leave your stuff outside, Heather." She glanced up to see Sam shaking his head at her. Mean mommy. Sonora closed her eyes and swallowed nausea. Too early for the ulcer, but here it was anyway. Lack of sleep. Unless it was something else, like . . . no, no. It couldn't be that. Sonora glanced at the calendar on her desk and realized her period was late.

"Mommy?"

"Look, Heather, I'm sorry you feel bad. Mommy's at work right now, but we can talk about this some more when I come home. Look under your bed and in your closet. Maybe you didn't leave it outside."

Tim's voice echoed in the background. "I bet it's under your bed. Come on, you dork, I'll help you look."

Sam settled on the corner of Sonora's desk as she hung up. "Now can we go?"

"I'm ready if . . . excuse me, Sam. There's Sanders by the cof-feemaker. Time out for baby training."

"Baby training?"

"Be right back."

Sonora leaned against the bathroom wall and folded her arms. Sanders gave her a nervous look, then turned to the mirror, dig-ging in her purse for a brush, lipstick. It gave Sonora a pang to realize that she made the other woman nervous. She thought of Flash, and girl conversations over the phone. Sonora grimaced. *Not the same*. Sanders looked at her, and she folded her arms.

"I'd say sit down, but for obvious reasons, I don't think either of us would be comfortable that way."

Sanders laughed and bit her bottom lip.

"I know this sounds offensive, Sanders, but you don't have a penis, do you?"

"*What?*"

"Now, you could buy yourself a penis in the back of one of those magazines they pore over down in vice, but it wouldn't be the same, would it? So save yourself some confusion and hurt feelings. You're not going to be one of the boys. This isn't woman-to-woman stuff. I'm telling you the same thing my sergeant told me eight years ago, okay? Don't let guys like Gruber interrupt you every two seconds. They're not going to take you seriously, you put up with that."

"I don't want to be rude."

"*They're* being rude."

"So you're saying I should file a complaint?"

"You want to file a complaint because you got interrupted?"

Sanders folded her arms. "Then what do I do?"

"You handle it, and you better do it now, because it's going to get worse if you don't. Draw a line and don't let anybody step over it, and don't hold a grudge. Oh, and Sanders, when you do take a stand out there, try not to smile."

"Smile?"

"My observation is that women always smile no matter what. I bet Bundy's victims smiled before he killed them. You're a cop. Don't smile when people are giving you grief."

"You've given me a lot to think about."

"Good. It's one reason I like working with women. They think."

29

A wooden carousel horse sat in the display window of Shelby's Antiques. The white enamel was chipped and worn, the red and blue roses painted round its neck drab and faded. For the first time in her life, Sonora had the urge to buy an antique.

A cluster of bells at the top of the front door jangled as she and Sam walked in. Sonora went directly to the horse and checked the price tag that hung around its neck. Her urge to buy an antique went away.

It was a large store, crammed full of furniture and shelves that held displays of dolls and bins of odds and ends—flea-market stuff, which Sonora always thought of as junk. She found the thick odor of old things unpleasant. There were tin trays that said Coca-Cola, Betty Boop postcards, tiny, colored-glass bottles, playing cards from New York City. Coke bottles, moldering books, World War II medals, china dolls, plastic dolls, a teeny little tea set. Much of the small stuff hailed from the forties and fifties, with an old-fashioned aura of tackiness Sonora found depressing.

She passed a rack of white gauze dresses that swayed when she walked too close. She fingered the smallest, touching the delicate cotton, the yellowed satin ribbon, the row of tiny pearl buttons.

"Blue Willow plates!" Sam moved to a table by a pile of books. "Shelly's got one her grandmother gave her. You've seen it, it's on the wall in the kitchen. Shelly would love this place. She would eat this up with a spoon."

Sonora walked deeper into the store, warped tile beneath her feet. She passed a Victrola and a stack of LPs in worn jackets. The one on top was *Carmen*.

A woman stood behind the counter, manning a polished-brass cash register. Her hair was very dark, parted in the middle, flipped under. Her figure would have been considered wholesome and fine in the fifties. She wore dark lipstick and had heavy brown eyebrows. A pair of glasses hung from a chain around her neck. She was studying a stack of papers, making notations in ink. Sonora would have guessed her to be a Ph.D., teaching anthropology or medieval literature at an Ivy League university.

The woman looked up and smiled, and Sonora reached for her ID.

"Morning. I'm Specialist Blair, Cincinnati Police Department, and the man over there admiring the Blue Willow plates is Specialist Delarosa. I'd like to ask you a few questions."

The woman put her glasses on, took her time studying Sonora's ID, cocked her head sideways to get a good look at Sam.

Sonora fumbled with her recorder, peeling cellophane from a fresh tape. "I'm a homicide detective. I'm investigating a murder."

"A murder?"

Sonora nodded. "I'm sorry, I didn't catch your name?"

"Shelby Hargreaves. I'm part owner."

"*H-A-R-G-R-E-A-V-E-S?*"

"Yes."

"Were you here last Tuesday? I was wondering if you waited on a woman that afternoon—I have a sketch. It would have been around . . . " Sonora glanced at her notes. "Sometime after lunch. Two, maybe three. You were here then?"

"I was here all day. I was in early, around seven, and didn't leave till after nine."

"This lady is blond, between twenty-five and thirty-five. Small boned. I've got the sketch here, but it's not one hundred percent accurate, you understand?"

"You could be describing yourself, Detective."

Sonora grimaced.

Shelby Hargreaves frowned over the drawing, then tapped her cheek with a short fingernail that shone with clear polish. "I think so. Yes, if this is the one I'm thinking of, I helped her myself. She came in a taxi."

Sonora kept her face noncommittal. "You noticed that?"

"It's unusual, don't you think? Most people drive their own car, or walk, or maybe take a bus. They don't take a taxi to go shopping."

"How about when she left?"

"I don't think I noticed. She didn't ask to use the phone, so she could call a ride. She just went out. Headed toward town, I'm pretty sure."

"Toward town," Sonora echoed. They could check bus schedules and cab companies. "How long was she here?"

"An hour and a half, maybe two hours. She was a browser. I think she'd been in before, because she had certain areas she went to—like she knew where we kept the things she liked."

Shelby Hargreaves slipped the glasses off her nose and rubbed her eyes. "She was very much in her own little world, that one. Came walking in all business, then wandered slowly down the aisles, like an enchanted princess. Antique magic."

Sam walked toward them down the aisleway, turning his head now and then as something caught his eye. "You watch all your customers that close?" he asked.

Hargreaves shook her head. "Not usually. But she had an acquisitive look. She wanted things, touched them, like a spoiled little girl at a candy counter. I call it greedy fingers."

Sam grinned, and Hargreaves gave him a particular smile.

"What kind of things did she look at?" Sam said.

Hargreaves leaned both elbows on the counter. "Dolls were the main fascination, and what I call the miniatures. Dollhouse furniture. She liked that little tea set over there, did you see that?"

Hargreaves moved from behind the counter and led them to a small child's tea set.

Sonora frowned. Something here that bothered her.

"This set is too small, really, for the size doll she wanted, but she wouldn't look at anything bigger." Hargreaves led them down the aisle. "She looked at these for a long time."

They were displayed on a mahogany sideboard—china dolls, exquisitely dressed, blue marble eyes fringed by thick dark lashes, lids that opened and shut. Some of the dolls wore earrings, and one had a parasol, trimmed in lace, and delicate bisque rouged cheeks.

"My daughter would love these," Sonora said.

Hargreaves nodded and grimaced. "It's only adults, collectors, who have these kinds of dolls nowadays. It's hard to remember sometimes that they were made for children." She pointed to a boy doll dressed in brown velveteen pants and jacket, ivory lace at the sleeves and throat. "She looked at this one quite a while. Too expensive, I guess. He's a German bisque boy. A character doll, see the painted eyes? It's a Simon and Halbig. But she didn't go for it. She didn't like the hair. It's blond, you see, and she wanted dark hair. I wound up getting her one I had downstairs. It wasn't in mint condition—it was missing an arm, and the cheek was scuffed. And it's not marked, so I can't be one hundred percent sure who made it, which decreases the value." She leaned close to Sam. "Most people, they don't like the missing limbs, and they use that as a major arguing point to bring the price down. Unless they work on dolls themselves, they won't buy. But this girl hardly seemed to notice."

"I wish I could see it," Sonora said.

"I've got another like it, a girl. Come with me, I'll show you that."

She led them into the next room, which was filled with larger pieces—furniture, spinning wheels, cabinets. A wide staircase led from the center of the floor to the basement. Sam motioned Sonora ahead and followed close at her heels.

It was musty smelling downstairs, and cold. The merchandise wasn't as choice. There were a lot of books—old, blue-jacketed Nancy Drew books, Hardy Boys adventures, military paraphernalia. Hargreaves moved purposefully past a dusty, vintage sewing machine, her heels noisy on the yellowed tile. She stopped in front of an open cupboard that was teeming with dolls—many of them missing limbs, some of them nude or headless, all of them battered and worn. The misfits.

"It's a very unusual doll, the one she selected." Hargreaves reached for a girl doll, about seventeen inches tall. It wore a blue plaid dress; a satin ribbon had somehow been attached to the painted-on hair. "This one is actually marked. It was made in Brooklyn by Modern Toy Company, sometime between 1914 and 1926. My guess is it's an early one, so I'd say 1915 or 16." She handed the doll to Sonora.

There was a brown stain on the front bib of the dress, but the white kneesocks were surprisingly clean, the yellow shoes unmarked. The arms of the doll were oddly muscular, like drumsticks, and the striated hair and porky little face were painted on. The doll had an oily look that Sonora did not like.

Sam took the doll and waved its little arm. "Sawdust."

"Right. The body and head are shaped with cork, but the limbs are stuffed with sawdust. They're jointed." Shelby Hargreaves pulled up the doll's dress. "See here? Disks at the shoulders and hips."

"How did she pay?" Sonora asked.

"Cash," Hargreaves said.

"Did she buy anything else?"

"Odds and ends for doll making. I have a box of stuff out in the back." She inclined her head toward two heavy swing doors. "I let her poke through that, and she picked up a few things. Come on, I'll show you."

Sonora took the doll away from Sam, smoothed its dress back over its knees.

The back room had a rough cement floor and was dark and drafty. Slits of sunlight shone through cracks in an accordion-style delivery door, which was shut tight and padlocked. A naked bulb hung from the ceiling, providing a cone of dim light and an abundance of dark and shadow.

Sonora looked at the exposed wires, the dust, the dry brittle furniture. Fire hazard, she thought.

Most of what was back in the storeroom looked broken and abandoned. An old metal baby crib, bars lethally wide at the top and narrow at the bottom, was stacked next to an iron bedstead, a wooden Indian, and a Coca-Cola sign. Shelby Hargreaves squatted next to a battered, avocado green storage trunk, opened the latch, and lifted the lid. Sonora looked over her shoulder.

A macabre collection, this motley conglomeration of doll eyes, sawdust-stuffed limbs, tiny, unattached hands, and doll heads. A threadbare baby bonnet lay next to a torn parasol and a pair of teensy eyeglasses. There were shoes and felt kits, a few paintbrushes, what looked like molds for heads. Sam reached in and picked up an odd tool, shaped something like a Tootsie Roll Pop.

"What's this for?"

Shelby Hargreaves touched the gray metal. "An eye beveler. Made by a company in Connecticut. It's used to make an eye socket. There's a better one in here." She rummaged through the trunk. "I *know* there's another one. Unless Cecilia sold it or moved it. It surely didn't get up and walk off by itself."

Sonora exchanged glances with Sam.

"Now that bothers me," Hargreaves said. "I'll have to check with Cecilia. I suppose she must have sold it."

"Did this girl buy anything from the assortment here?" Sam asked.

"She bought some eyes. Brown eyes. Blue ones are more popular, but she wanted the brown. I tried to sell her something to replace that arm." She held up a sagging sawdust limb. "This might have been made to work, but she didn't want it."

There came the faint but unmistakable jangle of the bells over the front door.

"Excuse me, I'd better get back upstairs."

Sam gave her a hand up, which made her cheeks turn pink. She dusted off her skirt.

"Look around all you like, detectives. If you'll close the trunk when you're done, I'd appreciate it."

Sonora waited till she heard the clatter of heels on the stairs, then squatted next to the trunk, picking things up, putting them down. "No eye beveler," she said.

"Reckon Flash took it?" Sam asked.

"No doubt in my mind."

30

S am's radio went off as they walked out of Shelby's Antiques. Sonora propped her feet up on the curb and leaned against the Taurus. She looked through the window at the carousel horse.

Sam put the radio back on his belt.

"What's up?" Sonora asked.

"Sheriff called from Oxton, about the security guard? Louisville ME did the autopsy this morning. Definitely a twenty-two, three bullets. And they found the car she took."

"Where?"

"Parked way out of the way, some rural road or other called Kane's Mill. They figure she stashed her car, crossed a railroad bridge on foot, and hiked about six miles into town to the TV station. Maybe changed clothes in a McDonald's or something—could be they'll find witnesses. She'd have to be hauling a good-sized pack for the video camera. Afterward, they figure she lost her tail on the back roads, doubled back to where she had her own car stashed, and switched. They found strands of synthetic black hair caught in the car door, and the driver's seat was set as far up as it would go—just right for shrimps like you and Flash."

"Thanks, Sam. Mind slipping your wrists into these handcuffs?"

He grinned. "The car was wiped, but they got one or two prints, not good ones. Plus they found an X-Acto knife that nobody from the television station claims. The kind of thing a hobbyist might use."

"I think we know what her hobby is. Did you tell Crick that our girl likes to play with dolls?"

"He thought it was pretty interesting that she made a point of getting a new one hours before she killed Daniels. A boy doll at that. And that it was important enough for her to pay cab fare, like it was part of some little scenario she had cooked up."

Sam's radio went off again. He raised one eyebrow; Sonora shrugged. She had a worried feeling, as if something important had slid by.

She rewound the interview tape, put the recorder next to her ear. Hargreaves's voice was distinct and pleasant—she'd be good on radio.

"*. . . and what I call the miniatures. Dollhouse furniture. She liked that little tea set over there, did you—*"

Sonora felt a hand on her shoulder and jumped.

"Girl, you okay?"

"Yeah, sure. What's up now?"

Sam frowned. "Dumpster fire, at the school where—"

"Keaton?"

He nodded. "Evidently Flash went after one of the teachers."

Sonora headed for one side of the car, and Sam for the other. She buckled her seat belt. "So what happened?"

"That's all I know. Daniels called it in himself. Blue Ash PD didn't want us pulled in."

"How long ago?"

"Couple hours. She's long gone, and Crick is pissed."

"So am I. Thank you, Blue Ash."

"Cut 'em some slack, Sonora, for them it's a routine Dumpster fire."

"There are no routine fires where Keaton Daniels is concerned."

"Why's she going to show up at his school, Sonora? Helluva chance she's taking."

"You understand the word *obsession*? Why do ex-husbands shoot their ex-wives at the office? I wish to God Crick would keep somebody with him."

"Live in the real world, Sonora."

31

The burned-out Dumpster was at the far end of the Pioneer Elementary School playground. Sonora stood on the hood of a Blue Ash patrol car and peeped inside. The fire had gobbled the top layer of trash. She wished Arson Guy was around. If the fire had burned deeply in one spot, it likely had smoldered, which might mean a cigarette tossed in. If, on the other hand, there was an accelerant—

She heard a recognizable click and turned her head.

"Just leave your hands where they are." The voice was female and shaking with excitement. Sonora got a quick look out of the corner of her eye.

The Blue Ash patrol officer was black, fine boned and slender, looking more like a teacher than a cop. She wore the uniform with spit and polish.

Sonora made sure her hands stayed put. "Excuse me, Officer. Sorry, can't read your name tag from here. Bradley?"

"Brady."

"Officer Brady. What the hell do you think you're doing, pulling your gun there? If this is your car, I promise, I haven't scratched the paint."

"Identify yourself, please."

It dawned on Sonora that the Blue Ash police would be looking for a short blonde. This was getting irritating.

"The woman you're looking for is thinner than I am, much as I hate to admit it. And her hair is shorter and lighter blond."

The uniform was looking around for help. No one was close. She pulled the radio off her belt.

Sonora laughed. "Come on, Brady, please, don't embarrass me like this. I'm a detective, I work homicide for the city. That's my partner there in front of the school, talking to the good old boys. You know him? Sam Delarosa?"

"Got some ID?"

"Right here on my belt."

"Keep your hands up."

"If I fall on my butt, it's on your head, so to speak."

Brady did not smile, and she kept her gun steady. Sonora turned sideways, hands in the air. She hoped Sam wouldn't notice, she'd never hear the end of this. Brady inched closer, squinting at the ID.

"If you're satisfied with the little plastic picture, I'd appreciate it if you'd holster your gun, Officer Brady."

"Sorry."

"Nah, you never can tell." Sonora sat on the hood of the car and swung her legs over the side.

Brady nodded glumly. Her hair was trimmed close to her head, and her face showed the uncertainty of extreme youth.

"You been here long?" Sonora asked.

"Since the call came in."

"So what's the story?"

Brady leaned against the car and began to talk. Good old girls, Sonora thought, as she listened.

The call had come in a little after two. Brady checked her notes. Two-twelve, to be precise, which Sonora could see she was. It had been physical-activity time, and there were two primary classes on the playground. Sonora looked around the lot. It was a nice school, and judging from the facilities, was run by a fat-cat PTA. A map of all fifty states was painted on the asphalt—educational hopscotch. There was a slide and a swing set and monkey bars, freshly painted in vibrant shades of all the primary colors, with cypress mulch cushioning the dirt beneath.

There had been two groups outside. One of them should have been Daniels's class, but they had traded time with Vancouver's primary so they could schedule in a performance by a traveling puppet show. Instead of being outside, Daniels and his kids were indoors, watching *Rumpelstiltskin*.

Vancouver had noticed a woman hanging around the edge of the playground, and was on her way over to check her out when one of the children fell off the monkey bars. When she got that settled, she saw the woman talking to one of the children. She challenged her. The woman came at her, scratched her face, shoved her to the ground, and ran away.

Sonora frowned. The playground was vulnerable, placed on the other side of the school parking lot, away from the main buildings. The school was surrounded by houses on two sides. A limited-access highway ran along the back, with a small hill and a thin strip of trees and bushes between. The back of the school was fenced with four feet of chain link, but there was no fence on the left side. Easy access, Sonora thought. Wouldn't even have to climb the fence.

"Any idea what this woman said to the child?"

"She wanted to know who his teacher was. He said Miss Vancouver, and this woman said wasn't he in Mr. Daniels's class? Then that's when the teacher came over."

"She hurt much?" Sonora didn't see an ambulance, but it would have come and gone by now.

"No, not really, just shook up."

Sonora looked for Sam. His shoulders were stiff, and he was waving his arms. The side door of the school swung open, and Keaton Daniels walked out with a man whose rumpled suit and air of authority said police. Trailing behind was a short man who wore his pants hitched below his belly and slicked back his thinning black hair with something sticky. The principal, Sonora guessed. Whoever he was, he did not look happy.

Neither did Keaton. His jaw was set, and he had that wary and guarded air she was beginning to know. Sonora slid off the hood of the car.

The cop in the suit eyed the ID hanging from Sonora's belt and gave her a hard look. She didn't know him. She got along with Blue Ash homicide people, but she didn't sense any rapport with this one.

The cop cleared his throat. "Excuse me, Miss—"

"Specialist Blair." Sonora held up both hands and pointed at Sam. "I'm just one of the troops, sir. The man you need to argue with is over there. Mr. Daniels, may I have a word?"

The cop gave Keaton a hard look. "We'll be in touch."

The principal's smile was tense. "Think about what I said, Mr. Daniels. We'll talk again in the morning."

Keaton jerked his head in an unfriendly nod. Sonora fell into step beside him, and they left the others behind.

"They want me to leave, you know that?" He looked at her sideways and kept walking. "Like I would. Like I can't protect my kids.

If I'd been out here I would have *had* her. God, it would have been so easy."

Not as easy as you think, Sonora thought. Now probably wasn't the time to bring it up.

They went across the playground, past the monkey bars and basketball goals. Keaton looked first left, then right.

"What are you looking for?" Sonora asked.

Keaton scratched his head. "One of the kids in my class said she saw a woman out here two days ago, watching us at PA. She said the woman was standing by the water. I'm trying to figure out what the hell she . . . surely it couldn't . . . " He moved off toward the line of trees that ran between the back of the school and the interstate, stopping in front of a deep puddle of mud, two feet by three, shadowed by a clutch of adolescent oak trees. Keaton looked down at the muddy water. "You think this is what she meant?"

Sonora shrugged. Looked for footprints. "Anything is possible, Keaton."

He glared at her. "She's not running me off, not me, babe. I'm not leaving my kids, or quitting my job, or changing my life."

"Can they make you? Quit?"

Keaton stared off toward the school. "They'd have to go through channels. Offer me something administrative downtown, and even then, I don't think they could force it. If the principal wants to get nasty, he can start shading my evaluations, but that takes time." He lifted his chin. "Why, you think I'm wrong? You think I'm risking my kids? I can take care of them, Sonora. If she comes back here, fine with me."

Sonora nodded at him. "School got smoke alarms?"

"Of course."

"How about your town house?"

He put his hands in his pockets. "Four as of last night."

"I'm up to five now, at my house."

He gave her a second look. "Your house?"

"Just paranoid. I've got two kids, remember. You change your locks yet, Mr. Daniels?"

"*Mr.* Daniels? What happened to Keaton?"

"What happened to the locks?"

"Using the mom-voice on me, Detective?"

"You think she's not dangerous because she's female, Keaton?"

"I think I can handle her."

"Your brother couldn't."

Sonora drank from a can of Coke as she headed toward her desk. The message light on her phone was blinking. Chas, no doubt. Constant, predictable, and annoying. Twice she'd returned his calls, but he never seemed to be home.

She remembered calling Zack, nights he worked late, returning calls to find he wasn't there. Guess where I am, Sonora? Let me throw it in your face. Only this time, the nasty tricks didn't work, because this time, she didn't care.

Her stomach went from nausea to pain. Ulcer or not? She'd picked up a test at the drugstore yesterday. Sooner or later she would work up the nerve to use it.

Sonora leaned against her desk, pushed the button. Not Chas, amazingly, but her brother, sounding perturbed.

". . . something funny with your phone. You got call forwarding to my place now or something? Because that woman who sings is calling over here at the saloon. Normally I wouldn't mind, but she doesn't sing all that well, okay, and 'Love Me Tender' isn't one of my favorites."

Sonora chewed a fingernail. Could this weird caller be Flash? Why would she call and sing? Flash was getting to her, big-time, maybe she was just seeing her everywhere. On the other hand, how many strange women were out there making calls to Sonora, and why now? There were no coincidences in a murder investigation. Just paranoid homicide cops.

Sam wandered in from the direction of the men's room, adjusting his belt. "Molliter's got his hooker, you want to go listen up?"

Sonora looked at him, frowned. "I don't have call forwarding."

"No kidding? Can we focus here, Sonora? Gruber and Molliter have her in the interrogation room right now."

"You mean interview room."

"I mean hot witness. Gruber says she may know the killer."

"Thank God for the witness fairy."

"Girl, you are so cynical. Your problem is you just don't like Molliter. Come on, let's peek."

The witness was small and rail thin, and she sat in the chair sideways, her feet curled under her. She smoked with hard, jerky motions, fingers trembling around the cigarette. Her jeans were shredded from stem to stern, and she wore red Lycra bicycle shorts beneath. Her dirty cowboy boots were brown suede with tassels, the heels showing a pyramid-shaped pattern of wear. She wore a red-and-black plaid shirt, eye makeup, and her spiked yellow hair was greasy.

Molliter sat near the tape recorder, a dark green monster that took up the right-hand corner of the table. Gruber said something about coffee and headed out. Sam intercepted him in the hallway.

"So what's she say?"

Gruber poured coffee in a Styrofoam cup. "She says black, and six packs of sugar."

Sonora nodded. "That ought to hit her good, she's already shaking. She needs something, but it's not sugar."

Gruber shrugged. "She works the trade, Sonora, and she's white, so that's like a given, you know? Course if she's no better at it than you were when we worked vice—"

"What's she say about the killer?"

"Hooker friend of hers, named Shonelle, who likes to work with cuffs. She's telling Molliter all about it right now. I better get back in there before he embarrasses himself."

"Physical description fit our girl?"

"Not even close. Taller, different complexion, and hails from 'Nawth Carolina.' "

"So how's this Shonelle wind up hooking in Cincinnati?" Sam asked.

Sonora pushed hair out of her eyes. "Maybe she's a Bengals fan."

Gruber folded his arms and gave her a lopsided smile. "Something to do with an *arson* thing. No conviction—no surprise, you know their hit ratio. Supposedly this Shonelle was getting hassled and brought in every time a fire broke out, so she decided she needed a change of pace. Came to Cincinnati."

Sam looked at Sonora, then back to Gruber. "How'd you get on to this? She just waltz in the door?"

"I told you, Molliter knows her, from vice. She says she and Shonelle used to be buddies. But I don't hear friendship when she talks, you hearing me?"

Sonora nodded.

"Says when Shonelle talks about the johns, she says she's going to set their pants on fire."

Sonora grimaced. "Oh, sure. Tailor-made. Lock 'em up, and I'm out of here."

Gruber waved a hand. "Don't sneer at me, that's what she says. Says she's been suspicious because Shonelle stole one of her regular customers, and this guy, who used to come around every couple of weeks, hasn't been back. And when Sheree—her name is Sheree La Fontaine—"

"Of course it is," Sonora said.

"It's on her driver's license. Anyway, when Sheree asks Shonelle about this john, Shonelle just gets a funny look, and kind of laughs, and says she took care of him for good. Roasted him."

"She actually used those words? Roasted him?"

Gruber nodded.

"She give you a description of this Shonelle?"

"To the wire, babe, right on down to the fuchsia orchid tattooed on her left shoulder blade."

"What's she like?"

"Black, redheaded, tall and curvy. Big bazooms—Sheree swears they're fake. Oh, and a trick knee."

"Say that again," Sam said.

"That's how *she* put it. They both work the other side of the river. Shonelle used to dance in a club called Sapphire, but can't anymore 'cause of the knee."

"No disability on that, huh?" Sam said.

"So did she give you a name on the john who got roasted?" Sonora asked.

"Said he called himself Superdude."

"*Superdude?*"

"Yeah, well. More imaginative than John Smith."

Sonora cocked her head sideways. "Smells worse than the morgue. She given you a description of Superdude?"

"Not yet, but hang around, and I'll ask."

He headed for the interview room, and Sam filled two coffee cups. Sonora didn't want it, but took it anyway so she would not have to field queries about the ulcer. The doughnuts were wearing off, and the pain was going from background irritant to foreground agony.

They headed for the two-way.

Molliter was still hunched over the recorder, and Gruber had pulled a chair close and was leaning forward, face friendly. Sheree glanced at the two-way now and then. Once she waved.

"They think we don't know that they know," Sam said.

Sonora grinned. Anybody who watched TV knew, little children knew. But the two-ways were useful because you could baby-sit a suspect a lot easier if you could peep in from the hallway—just to check on the little things, like whether they were climbing the walls or punching holes in the ceiling. They'd had one guy try to get out that way. Sonora always figured he'd have had a better chance with the front door. Or just by waiting it out. You couldn't keep a suspect forever without the DA nailing you to the wall. Not in real life.

Sheree took tiny sips of the coffee. Gruber was smiling and patient, and Molliter, as usual, looked sour.

"You sure you don't know any name other than Superdude?" Gruber said.

"He didn't use American Express, okay, he left home without it." Sheree pulled a cigarette from a new package of Camels that Gruber had given her along with the coffee.

Gruber lit a match. "How about what he looked like? He was a regular, so—"

"So yeah, I saw more than his face. No more than five inches. I'd say average."

Molliter coughed, and Gruber nodded seriously. "That's good, but we need something to tell him apart from all those other average guys. How about the rest of him? Like his face, build. Hair and eyes."

Sheree gave him a playful smile. "Pubic hair?"

"You want to tell me about it, I'll listen."

"Lot of things I could tell you about."

Sonora wondered how old Sheree was. Impossible to tell, with hookers, the streets aged them quickly. This one looked forty and acted fourteen.

The girl seemed bored suddenly, glanced again at Molliter, then took a deep drag of her cigarette. "He was kind of on the tall side, nothing major. Five-eleven maybe, six feet. Sort of skinny, you know, stringy kind of build. Hair was reddish brown, and I think his eyes were green."

"Anything else you notice about this guy?" Gruber said.

She shrugged.

"You told us all kinds of stuff on Shonelle. Do the same for me on the guy."

"I told you. Tall and skinny."

"So what kind of nose he have? Big nose?"

"Just a . . . just a regular nose."

"Tattoos? Dark eyelashes?"

"Sure. No. I guess his eyelashes were light."

Sonora blew air between her teeth.

"What?" Sam said.

"She's describing Molliter. There is no Superdude."

"Looks like Molliter's eating it up."

"Molliter would. They should see if she'll take a lie detector. Right now. See if she will."

"We can't do one today, anyway."

"I know that, but she doesn't. I'll be right back." Sonora went into the bullpen and veered left, sticking her head into officers' quarters. Crick was in front of the terminal, his sausage-thick fingers working the keyboard over with swift, heavy jabs.

"Sergeant?"

"Yeah, what is it, Blair?"

"Gruber and Molliter tell you anything about this witness they got?"

"So, what about it?"

"I been watching, Sergeant, and I'm telling you she's pulling their chain."

"What makes you psychic?"

"Come on. She says this missing guy is named Superdude, and when they asked her for a description she gives them Molliter. Let's just say I got a feeling. Looks to me like she's got it in for this Shonelle she's trying to pin."

"Oh, well, Blair, if you got a feeling say no more." Crick leaned back in his chair. "She give much detail on the description?"

"Precious little. Broad and vague, and when Gruber led she was happy to follow. The only thing that does strike me is the girl herself. She kind of fits the general description. Short and blond. Bent."

Crick pulled at his bottom lip. "How about we offer the lady a lie detector?"

"My thoughts exactly."

"Okay." He went back to the keyboard. Sonora stayed in the doorway. "What now?"

"That Dumpster fire makes it pretty clear. Flash is sticking close to Daniels."

"No, Blair. We do not have the manpower to surveil him round the clock."

Sonora leaned against the doorjamb. "What about that trip to Atlanta? That cop, Bonheur, has no problem with me going down there, looking at the case file, talking to the victim."

"How you going to do that? They using mediums, or making do with Ouija boards?"

"I told you, sir, the victim survived on this one. Untied his ropes and got away."

"No handcuffs?"

"No, but a lot of other similar elements."

"I'll think about it."

"Are you inclined to say yes?"

"Maybe. Are you inclined to go away? Listen, Blair, you talked to Sanders?"

"No, why?"

"She's onto something. Run along now, and bother her."

33

Sonora stood with her back to the bathroom door, bolt digging into her ribcage, thinking she might need to be sick again. The back of the toilet was littered with wadded cellophane packets, an empty box, a wrinkled instruction sheet.

She held the white wand limply, tears rolling down her cheeks. Both windows pink. Why pink, she wondered, why not black? This could not be happening, not to her, not now. Men like Chas should not be spreading genetic material.

Sonora picked up the instruction sheet, hand shaking. She studied the succession of little pictures in the directions, vision blurred by tears. The outside door opened, and she heard footsteps.

"Sonora? Sonora, you in here?" Sanders. Sounding chirpy and excited. "Sonora?"

"Yeah, yeah, I'm here."

Sonora reread the instructions. Took a breath. Both windows were supposed to start out pink. For negative results, wait five minutes and pray the window on the left turns white.

There was still hope. She looked at her watch, wondering how long it had been.

Sanders's voice was melodious. "Crick said to talk to you and let you know, because I think I may have found her."

"Who?" Sonora leaned against the wall. Breathed in and out. Listened to the beat of her heart. Time to look, time to check that little window, or wait another minute?

"Who? Oh, you're kidding. I was checking community colleges in those parts of Kentucky that Detective Delarosa—"

"Sam."

"Sam was talking about."

Sonora's grip tightened on the wand.

"And I've got a possible that looks really good—fires *and* a suspicious death, and there's a picture, a yearbook picture. They faxed it, and it came through pretty good. Could you come out and look at it, please?"

Now. It was time. Sonora swallowed, felt her stomach flip-flop, and raised the wand in a shaking hand.

Left window white.

Sonora closed her eyes and leaned into the metal door. "Thank God, it's an ulcer."

"What?"

"Just one second, Sanders." Sonora took a deep breath. Nah. She was done being sick. She pushed hair out of her eyes, came out of the stall.

Sanders held up a thin white slip of fax paper. "You think this might be her?"

"Give me one minute." Sonora bent over the white porcelain sink, grimaced at the familiar rust stain that circled the drain. Her knees were weak. She cupped her hands under the faucet and rinsed her mouth.

A small idea came to mind. She could make those calls and visits from Chas disappear with one message left on his machine—just tell him her period was late. Sonora looked at her reflection. Was she that much of a bitch? She thought maybe she was.

Sanders tapped a toe in a soft, annoying staccato. Sonora looked in the mirror.

"Okay, Sanders, what's her name? This girl in the picture?"

"Selma Yorke."

Sonora decided that Sanders was holding her breath. She wiped her hands on a brown paper towel.

"Give it here."

34

Sonora had that feeling she got when the case was finally break-ing. They had a name. They had Selma Yorke.

It was definitely her picture in the yearbook. Sans wig, but Sonora knew the face, the *look* of her.

She had been featured twice. Once in the traditional rows of stu-dents, unsmiling and shy, hair waving in pale blond rivulets, bangs longish and combed to one side. The other picture was a group shot of young girls in long white dresses, posing on a wide sweep-ing staircase. Perfumed and made up, eyes shiny with excitement, each and every one with a bouquet of tiny pink roses. Selma was the standout, the one who ignored the camera, looking off in the distance with a sour expression. She held her bouquet tightly in one hand, letting it trail to the side, as if she couldn't care less about the flowers but had no intention of letting them go. Her bangs were ragged and short, angled awkwardly as if they'd been snipped by an angry child. Sonora remembered when Heather had cut her bangs with little plastic safety scissors. They had looked much the same.

Selma Yorke.

Sanders hunched over the phone book, limbs loose, eyes down-cast. "She's not in here."

Sam looked at Crick. "We going to pick her up or circle?"

"Pick her up, if we can find her." Crick squinted at the computer terminal. "Never been arrested in Cincinnati. No Ohio driver's license. We can run it and see if she's got a Kentucky or Tennessee license."

Sonora crooked a finger. "Come with me, Sanders. Sam and I will show you how it's done." She glanced at her watch. "You guys just give me half a minute to make one quick call."

"Didn't you just talk to your kids?" Sam asked.

"I have to leave one short message for Chas. Only take a sec."

Sonora put a videotape of *The Crying Game* up on the counter. It was a slow afternoon, so there wasn't a line.

Sanders stood beside her, looking nervously over one shoulder. Sam was in front of the popcorn machine. He bought a large bag, crammed a handful of kernels into his mouth. Sonora opened her purse and dug in her wallet.

"Do you have an account here?" The clerk was male, in his late teens.

Sonora nodded. "I forgot my card."

"Name?"

"Selma Yorke."

He tapped the keyboard. "Is your account at this location?"

"No, it's at the other one."

"That's Selma Yorke at 815 Camp Washington?"

Sonora nodded, smiled, paid $3.50, and signed for the movie. Sanders was bouncing again. They headed for the parking lot, and Sam wandered out with them.

"Popcorn?"

Sonora took a handful.

"How can you *eat*?" Sanders looked at them over her shoulder as she headed into the road. Sam grabbed her elbow and held her back, pointing a salty finger at an oncoming brown truck.

"UPS stops for no man, or woman."

Sonora licked salt off the palm of her hand. "No one, Sam. Sounds better if you just say no *one*."

The truck moved by in a cloud of exhaust, and Sanders danced ahead. "What now?"

"We could watch the movie," Sonora said.

Sanders laughed, and Sam looked at Sonora. "We were young once."

The sign said WELCOME TO CAMP WASHINGTON. The tiny group of houses lay just under the interstate, one street over from the slaughter yards. Railroad tracks were in spitting range, and old brick warehouses were a couple of blocks away. Sonora rolled the car window down and listened to the backdrop roar of traffic. It was still light out, drizzly. Humidity made the air thick and sticky, in spite of the chill. Sonora heard the whine of a train, the metallic squeal of brakes on track. She closed her eyes. This was what Selma Yorke heard at night when she lay in her bed. These were the noises and smells that framed her life.

Sanders leaned over the back of the seat. "We could knock on the door and see if she's home."

Sam raised an eyebrow at Sonora. "What you think?"

Sonora gave Sanders a look. "Remember. She's not under arrest. We don't have a warrant. We just want to talk."

"Got your gun, Sanders?" Sam said.

Sonora opened her car door. "Leave her alone, Sam."

The house was old, two stories, nearly hidden behind a large leafy oak tree and caged by a tall ragged hedge that almost concealed a rusting chain-link fence. The lawn was scrubby, weed-infested bare dirt. The windows of the house were crusted with grime, the interior secreted behind gauzy curtains that looked filthy, even from a distance. A tire swing sagged from a tree in the front yard, suspended by a rotting rope.

An empty bird's nest sat in the crook of a rusting gutter pipe under the eaves of the house. Sonora heard the coo of a dove. She walked across the spongy grass, boot heels sticking.

She's not here, Sonora thought. But her heart was pounding and her palms were coated with sweat.

She stood away from the window and the door, letting Sam knock. A significant number of police officers were killed on front porches, even on minor calls.

No one answered.

35

Sonora was alone when the call came through. The paperwork was done, and she was listening for the umpteenth time to Gruber's interview with the woman who'd spotted Flash's car. She came out of her daze on the second ring, looked around, and realized that the guy on night shift was at dinner.

"Homicide, Blair."

"Girlfriend, we need to talk. Phone booth half a block down by the parking lot. Get over there now."

Selma. Sonora caught herself before she called Flash by name. "Let's talk here."

The line went dead. Sonora ran her hands through her hair, grabbed her blazer, and headed for the elevators.

The streetlights blazed over deserted sidewalks, office buildings lit and empty. Sonora was glad to have the Baretta in her purse. A car cruised slowly, muffler loud. Sonora made eye contact with the driver—lone male—who speeded his car and disappeared.

The ring of a phone sounded as the throb of the car's engine trailed away. Sonora ran the last few steps. Picked up the receiver.

"You'uns didn't have much of a childhood, did you?" The words were flippant, the tone was not. Selma Yorke's voice was thick and draggy.

Sonora shivered. "I'll see you my childhood and raise you yours. You're getting us mixed up."

"I did it for you, you know. I felt sorry for you, after talking to him. I mean, it was all threes for you, wasn't it, girlfriend?"

"What do you mean, threes?"

"People have personalities and bad luck, just like numbers. You never notice that before? Three is bad news. And that brother of yours a one."

"A one?"

"You know, a *one*. Shy and outcast, nobody liked him. That bothered you a lot, didn't it? Kids are mean, he was all the time getting beat on, and then your daddy getting mad at him for not sticking up for hisself."

Sonora's purse strap slid down her arm. "Tell me about *your* daddy."

She might never have spoken.

"Then you go and marry a man just like him, just like they say in the shrink books. Make you happy, he's dead now?"

"Does it make you happy, the men you've killed? Is that why you do it?"

"You'uns think I'm a total mess, don't you, you think only good girls have nice feelings. I tell you this. I knew a boy once, just a boy, like Keaton. Made me feel like I was . . . like I was important, like I was a part of him. The thing is, I always have been all by myself. And I liked it that way, except sometimes I'd get to feeling funny. Like I was going so far inside myself I wanted to scream? You ever feel like that?"

"No," Sonora said.

Silence again, then a choked laugh. "That's why I like you, you always say just what you think. Maybe you don't know how it feels. But it's noises, inside of me. Like Mama in the fire."

Maybe it's your conscience, Sonora thought.

"You ever hear whale songs, Detective? That's what it sounds like, inside of me. Look, I know I'm different. I've always known that, always been on the outside, looking in. This boy, Danny, he was like Keaton. He made the bad feelings go away. Being with him was like . . . like being high. It felt good. I didn't think I'd ever feel that again. I see men, and they look like him, like Danny, but they don't work, they don't give me that feeling."

"Does Keaton give you that feeling?" Sonora said.

"Good to know you're catching on."

"What was that business on the playground?"

"I was missing him. I had to see him."

"Don't give me that," Sonora said. "What you're doing is hunting him."

"Don't you see?" Selma said. "That's where you come in. I helped you. Now you help me."

36

By the time Sonora made it back to the squad room, the phone was ringing again.

"Homicide, Blair."

"Ms. Sonora Blair?"

"Speaking."

"Ma'am, I'm calling from University Hospital, concerning a Charles F. Bennet. Are you a relative?"

Ex–significant other, Sonora thought. "I'm his, um, his friend."

"Ma'am, Mr. Bennet has been in an accident and—"

"A fire?"

"No ma'am. A car accident."

"How bad is he?"

"He's in emergency now, but—"

"I'm on my way."

It was raining again, just like the night Mark Daniels was killed. Sonora felt like she was dreaming as she went through the automatic doors into the waiting room.

Quiet night. Two people watching television, one uniformed police officer on the phone.

"Sonora Blair, here about Charles Bennet."

The clerk was middle-aged and tired, eyes blue and bloodshot. "Yes ma'am, if you'll take a seat, someone will be right with you."

The police officer looked over his shoulder. "Excuse me, ma'am, did you know Mr. Bennet?"

Did? Sonora nodded.

"I wonder if I might ask you a few questions."

Sonora brought her ID up out of her purse. "All you want, but I'd appreciate knowing what happened."

"You're homicide?"

"Yeah. He's dead, isn't he?"

The uniform hesitated. He was an older man, close to retirement, and his eyes were sad. "I'm sorry, he was DOA."

Sonora nodded, feeling stiff and numb.

The uniform put a hand on her shoulder. "Hit-and-run, he never saw it coming."

"Any leads on the car?"

The officer shook his head. "No witnesses. Got shards of broken headlights in his shirt pocket, and tire marks on . . . "

"It's okay." Sonora straightened her shoulders. "I think I better have a look."

The pretty face was gone. There were tire marks on the crushed chest, windpipe, and larynx. For the first time in a long time, Sonora looked at death and felt ill.

She turned away, saw the clothes piled on the counter. The shoes were in good shape, pants in tatters, shirt all gore. The familiar jacket was stiff with blood. Sonora fingered the sleeve, then gave it a second look.

There had been four leather buttons—one had been torn away, leaving three. She checked the other sleeve. Three buttons again, one missing.

I helped you, now you help me. Three and three. Proof of what she already knew.

Selma Yorke.

37

Sam handed Sonora a beer and sat on the end of the couch. He scratched Clampett behind the ears. "You doing okay over there, Sonora?"

"I don't know. Tell you the truth, I don't feel so good."

"Tell you the truth, you don't look so good. Have a big drink of that beer."

"Hang on a second, I think I hear Heather."

"She's fine, the kids are asleep, I checked them both just a minute ago."

Sonora took a sip of beer, leaned back, and closed her eyes. "This is so unbelievable. It's hard to . . . I'm not happy about this, Sam."

"I didn't figure you would be."

Sonora opened her eyes. "I mean, I may have been pissed and all, but I'm not glad he's dead. He was . . . it made me sick to look at him."

"What's the matter with you, hon, nobody's going to think you're happy over this."

"Selma does."

Sam sat forward. "You talked to her?"

Sonora swallowed. "A couple of times."

"You mean stuff we don't have recorded?"

"Once on a pay phone. Once on my car phone."

"And you didn't *say* anything? What the hell's going on with you?"

"I . . . she . . . she knew things, Sam, really private stuff."

"Private? What are you playing at, girl, there's nothing private between the two of you."

Sonora blew air between her teeth. "Wrong, Sam. She knows things, *personal* things, stuff she's got no business knowing."

Sam put a hand on her shoulder. "Okay, Sonora, let's take this slow and think it through. Tell me what she knows."

"Things like . . . like my parents. You remember that business when my mom died?"

Sam set his beer on the end table and gave Sonora a sideways look. "You saying she knew that you think your dad—"

"Yeah. She knew that. *All* about that."

Sam got his thoughtful look. "What else? Anything?"

"About my brother, growing up. And about Zack."

"You talk about this kind of stuff to just *anybody*, Sonora?"

"Jesus, Sam, of course not. You. Just you. And you didn't tell her, did you?"

"You have to ask?"

"I haven't told anybody else. Well, my brother. But he wouldn't talk to her."

"What about the obvious here, Sonora, boyfriends? You were over the moon about Chas for a while there, you give him all the intimate details?"

Sonora picked her beer up, put it back down. "Oh."

"'Oh,' she says. I take that as a yes."

"But why would he, I mean how could she . . . you think she's been, like, dating him?"

"I admit it's a stretch, but who else could it be? Any signs he's been seeing somebody?"

"Yeah, right, I should know them by now."

"Would Chas tell all that to somebody he barely knew?"

"I think maybe so, especially since he was so mad at me. Jesus, this is so weird."

"You ought to pick your fellas a little more carefully, girl."

"So she did do it. She killed him. If you could have heard her on the phone, going on about threes."

"I wouldn't know about that, would I, since you been holding out? But, Sonora, jacket buttons don't prove murder. Can't build a casebook on something like that. We need to get a look at her car, get the physical evidence. We'll run this by Crick in the morning, play up the sympathy bit over Chas so maybe he won't kill you."

Sonora put her head in her hands.

"You okay?"

"I feel lost, Sam. Like I'm falling. I don't know how to put it, I just know it feels really bad. It makes me wonder."

"Wonder what?"

"If this is like the way she feels."

38

Records from Selma Yorke's alma mater showed that she had gone to high school in Madison, Kentucky—a small town, barely on the map, resting in a valley at the foot of a mountain raped by strip-mining. Sonora looked at the raw wound of land, thinking that Selma had grown up with it.

There was one restaurant on the outskirts of town. A Pizza Hut.

The two-lane road twisted and turned, leading them downward toward the river. Woods pressed on both sides, relieved now and then by a sprawl of mobile homes and boxlike whitewashed houses. Men sat outside on front porches and smoked.

Sonora stared out the window. "What are these guys doing? It's a working day."

"Maybe they work night shift. Maybe there is no work."

"And maybe they're just watching the marijuana grow."

"Watch your stereotypes, girl."

"Lookit, Sam, there are dogs under that porch."

"Don't point, Sonora, it's not polite."

Sonora pushed her nose against the glass. "You know, I think I've seen that house already."

"They just look alike."

"This is the second time that woman in lavender pedal pushers has waved at me, Sam."

"There's a little grocery about a mile down the road. We'll get directions there."

"How do you know?"

"'Cause we passed it a couple times already."

✳   ✳   ✳

The sign over the screen door said Judy-Ray Food Mart. It was warm inside, poorly lit. Almost everything was old—the linoleum, the shelves, the dairy case. Only the stock was new—bright-colored wrappers on old metal shelves. There was a large selection of cigarettes and chewing tobacco. Sam helped himself to both, along with a packet of peanuts, a Moon Pie, and a bottle of Ale-8 One.

"Hidee," he said to the girl behind the counter.

She wore acid-washed jeans and a woven belt that said DONNIE'S GIRL on the back. Sonora stepped aside and let Sam do his stuff.

She was hungry. She eyed the counters and settled for tiny white powdered doughnuts, a packet of cashews, and a Coke. Sam opened his packet of peanuts and poured them into the bottle of Ale-8 One.

He grinned at the girl behind the counter. "Wonder if you could help me out some."

Sonora wandered to the back of the store, opened her pack of doughnuts. Checked out the movie rentals.

All the latest films. Rural wasn't rural anymore.

"Sonora?"

She swallowed a mouthful of doughnut. "Yeah?"

"Come on, girl. We took a wrong turn, but I know where I'm headed. It's out of town, no more than fifteen minutes away."

Sonora settled back in the car, wondering what Sam meant by town. The grocery store? The mobile homes?

He sat beside her, drinking Ale-8 One and crunching peanuts. He seemed happy.

"I'll be damned, they *said* a chicken on the mailbox. This has got to be it."

A faded plastic chicken sat on top of a dented mailbox. Some joker had shot a bullet through the chicken's head. Sam turned into the drive, and gravel crunched beneath the tires of the car.

The house was small, two stories, painted blue with white shutters. Children's toys, bright-colored plastic, littered the sagging porch and the sandy, dirt-packed yard. Clumps of grass and weed had turned brown. Sonora could see a tire swing and a burned-out barn behind the house.

"This looks a lot like where she's living now," Sam said.

"Yeah, and see that, Sam?"

"The barn? Fire follows this girl, doesn't it?"

There was no screen in the storm door, just a warped metal frame. Sam knocked on the sun-bleached wood.

They waited. Sam knocked again, and the door was opened by a woman in a blue cotton dress. The thick hams of her calves were encased in heavy stockings and showed like stumps beneath the hem of her dress. Her navy blue leather shoes, Pappagallos, looked brand-new.

She opened the door wide. "You'uns must be the police. Come in, won't you?"

You'uns. Sonora exchanged looks with Sam. They were in the right place.

"I'm Marta Adams, Selma's aunt. Ray Ben, the police are here."

The living room was small, the wood furniture polished and slick. A braided rug gave a cozy Early American look. The furniture was maple, and there was a profusion of end tables, coffee tables, side tables—all covered with ceramic animals, seashells, ashtrays, and coasters. There were doilies on the arms of the floral chintz couch. Heavy green curtains kept the sun out.

Ray Ben Adams sat at the edge of his recliner. In spite of being skinny everywhere else, his belly bulged over his belt buckle. He wore black leather work shoes, the lace-up version, and a blue, oil-stained work shirt that had his name printed on the pocket. He had sideburns, an angular, sun-burnished face, and his hair was gray-streaked and greasy. His brown eyes were bloodshot. Oil and dirt had permanently stained the cuticles around his fingers.

He took a deep drag of his cigarette, smoking it down to the filter, and stubbed it out in an ashtray that said Myrtle Beach, South Carolina. He stood up to shake hands.

Marta Adams fanned her blue dress out behind her and sat on the edge of the couch. Beside her, on an end table, was a large, worn black Bible, reading glasses folded neatly to one side. Marta Adams crossed her legs, and the nylon sang.

"You'uns want to talk about Selma, that right?"

Sonora nodded, thinking that Marta Adams was the kind of woman you could imagine waiting tables, calling people honey, and snapping gum. Her favorite brand would be Dentyne.

"What's she done?" Ray Ben asked.

Sonora set the recorder on the coffee table and slid in a new tape. She was on the verge of saying "nothing," then decided that would be an insult. She and Sam hadn't come all the way out here for nothing.

"We're homicide detectives, Mrs. Adams. We think Selma may be involved in a case we're investigating."

"Homicide? You mean murder?"

Sam nodded. "Yes, ma'am, we mean murder."

Ray Ben pulled a package of Winstons from his shirt pocket. "You think she done it?" He offered the package to Sam, who looked wistfully at Sonora, then declined. Ray Ben struck a match and inhaled tobacco. Sonora's head began to hurt.

"That's what we're trying to figure out."

"What'd she do?"

Sonora looked at him steadily. "Handcuffed a man to the steering wheel of his car, doused him with gasoline, and set him on fire. Sir."

Ray Ben sagged in his chair. Marta Adams tightened her lips and settled back against the couch. Large tears rolled down her cheeks.

She took a crumpled wad of tissue from the bosom of her blue dress.

"When's the last time you talked to Selma?" Sam's voice was gentle.

Ray Ben cleared his throat. "Mama, maybe we better not talk to these folks. We don't have to say a word, if we don't want to."

Marta Adams patted her husband's knee. "We'll do what the Lord would want us to, Ray Ben. She's beyond us, we known that a long time."

He swallowed hard and took a deep drag of his cigarette. Sonora was tired, and the tobacco smoke irritated her eyes. She thought of her children. Stuart would look after them. They were okay.

"What you want to know?" Marta Adams asked.

"Just tell us about her," Sam said. "Anything you can think of."

Marta Adams fiddled with the top button of her dress. She blew her nose delicately and with apology, and began to talk.

Selma had come to them at age five with nothing more than a doe-eyed baby doll that played Brahms's "Lullaby" and the soot-stained nightie she had been wearing when a fireman carried her out of her burning bedroom to safety. Both parents, Marta's sister, Chrissy, and her husband, Bernard, had died of smoke inhalation.

It had been a fire of suspicious origin, starting in the living room. There had been speculation that little Selma was playing with matches, but the final conclusion was that a cigarette had ignited the couch. Bernard had smoked.

The baby doll had reeked of smoke, but Selma pitched a fit when they tried to wash it or get her a new one. They let her keep it. It was all she had.

She did not smile or talk the first year she was with them. Shock, they were told. She was an intelligent child. Her parents—Bernard in particular—had been "yuppies" (this confided in an embarrassed whisper) and had started her in Montessori schools by age three.

After she was with them a year, she resumed talking. They did not make a big deal of it, they were warned not to. The smiles never came.

She had been an uncomfortable child.

Selfish. They hated to say it, but it was true. She didn't like to share, but Marta and Ray Ben had five of their own, and sharing was par for the course. She liked pretties, not necessarily valuable. There was no predicting what would catch her eye, but whatever did had a way of migrating to her secret stash. Sometimes she buried things, then forgot where, and would dig the yard up trying to find them. Made little holes everywhere.

She was mesmerized by mirrors and water, puddles and lakes. She'd sit and look into the river for ages, not moving a muscle. But she hated the ocean.

"The waves scared her. We went to Myrtle Beach once, and she wouldn't go in the water. Said it was too big and too noisy." Marta Adams looked at Ray Ben, and he nodded.

No, she did not get along with other children. She was uninterested in the other kids, preferred her own company, and played alone for hours, taking inventory of all of her treasures.

Dolls? Oh, yes, she loved dolls. She would scream till her face got red if you touched one of her dolls. Ray Ben had tried to fix one once, they were always losing the arms and legs, and Selma had not liked it one bit. She hadn't cared about the missing limbs, not like Marta's little girls, who would die a thousand deaths over a Barbie who'd lost a leg.

Sometimes, Ray Ben spoke up suddenly, she secretly mutilated the other girls' dolls, so they would pass them on to her.

"You don't know that," Marta told him.

"I seen her do it once."

No, no, the barn had burned a couple years after Selma had gotten there, but she'd only been seven at the time. Seven years was too young to blame. It had been a terrible fire. They had lost an old milk cow and a goat, and their entire crop of tobacco.

The kids had cried for weeks about the animals. Except Selma. She didn't cry unless she was mad.

They tried to give her religion. The minister of their Baptist church went the extra mile with Selma, but she was never grateful. They had church on Wednesday night, Sunday morning, and

Sunday evening. They said grace at every meal and had a Bible reading after supper most nights.

None of it rubbed off on little Miss Selma Magpie.

Sonora looked at Sam. There was spite in the way Marta Adams said "Miss Selma Magpie."

"That was her nickname?" Sam's voice was honey.

Marta Adams laughed, but her eyes were cold. "I guess we did call her that, a few months after she come. Most of the kids had nicknames."

"What was she like as a teenager?" Sonora asked.

Ray Ben stubbed out a cigarette. "She was trouble, that's what she was."

"Now, Ray—"

"You said tell them the truth, Marta. Tell them the truth."

Marta looked at the wall. "Those were difficult years."

"I'll say they were. She drank and she smoked, refused to go to church with us on Sunday, and did things with boys by the time she was thirteen."

Marta Adam's face turned dark red. "Ray Ben."

"It's true. We caught her, didn't we?"

"Not *boys*. That one boy." Marta Adams bowed her head. "It's a wonder that child never got pregnant. The truth is, no matter how much I punished that girl, she done as she pleased, even when she was little bitty."

"When did Selma leave home?"

Marta sniffed. "Two months after she turned fifteen, she walked out this house and down that road, and we never seen her again."

Ray Ben shook his head. "She never called, she never wrote, never so much as sent us a card. We ain't heard word one out of that girl since she left."

"Did you adopt her?" Sonora asked.

"We always meant to, but just never got around to it. She always went by Adams, though, like the rest of our kids."

Sonora frowned. "That was how long ago?"

"When she up and left? Been, oh, gosh, eleven years. November, I think, 'cause she went with no coat and it was cold. Just took that old worn-out jean jacket and her doll."

"And the roll of money I had on my dresser, *your* best earrings, and Jester's little pistol." Ray Ben did not seem to have fond memories.

"A twenty-two?" Sam asked.

"Sure was. Cute little thing."

Sonora looked at the thick curtains, wishing she could see outside. She pictured Selma aged fifteen, going down that gravel drive for good, all alone in the world. Three years later she had enrolled in Ryker Community College under the name of Selma Yorke. Where had she gotten tuition money? ID? High school transcripts?

"Did she graduate from high school?" Sam asked.

Ray Ben shook his head. "She was smart, but she didn't do nothing with it."

Sonora would have given a lot to know what had happened in the three years from fifteen to eighteen. Selma had taken college courses in business and accounting for close to two years, leaving in the middle of her last semester, after a dorm caught fire just before Easter vacation. A boy had died in the fire—a dark-haired, brown-eyed boy. Sonora had seen his picture in the yearbook. He had been studying business administration, was on the intramural football team. He'd been on the swim team and was accounted a champion at table tennis. Dead now, eight years, in a fire of suspicious origin.

"Your sister's last name was Yorke?" Sam asked.

"Yes. She married Bernard Yorke. He worked for Ashland Oil. Had a real good job, made good money."

"More than we ever did," Ray Ben said. "For all the good it did him. We still wound up raising his daughter."

And what a fine job you did of it too, Sonora thought.

Sam leaned toward Marta Adams. "What was it that made her leave all of a sudden?"

"We didn't say all of a sudden," Ray Ben said.

Sam smiled gently. "Middle of the school year. It's cold out, she's fifteen years old. Must have been something."

Ray Ben shrugged.

Marta Adams looked at the floor. "That was just Selma. She did stuff like that."

39

The principal's office of Jack's Creek High School was a square box, the walls concrete block, the floor overwaxed linoleum. The yellow pinewood desk was cluttered, and one of the filing cabinets hung open. The chair behind the desk was undoubtedly the most comfortable in the room, but it was empty.

Sonora sat in a straight-back wood chair next to Sam, waiting for the next teacher.

"Get the feeling she wasn't much liked?" Sam was saying.

Sonora nodded. The principal had been new and young, and did not know Selma Yorke, but he had lent them his office and instigated a parade of teachers who did.

Someone knocked at the door.

Sam looked at his watch. "Last one."

The woman was past retirement age, tall and broad shouldered, with well-rounded hips but no extra weight. She wore a blue print dress that hung loosely to mid-calf, thick cotton socks, and scuffed deck shoes. Reading glasses hung from a chain around her neck. Her hair, gray and white, was thickly plaited and hung down her back.

"I'm Ms. Armstead, the art teacher."

Sam stood up and shook her hand. "Specialist Delarosa, and this is Specialist Blair."

Armstead nodded at Sonora and sat down. She inclined her head toward Sonora's recorder. "Are you taping this?"

Sam smiled at her. "We record all our interviews, it's standard procedure."

Sonora leaned forward. "Ms. Armstead, the principal talked to you already, didn't he, about a student named Selma Yorke?"

"I don't remember all of my students, Detective, and this *was* over eleven years ago. But the fact is, I do remember Selma, very well."

Sonora and Sam exchanged looks.

"Why very well?" Sam asked.

"I'm an art teacher, and Selma was very talented. Talented and . . . tortured."

Sonora settled back in her chair. "Why do you say that—tortured?"

"I'm speaking internally. Let me give you a for instance. We always do a unit on portraiture—one student models and the others sketch. Selma couldn't do it, she could not draw another human being. Sometimes she would sketch a number, instead of a face. It was weird, it made the other children uncomfortable. She was not well liked. She tried, I'll give her that. I saw the child sit there, time after time, pencil in hand. She would break the lead, tear the paper. One particularly bad day she went to the restroom and . . . and cut off her bangs." Armstead's voice went breathless. "I went to her. I took her aside, but she was a difficult child to get close to. I will tell you honestly that I did not like her. But I did respect her talent. I haven't had another student like Selma."

Good, Sonora thought. But Armstead looked bereft.

"Had she done anything like that before? Gotten mad and cut her bangs?" Sam asked.

"When I gave them the self-portrait assignment, Selma couldn't even begin. She got very angry, then came in the next day, bangs chopped right off, the same thing. She was very apathetic. Said she'd take a failing grade for the project, moped around the room while the others were working. Then she came to me and asked if she could draw Danny instead."

Sonora looked at Sam. "She mentioned a Danny. A couple of times."

"Tell us about him," Sam said.

"Daniel Markum. He was older than she was, twenty-two, twenty-three. His brother went to school with Selma, and he worked the family farm and ran a repair shop from the house. Some of the teachers thought he shouldn't have been fooling with a girl as young as Selma, but she was crazy about him."

Sonora leaned forward in her chair. "Did she do it? Draw him?"

Armstead nodded. "A very credible job; she *was* talented. She did him, but never anyone else."

"Have you seen her since she left? Heard from her?"

Armstead shook her head. "I did what I could when she was my student, but we were not close. I kept things, some of her work, locked away in my private cabinet. Would you like to see?"

A bell rang just as they left the principal's office, and the hallways flooded with kids in blue jeans. Armstead led them past a thinly populated trophy case, through double doors into 101-A—the art room.

The walls were covered with vibrant masks of papier-mâché, bright greens, yellows, blues. Armstead went past a paint-streaked sink and opened a locked cabinet. Her head disappeared, and Sonora heard rustling noises.

A girl peered in the doorway and looked at Sam. She grinned and left.

"Here we are." Armstead brought out a fabric case and unzipped it over her desk, took out a canvas, and held it up.

It was thickly painted with throbbing, dark color.

"Selma loved to paint. Disturbing things, hot hard colors as you see here, very abstract. The other students, the other teachers, thought it was just splatters on canvas. Ignorance." Her voice sounded clipped and irritable. She rummaged in the satchel and pulled out a square of canvas paper. "This is the sketch she did. Danny Markum. The likeness is good."

Sonora held the sketch by the edges. It had been done in charcoal, by a hurried, almost frantic hand, and something about it disturbed her. The likeness to Keaton Daniels was superficial, but marked. She passed it on to Sam.

He looked up and caught Armstead's eye. "What happened with her and Danny?"

Armstead winced. "She did this just before the . . . that business at the river."

"What business at the river?" Sonora asked.

"You don't know?"

Sam shook his head.

Armstead settled slowly into the chair behind the small square desk. "Nobody really knows for sure what happened that night, and there were a lot of versions flying at the time, let me tell you." She looked out the window, seeming far away. "I told you Danny had a brother, Roger, and he was in Selma's class. Selma was jealous of Roger. She was jealous of anybody that went near Daniel, but Roger in particular.

"The two of them, the brothers, had a habit of going night fishing once a week. It was a sore point with Selma. She had a thing about the river. Anyway, Selma was always agitating to tag along, but Roger usually talked Daniel out of letting her go. This one night, Roger said Selma came anyway, fought with Danny, then stormed off. The story goes that after Selma left, Roger went back to the car for more beer. And when he came back, Danny was gone. Nothing there but his fishing pole and bait, and a half-empty beer can."

"They doing a lot of drinking?" Sam asked.

"Probably. More than they should, no doubt. They dragged the river and found Daniel's body. The official ruling was that he waded out over his head and drowned. He couldn't swim. Most of the kids around here can't."

"Then the rumors started," Sonora said.

Armstead propped her chin on her elbow. "More than just rumors. Roger made a big fuss. He said Selma came back and pushed Danny in. But the sheriff let it go. He said that Selma loved Danny and, after all, she was a little thing, and Danny was a solid six foot. But they . . . they found one of Selma's earrings in the mud. Selma said she lost it the first time, when they had words."

Sam looked at Armstead. "The *first* time? She said that?"

Armstead nodded. "I heard her say it, here in class."

"You tell the sheriff?"

"I . . . yes." Armstead traced a finger across the desk. "Roger wouldn't let it be."

"Is that when she left?" Sonora asked.

"Not exactly. Not long after that, Roger had an accident. He was working late in the family tobacco barn, and a fire started. He didn't make it out."

Sam spoke gently. "Any ruling on how the fire started?"

Armstead spoke through clenched teeth. "Someone emptied a gas can that was there for the tractor, and then dropped a match. Roger never had a chance." She looked up at Sam. "Everyone said Selma did it. And *that* was when she left."

Sonora and Sam exchanged looks.

Armstead took the canvas paper from Sam. "It's a very focused sketch, don't you think?"

Sonora thought obsessed would be a better word. "Ms.

Armstead, do you think Selma killed Roger? Do you think she killed Danny?"

Armstead raised a hand in a gesture that looked hopeless and tired. "I wouldn't—I couldn't know. I will tell you that after Danny died . . . she tried to draw him, but she couldn't."

40

Sonora looked up at the fifth floor of the Board of Elections building, saw that all windows were lit. She looked at Sam.

"Go home, babe, see your kiddo. How's she doing?"

"They're still running tests, Sonora. Always running tests." He chewed his lip. "Naw, I better——"

"Go *home*, Sam."

"Go home, okay. Call if you get something." He leaned across the seat and kissed her cheek. "You're looking tired, Sonora."

"I am tired, Sam."

He watched her walk from the car to the side door—cop watching cop in at cop headquarters. Sonora glanced up at the video camera in the doorway.

The elevator was slow. She rested her head against the wall, thinking she would like it if Sam kissed her more often.

Her phone was ringing as she walked in. She almost passed it by, then thought it might be Stuart or the kids.

"Homicide, Specialist Blair."

"Hello." The voice was high and fluting, vaguely familiar against a noisy background. "This is Chita Childers. You know, from Cujo's?"

Sonora's heartbeat kicked in hard and heavy. Tell me she's there, she thought. Tell me she's there.

"He's here."

Sonora leaned against her desk. "He?"

"Yeah, um, that guy, you know? The one in the picture?"

Sonora felt a chill, then her heart settled. Keaton, of course. "Solid build, dark curly hair?"

"Yeah." Chita was chewing gum, which over the phone sounded like a wad of plastic in her mouth. Sonora wanted to tell her to spit it out.

"Thank you, Ms. Childers. I appreciate the call."

"Should I try to keep him here or something?"

"No. He's not a suspect."

"Just a law-abiding citizen having a drink, huh?"

Sonora pictured Chita Childers behind the bar, hands on her slim hips.

"You might want to know that he's asking after her. That blonde in the jean skirt. He's not a cop, is he?"

"Did he say he was?" Sonora asked.

"No."

"He's not."

"So I shouldn't have called, huh?"

"Certainly you should have. I appreciate it." Women always needed to be reassured, Sonora thought. "If you see the other one—"

"The girl?"

"The girl. Don't approach her, and call me right away."

"Will do."

Sonora called home. "Stuart? Don't wait up, I'm going to be late. Can you stay?"

"Bartender went home with the flu twenty minutes ago. I was going to wait till the kids went to bed, then take off. You think they'll be all right, or you want me to stay?"

"They should be all right, just make sure they're all locked up and the alarms are on."

"No problem. Case breaking?"

"Side issue. Trying to keep John Q. Public out of trouble."

"Maybe John Q. wants trouble."

"He's going to get it, he doesn't watch out."

41

Sonora ran a pick through her hair and reapplied her makeup, smearing Sulky Beige heavily across her lips. She looked in the rearview mirror. Nothing she could do about the hard exhaustion in her face and the newly acquired slump to her shoulders. She straightened her tie when she parked the car, then changed her mind and stuffed the tie in the glove compartment.

Cujo's was winding down—it was late, a weeknight. Sonora wondered if Selma was around, watching him, watching her. She paused in the doorway, and people stared. Something about her always said cop. Keaton sat by himself a few feet from the bar where he could see the front door, the restrooms, and the television. He was close to the end of his beer. His khakis were wrinkled, but his shirt was freshly pressed and he had shaved after five. He looked tired and pale and wonderful.

Sonora rested a hand on the chair across from him. "Hello, Keaton Daniels."

"Sit down. I saw you on the news tonight, and I was wondering about all those developments you mentioned."

Sonora sat and smiled sadly.

"It's all hype, isn't it?"

"It's not breaking yet, I won't lie to you. But it's moving and picking up speed. And I *will* catch her." She tilted her head sideways. "Provided you don't beat me to it."

He smiled, and she liked it that he didn't try to deny it. "Am I in trouble?"

"You got a gun, Keaton?"

"Yeah, you mind?"

"Got a permit? Know how to use it?"

He nodded.

"Then no, I don't mind. Just don't take it to school with you." She leaned back in her chair. "Been here a long time?"

"Since eight."

"Long night."

Chita Childers leaned across the bar, trying to get their attention. "Last call! Either of you want anything?"

"I was thinking about toast," Sonora said. It was out of her mouth before she had time to think. Bad girl. No can do. Brother of victim. Be smart.

Keaton stood up and took the jacket from the back of his chair.

God he looked good, she thought.

Chita Childers stared at them. "Going to call it a night, huh?"

Keaton smiled at Sonora.

"I'll follow you home," she said. See him in safely, she thought. Yeah. Right.

The streets of Mount Adams were lined with parked cars, giving the neighborhood a tight, squeezed feeling. Keaton took Sonora's hand and led her up the walk to the front porch. He fumbled with the house key, and Sonora wondered if he was nervous. She was.

"You ever get those locks changed," Sonora asked. She looked over her shoulder. Scanned the dark streets.

Nobody, no movement, no car out of place. Selma couldn't be everywhere at once, one person couldn't do twenty-four-hour surveillance. Maybe she wasn't out there.

And maybe she was.

"Yeah, I got the locks changed. We're safe."

The house was dark, just a light over the sink in the kitchen. Keaton headed for the lamp, but Sonora put a hand on his arm, and he left it dark. The blinds were open, and the streetlights gave the room a shimmer of illumination. Keaton closed the front door and locked it.

He took Sonora's hand and led her to the edge of the couch. "Stand close to me, like you did the other night."

Sonora let her purse slide off her shoulder and drop to the floor. She draped her blazer over the arm of the couch, then moved toward him, not quite touching. Was she really going to do this? She studied his face, shadowed by darkness. Yes. She was.

Keaton put his arms around her, and she stood on her tiptoes and dipped her tongue into the hollow of his throat, a butterfly flick. He kissed her, swiftly and hard, and after a while she broke free.

They stood still for a moment, breathing deeply. Keaton put his hands on her hips and pulled her tight against his body. She closed her eyes, feeling his warmth, his hardness, the beat of his heart against her chest.

He traced the line of her neck and shoulder with the thick pad of his thumb. She placed a finger against his lips, parting them slowly, touching his tongue, lightly grazing the bottom edge of his teeth.

With her other hand she unbuttoned the top buttons of her shirt and unlatched the front hook of her bra. She arched her back, felt her hair slide across her shoulders, bit her bottom lip when he bent forward and put his mouth on her breast.

They shed their clothes quickly, awkwardly. Light spilled in from the street and turned their flesh milky white.

Sonora sat on the couch and pulled him close in front of her, took him into her mouth. He wrapped a hand in her hair and said her name so softly she thought she imagined his voice.

His breath came in short gasps, and the hand tangled in her hair tightened into a fist.

"*God.*"

Sonora laughed.

"Come upstairs," he said.

The stairs were bare wood and caught the light. Sonora's hand slid against the banister on the way up, and Keaton guided her through the open hallway toward his bedroom.

Outside, a car door slammed.

"You okay?" Keaton asked. He stroked the small of her back.

"Just jumpy."

It was dark in the bedroom, blinds drawn tight. Sonora saw the white glow of a digital clock. Keaton put both hands on her shoulders and pressed her back against the edge of the bed. He pushed her legs back till her knees were high, then traced the inside of her thigh with his tongue.

She grabbed the headboard and shut her eyes. His touch made her jerk, and he paused for a moment before he resumed, relentless and slow. He moved on top of her, his mouth over hers. She grabbed his shoulders.

"Keaton."

She shut her eyes and tried to hold him back. Now was probably a bad time to tell him she wasn't on the pill. She relaxed and let him resume, just once or twice more, and then she thought of pregnancy and babies and how easily she got caught.

"Keaton, I can't—"

He kissed her neck. "Yes, you can. Yes, you can."

"Keaton, I get pregnant at the drop of a hat." The words came out in a strangled rush. He stopped moving inside of her and raised up on his arms. "So to speak," she said.

"Sorry. Should have asked."

The bed creaked when he got up. She heard a drawer open and close, the crinkle of a foil packet. He climbed back into bed and stretched out beside her, kissing her again. She swung her legs over his hips and sat on top of him. He put a hand on her belly, and then he was inside again, and now it was safe, and she rocked on top of him, slow and sure.

And then she was overwhelmed, suddenly, and closed her eyes, lost just before his soft groan.

Sonora sank slowly to Keaton's chest. He put his arms around her, scratching her back lightly, making her shiver and smile.

"You hungry?" He sounded sleepy and peaceful. Kind.

"Starved, how'd you know?"

"Your stomach's growling." He turned a lamp on beside the bed. The room was all dark wood and masculinity. He opened a dresser drawer and pulled out a large white sweatshirt. "Put this on if you're cold."

She slid the shirt over her head. The cuffs hung past her wrists.

"Be right back." He went into the bathroom. Shut the door.

Sonora went to the dresser, checked her hair in the mirror, noticed a newspaper clipping with her picture. Next to the clipping was a hardbound notebook that had JOURNAL OF INVESTIGATION printed in bold black letters on the front.

Private, of course. She turned the cover.

My brother is dead now, the police are tracking the killer. The detective in charge is a woman. She strikes me as tough and capable. She has a smart mouth, but underneath I think she is kind.

Sonora grimaced, then smiled. Interesting to get those first impressions.

I will be dogging her every footstep. I want Mark's killer caught. But I am getting ahead of myself. I think this all started with phone calls, right around Easter, when Ashley and I began falling apart.

Sonora heard the toilet flush. She closed the journal and moved away.

Keaton came out of the bathroom wearing a dark blue bathrobe. He took her hand, leading her down the stairs through the dark silent house, and they laughed for no particular reason. Sonora felt like a child who was getting away with something.

He turned on the lights. Darkness was thick against the windows, and Sonora blinked at the harsh, cheery brightness of his kitchen.

"I was hoping you would come, so just in case." He opened the refrigerator and waved an arm.

Chocolate-covered strawberries, frozen yogurt, egg rolls. Classic Coke in bright red cans.

Keaton Daniels smiled proudly. "Girl food."

42

Sonora left Keaton's town house well before dawn, with a full stomach, a sleepy ulcer, and a long hard kiss.

"You really go to work this early?" he asked as she hunted through the living room for her clothes.

"Umm. Where is my . . . oh, there it is. Here's your towel back, and thanks for the use of the shower."

"Can I talk you into some breakfast? You said last night you wanted toast."

"I lied."

The phone rang. Keaton frowned, looked at her. "Think it's for you, some cop thing? Nobody calls me this early."

Sonora shook her head. "I didn't give your number out. Nobody knows I'm—answer it, why don't you?"

He took the extension in the living room. Said hello. Listened.

She knew who it was by the sudden set of his shoulders, the hand by his side closing into a fist.

He hung up.

"It was her," Sonora said.

"Yeah." His voice was tight, so different from the way he'd sounded minutes before.

Sonora yanked her boot over her foot. "What, Keaton? What'd she say?"

"She said she'd pay me back. She'd pay both of us back good."

Sonora drove through the dark streets—it was garbage day again, and plastic bags clogged the curbs. She had called home, of course. All was well. She cruised out of the Mount Adams area and wound down to Broadway onto the bridge, just as the sky got lighter. She glanced over her right shoulder, saw the mountains were fogged in. A train whistled. Three large road locomotives strained at the upgrade, pulling a fully loaded unit train—Kentucky coal, headed north.

She wondered how adults—herself in particular—expected teenagers to be sensible about sex, when they were dumb themselves. Do as I say, not as I do.

It started to rain, and Sonora turned on her windshield wipers, squinting through the gray haze and drizzle. The river was greenish at the edge, brown toward the middle. The local access bridge was brightly lit, and Sonora passed through the stone crossing. Lights from the parking lots at Riverfront Stadium made reflections that looked like torches coming up from the water. The roar of trucks on the interstate sounded lonesome.

Sonora glanced at her brother's saloon, snug in its berth on the waterfront. She had no regrets about investing Zack's death benefits in Stuart's business, but had lately been wondering what she was going to do about sending the kids to college. Surely by the time Tim was out of high school, she and Stuart would have enough return on investment to send Tim to Harvard. Provided he passed algebra.

Sonora took the exit to Covington. The steep hilly streets were quiet. She drove past tall narrow houses, packed close together, painted in an astonishing range of colors—stately red brick to lime green. All of them looked dingy in the gloom. There were high-rise hotels, the big clock tower, Super America, Big Boy Burgers, Mainstrasse Village, and the sign for the visitors center. Cincinnati kept its sin on this side of the river, and Covington was a small town, big-city-satellite mix of stately churches, dingy houses, motels, and bars that featured GIRLS, GIRLS, GIRLS and XXX MOVIES.

Sonora passed Smith Muffler shop *(Free Installation)*, KFC *(Finger-Lickin' Good)*, and Kwik Drive-in *(Kools, Camels & Savanna Lights)*. She breezed past Senior Citizens of Northern Kentucky and turned into the empty parking lot that served the legal offices of McGowan, Spanner & Karpfinger—uncomfortably located across from Red & Orange Liquor Shoppe and Angel's Bar, featuring GIRLS DAY & NITE.

Sonora saw a hunched figure in a black leather jacket through the glass of a brightly lit booth. The lawyers were not pulling all-nighters, but if they had been, their BMWs would be safe. Ruby was on shift.

Sonora walked across the freshly patched asphalt, finding nothing much and everything in particular of interest. Cop attitude. Ruby, as always, had her head bent over a book.

A tiny CD player spewed jazz with a state-of-the-art quality that had cost thousands in speakers and amps just ten years ago. A pink-and-white box of Dunkin' Donuts was open and empty, and Ruby was sipping Evian water and scoring notes on blank sheets. Ruby acknowledged Sonora with a nod and put out her cigarette.

Sonora opened the door of the booth and leaned her shoulder against the edge. "Hey, girl. Have I come at a bad time?"

Ruby gave her a sideways sloppy smile. "The great composer at work. I'd offer you a doughnut, but I ate them already."

Sonora had never been able to pinpoint Ruby's age—somewhere between twenty-eight and forty-eight. She was big boned and fleshy, skin a deep blue black, and her hair was thick, abundant, and rigid with tight curls some women paid big bucks to achieve. She was deft with makeup, and wore purple lipstick and a nightstick on her belt as if the two always went together.

"Ruby, you ought to be studying."

"I know. What you smiling about, you just get laid or something?"

"I've been over there at girls girls girls, dancing on tables all night."

"I have to say it agrees with you."

"Speaking of dancing. You know a working girl named Shonelle?"

"Shonelle, hmmm. She danced at the Sapphire, didn't she? The one jacked up her knee?"

"Jacked up?"

"*Messed* up. Sonora, you are so *white*."

"Yeah, yeah, be a bigot. How about Sheree La Fontaine, you know her?"

Ruby shut her eyes. "Skinny little girl with fake blond hair that she doesn't wash good more 'n once a week?"

"That's the one."

"What's going on? I've seen that evangelist cop hanging around, what's his name, Molliter?"

"Molliter."

"I hear he has an AK-47 stashed in his basement in the burbs. Cincinnati's finest. Who protects us from you guys?"

"You need protecting, Ruby?"

Ruby patted her nightstick and the huge revolver on her hip.

Sonora flipped open the lid of the Dunkin' Donuts box and scooped up a crumb of chocolate frosting.

"This have anything to do with that dude got roasted in his car?"

Sonora licked her finger and nodded. "Tell me about this Sheree La Fontaine and Shonelle."

"No love lost, that's for sure. Always fighting over . . . get ready. Clothes."

"Clothes?"

"See, they both work the streets, right? And some of the girls, I'm talking about Sheree here, stash clothes in out-of-the-way places around their hangouts. Might need a switch during the night, sometimes they change if the cops run them in, you know the drill. And Sheree says Shonelle keeps taking her stuff, and buddy, they got into it big-time last month. I'm talking a hair-pulling, cussing, spitting cat fight."

"What's the dope on this Sheree, anyway?"

"From down south somewhere, the Carolinas I think. I hope she's not par for the course, because if she is and the South does rise again, we all be in for some shit."

"Could you get a little more specific?"

"Weird, Sonora, even for an addict. Sits in the bars and lights matches. Shonelle is twice her size, but went after her, digging with those fingernails like a maniac. Course, hooker addicts aren't exactly your average bear, you get me?"

"You see her around the night the Daniels kid got killed?"

"Let me think. That was . . . Tuesday week, that right?"

Sonora nodded.

"You know, come to think, I did see her. Around midnight, getting in a car with some john. I didn't get much look at the guy, so I don't know if it was your boy."

"My guy was up in Mount Adams at midnight. On his way to die."

Ruby looked grim. "Yeah, well."

Sonora yawned. "I got to go home and kiss my kids before they go to school."

"How they doing?"

"Good, except my son's flunking algebra. How's yours?"

"She's fine. Potty trained, finally, thank you, Jesus." Ruby glanced down at the page of notes, then looked back up at Sonora. "Me and my ex, you know, we just don't go good together. But he's helping me with tuition, and he keeps the baby sometimes. Now, most girls I know, their ex just walks off and leaves them with the babies, never even looks back. Lot of anger out there, Sonora. Lot of girls I talk to just nod and say maybe this guy got burned up, maybe he brought it all on his own head."

"He didn't, Ruby."

"Hell of a way to go."

Sonora nodded. "Listen, there's no food in my house. There an all-night grocery store anywhere close?"

"Nothing but that Kwik Stop, and they charge an arm and a leg."

"I look rich to you?"

43

Sonora was thinking that she had bought everything except milk, when she turned the corner toward home. In a split second of clarity she saw the flashing blue lights, the police cars, the open front door.

Remembered Selma's words—*I'll pay you back good.*

Sonora slammed on the brakes, opened the car door, and was on the pavement as the parking gear caught and the Nissan rocked backward. Out of the corner of one eye, she could see the wary stance of the patrolman in the second car, see his hand cover the gun on his hip as she ran toward his partner.

"What the hell's going on here?"

The uniform on the radio was young, dark hair cropped short. He clicked his radio off, blinked. "Everything's all right, ma'am."

"This is my house, okay? I've got kids inside."

The screen door slammed. Stuart headed her way, taking the porch steps two at time. His shirttail hung over his jeans, and his shoelaces were untied.

"Where are the kids?"

"They're all right, Sonora. Everybody's okay." He ran a hand through his hair, making it stick up on the side.

Sonora folded her arms, closed her eyes a short moment, took a deep breath.

"Ma'am, did you say you live here?"

It was the one who had touched his gun. Light brown hair, thick neck.

"Detective Blair, I work homicide. And yeah, I live here."

The dark-haired one, the steady one, was nodding at her. "We got a call, nine-one-one, possible intruder—"

Sonora heard the door open. Heather ran toward her, arms out, face tear-stained and pale. Something bad.

Sonora looked at Stuart. "Where's Tim?"

"Right here." Tim shut the front door and followed his sister down the steps.

Sonora put her arms around Heather, gave Tim a hug. He did not pull away. She lifted Heather up in her arms, groaned as the weight of her growing child hit her in the small of the back.

"So, what's up kidlets?"

"Let me tell it," Tim said. "We heard somebody outside the house, and—"

"She pulled on the knob, Mommy! On the back door, we saw her."

"Her?" Sonora swallowed hard.

Tim folded his arms across his chest. "I thought it was you. I almost opened the door. But Clampett was barking, and he yelped and I looked out the curtain, and it *wasn't* you."

"So then what?"

"She knocked on the glass real hard!" Heather burst into tears and buried her face in Sonora's shoulder.

Tim looked tense and young. "I called Uncle Stuart, and he called nine-one-one. That was right, wasn't it?"

Sonora put a hand lightly on her son's shoulder. "It was perfect."

He nodded, cheeks flushed, lips tight. "We can't find Clampett."

Stuart bent down to tie a shoe. "We'll find him, Tim."

Sonora set her daughter down. "Did you get a good look at this woman, Tim?"

"Short hair, like to here." He touched his collarbone. "Blond. She was little, like you, Mom. She looked funny."

"Funny?"

He shrugged. "Weird."

The patrol officer grinned and tousled her son's hair. "I bet I could put my feet up and let him write the report."

Sonora looked at her brother. "You get a look at her?"

"Long gone by the time I got here." He bent down, picked up Heather, balanced her on his hip. She wore nothing but a night-gown, and her long thin legs had chill bumps.

"Cold, baby?" Sonora put her blazer around her daughter's

shoulders. She looked at the uniforms. "You guys had a chance to take a look around?"

"Just a quick one." Thick neck.

Sonora nodded. "Stuart, why don't you take the kids inside and—" Sonora heard a whimper and looked over her shoulder. The three-legged dog bounded toward her, something yellow streaming from the side of his mouth. Clampett barked, doggy breath frosting white in the chill air.

Sonora braced herself as the heavy muddy paws landed against her shoulders. Clampett's tail swished back and forth, thumping Heather's bare legs.

"Want to dance, pup?" Sonora put her hands on the dog's soft muzzle, pried open the black-rimmed jaws, wrestled a large round lump off the back of the thick ham tongue. Clampett barked and jumped, and Sonora twisted sideways, playing keep-away.

The dark-haired cop looked pale. "What is that?"

Sonora held up the soggy blond head so he could see. "Barbie. Or parts thereof." She studied the wet, plastic doll head, wondering about prints.

It was muddy out in the yard. Stuart took the kids inside to make hot chocolate while Sonora walked the perimeter of her property, circling closer and closer to the house, the dark-haired uniform at her heels. The volleyball net sagged across the middle of the backyard, and the lawn was overgrown and brown, thick grass limp with dew.

She wondered what Flash had thought of the plastic kiddie pool filled with trolls and algae-coated water, the basketball wedged under the rusted-out slide, the plastic playhouse so full of old toys the door bulged open.

There were footprints outside Sonora's bedroom window and another set by Heather's.

The thick-necked cop rounded the corner of the yard and jogged over, hand holding the radio snug to his belt. "CSU van is on the way. I asked your brother to stay inside with the kids for the time being."

Sonora nodded and sat down on the bottom porch step. The uniforms moved discreetly away and talked together in low voices, pretending not to notice while Sonora put her head on her knees.

44

Sonora slopped coffee into her lipstick-stained mug. She was late, the task force had already assembled. Her phone rang before she could get away from her desk. Sonora sighed and picked it up.

"Hey, girlfriend, how's the kids?"

Sonora sat back down. Gritted her teeth. "You listen to me—"

"No, you. I'll make you'uns a deal. Leave Keaton alone, I'll leave them alone. Think about it."

The line went dead. Sonora's palms were slippery on the receiver, and the phone smacked hard on the desk when she lost her grip. She took a breath, hung the phone up gently. Closed her eyes, opened them. Took a notepad off her desk and headed for her meeting.

They were watching a videotape of the latest press conference. Sonora squinted at the screen, wondering if it was her imagination, or if she was showing just a hint of double chin.

Gruber looked up. "That's a nice tie, Sonora, but what happened to the one with the catsup on it?"

Crick shushed him. "Watch for the next part, it's good."

On-screen, Sonora cocked her head to one side and told the reporters that the investigation was moving forward swiftly and it was only a matter of time. Yes, she was the case detective and would make the arrest herself. The DA's office was waiting for lab results, merely a formality. They had been lucky with witnesses, and, quite frankly, the killer had made a number of careless mistakes.

If the killer wanted to talk, Sonora was certainly available, and she gave her number. It would be in the perpetrator's best interests to turn herself in. She would be handled sympathetically, the police department would see that she got the proper help, and a lawyer would be provided free of charge.

Yes, the perp was a woman, a sad case, very disturbed, pathetic really, not particularly bright.

The room got quiet. Normally, this last would bring a howl of laughter and the theory that Sonora would be the next victim. Sonora rubbed her eyes and wished she was as close to arrest and wrap-up as the confident woman on-screen.

"Good job, Sonora," Crick said.

Gruber crossed a heavy foot over one knee. "Yeah, too good. I don't like what happened at Sonora's house this morning, kids and all. I think you're throwing her out there, sir, and look what we get."

"Action, reaction," Crick said.

Sonora felt her face get warm and pink.

"Yeah, with Sonora's neck on the line." This last from Molliter.

Sonora was surprised. Then wary. Was this camaraderie, or over-protection? Did it matter, with her children caught in the middle? What would they say if they knew where she'd spent the night?

Crick looked at Sonora. "CSU get anything?"

"Not a lot. Partial right thumb on my daughter's window. Toe smear in the mud. Terry also told me Sheree La Fontaine's prints don't match the one they took off the Polaroid that Flash sent to Keaton Daniels." Sonora did not look at Molliter.

Sanders tapped her chin. "Sir, I was wondering if we could utilize the feds on this."

Gruber hooted with laughter. "Utilize the feds? That's sweet, honey. Then maybe we can teach the Aryan brothers to sing 'We Shall Overcome.' "

Sonora rubbed her eyes, kept her voice low-key. "We've asked for help in that quarter, Sanders, but it's just a formality. Leave no stone unturned, you know? FBI doesn't come in unless there's a signed warrant with the suspect's name."

"Yeah, they're happy to take the collar, long's they don't have to put out."

Molliter folded his arms. He looked unhappy. "Look, Sonora, maybe you're overdoing it on this Daniels guy."

"What's that supposed to mean?"

"She may just move on to the next victim."

"I think it's pretty clear she's fixated," Sam said.

Sonora kept her mouth shut. Dangerous ground.

Gruber waved a hand. "Okay, but why has she got this thing with Sonora? It's almost like they're rivals or girlfriends or something. I mean, Sonora's a cop—"

"I told you, it's catch-me-if-you-can," Sonora said. "It happens."

Crick folded his arms. "It happens when the perp is flipping out. Which makes her that much more dangerous." He pointed at Sonora. "You still want to go to Atlanta?"

"Sir?"

"Been talking to your buddy down there, Bonheur. Selma Yorke's name showed up in the file of possibles they put together after the attack on James Selby."

Sam put a hand on Sonora's shoulder. "*Here* we go, darlin'. Here we go."

"Blair," Crick said. "About what I said earlier—action, reaction. What do *you* think set her off?"

Sonora swallowed. "TV interview, obviously, sir." Bad policewoman, she thought. Her chest was tight. Was that what guilt felt like? Had Zack felt this way when he cheated?

Crick was nodding. "What would you say to one of those radio call-in things? Think she could resist talking to you?"

Sam shook his head. "I don't like this."

"We'll have somebody with her kids," Crick said.

Sonora cleared her throat. "It's just—"

"Just what? If she reacts that much to a taped interview, I think she'll go nuts to talk to you live."

"Talking on the radio would make me nervous, sir."

"Get over it, Blair."

45

The city of Atlanta throbbed with sunshine and noisy traffic. Sonora squinted and put on a pair of dark sunglasses. An unmarked police car pulled into the circle drive in front of the hotel and parked illegally. A black man in a lightweight tan suit got out of the car, leaving the driver's door hanging open.

"Detective Sonora Blair?" He pointed large fingers at her like a gun.

"You must be Bonheur."

They shook hands. He wore a diamond-encrusted wedding ring and his grip was firm. He was built like a football player, hair close-cropped and balding at the top. He opened the passenger door of a pale blue Taurus and motioned Sonora in. She would have thought it was funny he drove the same make of official car she did if her head hadn't been pounding so hard.

"Thought there was going to be two of you."

"My partner had to stay behind. Little girl is in the hospital."

"Too bad. Got your suitcase and everything. You all checked out?"

She nodded, slung the suitcase in the back, and settled in the front seat.

"What time you get in?"

"Three A.M. Fly back out tonight around six."

"Running you ragged, aren't they? First name's Ray."

"Sonora."

"You like Atlanta, Sonora?"

Sonora took her sunglasses off and looked at him. "Ray, I *love*

Atlanta. It is vastly superior to Cincinnati, which when I left it was gloomy and gray."

"That's the North for you."

A horn honked, and Ray switched lanes quickly. He drove the car in short jerky spurts, and Sonora put a hand on her stomach.

"You know, talking on the phone and all, I kind of got the impression you were white."

"Excuse me, Ray?"

"White, you know, not green, like you are now. You feeling bad or something?"

"Having a Maalox moment."

"Ulcer, huh? You know, my wife has a cure for that."

"Maybe I should give her a call."

Bonheur changed lanes again, cutting off a Subaru. The driver flipped a rod and Bonheur shook his head. "You don't want to. My wife's cures are usually worse than the disease." He gave her a sideways glance. "How about we go downtown and let you get a good look at the case file. Then we can go out and see the crime scene. Maybe grab an early lunch. We have an appointment with James Selby around twelve-thirty, quarter to one."

"He okay about talking to me?"

"Yeah, but it's been a long time since it happened. He blocked a lot of it, right after."

"You have him hypnotized?"

"DA nixed it. Said too much chance of planting suggestions that would seem like memories. Didn't want to muddy his credibility as a witness, not that it ever came to court—we didn't get close. But I've talked to this guy since, and he's been filling in the gaps. Hard to know, though, if it's real or not. You can read the transcripts of what he said right after it happened, and decide for yourself."

"She ever get in touch with you?"

"She? The killer?"

"Yeah."

He looked at her. "You mean like some woman on the edge of the investigation, trying to help or be involved?"

"Yeah, sort of."

He shook his head. "We watch for that, with the weird stuff, but I don't think it ever came up. Why, you got somebody?"

"She calls me."

"The killer does? You sure it's her?"

"I'm sure."

"What's she say?"

Sonora talked. He listened. Frowning. Then rubbed his chin.

"Sounds like it's got to be her. Sounds like she's losing it, too. Happens sooner or later. Takes more risk, more fantasy, to keep 'em happy."

"You think she wants to get caught?"

"Hard to tell. That business with her coming to the house, that's creepy. Your kids safe right now?"

"Oh, yeah."

"She wants to get caught, she can always turn herself in. I think she likes the game."

"I think she may be . . . trying to connect. She's angry."

"They all are."

"Serial killers?"

He grinned at her. "Women."

James Selby lived in a brick Cape Cod on the opposite side of town from the crime scene—which in Atlanta during afternoon traffic meant a two-hour drive. Waxy-looking ivy hugged both sides of the house. There was a square plaque in the front yard, announcing the name of the security firm that watched the premises. Sonora had noticed similar plaques in a lot of the yards. Atlanta had a crime rate that thrived with the magnolia blossoms.

Selby's front door was wood plank and horseshoe shaped, with black metal hasps at the top and bottom that made Sonora think of Lutheran churches. The door had been painted dark red sometime in the last month, and a new, freshly polished brass kickplate ran along the bottom. Sonora heard wind chimes.

Bonheur galloped up three red-brick steps to the tiny front porch and rang the doorbell. Sonora followed slowly, hand on the wrought-iron railing. Off in the distance came the burr of a lawn mower.

Bonheur touched her shoulder. "Brace yourself. He's been through a lot of operations. Spent the better part of three years in the hospital, and if you think he looks bad now, you should have seen him then."

The door opened and swung inward, and a man appeared in the shadowed hallway.

"James. My man."

"Ray. Good to see you, come on in." The voice was the low rasp of severely damaged vocal cords.

Sonora followed Bonheur up the front stoop into the dim, tiled hallway.

Even in the thin light, James Selby was startling. Sonora felt her stomach sink as she took in the elongated, scarred features, one sightless eye lower than the other. His hair grew in a patch on the back of his scalp, blending with a bad toupee. His face looked like it had melted, smeared, then frozen. The neck was thickly scarred, one hand misshapen, the forearm curled forward.

Bonheur touched Selby on the shoulder. "Standing beside me here is Detective Blair. I told you about her."

Selby's thin, slash lips stretched into a smile. "Good to meet you, Detective. Forgive me, do you use Pond's moisturizing cream?"

"Yes."

"I like the way it smells. Very fresh, better than perfume. My sense of smell is fantastic since I lost my sight."

"Please don't tell me what I ate for lunch."

Selby laughed, a raspy bark. "Come in, we'll sit for a while."

He led them into a dark living room and switched on a lamp. Late-afternoon sun slanted in from French doors that opened onto a brick patio. A golden retriever lay like a sphinx next to a shabby green easy chair. The dog wore a thick leather harness on her back and watched James Selby's every move, tail thumping the floor.

"That's Daffney, by the way. She'll play cute and show you her tummy, but I'll have to ask you not to pet her. She's a working dog and she's on duty."

Daffney immediately rolled to her back, front paws paddling the air. Sonora thought of Clampett and hoped the kid next door was being diligent about letting him out.

"I think that bulb's burned out, on your lamp there," Bonheur said.

Selby looked up. "Is it? Let me get another one."

"Don't bother, James. We got enough light from the window."

"If you're sure." He held up a plastic board. "Look at this, Ray, this is something new." He turned his head toward Sonora. "It's a Braille writer—works so that you can write and read left to right, instead of backward. I'm testing it. They have this great question-naire for feedback. Not in Braille, though." He laughed again, hoarsely.

Sonora glanced around the room. There were no knickknacks and precious little furniture. A grand piano sat in one corner, black, highly polished. Sonora and Bonheur sat at either end of a floral patterned couch that had the look of a valuable antique. There were food stains on the upholstery.

The fireplace was choked with charred lumps of wood and thick gray ashes. A green rag rug in front of the hearth was thickly coated in dog hair. Sonora pictured the man and the dog, sitting in this room on chilly nights, the only light from the glow of the fire.

Shelving along the wall held stacks of CDs and one picture in a wood frame. Sonora crossed the room for a closer look.

Selby cocked his head to one side, and the dog watched, eyes alert. "You're interested in the picture, Detective Blair? I'm afraid that's my vanity showing, leaving it out. I like people to know what the man inside looks like."

Sonora picked up the frame. The print was eight-by-ten, black-and-white. The focus was slightly off.

"That was taken a few months before it happened."

They all knew what "it" was.

The photograph showed James Selby sitting at the piano. A girl sat beside him, her arms wrapped tightly around his waist, her heart-shaped face porcelain pretty. A fire flickered in the fireplace, and the photographer had caught the reflection of the flames in the surface of the polished piano.

Sonora felt a twinge of dread. This could be Keaton, she thought, looking back at James Selby. They had been so very alike—brown eyes, dark curly hair, that solid presence.

Sonora stared through the French doors to the algae-scummed birdbath, the snarled cluster of rosebushes, the weeping willow tree—James Selby's backyard that she could see and he could not. She took a breath and sat back down on the couch.

He looked different to her now. He was the man in the picture.

"Tell me your story," she said.

Selby waved a hand self-consciously, as if she had not come cross-country to hear him. "Ray's heard all this before."

Sonora wondered what his voice had been like. Low and sexy? Had he sung in the shower? She opened her purse and set out the recorder.

"Forget Bonheur, he can always take a nap. Take your time, Mr. Selby. Tell me everything you remember, and I'll bring you her head on a stick."

Selby looked up sharply. "Ray, I like this woman."

"No doubt she earns her ulcer."

Selby tucked a small cushion under the curled arm, then draped his good right arm on the side of the chair.

"In the beginning, Detective Blair, there were phone calls."

He had practiced this, Sonora thought. He had everything thought out and worked through.

"The calls began after Easter, lots of them, calling and hanging up. Sometimes she would talk. She'd say, hello there, James. Nothing else."

Sonora put a fist under her chin.

He had met her at a bar, his usual place. He'd had the vague feeling he'd seen her before.

He had moved away fairly quickly. He was pretty good-looking, and it wasn't unusual for a woman to strike up a conversation. But that night he was there with the guys, and he wanted nothing more than the traditional beers after Wednesday-night softball.

Sonora heard pain in his voice. And pride. She wondered about the girl in the picture.

He left the bar around ten. It was a weeknight, and he had to be at work by eight.

Where did he work?

A bank. He was a teller, on his way up. He'd liked the job a lot.

She'd approached him in the parking lot, hands nervously twisting the strap of a large leather bag slung over her shoulder. It was an old mailbag, scuffed and worn, and he'd asked her about it. She said she'd gotten it at a flea market.

"Flea markets and antiques," Sonora muttered.

Selby shifted the crippled arm.

She had car trouble. She'd had her transmission replaced and now the engine wouldn't start. He'd offered to take a look—a skiffy transmission shouldn't keep the engine from catching—but she'd said no. It was under warranty. She'd have somebody come out and take a look at it in the morning, could he just give her a quick ride home?

She had looked over her shoulder when she asked him, and had seemed small and scared. Selby laughed here, saying he'd thought she was nervous of him. He was a big guy, six feet and solid, and he'd offered to lend her cab fare.

That had seemed to reassure her. She'd nodded shyly, not smiling, and opted for the ride. That was why he was so sure she was nervous of him, because she never smiled. He thought she was afraid.

"James, did you see her car, at the bar?" Sonora asked.

"Uh . . . I didn't check under the hood or anything. She said it was a transmission thing. I didn't get the feeling she wanted me to take a look or anything. She seemed resigned, you know?"

"So you never actually saw the car?"

Selby was quiet. "Guess not. I don't really remember."

Bonheur shifted sideways in his chair. "We followed up on the car angle. Checked the lot at the bar the next morning. Went to repair shops. Never got anywhere."

"Her car was in the subdivision, dropped off ahead of time," Sonora said. "Don't you think?"

Bonheur scratched his chin. "Could've had two."

"Maybe. We place her using cabs, maybe buses."

"You saying she stood outside that bar crying car trouble but no car?"

Ballsy, Sonora thought. "Takes your breath away, doesn't it?" She looked at Selby. "So she's got you feeling protective, and you offer to take her home. Then what?"

Selby settled deeper into his chair. "She gives me the address, but I couldn't place it. She told me the subdivision was new, no way I'd know it. Actually, she said you'uns. No way you'uns would know it." He swallowed. "The way she said it. Made her seem . . . smalltown, kind of. Vulnerable."

Sonora nodded here. This was Flash.

They wound up on the outskirts of the city, in a remote area where they were just starting to build houses. Only a smattering of new homes in the front of the subdivision were occupied. He had protested, thinking they'd gone the wrong way. He began to wonder if this woman was some kind of mental case, or if he was being set up for a robbery. He was getting worried, and very sorry he'd picked her up.

Pull up here, she'd told him. And suddenly she had a gun, a twenty-two derringer, small even in her delicate little hand. This is a robbery, she'd explained, unsmiling, voice soft. She wanted his wallet, that was all. He'd handed it over without a word, annoyed with himself for picking her up, thinking this would be too embarrassing to report to the police. Wait till he told the guys at the next softball game.

She kept reassuring him over and over that she wasn't going to hurt him—that she was afraid of him, and needed getaway time. She tossed him a looped clothesline and told him to wrap it around his wrists, legs, and belly, and thread it through the steering wheel. She took the keys out of the ignition and the car registration out of the glove compartment. Then she'd looked up at him and said, by the way, before you get fancy with the rope there, hand over your clothes.

That was where he'd turned balky. No way was he taking off his clothes, too weird. She'd explained in a firm, matter-of-fact voice that she would put his clothes and car keys together about a hundred feet from the car. That would slow him down and give her plenty of time.

But she had gone strange on him in a way he could not explain. Her eyes were empty, her speech mechanical, as if she wasn't seeing him, as if he wasn't there. Somehow, they weren't connecting.

He stood his ground. She shot him in the leg. Selby's voice still echoed surprise after all these years. He never believed she would shoot him, not without working herself up to it. But she hadn't hesitated.

Sonora nodded slowly. So this was how little Flash had gotten the man tied up.

At first, Selby was saying, he had been so shocked he hardly felt the pain. Flash demanded his shirt, and he handed it over. He remembered he fumbled one of the buttons and she had leaned over and ripped it off, and kept it clutched in her left fist, right hand steady with the gun. He'd grabbed at her when she got close, and she'd shot him again, the bullet hitting his shoulder.

He was bleeding and hurting, so she'd helped him loop the clothesline around his hands and waist, passing it through the steering wheel. She had tied the knots herself—not very well. He'd done a half-assed job looping the rope around his hands, but she hadn't protested.

She rolled down her window, grabbed her bag, and got out of the car. He watched her from the rearview mirror, though he was getting dizzy and had to concentrate not to pass out. She went to the gas tank, tried to open it, but it was the locking kind. She found the key on his ring—very cool about the whole thing—then pulled plastic tubing and an empty Coke can out of the bag. She put the tube in the gas tank, sucked the end of it, and inserted it through the keyhole opening of the Coke can, filling it with siphoned gas from the tank of his car.

The whole time she worked she hummed. A small part of his mind kept trying to place the song.

She took the dripping Coke can and splashed gasoline in his eyes.

He remembered crying out, rubbing his face on the bare skin of his shoulder, while she splashed gas into his lap, the front seat of the car, and all along the loose end of the clothesline that she pulled out of the window to the pavement below.

He heard her fumble in the bag, saw a flash, and opened his eyes long enough to see that she had a camera and had taken his picture.

He was sick now, the gasoline fumes making him nauseous and dizzy, and his thoughts weren't connecting too well. He smelled the burnt head of a match. He opened his eyes to the nightmare vision of a ribbon of flame eating its way up the clothesline, and— he hesitated here—the woman pulling up her skirt and wedging a hand between her legs.

Seconds, was the thought in his mind. He only had seconds. And suddenly the gun didn't seem to matter a hell of a lot.

He got untangled from the rope fairly quickly, but it took some fumbling to unlock and open the car door. That was where he'd made his second bad mistake. If he'd gone through the window he might have made it out in time—at least not been burned quite so badly. Maybe saved his face. But the gasoline fumes exploded just as the car door opened, and he was engulfed in fire.

Here the memories got sketchy. He thought he'd dropped to the ground and rolled, and he'd swear she'd stayed to take pictures.

After this point, everything in his mind was dark and vague, but he had the impression that someone had driven by, honking their horn. He'd always wondered about that. Had it been somebody trying to summon help . . . or had it been her?

Her, Sonora thought, but said nothing. The dog snored, the clock ticked. Dusk was gray in the room.

Ray got up, put a hand on Selby's shoulder. "You all right there, James? Can I get you a beer, or a glass of water?"

James Selby covered the scarred hand with the good one. "Funny how it comes back so clearly. I even remember what she was humming."

Sonora nudged the dog with her foot.

Selby turned his unseeing eyes in her direction. "It was that one Elvis used to sing. 'Love Me Tender.' "

Sonora sat forward on the couch. "You *sure*?"

Ray was watching her, the wary cop look. "What?"

"Someone's been calling my house, that's all. Singing that song."

"A woman?" Ray asked.

"Yeah, a woman."

Selby leaned toward her, face folding into the semblance of a frown. "Be careful, Detective."

S onora was restless on the flight back from Atlanta. She had asked Selby if there had been anything after the attack. More phone calls. Notes, maybe. Pictures. The question took him by surprise and earned her a sharp look from Bonheur.

Nothing else, he had assured her.

She hit the bathroom before they landed, running a pick through her hair, leaving it draped over her shoulders rather than tied back. She took a moment for a coat of bronze lipstick. There wasn't much she could do about the greenish pallor; air travel never agreed. She'd feel better once her feet were on the ground.

The flight landed on time. Sonora ignored the baggage pickup snarl with the superior air of one with only carry-on luggage. She paused in front of a bank of phones. Selby had looked too much like Keaton, before the fire had eaten his face.

She called the Mount Adams town house, and a voice answered after the third ring—a voice she knew well.

"Sergeant Crick?"

"Speaking."

"This is Blair, what the hell's going on?"

Crick's tone was grim. "She's been here."

Sonora's knees went weak.

"Daniels got home from school around four-thirty this afternoon—"

Flash had been waiting for him, Sonora thought.

"—and found the door partway open, the side window smashed."

Why? she thought. Why did he go in? Idiot. Keaton.

"So he went to a neighbor's house and called. Sonora? You still there?"

Sonora leaned against the wall, the tile cool on her cheek. "Listen, Sergeant Crick, this connection's bad, I can hardly hear you. Is Daniels okay?"

"He's shook, but he's all right."

"I'm coming out."

A CSU van and a swarm of official cars were stacked along the streets near Keaton Daniels's town house. Sonora was stopped by a uniform on the sidewalk out front. The officer eyed her blue jeans, dusty boots, leather jacket.

"Can I help you, ma'am?" His voice was stern—one of the uniformed types who used courtesy like a blunt instrument.

Sonora flashed her ID.

The officer apologized but stood his ground. Sonora gave him a second glance, and he moved reluctantly off the sidewalk, into the grass and out of her way. She went up the front step slowly, boot heels loud on the concrete, and walked into the living room.

Keaton Daniels was on the couch, looking stunned and being ignored by the bevy of crime-scene officers. Sonora heard Molliter's voice, saw Sam headed down the stairs, two at a time. He gave her a warning look.

"Blair." Crick's voice was a bark, and he didn't seem happy.

Sonora raised an eyebrow. "I told you he needed protection. Keaton?" She touched his shoulder and took his hand—ice cold. She sat on the edge of the coffee table and leaned close. "You okay?"

He nodded, looked relieved to see her.

"Keaton, are you cold? You want a sweater or jacket?"

"I'm okay, Detective." His voice sounded dull, a monotone.

Sonora looked over her shoulder. "Anybody found this man a cup of coffee?"

Crick was watching them, eyes narrowed. He singled out a patrolman. "Find the man a cup of coffee." He motioned Sonora up the stairs. "Crime-scene guys are still working things over, but let me give you the tour. The bathroom is the worst."

Sonora pretended to be confused about which way to turn.

"She took a shower, used the toilet."

"How'd you figure that out?" My fingerprints will be all over this place, Sonora thought, peering in through the doorway.

"How do you think, Blair? Hey, be careful, don't touch."

The guest bathroom, so tidy before with fresh towels and expensive peach soaps, was now a mess. Sonora stayed in the doorway, thinking that she was likely the last person to use the bathroom before Flash. She felt queasy suddenly, and her head hurt.

The bath mat, thick, white, and fluffy, had been rolled up and jammed in the corner behind the commode. One of the drawers under the sink was open partway. The toilet lid was up, and Sonora took a quick look. Yeah, okay, Flash had used the toilet and left a wealth of clues as to her current dietary habits.

The shower curtain had been yanked sideways, and one corner had torn loose from the rings and sagged into the tub. A sopping-wet washrag had been thrown on top of the bath mat, and the soap was in the bottom of the still-wet tub, melting and stuck to the porcelain.

Wadded into the corner of the stall was a thick blue towel. Sonora wondered if Keaton had changed the towels. Please God, he had changed them.

"Blair?"

"Sir?"

"I said we got pubic hair out of the drain and . . . you with me here?"

"Yes sir. Excuse me, I've been to Atlanta and back in the last twenty-four hours."

"You should have slept on the plane. Anyway, we may get something off the towel. God knows, this place is lousy with physical evidence, which will do us no good whatsoever, unless we catch this bitch." Crick grimaced. "Terry says she's a natural blonde."

Sonora opened her purse and dug out a bottle of Advil. She poured three tablets into the palm of her hand and swallowed them dry.

"Take a look over here in the bedroom. Something you better see."

Terry was stripping the sheets from the bed as they went in. Sonora felt her knees go funny as she looked around the room. Dark bronze lipstick had been smeared across a pillow case, the shade close to Sonora's own.

Sam was pointing a flashlight onto the dark floor of the closet. "She took his *shoelaces*. And tore buttons off some of the shirts."

He squatted down on his haunches, touching nothing. "Looks like a tennis shoe outlet in here."

Crick touched Sonora's arm and pointed her to the clothes dresser. The newspaper photo of Police Specialist Sonora Blair had been wadded, then ripped into three pieces. Keaton's journal of investigation was gone.

"That all?" she asked.

Crick put his hands behind his back and cocked his head to one side. "'That all,' she says. I would think it would get under your skin a little, Blair. Because this is a dangerous woman, and I get the *serious* feeling she doesn't consider you good people."

"This surprises you, sir? After coaching me through the press conferences? I would have thought you'd be happy."

"You just be careful, Blair."

"What else did she do?"

"Went in the kitchen and took a fistful out of a macaroni-and-cheese casserole. Ate some of it, we think, and smeared the rest on a dish towel."

"She'll be in trouble looking for leftovers at my place. I got a thirteen-year-old."

"Funny girl."

He crooked a finger and ushered her into Keaton's tiny private bath. Sonora frowned, followed.

The countertop was crowded—Braun electric razor, worn black toothbrush, deodorant. No peach soaps shaped like roses. Crick shut the bathroom door. He closed the lid on the oak toilet seat and waved a hand.

"Go ahead, Blair, make yourself comfortable."

Sonora perched on the edge of the tub, folded her hands in her lap. "Yes, Sergeant?"

Crick scratched the side of his neck. He was a big man, and he took up a lot of room. His knees were too close, and Sonora pulled away.

"Look, Blair, I ought to call you in my office and come up on this in a more delicate way, but we've worked together a long time. I want you to consider this an *unofficial* question. And be honest, Blair, for your sake and mine."

She was cold suddenly. She swallowed.

"Is there something going on between you and this Keaton Daniels?"

Sonora cocked her head to one side. "Something going on?

He's Mark Daniels's brother, Sergeant, and I think he was the intended victim all along. Sam and I have questioned him silly, and spent some time trying to gain his trust. We're trying to keep him alive. I consider that part of the job."

Crick rubbed the top of his forehead. Sonora noticed that his eyes were bloodshot, lids swollen.

"Look, Blair, I've been in touch with Renee Fischer. You heard of her?"

"Forensic psychiatrist. Used her on the Parks thing, didn't they?"

Crick nodded.

"I hear she's good," Sonora said.

"She is. She's just getting started on Flash, but she called me early this morning. Said she'd been up all night, going through what I gave her."

"And?"

"She says there's obviously something about Daniels, something different from the usual victims."

"We knew that."

"Yeah. And she's looking at you as a cross between a confidante and a rival."

"I'm the cop trying to bring her in, makes perfect sense."

Crick looked at her.

"Your point? Sir?"

"Okay, you're the one after her hide. Fine, Blair, if that's as far as it goes. But that's your picture there, on top of the dresser in this man's bedroom, and Flash didn't cart it up here. I asked."

"What did Keaton say?"

"He said he clipped all the articles about the investigation."

"There you go."

"I didn't see any other articles."

"I guess he hasn't had time to put together a scrapbook, Sergeant. Why don't you get specific, sir, and tell me just what the problem is. Or is there a regulation against my picture on this man's dresser?"

"No, Blair, and there's no regulation against fucking him either, but you damn well better *not* be."

Sonora spoke through clenched teeth. "You don't have these little talks, these kinds of suspicions and speculations, when it's male cops and female witnesses."

"Don't give me that sexual harassment crap, unless you want to make it official. I want you to listen to me, Blair, and for once in your life don't interrupt. If there *is* something going on between you and Daniels, we got problems. The woman is dangerous, and I want her before she goes off again." His voice lowered and went gentle. "I've known you a long time, Sonora. I've never seen you dump a case, I've never seen you cross the line. If something's going on, I want you to tell me, and tell me *now*."

Sonora stared at him, stony faced.

Crick threw up his hands. "You fucking Daniels or not?"

Sonora folded her arms. *"Not."*

47

Sam, I'm in *trouble*."

"Sonora—"

"*Shit*, Sam."

"Don't panic, girl. Get yourself together, before somebody hears us. We'll talk later."

Sam lit a cigarette, and Sonora didn't complain. They sat in the parking lot of the Sundown Saloon, looking at the still sludge of the river. Sam flicked ash out the open window.

"You should have told him the truth."

"You said that already."

"Yeah, but, Sonora, he's right, it does affect the investigation. You were the last one in the bathroom before Flash. Suppose those are your hair samples?"

"You think that hasn't got me worried?" Sonora took a deep breath and looked out the window. "What are you going to say if Crick asks you about it?"

"You mean if I know you slept with the guy? You want me to lie for you?"

"Yeah."

Sam flicked the cigarette butt out the window. "Remember back when we thought we were the good guys?"

"Thanks, Sam, you always know how to make it all better."

"You okay now? I'd like to go home."

"I'm going to get the kids and go back to the house."

"You're going to get them up? It's two A.M. Let them sleep at your brother's."

"I promised I'd get them tonight. Besides, I want them home in their own beds so I can get them off to school okay."

"Come on, then. You herd Tim and I'll carry Heather." They closed the car doors softly—habits acquired on stakeouts. Sonora felt bad suddenly, the ulcer again, and she leaned against the side of the car.

Sam turned to look at her. "You coming?"

"In my own good time. Sam?"

"What?"

"Something I was wondering. This guy in Atlanta, this Selby. He said the calls started up after Easter. And it just dawned on me that Keaton said the same thing."

"I don't remember him saying that. And I've gone over all the transcripts at least four times."

Sonora remembered that she had read it in Keaton's journal of investigation. "He said it, Sam, okay?"

"Pillow talk?"

"It's interesting, don't you think? I mean, what's the big deal about Easter?"

"Eggs, bunnies, religion. Could be a lot of things. Sonora?"

"Yeah?"

"Let me know, will you? When you find out?"

"Find out what?"

Sam grinned. "Whether or not Keaton changed the towels."

48

The kids slept in the car on the way home. Sonora carried Heather to her bed and guided Tim into his. Clampett had made three messes, in spite of being let out regularly by the boy next door, who had dutifully deposited the mail and newspapers on the kitchen table as instructed.

Sonora left her carry-on bag in the hall. She flipped through the mail in the kitchen, finding monthly greetings from MasterCard and her utility company, and a reminder that it was time for the children to visit their dentist.

She paused in the dark hallway, feeling the ulcer, too tired to move but too wired to sleep. A long soak in a hot bubble bath would be good right about now.

She had just belted into a bathrobe when the phone rang. Please be Keaton, she thought.

"Sonora?"

It was him.

Sonora kept her voice formal. "Thank you for checking in, Mr. Daniels. Are you at your wife's house?"

"No. Red Roof Inn, exit seven off seventy-one north."

"I'll be in touch as soon as I know something."

"Sonora—"

"I'll be in touch, Mr. Daniels."

"Oh. Thank you, then."

"Good night." Sonora hung up, switched the phone to the children's line. Called information, Red Roof Inn. He answered on the first ring.

Sonora caught her breath. "Sorry, Keaton. My line is monitored right now. I'm calling on the kids' phone. You okay?"

"No."

"We need to talk."

"How about dinner tomorrow night?"

"Not possible. Keaton, I'm in trouble here, about you and me."

"I was getting that impression tonight. You acted funny."

"I lied to my sergeant. About us. I told him it was strictly business."

"Is it?" He sounded cold suddenly, wary.

"I don't usually sleep with witnesses. Look, I have to ask you about the towels."

"The towels?"

"In the bathroom. When we . . . got together. After I took a shower, did you change the towels?" She held the phone clamped tightly in her fist.

"Oh. Sorry, no I didn't. Is it a problem?"

"There's physical evidence, Keaton. Hell, they found pubic hair in the bathtub drain. It could be mine or hers. They think it's hers, but we know better. It could be either of us."

"What did your sergeant say?"

"I didn't bring it up, Keaton. I'd prefer not to get fired, considering my kids and the state of my bank account. Mortgage and all, you know?"

"Sorry, I must be dense, this really is trouble."

"It really is. Another thing I need to know. I saw on your dresser before I left for Atlanta your journal of investigation."

"That was private."

"I didn't read it." Just the first page, she thought. "Was it there when Flash got into your bedroom?"

"Flash? Is that what you people call her? Is this some kind of a cop joke?"

Sonora winced. "It's slang, and it's not a joke, it's real life in the world of a police officer. I'm sorry if you're offended. Was the journal out when Flash came through your town house? Did she take it, or did our lab people get hold of it?"

"She took it."

"I see. What was in there?"

"Personal things I'd just as soon no one else read. It started out as a log of investigation, but there's also things about my brother. And about you."

"About me?"

"Yeah."

"Damn. That journal is going to piss her off big-time. You take care of yourself, Keaton, and watch your back. Call me at the first sign of trouble."

"Do I understand you to mean that's the only time I call you?"

Sonora closed her eyes. "Afraid so."

"For how long? That we can't see each other?"

"Till I catch her, Keaton. And bring her to trial. And convict her ass."

"Yeah. I see." He hung up.

Sonora set the phone down gently. Maybe not the bubble bath routine. Maybe just a very hot shower.

She checked the kids—both sound asleep. Clampett was stretched in the hallway between their rooms. He lifted his head when Sonora walked by. Whimpered.

"Want to go out?"

He wagged his tail and got up with a painful, jerky movement that made Sonora notice the white fur rimming his black lips, the sagging muzzle, rheumy eyes. She crouched low and hugged the dog, thinking from the smell of him it was high time for a doggy bath.

"Go out, Clampett?" She headed down the hallway, turned off the alarm. A cold shock of air wafted through the door, and Clampett slowed. Sonora nudged his hind end with her knee, and the dog kept going. Slowly.

"Good boy."

She flipped on the back porch light. Waited. Clampett disappeared into what was left of the garden. Sonora reset the alarm and went to take her shower.

The bathroom was still neat—the kids had not had a chance to shed clothes, pull down towels, toss washrags, and leave lumps of toothpaste in the sink. Sonora turned the shower on hard and hot, closed her eyes as water streamed across her shoulders.

She was rinsing shampoo out of her hair when the burglar alarm went off.

Sonora left the water running, grabbed a towel, and stepped over the side of the tub, wiping suds out of her eyes. Her robe hung from a hook on the back of the door. She grabbed it just as the doorknob turned, then caught on the snap lock.

Sonora froze, jammed wet arms into the sleeves of the nubby terry-cloth robe, belted it quickly, and opened the door.

The hallway was empty.

She checked the children—mother first, cop second. Tim was asleep in spite of the alarm. Heather sat bolt upright in bed, clutching a stuffed penguin.

"Stay put," Sonora said.

Clampett barked, the hysterical bark, guard dog aroused. His toenails raked the back door.

Sonora smelled smoke just as the detector went off. The earsplitting buzz made the hair stand up on the back of her neck.

She ran down the hallway. The front door stood open, broken panes of glass in the foyer. She heard footsteps—someone running across the sidewalk. She was torn, but she'd seen enough fire scenes to know how quickly a house could go up.

A car door slammed as she headed into the kitchen.

The fire was on top of a pizza pan, pictures curling into flames. Sonora grabbed a dish towel and smothered the tiny blaze. She heard footsteps, saw her son.

"Fire's almost out. Go see to your sister."

The dish towel was blackened and smoking, and she tossed it into one side of the sink and turned on the water. Outside, Clampett sounded suddenly far away.

Sonora looked down at the Polaroids. Saw her son's face, this time sound asleep. She frowned. Recognized the bed she'd just hauled him out of. Stuart's place. Her hand trembled as she flipped the second picture.

Heather, clutching the penguin, cheeks round and soft in sleep. Same nightgown she wore right this minute. The pictures had been taken hours ago at Stuart's.

Sonora took another dish towel and waved the air beneath the smoke detector. The alarm stopped. Silence, except for the shower running. She took a deep breath. Went to the phone, hit the automatic dial button for her brother. The squeal of a disconnected line was loud in her ear.

"I'm sorry, the number you have called is not in working order. Please—"

Tim and Heather stood in the doorway, close together. They asked no questions, which told Sonora how shook they were. She clutched the edge of the kitchen counter.

"Somebody broke in, and I'm worried about Uncle Stuart. I'm going to call for help, then all of us are going to get in the car and go check on him. We're staying together, got that?"

They nodded.

"Can Clampett come?" Heather asked.

"You bringing your gun?" Tim said.

Sonora bit her bottom lip. "Yes to both questions."

Both children looked satisfied.

49

The windshield fogged as the car spiraled downhill. Sonora opened the window, smelling the river, listening for sirens. Her hands were unsteady on the steering wheel, and Clampett's doggy breath was moist on her shoulder as he leaned over the back of her seat.

"Heather. Get the dog."

"Mommy, are you okay?"

"Drive faster," Tim said.

"Everybody's seat belt fastened?"

The riverboat rose out of the water, a smoking black skeleton. Blue lights from police cars strobed across red pulses from the ambulance and fire trucks.

"Mommy."

Sonora caught her breath. "Maybe he wasn't home. Stay in the car, I'll go check. Hang on to the dog."

The first person she recognized was Molliter. She was about to call to him when a uniform stepped into her path.

"I'm sorry, Miss—"

"I'm a cop," she said.

He looked dubiously at her wet hair, still sticky with shampoo, the sweatshirt, blue jeans, Reeboks, no socks.

"This is my brother's place."

His look went from tough to pitying. "Could you step over here please, ma'am?"

It was Molliter who came to the rescue. Molliter who waved the uniform away and sent someone to sit with the kids. Molliter who took her to a smoke-grimed fireman who offered her a blanket and a sweaty handshake.

"Did you bring anybody out?" she asked.

He hesitated. He had blue eyes, big shoulders. He looked past her to Molliter, who said, "Best tell her what's going on," in a flat tone of voice.

Cop tones, she knew them.

"You say your brother was inside?"

"Maybe. He lives on the third floor. There's a storeroom up there, next to his apartment."

"Right about where would that be, ma'am?"

Sonora pointed.

The fireman gave her a look of sympathy. "I'm sorry. We weren't able to get him out in time."

He glanced over her shoulder at the waiting ambulance. Sonora followed his gaze, aware, for the first time, that the paramedics were standing around. Waiting.

"He's in the ambulance?" Sonora said.

"Uh, no. Actually, our man went in and—" The fireman cleared his throat. "Clearly, the victim was dead, and it was . . . it was obviously a matter for the police."

"Obviously a matter for the police," Sonora echoed. She wondered what the fireman had seen that made the upstairs apartment so clearly a matter for the police. "When can we go in?"

"Still pretty hot up there, ma'am."

Molliter touched her elbow. "Let's find you a place to sit, shall we?"

Sonora agreed that would be nice.

Her hair was dry by the time Sam and Crick arrived.

"Long time no see," she said.

"You don't have to be tough tonight, Sonora." She didn't know Gruber was there till he touched her shoulder.

"She can't help it." Sam crouched down on one knee. "Shelly's here."

Sonora let a breath escape. "Good. Where?"

"In the car with your kids."

"What about Annie?"

"At the hospital."

"Of course, Sam. Sorry. Can't believe I forgot."

"That's okay, honey." He squeezed her shoulder, and she put her hand over his. She thought for a minute she might like to cry, but the urge quickly passed.

Crick edged close. "Sonora, I can't believe this is happening. Did I hear right? Flash was at your place tonight?"

Sonora nodded.

"Thank God your kids are all right." He shifted his weight. She realized he was talking to her in a tone of voice she'd never heard. Maybe it was the voice he used with the babies in the church nursery. "Sonora, we're going in now. I want you to—"

"Please, Sergeant Crick. Let me come in."

He got that look of infinite patience. "Not a good idea."

"Your brother, you'd go in."

"I'll leave it up to you, Sonora. My advice is stay away."

She nodded. Dropped the blanket that had been around her shoulders. She picked it up off the ground, shook it out, folded it, then frowned, not sure what to do. Crick waited as if he had all the time in the world. Gruber took the blanket from her matter-of-factly.

"Let's go," Crick said.

He had a flashlight. Sonora followed, Sam on one side, Gruber on the other, Molliter bringing up the rear.

It was hot inside, acrid with smoke. Sweat filmed the back of Sonora's neck, dripped down her spine. She felt hot and cold, a tense flutter in her chest. She was breathing hard. Tasting salty sweat on her upper lip.

She went up the side of the stairs, thinking how much her brother had loved this place. The smoke-singed tables and charred wet carpet seemed vaguely familiar. She glanced over her shoulder at the bar. Thought of Stuart developing his palate during his restaurant days, sampling leftover drinks from the night before while cleaning the bar the next morning. Thought of him looking after the kids, feeding them TV dinners, playing Monopoly, giving horsey rides.

Thought of him in the bad old days, walking home alone every afternoon.

Crick faltered at the top of the stairs, and Sonora took the lead, first one in the tiny, well-equipped kitchen. The pictures that Heather had colored and taped to the refrigerator were torn and shredded. The round glass table was over on its side, and the drawer that held kitchen knives gaped open.

"The oven's still on," Sonora said.

Sam looked thoughtful. "They were baking cookies tonight, weren't they? Stuart and the kids?"

Sonora nodded. Opened the oven door. Cookie sheet, no cookies. "My guess is he was in here baking when she surprised him. Looks like they fought."

"Mess could have been made by the firemen," Gruber said.

"They're not going to rip the pictures off the refrigerator." Sonora pointed. "Bedroom's that way."

Gruber and Molliter headed down the dark hallway. Sam patted Sonora's shoulder.

"Let me go in first a minute, okay?"

She nodded, reluctant now.

"You all right?" Crick said. He wiped a handkerchief across the back of his neck.

Sonora said yes, heard the snap of rubber gloves from the bedroom, the drip of water down the wall, the roar of traffic on the bridge across the river.

She looked at her feet. "I think I'm going in now."

"If you're sure." Resignation and fatigue in Crick's voice.

She started in just as the others came out.

It was Sam's face that changed her mind. He put an arm around her and turned her away. "Don't be going in there, honey. It was pretty quick. He didn't suffer long."

Sonora hid her face in Sam's shoulder and squeezed her eyes shut, thinking how kind he was to lie.

50

The children did not know what to make of her. She had laughed when she broke the news of Stuart's death, then apologized and laughed again. Tim had looked at Heather and said, "You know, we may have to commit her." Then all three of them had burst into tears.

Sonora still had her funeral dress on, but the kids had changed into blue jeans.

Tim looked at the clock in the airport restaurant. "Baba's going to make us miss the flight."

Sonora grimaced. "She'll come rolling in at the last minute. No one in your father's family is punctual. It's genetic."

Heather waved her new Barbie doll. "Thank you for all the presents, Mommy, and my new jeans."

"You sure we can afford this?" Tim asked.

Sonora gave him a look. "You like the Walkman?" They were young, she thought. Young enough to be distracted by pretties.

"I wish you could come with us, Mommy."

Tim ate a large bite of hamburger. "How come you can't? You're off the case, aren't you?"

Sonora put her finger in a wet mark on the table. "Yeah, I'm off."

"That's mean, Mommy, when you work so hard."

"No, hon. I can't work it anymore. Them's the rules, and they're good ones."

"It would be upsetting, dork." Tim looked at Sonora, grimaced, and exchanged looks with Heather. "She's doing it again. *Mom.* Why are you looking like that?"

"What's wrong, Mommy? And don't say nothing."

Tim put his french fry down. "Is it because of Stuart, or because we're going? We can stay with you, Mom. I'm not afraid."

Sonora rubbed her eyes. "It's Stuart. I'm going to be upset about this awhile, okay? Aren't you guys upset?"

Heather stuck her thumb in her mouth.

Tim shrugged. "I loved him, okay? But I never miss people. When they're gone, they're just gone. I still have my life."

Sonora chewed the knuckle of her left fist. Hard words from a thirteen-year-old. Which worried her more than tears. "Eat up, kids."

Heather put her hands demurely in her lap. "It's very good, but I'm not hungry. Mommy, are you going to be lonely?"

"Clampett will keep me company, and I've got some stuff to do that's going to keep me busy."

"What stuff?" Tim said.

Sonora wiped her hands clean on the thin and unsatisfactory paper napkin. She poured salt in her palm and ate it. She hadn't done that since she was Tim's age.

"But where are we going?" Heather said.

"Atlanta," Tim told her.

"But after Atlanta."

Sonora squeezed her daughter's hand. "Won't know till you get to Atlanta. Baba's going to pick. Why don't you talk her into taking you to a beach?"

"The ocean?" Heather said.

"That's where beaches are."

Sonora scowled at her son. "Be nice. I'm counting on you. I'm counting on both of you. Look after each other and be good. And do your schoolwork."

"How long are we going to be gone?" Tim asked.

Sonora frowned. "I don't know, I haven't thought that far. Probably till Visa cancels my card."

The first picture came in the mail late that afternoon. Two more arrived the next day.

Sonora sat on the couch in the living room, thinking about walls. The phone rang. She did not count the rings, or notice when they stopped.

Walls were not the sort of thing one normally noticed. She knew that, in the back of her mind—knew that so much time staring at walls was not a good thing. But there was something about a wall that was steady and undemanding, muting somehow. Walls dulled the senses, which in turn dulled the pain.

She was glad the kids were gone. It was good to know they were safely tucked away at the seaside with a grandmother who might smoke too much, and make Heather sneeze, but who would nurture them. Nurture was hard right now. Sonora was relieved not to have to nurture.

And dealing with the kids would definitely take away from wall time.

She heard a bark. Got up to open the back door, felt the wind across her face, sniffed it like a bouquet.

So much for her quota of daily activity.

Clampett nudged her knee, licked her fingers. Sonora scratched his neck under the worn leather collar. The angels might turn their backs, but not her trusty dog.

53

Sonora was asleep on the couch when the doorbell rang. She opened her eyes. Rubbed a hand over her face, licked dry lips. She looked at her watch, saw it was two o'clock—A.M. or P.M.?

The doorbell rang again; P.M., she decided. Felt like afternoon.

She opened the door, blinked at the man who stood on the front porch. Felt Clampett's presence by her side.

The man was somewhere between twenty-eight and thirty-eight, which was a nice age bracket for a girl who was interested, which she wasn't. He wore jeans and a white cotton shirt, had high, broad cheekbones, a baby face, wavy brown hair.

Nice shoulders, Sonora thought.

The man picked up a rose petal from the soft stems and pieces that littered the front porch.

"Somebody been sending you flowers, pretty girl?"

Sonora wondered if she should tell him that the rose petals had spilled from funeral flowers. She looked down at her worn jeans, thin white T-shirt, thick white socks. She decided that she was not a pretty girl and that this man annoyed her.

"I don't want any," Sonora said.

"Now hang on and give me a chance. See, your dog there hasn't barked or growled once. Dog knows I'm good people."

Sonora put a hand on Clampett's collar. "This is the world's best dog. In honor of this dog, I'm going to give you thirty more seconds."

He grinned. "I'm from across the river, honey, I'm not sure I can talk that fast."

"Give it a shot."

He rocked back on his heels. "You're Blair, aren't you? Homicide cop working the case where the guy was cuffed in his car and burned up?"

Sonora straightened her back. "Let's see some ID."

He reached into his back pocket, and she tensed. "No room in there for a weapon, honey, not in this pair of jeans." He handed her a badge, and she looked it over, squinting.

"Deputy Sheriff Jonathan Smallwood. Calib County, Kentucky?"

He propped an elbow on the wood rail of her front porch. "Sorry about what happened to your brother."

She nodded. Word like that spread quickly, cop to cop.

"That's the main reason I drove up here. After I heard about your brother. I got a story to tell you."

Sonora opened the screen door. "Maybe you better come in."

Smallwood paused at the edge of her living room, gave her a look over one shoulder, and shook his head.

"You been eating anything at all?"

Sonora curled up on the couch, cross-legged, pretending not to notice when Clampett jumped up on the next cushion and laid his head in her lap. House rules for dogs had gone to hell.

Smallwood opened the curtains, stirring the dust, letting a latticework of sunshine in so bright Sonora blinked. He gathered up glasses, wadded tissues, pizza boxes, and disappeared into the kitchen. He stacked newspapers and set them on a chair.

"Feel better?" Sonora said.

"No, but you will." He settled into her rocking chair. Crossed one ankle over his knee. "Once upon a time."

Sonora leaned close.

It had been five years since he'd come across the car burning hotly on an out-of-the-way county road where the savvy parkers knew to go. It had been hot out, early September, and he shuddered when he described the blackened figure fused to the steering wheel—eyeless sockets, arms pulled forward, pugilistically locked.

The car had belonged to one Donnie Hillborn, and dental records had confirmed that the blackened body was indeed Donnie, the older brother of Vaughn Hillborn, hotshot football player, currently being courted by the University of Tennessee, the University of Kentucky, Duke, and Michigan State.

Donnie had been a local embarrassment. Donnie had been gay and proud of it.

There had been numerous oddities at the scene. A key in a charred fist. The smell of gasoline inside the car. A Coke can in the weeds nearby that had held gasoline and not Coke. No shoes, belt buckle, or signs thereof, anywhere on or around the body.

"Could've burned up, I guess." Smallwood glanced at Sonora.

"Not if the body didn't."

He looked thoughtful. "Officially listed as a traffic fatality, despite the lack of tire marks or collision damage."

"Autopsy?" Sonora asked.

"Wasn't one."

"Why does this smell so bad? Why cover it?"

Smallwood rubbed the back of his neck. "It's the sports thing."

"You've lost me."

"The family didn't want it investigated. They figured it was some kind of hate thing. Because Donnie was gay."

"You've *got* to be kidding."

"This is a very out-of-the-way county in Kentucky. A man can go to LA and walk around with false eyelashes and a cosmetics bag and people don't look twice. But where I come from . . . don't tell me Cincinnati's an oasis of tolerance. You people just concentrate your vice on the other side of the river in Covington."

"We let Mapplethorpe stay."

"Been lynched in Calib County."

"I take your point, Deputy. How'd the family manage to swing it? Money?"

"You birth a football player, it puts you in the catbird seat."

"Come on, I don't get this." Sonora tickled Clampett just under his left ear. "Nobody's going to cover up a murder because somebody's kid plays good high school ball."

"And you looked so intelligent, too."

"Explain it better," Sonora said.

Smallwood rocked back in his chair. "I'm not saying who the family talked to, or where the pressure connected. Could have been local, could have been the sheriff. Could have been somebody at the university, some alumni. All I know is, the death of Donnie Hillborn becomes a tragic traffic fatality, and Vaughn gets pretty serious about going with UK."

"And did he? Might give you a clue as to who put pressure on who."

"We'll never know. Six weeks later, he was dead too."

Sonora lifted her head. "Of what?"

"Accident, out on the farm. Hillborns had a little place, way out from town. Barn caught on fire. Vaughn was inside, trying to get his horse out. Ironic, isn't it?"

"It's crap, and you know it."

Smallwood looked at her. "They found a cigarette butt."

"Kid played football, he didn't smoke."

"It's Kentucky, everybody smokes."

"So what did you do, Smallwood, you leave it alone?"

Clampett jumped off the couch and put his nose on the deputy's knee. Smallwood rubbed the dog on the side of the neck.

"Believe me, I tried, and I caught hell for it." Even now, five years later, Sonora could hear the frustration in his voice. "The thing is, these people never went anywhere, except to Lexington now and then to shop at the malls. Hillborn was a good kid, studied hard, worked the family farm. I've looked at every face in town, more than once, and I can't make sense of it. I thought at first it was some kind of nutcase passing through, but Vaughn died too, so that don't hold up."

"What did Donnie Hillborn look like?"

"Big guy, solid. Six-two."

"Dark curly hair and brown eyes?"

Smallwood looked at her. "Yeah."

"Sounds like my girl's involved."

"I thought so, that's why I'm here. What do you know about her?"

"Selma Yorke. Small, wavy blond hair. Never smiles."

"That's it?"

"Watching men burn up in their cars brings her to sexual highs. She takes pictures."

"Where would she run across Hillborn and his brother?"

"She likes brothers." Sonora's throat closed. She swallowed.

Smallwood's look was full of pity. "I've never seen anybody like that in Calib County, and I'd know."

"You said Vaughn went into Lexington. Maybe he caught her eye there."

"I checked. He'd been doing recruiting trips for months, training, studying, and working on the farm. He hadn't been to Lexington since Easter, and the only place he went was Sears, to get some Craftsman tools and his taxes done at the H and R Block."

"Why didn't you call me three weeks ago?"

"You're not listening, are you? The case is closed and I'm not here, and the investigation does not go on. But I have copies of the investigation reports in the trunk of my car, and if you want them they're yours."

"I'm not working the case. Why don't . . . Hold up a minute. You said he went to Lexington around Easter?"

"Yeah."

"To get his taxes done?"

"Yeah, at H and R Block. At the Sears."

"Sears. Hell, yes, next to the Allstate booth. Ashley Daniels works for Allstate, in a mall. It's *taxes*. April fifteenth. It's not Easter at all, it's the tax thing. It's H and R Block." Sonora put a fist under her chin. "Be interesting to find out how many of Selma's victims got their taxes done there."

"Don't mind my look of confusion, honey, but have I helped you out?"

"Yeah, you've helped me. Thank you very much, Deputy Smallwood. I didn't see you, I didn't talk to you, and you can clean up my living room anytime you want."

He shook her hand warmly. "Your rocking chair is real comfortable, and I'm nuts about this dog."

54

The office was familiar and strange—her desk unnaturally clean, no messages on the answering machine. Sonora smelled old coffee and felt like she'd left yesterday and a hundred years ago.

She ducked into Crick's office before anyone saw her.

He was frowning at a computer printout, but when he saw her he smiled.

"Home from the wars," he muttered and motioned to a chair. "How are your children?"

She sat down. "Taking it so well it scares me."

"Kids are tough. How are you progressing on the nervous breakdown?"

She laughed. Realized she hadn't in a while. "Very well, thank you, sir."

"I see you're wearing a clean shirt and tie. This mean you want to ease back into some work time?"

Sonora nodded.

"Good. You know you can't do active work on the Daniels case, but we can use you to consult. Or you can wash your hands of the whole thing, and nobody'd blame you a bit."

"You know better. Get prints, anything off the pictures?"

Crick shook his head. "We've been watching Selma's house, but there's no sign anybody goes there. We're trying to get a court order to search the premises. So far judge says no go."

"I've had to get my kids out of town, my brother got torched, and the judge says no go?"

Crick's face was expressionless.

"What happened to Molliter's big witness?"

"Got a body turned up at the morgue, looks like it may be her. Molliter had court today. He'll ID it tomorrow."

"I could go. I saw her in interrogation."

"That would help."

They looked at each other.

"Would a cup of coffee help you work your nerve up, Sonora?"

"Sir?"

"So you can say whatever it is you've got on your mind."

Sonora tilted her head sideways. Took a deep breath. "You remember that conversation we had in Keaton Daniels's bathroom?"

Crick's eyelids drooped slightly, but he stayed quiet.

Sonora sat on the edge of her chair and looked at the floor. "I slept with Keaton Daniels, and used his shower. The physical evidence you got out of the bathroom—it could be her or it could be me."

"I see."

"Selma was out there. Watching. She knew I spent the night. She called and said she'd pay us back, both of us."

Crick looked at her.

"That's why she showed up at my house. And his."

He placed his fingers together, carefully. "No wonder you were worried."

"Still am."

"Sonora. It's a wonder she didn't take your babies out with your brother."

She gritted her teeth. "Not a minute goes by, I don't think about it. Maybe she's getting a conscience."

Crick pointed a finger at her. "Pay attention. They never, *ever*, get a conscience. She didn't kill your kids because it didn't suit her at the time. Maybe it didn't fit in with her fantasy. Because that's what these killings are, they're her fantasy. That's why she does what she does, she's acting it out. And she's got no limits on what she'll do to make it happen. Make no mistake. If she'd felt the slightest urge to kill them, she would have, without a second thought."

Sonora nodded, sat back in her chair. "There's more."

"I don't want details, Sonora."

"I had a visitor. A deputy from a remote part of Kentucky who had a story to tell me."

"He slept with Keaton too?"

"Selma hit there. Two brothers, both dead in fires, one burned up in his car. A few months before it happened, one of them had his taxes done at H and R Block."

"So?"

"So. H and R Block in a booth at Sears. These booths are usually located next to the Allstate counter, or they used to be. You following me?"

Crick frowned. "Not really."

"Daniels's wife, Ashley, is an Allstate agent. Her booth is right next to the H and R Block office every year. I checked. These killings happen in the fall, but it's usually after a few months of phone calls and stalking. Keaton said his calls started in April. And Selby, that guy in Georgia, that's when his started. April. Think April fifteenth. Taxes. H and R Block. You get it?"

"You saying she's some kind of tax accountant? Works for the IRS?"

"For H and R Block. Not hard to get on there, it's seasonal, they train people. Perfect for her psychological profile—intermittent, undemanding employment. When tax season is over, she's got time and a long list of possible victims. Name, address, income. Deductions."

"Yeah." Crick rubbed his chin. "Ties in with that weird thing she has with numbers. What is it, threes and nines?"

"Threes are evil, ones are shy."

"Obviously not your average bear, this girl."

Sonora looked at him. Waited. "Crick, drop the shoe, will you? Yell at me now, please, and get it over with."

He leaned back in his chair, gave her a sad smile. "Normally I'd transfer your ass, the very least. I'm cutting you a lot of slack. I think you've had enough grief, Sonora."

She stared at the floor. "You don't seem surprised. I take that to mean I'm a lousy liar."

"Not at all. It's her that convinced me. Something set her off enough to stalk you, and kill your brother. Could be the cop angle, could be more than that. I thought there might be more. Your kids came damn close to the edge there. If it gives me nightmares, God knows what it's doing to you."

Sonora chewed her knuckles.

"Look, Sonora, it's good your kids are out of town, but they can't stay away forever. We need to keep Flash stirred up and angry. We need to keep her off balance."

"You want me to sleep with Keaton again?" The look he gave her made her sorry she'd said it.

"Radio call-in show, remember? We decided to let Sam take your place, but you know it'll work a hell of a lot better with you. Problem is, this business with your brother. It'll draw a lot of attention."

"That's what you want, isn't it?"

"Might not be what you want."

"What I want," Sonora said. She let her hands rest between her knees. "What I want is to catch her."

55

S onora walked carefully on the freshly mopped tile floors, watchful of wet spots. The morgue was quiet, the lights off in most of the offices. From somewhere came a voice that sounded like Eversley.

"Yeah, sure, another mysterious disappearance. First my chicken coupon, now this. You telling me the DBs are taking this stuff?"

Sonora passed the refrigeration unit. The thermometer showed a temperature of fifty-five degrees. Inside the viewing window, she saw the forlorn body of Sheree La Fontaine, lying like a ramrod on a gurney, a towel balled around her feet.

Marty stood patiently beside her. "Hate to say it, Detective, but we've had DBs in here that looked healthier than you do."

"I'm in the right place then, aren't I?"

He inclined his head toward the body. "That her?"

"That's her. Sheree La Fontaine. Working girl from the other side of the river, hails from North or South Carolina."

"Wasn't she a suspect in that Daniels thing?"

"Not anymore. I take it cause of death would be the stab wounds to the throat?"

"We'll make a pathologist out of you yet." Marty made a notation on a chart. "Sign."

Sonora scrawled her signature.

"I thought Molliter was coming in."

"His day off and he had to be in court, so they're already paying him time and a half, plus I was in the neighborhood. On my way to do a radio thing, call-in show. I'm a celebrity expert. Cop and victim."

Sonora sat back in the chair, loosened the high heels on her feet, decided that when she got home she would throw them away. She looked out the window. It was dark. She had talked to the kids right before she left. They were fighting with each other and enjoying the beach.

She took a sip of water and wondered if there was time to go to the bathroom.

A man in blue jeans and an olive green pullover sweater sat behind a board of controls. He smiled at her. He knew she was nervous, and he'd been working hard to do the impossible and make her feel at ease.

He stroked the thick black mustache over his lip. "Don't forget the ten little words we can't say on the air."

"You'd just lose your license, I'd lose my job."

He looked reassured. "Here we go, then. If you have an uncontrollable urge to cough or throw up or something, just hold up one finger and I'll cover. Ready, two, three . . . and this is Ritchie Seevers on the air tonight with Specialist Sonora Blair of the Cincinnati Police Department's Homicide unit. Specialist Blair is . . . I'm right, aren't I? The lead detective on the Mark Daniels murder investigation?"

"I was the lead detective, yes. Not anymore."

Seevers touched his forehead. "Of course. For those of you who've been living in a vacuum, Specialist Blair's brother was the latest victim of the Flashpoint killer. Detective Blair is here to talk to us about the ongoing investigation of the truly heinous murder of Mark Daniels, who, as you likely remember, was burned alive in his car. She's also going to give us guys some safety tips." He laughed here, at the notion of men needing safety tips. "And if any of *you* out *there* have questions for Specialist Blair, be sure and give us a call."

Seevers paused, and Sonora wondered if she was supposed to make a comment. She could not think of anything particular to say.

Seevers smiled and went on. "Detective Blair, do you . . . let me interrupt myself, I think we have someone on the line."

"Hello?"

The voice was female. Sonora felt her heartbeat pick up.

"Yes, hello, you're on the air with Ritchie Seevers and Specialist Blair of the Cincinnati Police Department's Homicide unit."

"Oh. Hi, Ritchie. I listen to you all the time. And I wanted to ask a question."

"We're all ears here, but first would you tell us your name."

"Rhonda Henderson."

"How you doing, Rhonda, and thanks for calling in. What's your question?"

"My question? I just wanted to ask. Umm. So you're a girl and you're a police officer. Do you carry a gun like the men?"

Sonora crossed her legs and leaned back in the chair. "All police officers are required to carry a gun."

"Do you like, know how to use it?"

Sonora sighed, realized the big exhale was not such a great idea on live radio. Seevers went through a round of patter. Answered another caller, this one male. Sonora shifted her weight, trying to ease a knot of tight muscles in the small of her back.

"Ma'am, are you the police officer whose brother got killed in the saloon fire?"

"Yes, I am."

"You must feel awful."

Seevers shot her a sympathetic look. "Thank you for calling, sir. We appreciate your sympathy."

"You going to kill her when you run her down?"

Sonora crossed her legs. "It's my job to uphold the law, sir, not break it."

"But if it was my brother and I was you, I'd break her neck."

"I'm mainly interested in seeing she gets off the streets."

"How long's that going to take? I guess since she's killed one of your own, so to speak, I guess now maybe you folks will do something about bringing her in."

"No one understands your frustration better than I do, sir, but we've had a team of very fine officers tracking this woman from day one. All of them have worked around the clock, and will continue working long hours till she's caught."

"Yeah, but . . . "

Sonora felt heat rising in her cheeks. She tried to focus, thinking this was too soon after Stuart, that she was going to lose it and screw everything up. Seevers was waving at her. Another caller.

"I just want to know, where is your sympathy for this poor girl?" The voice was older, female with an angry edge. But not Flash.

Sonora sat back in the chair, mouth open. Where was her sympathy?

"I mean, get real, why don't you? You know and I know that only *men* kill for no reason. I assure you this poor girl's the victim here."

Sonora leaned close to the mike. "Ma'am, I sat in emergency with a twenty-two-year-old college student right after he was pulled out of a burning car. I guarantee you *he* was the victim."

"You just say that because he's your brother."

"He was not—"

The woman's voice jumped an octave. "You don't know what these guys did to this poor girl. Maybe they *forced* themselves on her."

Sonora made an effort to sound calm and steady. "Ma'am, I'm going to have to stop you, and make it clear that the Flashpoint killer stalked her victims, that she—"

"You know, you're not exactly an objective party, though, are you, Detective?" The voice was low now, tight.

Sonora bit the inside of her cheek. Selma had twitted some dark pool of feminine rage. There'd be no dealing with this one. Sonora wondered how many more like this there were out there.

"And I mean, no matter what *you* say, which we really can't trust 'cause of your brother and all, but no matter, you know very *well,* miss, that this girl probably got the shaft all her life. She could've been raped, you just don't know what kind of horrors might—"

Who are we talking about here, Sonora thought. You or her? She set her jaw.

"I do know, ma'am, that whatever her background, she's got no right to tie innocent men up and set them on fire. And that objectivity has nothing to do with tracking this woman down like the *dog* she is, which the Cincinnati Police Department *will do.*"

Seevers's voice came through with just the right touch of mellow, belied by the sweat on his brow. "And we thank *you,* ma'am, for sharing your viewpoint."

Sonora leaned back in the chair. She had made it through Stuart's funeral without shedding a tear, enduring the looks and whispers of everyone who watched and waited for her to crack. Seevers handed her a wad of tissues.

"We have time for just one more—" Seevers was looking a question, and Sonora swallowed and nodded her head. "Ritchie Seevers, with—"

"Hey, girlfriend, it's me."

Sonora's throat went dry. She looked at Seevers. His eyes were large, and a sheen of sweat popped across his forehead. He had exactly what he wanted, Sonora thought, and wasn't sure what he was going to do with it.

"I just called to tell you bye," Selma said.

Sonora frowned. "Why good-bye? You going somewhere?"

Selma laughed. "You'uns don't ever miss a chance, do you?"

"Why are you leaving?"

"You know why. It's gone bad. I got to go looking."

A victim, Sonora thought. She'd be stalking again.

"What is it you want, Selma? What you looking for?"

Long silence, and when the words came, they came slowly. "A place that makes me happy."

"Happiness comes from within," Seevers blurted, pop radio psychology bubbling forth.

There was a pause. "Not in me," Selma said. Like she was sleepy.

56

Crick rubbed the back of his neck. Gave Sonora a look. "Track her down like a dog?"

Gruber cleared his throat. "I believe the actual words were 'like the dog she is.' I got to say, sounded good to me."

Crick turned sideways. "Lieutenant Abalone did *not* agree."

"Hey, she's human," Molliter said.

"I am not."

Sam looked at her. "You're not human?"

Sonora frowned. Realized she was tired and not making sense. She had that awful feeling—tight chest, panicky flutters, hot and cold chills. "She sounded so weird, don't you guys think?"

"You're the expert," Sam said, "she talks to you."

"She was weird. Like . . . sad. Toned down. Almost pathetic." Sonora looked at Crick. "You talked to Dr. Fischer about this?"

"Yeah, but I don't have to. You're not feeling sorry for her, are you?"

"No. Course not."

"Good. That poor-little-me voice is just a nice piece of work that'll come in handy if we ever jerk her butt in front of a jury."

"That sounds like Crick talk, not shrink stuff."

"Yeah, well, Fischer talked a lot about degrees of stimulation, depressed states of—"

"What's that got to—"

"Let me finish. In a nutshell. Flash is fading. She needs a jolt to pick her up."

"Maybe she'll go home," Molliter said.

Sam shook his head. "She's depressed, not stupid."

Crick shrugged. "Been watching the place from the get-go. She knows we're there, she won't come back."

"Let's go in then," Sonora said. "Take Fischer's opinion to the judge."

Crick shook his head, opened his mouth. "They won't—"

There was a knock on the door, and Sanders poked her head in. "Sir?"

Crick ran a hand under his shirt collar. "Why the hell are we all crammed in here? No, don't back away, come in, Sanders."

"She can sit in my lap," Gruber said.

Sanders put a hand on her hip. "If you didn't eat so many doughnuts, you might have a lap."

Sonora saw Gruber's look of shock, closed her eyes, smiled a little.

"Ashley Daniels just called," Sanders said. "A woman who identified herself as Police Specialist Sonora Blair stopped by her office, her Allstate booth, just a little while ago."

Sonora scooted her chair sideways. "What's this?"

"I got her to describe the woman. She was small and blond, and Mrs. Daniels thought she looked familiar, but she knew it wasn't Sonora."

Crick cracked his knuckles. "You ever meet Ashley Daniels face-to-face, Sonora?"

"Briefly."

"It's Flash," Sam said.

Sanders nodded. "The woman wanted Ashley Daniels to go with her. For questioning. But when Mrs. Daniels asked to see ID—"

"Good girl," Gruber muttered.

"The woman said she'd left it in her jacket in the car. She tried to get Mrs. Daniels to go with her down to the parking lot, but she wouldn't go. So the woman said she was going to go get it, and she'd be right back. But she didn't come back."

"Okay," Crick said. "She went for the wife. She's going to blow."

"We got to put somebody on Keaton, sir."

"Yeah, we'll have to. We stirred her up. I don't want his death on my head."

Everyone was moving, on their feet.

"But why's this woman seem familiar?" Molliter said. "Ashley Daniels thought she looked familiar, right?"

Gruber waved a hand. "Probably because they worked within

thirty feet of each other for several months. We confirmed. Selma Yorke worked at H and R Block in the Sears at Tri-County Mall. All her coworkers say she had black hair."

"Wig. Probably same one she wore to Mark Daniels's funeral," Sam said.

Gruber looked at Sonora. "We also got her connected up to an H and R Block in Atlanta. Lennox Square, mile away from the bank where James Selby was a teller. It's a definite he got his taxes done there."

"She used the same name?" Sonora asked.

"Workers get bonuses if they continue one year to the next."

"All right, surveillance on Daniels." Crick looked at his watch. "Judge Markham leaves for Hilton Head and a week of golf in one hour, after which Judge Hillary Oldham will be on call. Oldham used to practice law with Lieutenant Abalone's brother Samuel, and she likes cops. I'm going to get a court order out of this. I want a look inside that house."

"Can I ride along?" Sonora asked.

"Sonora—"

"Please. In appreciation of doing the radio thing."

"I'm supposed to thank you for that?"

57

They took exit 1846—passed a chili place, Isadore's Pizzeria, warehouses, old stockyards. The Camp Washington Community Center had bars on the windows. A sign on the door designated it as a child safe place. A worn poster on a telephone pole touted THE ULTIMATE CHALLENGE—THE MEANEST MAN CONTEST.

Overhead came the roar of cars on the interstate. It was gray out, a fine mist of rain in the air. Sonora rolled down her window, heard the squeal of brakes on railroad tracks.

She glanced at Sanders, who sat on the edge of her seat in the back of the Taurus. "Sam, we need to make a stop on the way back. Sanders wants to get Gruber a dozen doughnuts."

Sanders giggled and Sonora grinned. Good old girls. Sonora glanced out the window at a billboard that said EVER TOAST A FRIEND? and showed a car in flames. The warning on the bottom said: FRIENDS DON'T LET FRIENDS DRIVE DRUNK.

Her smile faded.

The house looked worn and bleary, here at the end of the day, tucked behind a cluster of trees that were leafless and forlorn. Sam eased the Taurus into a tight spot behind a rusting, mustard yellow Camaro. A large woman in maroon polyester pants and a black sweatshirt watched them from her front porch. There was a plastic Santa Claus hanging under the woman's porch light. Sonora wondered if it was left over from last year, or if the woman was early with her decorating.

Sam got out of the car, stiff legged. "Crick made sure to let the guys watching the house know we were coming, Sonora. Didn't want 'em getting excited and taking you into custody."

"Thank you so much."

This time she knocked at the front door. No answer. Sam used the key he'd gotten from the landlord. The door swung open with a creak and sagged sideways—warped, ancient, and unloved. Sam motioned Sanders around to the back of the house, then stepped forward, gun ready. Sonora followed at his back.

The living room was tiny and coated in filth, and it looked like the world's biggest flea market, garage sale, basement from hell. Sonora took a breath of stale, sour air, thinking that Selma Yorke could be three feet away and they'd never know it. Cardboard boxes, sagging and old, were stacked in every available space, most of them filled with old magazines and dusty, yellowing newspapers. Plastic laundry baskets brimmed with old clothes, jewelry, worn shoes, hats, purses, books—everything that was ever in the bottom of a closet or stuffed back in a drawer.

Sonora poked through a laundry basket with torn webbing, finding old baby clothes, a high-button shoe, a strand of bright orange beads—the kind children would stash in a dress-up box. Everything was coated with a fine layer of grime.

Things were acquired and abandoned. Owning was enough.

The kitchen was neat and clean. The appliances were old, the white enamel chipped in places, rusting around the chips. The linoleum was cracked and had holes and creaked loudly beneath their feet. The countertops were crowded. Sonora counted five bread boxes—most of them old, battered, and ugly. A chipped plate, mug, and fork sat in the white, rust-stained sink. The dishes looked clean. Sonora touched them. Dry. She ran a finger along the bottom of the sink. Dry again. She went to the refrigerator—a short, old-fashioned box shape with a wide metal handle.

Not much inside. A large can of Hawaiian Fruit Punch, the triangular openings on the metal top orange with rust. Juice had dried and formed a pink crust in the edges.

The shelves were stocked with white Styrofoam take-home boxes, wrinkled McDonald's bags, a red-and-white box from KFC. A white bag was full of stiff, cold hamburgers in blue-and-white cardboard boxes—White Castle.

The crisper was empty. No fruit. No vegetables. Sonora checked the freezer. Popsicles and freezer pops. Fudgsicles. Dixie cups with ice cream—vanilla with swirls of fudge, vanilla with swirls of strawberry. Jell-O pops. Pudding pops. Ice cream sandwiches from Sealtest. The kind of treats a child would pick. No Breyers, no Häagen-Dazs, no Chunky Monkey from Ben & Jerry's.

The laundry room was a revelation—empty Coke cans lined neatly on the shelves, three fresh new bundles of clothesline, looped and held together by a sticky paper wrapper.

"It really is her," Sam said. He went to the back door and waved at Sanders.

Sonora headed up the bare wood stairs. They were warped, impossible to climb quietly. She paused in the narrow, dark hallway, smelled dust, heard the tick of a clock. Heard Sam, coming up the stairs behind her.

"Bathroom," Sam said, pointing.

The room was tiny and smelled of mildew. The woodwork had been stripped from the wall, showing a dark grungy gap between the warped end of the brown-stained linoleum and the water-spotted plaster wall. The medicine cabinet hung open, empty shelves orange with rust and dirt.

Selma Yorke had left a handful of cosmetics. A fat pink tube of Maybelline mascara, black-smudged, lay sideways by the sink. Sonora spotted the stubby end of an eyeliner pencil, no cap, and a tube of brownish red lipstick. Talcum powder spotted the dry sink, caked in the lumps of aqua toothpaste that dotted the basin. Sonora looked in the trash can.

"What you got?" Sam stood in the doorway, one eyebrow raised.

Sonora looked at him over her shoulder. "I hate it when you do that."

"Sneak up on you?"

"Raise one eyebrow."

"That's 'cause you can't do it."

Sonora tilted the trash can forward. Wads of pink bubble gum. A Fudgsicle wrapper, streaked with dried chocolate. And a sprinkling of baby-fine blond hair.

"She cut her hair. Looks like she just snipped the bangs. Old patterns, Sam."

"Old patterns and new trouble."

A soiled towel showed smears of brown, orange, and blue. Sonora sniffed and smelled turpentine. Black mildew spotted the caulking along the sides of the tub.

Sam flicked a finger. "Reckon there's pubic hair down there in the drain?"

"Yeah, yeah, have your fun."

They split up. Sonora walked into the bedroom on the left, finding an unmade, wrought-iron single that brought jailhouse bunks to mind. The sheets had pulled from the foot of the bed, exposing a yellow-stained blue-striped mattress. The pillow was flat, trailing feathers from an open seam. There were no blankets.

The walls were plaster, dirt over old avocado green paint. The carpet was thin, green, sculptured.

The dresser was cheap, the top drawer empty. The other three drawers were stuffed with wadded clothing, so full they did not close. Bits and pieces swelled over the edges—jeans, underwear, nylon shorts. Sonora went to the closet.

The double metal doors were shut tight.

Sonora put a hand on a loose plastic knob and yanked. The door stuck, squeaked, then gave way to a rumbling avalanche that tumbled to her feet.

Dolls. Old, new, modern, antique. Barbie, Chatty Cathy, Thumbelina. China, plastic, and bisque faces. Stray arms, legs, heads, little dresses, little shoes, marble and painted eyes, wide-open, unseeing.

Sonora heard footsteps, Sam calling her name. She stirred the mass. Nothing real. Just dolls and doll parts.

"Sonora?" Sam stood in the doorway, gun at the ready. "You okay? I heard you squeal."

"Did not."

"Looks like Annie's room in here." He jerked his thumb toward the other bedroom. "You better come see."

It was the better of the two bedrooms, and ran along the entire back of the house. It had originally been two rooms, but the separation wall had been knocked out. There were two windows along the back, ragged curtains thrust to one side to let light in through grimy panes.

On the left-hand side was a workshop—hammer, nails, scraps of wood in one corner, a portable Black & Decker table saw. A sturdy easel had pride of place in the center of the room, and a wood shelf held paints, brushes, turpentine. Stacks of canvases were propped against the wall and stuffed in the closet.

Sonora studied the work, unfinished but long dry, on the easel.

The colors were angry. Dirty reds, orange, and brown. The paint was thick and full of chunks—plastic buttons, shoelaces, little bits of clothes glued on. A patch of cold ice blue was incongruous on the left-hand side, oddly unrelated to the rest of the picture.

"Look at this, Sam. Look at this stuff."

He turned the stacks of canvases facing the wall. "Jesus H. Christ, Sonora, this is weird-looking shit."

"Now we know why she takes the clothes."

"Take a look over here."

Wood boxes were stacked four high and three across, most of them two feet by two square, joined together in a huge and bizarre dollhouse.

Each box was a still life, and all the dolls were male, dressed in clothes that had been rudely cut and stitched from men's blue jeans, cotton shirts, khakis. Some of the dolls sat at desks, some played baseball. The first one stood behind a roughly constructed counter in a crude facsimile of the lobby of a bank.

James Selby, Sonora thought.

She stretched out a hand, but did not touch the brown-eyed doll that stared blankly from behind the counter.

There was a gap in the dollhouse. The next-to-last wood box was missing—had that been Mark Daniels? The last box was empty, the wood raw and newly sawn. Sonora wondered who had been slated to go inside. Stuart? Keaton? A shoe box sat in the windowsill over the empty wood box. Sonora peeped inside.

The tea set was tiny and made of porcelain, perfect for the fingers of a very little girl. It was too fragile for a young child; it would not be a practical gift. But it was sweetly painted with blue forget-me-nots and had a tiny teapot with a lid, six round plates, and four cups and saucers. When Heather found it beneath the Christmas tree last year, she had left her other gifts in a pile of colored paper and ribbon, lined up all her tiny horses, and become lost in a child's fantasy where ponies drank out of teacups, wore ribbons in their tails, and conversed with little girls in nightgowns.

Sonora clutched the edge of the windowsill and sat down on the floor. In her mind's eye she saw Selma Yorke drifting through the lawn around her house, where Tim and Heather slept and played and took their baths. She saw Selma's greedy fingers on Heather's little tea set and wondered if one of the Barbies in the closet full of dolls had been abandoned outside by her forgetful daughter, then snatched up by a woman who handcuffed innocent men to steering wheels and burned them alive in their cars.

"Sonora? You just get tired all of a sudden?" Sam crouched beside her, looking unhappy.

"It's not like I didn't already know she was hanging around the house, right? I just need to sit down for a minute."

"Honey, you are sitting down."

58

Sam and Sonora sat in the parking lot of a Taco Bell, engine idling.

Sam patted her shoulder. "You cold, Sonora? Want my jacket?"

She did, but shook her head no. Watched raindrops trickle down the car window. "It's more comfortable to think people like Selma don't have feelings. But they do."

"I know. But, Sonora." He touched her knee. "Lots of kids are abused. Only a rare few turn into killers. If you could be there when she does what she does, if you could see her face when she kills. You wouldn't have sympathy for her at all."

"I know." She squeezed his hand. Sam winked and eased the car toward the drive-in window.

"Come on, girl. Eat something, you'll feel better."

"Get me some rice." Sonora dug the cellular phone out of her purse.

"What you doing?"

"Checking messages."

"Why don't you take it easy for ten seconds while we get something to eat?"

Sonora sat with the phone in her hand. Punched in numbers and listened. Sam took a plastic bag of food from the window.

Sonora looked at Sam. "Shelby Hargreaves."

He parked the car next to a handicapped spot. "Woman at the antique store?"

Sonora nodded. "Wants me to call. Give me your pen, let me write this number down."

"Here." Sam handed her a Coke.

She unwrapped a straw and stuffed it through the slot. Liquid bubbled up over the plastic lid and spilled on her pants. She took a drink, then propped the cup against the back of the seat.

"You're going to spill that," Sam said.

Sonora put the phone to her ear. "Ms. Hargreaves, this is Specialist Blair, Cincinnati PD."

"Detective Blair. Good."

Sonora watched Sam bite into a bean burrito. He ate them bland, no salsa.

"Look, it's that doll I told you about—the German bisque boy that this woman looked at, but didn't buy? It's missing. It's got to have been stolen."

Sonora rubbed her forehead. "You're sure?"

"It was here last night, but when I came in this afternoon, it was gone. I've looked all over for it, and nobody remembers selling it. And it's not in the inventory receipts."

Sonora felt nervous flutters in her chest, the panicky hot and cold feeling. "It was good of you to call, Ms. Hargreaves."

"I just—"

"No, I appreciate it. You've been a big help." Sonora hung up, saw Sam was looking at her. There were bean smears on the edge of his mouth. She handed him a napkin. "Selma went to the antique store and took the other doll. It's now, Sam, she's gearing up for another hit. She's going after him."

"She took the other doll?"

"*Somebody* did, and we both know who."

"Okay, stay calm, girl, we got Daniels covered. Just need to get hold of Blue Ash and let them know."

"I'm calling the school." Sonora made the call, went through the rigmarole of identifying herself, asking for Keaton.

"I'm sorry, Mr. Daniels is in class. I can take a message."

"This is an emergency. Call him to the phone, please."

"Just a moment, then."

Sonora rubbed a fist on her left knee. Took a sip of Coke. Sam ate another bite of burrito, chewing slowly.

The voice came back to the phone, sounding breathless. "I'm sorry, he doesn't answer his intercom. The Chapter One reading teacher is in the room and says he'll be right back. I'll have him call you then."

"I'll wait."

"But . . . I think he's in the little boy's room!"

"For God's sake," Sonora muttered.

"Pardon?"

"No, pardon me. I need you to give him a message just as soon as he comes out. No, wait, let me talk to your principal."

"He's at Central Office."

"Okay. You're aware of Mr. Daniels's situation?"

"We all are."

"Good. You can understand, then, that it is important for him to get this message. Tell him not to leave the school under any circumstances. Not until he hears from me, by phone or in person. My name is Blair. Detective Sonora Blair."

"Detective Blair. Got it. I'll deliver the message myself."

"Do me a favor, will you? Go stand outside the men's room, and see he gets it as soon as he comes out."

The woman promised she would in a very small high-pitched voice. Sonora hung up and chewed her lip. "I got a bad feeling, Sam."

"He's okay, don't panic here. We got him surveilled."

"I want to go to the school."

"Crick wants you out of the way, you know that."

"Sam, Blue Ash? This is their territory and they're doing the surveillance at the school, right? Our people don't pick him up till he's on the way home. I want to go over there. I want to see him, I want to warn him. I got—"

"A bad feeling, I know." Sam wadded the burrito wrapper and tossed it into the backseat. "Okay, we're going. Eat your rice on the way."

59

The parking lot of the Blue Ash Pioneer Elementary School was a gridlock of buses and parents picking children up in the rain. Two Blue Ash patrol cars blocked the circle drive, blue lights flashing.

"For God's sake, girl, quit chewing the strap of your purse."

"*Something's happened,* Sam."

"Wait till I stop the car, Sonora!"

She left the door hanging open. The concrete walk was wet. Small children with backpacks and lunch boxes huddled beneath the overhang. Sonora forced herself to slow down.

A uniformed officer stood in the front entrance, hand on her hip. Officer Brady. She recognized Sonora and waved her on.

"They're in the office."

Sonora nodded, didn't break stride. She turned the corner and went through the doorway.

"It's *her.*"

Sonora heard the gun being drawn and put up her hands. "Hey, I'm a *cop.*" She had their attention, anyway, a knot of uniforms, two men in plain clothes, several women in suits.

Sam ran in behind her, waved his ID. "*Damn* good way to get yourself shot, Sonora."

"Leave me alone."

"Or hit by a car. What you doing jumping out like that? You—"

Sonora felt someone tap her shoulder. The man was short and round, had a thin wedge of white hair and a red face that probably meant high blood pressure.

"Excuse me for interrupting your argument. I'm Detective Burton, Blue Ash." He looked at Sam. "You guys partners, married, or what?"

"Same difference," Sam said. "Is Daniels okay?"

Burton touched the top button of his shirt and loosened his tie. "Daniels is gone."

Sonora sagged against Sam. "I knew it. I told you I had—"

"A bad feeling. I know."

Burton motioned to a black plastic couch. "Why don't the two of you sit down, and let's see if we can't get to the bottom of this."

He turned to a woman sitting in a chair that had been pulled away from a desk. He was gentle and he talked slowly. "Mrs. Sowder, there's no need to feel bad. Nobody's blaming you."

The teacher was white faced and grim. She nodded.

"Now he told you he was just going to be gone a little while, and that he'd be back shortly, that right?"

"That's right."

Sonora stood up. "Excuse me, Mrs. Sowder, I'm Specialist Blair. Did you get the impression—"

Burton waved a hand. "Detective, I'd—"

"Burton, look, this is your jurisdiction, okay. I know I'm jumping right in the middle here, but it's my investigation, and while you and I squabble, this killer is going to off Keaton Daniels. Just let me talk to her a minute, *please*."

The please stuck in her throat, but turned the trick. Burton waved her on.

"He didn't check out with the front office, Mrs. Sowder, that right? Did you get the impression he was sneaking away?"

The teacher rubbed her eyes. "It wouldn't surprise me. He seemed really upset. And he also . . . he asked to use my car."

"Your car?"

"He said his was stalling out, and could he take mine. He said he'd be back in about twenty minutes."

"But he didn't say where he was going?"

"No, but he was . . . compelling. He was frantic."

Sonora frowned. "And he knew that if he didn't come back in twenty minutes you wouldn't walk off and leave the kids."

"Of course not."

"So he knew they were safe."

"Yes. I've been teaching in his class all year. We have a good working relationship. We're friends."

"And he did take your car?"

"Yes."

"But didn't say where he was going or why?"

"I think it had something to do with his wife."

"His wife? Why?"

"He had a message from her, so he called her from the office. That's when he came back and said he had to go out just for a short time, and would I watch the kids."

Sonora peered into Keaton Daniels's rental. Rain drenched her head and shoulders and dripped off the end of Sam's nose.

"Three things we know," Sam said. "One, he didn't want to take his car, or check out officially, which means he wanted to sneak away. Two, he left in the middle of the school day and didn't tell anybody he was going except that Mrs. Sowder. Three. What was three?"

"His wife."

"Yeah, his wife called. A woman who said she was his wife, anyway."

"It was her. Secretary recognized her voice."

"Come on, girl, let's get out of the rain."

Sonora leaned back against Keaton's car and bit the back of her hand. "Just let me *think*, Sam."

"That's the problem, Sonora, you can't think, you're too upset."

"*This* helps?"

They stared at each other. Sam's tie was plastered to his shirt. Sonora's hair hung in wet wavy strands along her shoulders.

"God, Sam, Flash is going to kill him. He may already be dead."

Rain splattered the pavement, and a steady stream of cars flowed through the circle drive. The crush of children gradually began to dissipate.

"Let's try the Allstate booth," Sam said.

Burton surrendered the phone like a gentleman. Sonora reached into her jacket pocket, found the business card Ashley Daniels had given her that first day. She twisted the phone cord, counted three rings.

"Allstate, Beatrice Jurgins."

Sonora identified herself, asked for Ashley Daniels.

"I'm sorry, she's out of the office. Can I take a message or can I help you?"

"Look, this is an emergency. I have reason to believe Mrs. Daniels is in some danger, and I need to speak with her at once."

The voice on the other end went up an octave. "She's not here."

"Where is she, do you know?"

"She had an appointment. Somebody called, and she asked me to cover for her in the booth. A hot lead, she said. I figured it must be life insurance."

"When was this?"

"She got the call this morning. She said she had to meet a prospect on their lunch hour."

"She give you a name?"

"No, but . . . hang on a sec. Maybe she put it down in her book."

Sonora waited. Looked at Sam. His hair was wet and sticking up on one side. She smoothed it back in place.

"Hello? You there?"

"Right here," Sonora said.

"Okay, I looked on her desk. She's got her book with her—"

Sonora's stomach got tight and painful.

"But," the tone was triumphant, "she wrote Ecton Park on a scratch pad, and I'll bet that's where she went."

"Ecton Park? Seems strange for her to be meeting a client in Ecton Park, don't you think?"

"Not if you can sell some life. And she did say she was catching them at lunch."

"Them or her?"

"It must have been a her, because she put on the fake glasses. She does that when she writes a woman, because Ashley's a dish and she likes to tone it down."

"She make a habit of meeting clients in out-of-the-way places?"

"Ashley's careful. If she doesn't know somebody, she tries to meet them in the office. But we have the fall life contest going right now, and Ashley's really close. Could mean a trip to Hawaii."

Sonora sighed. "When is she due back?"

There was a long silence. "She's already late."

"Not careful enough, then. Thank you, Ms. Jurgins."

Sam wiped his face with a handkerchief. "You say Ecton Park? That's in Mount Adams, right where Keaton lives."

"Yeah, and it's outdoors and wooded. Just exactly what appeals to Flash. I think Selma's got herself a hostage, and Keaton's gone to rescue his wife."

Sam was nodding. "I'll call Crick."

"Do it from the car. Let's hit the road."

"*I'm* driving."

60

It's a big park," Sam said.

"She'll be by the water."

"Fine, Sonora. That could be one of about five different places."

"What kind of car did that teacher drive?"

"Sowder? Toyota Corolla."

"Find the car, find Keaton."

Sam drove past the conservatory and a rusted-out water tower. Sonora saw a pool of shallow greenish water next to an empty gazebo. Raindrops spattered the surface.

"What's that?" Sonora asked. "A skating rink?"

"No, fountain. Turned off for the winter."

The Taurus glided close. Made a shark pass by a lone car parked by the fountain—a shiny black Datsun Z.

Sam looked at Sonora. "You know the make of car Ashley Daniels drives?"

"Black Datsun Z."

"Anybody inside?"

Sonora squinted through the rain-streaked window. "Hard to tell, the windows are fogged. I'm getting out."

Her leg brushed the wet back bumper of the Datsun, and her jacket plastered to her back like a second skin. She shivered, looked in the window, knocked on the glass. Tried the handle of the back door and found it unlocked.

Sonora wrenched the door open and crouched close to the ground, gun at the ready.

Nothing but the sound of rain. Insurance manuals and a brief-case were scattered across the back cushions. A red leather purse lay on the front seat, passenger's side. A console in the middle held a large paper cup from Rally's and a mounted car phone. A dark stain ran down the side of the upholstery.

Sonora opened the driver's door.

There were dark brown smudges on the rim of the steering wheel, and blood pooled over the accelerator and gas pedal. A black slingback pump, left foot, sat on the car dash.

Sonora heard footsteps and looked up into Sam's face. Rivulets of rain ran down his cheeks. She took a breath.

"This does not look good."

Sam grimaced. "Just talked to Crick. Park patrol did an extra round a few minutes ago, spotted the secretary's car up the road, near the main park entrance at an overlook."

"Anybody inside?" Sonora closed the door of the Datsun and headed for the Taurus.

"Guy wasn't sure, he didn't think so. Crick told him to glide in and out, business as usual."

Sam backed the Taurus out of the circle drive and made quick work up the hill. Crick was there ahead of them, looking into the empty Toyota.

Sonora put a hand on the door handle.

"*Wait* till I stop, Sonora."

Crick turned when he heard their footsteps.

"Nothing," he said.

"Look in the trunk?" Sonora asked.

Crick shook his head. "Not yet. Crowbar's in the back of my car."

"I'll get it," Sam said.

Sonora paced the parking lot, went to the edge to look out toward the river. It was hard to see in the drizzle, and she held the palm of her hand up, shading her eyes from the rain. Concrete stairs led from the overlook to another parking lot below, where there were cars, a swing set, another fountain that had been turned off. An overlook at the end of the lot gave a less lofty view of the river, which was gray now, churning with rain.

The steps were steep, leading down the side of the cliff. A man and a woman slipped into view, then disappeared.

"That's them," Sonora said.

Sam and Crick were at her elbow. "Where?"

She wasn't sure who had asked the question, maybe both. "On the stairs."

"I looked when I got here, I didn't see anybody," Crick said.

"They passed into view just a second ago."

"You sure?"

"Hell yes, I'm sure."

Sam started for the stairs, but Crick held his arm.

"You go charging off after them, she'll shoot him, and you."

"I'll shoot her first."

"Let's try to keep Daniels alive. We'll drive down, then go on foot."

Sonora looked down the cliffside, squinting. Something there, a path of some sort. Which made a certain sense. People never stuck to the stairs.

She pointed. "I'm going that way."

"Sonora—"

"Just to keep them in view. Everybody gets in the car, they could go anywhere. They're close to the bottom already. I won't approach, Crick, I'll just keep them sighted."

"Okay, go."

"I'm with her."

Sonora headed for the path, Sam at her heels. The closer they got, the steeper it looked.

"Shit, Sonora, we're never gonna make this."

Sonora grabbed the trunk of a tree, knees aching at the incline of the hillside. The dirt had turned gluey in the rain, slippery on the top. Her shoes sank in the brownish black sludge.

Six feet down the slope her feet stuck, then slid. She landed on her knees in the mud. Sam grabbed her arm and pointed. Spoke in a whisper in spite of the distance and the rain.

"Look, see? There they are."

Two drenched figures headed toward the river overlook.

"Run, Sonora."

Once they got their momentum going there was no way to stop. Rainwater pooled at the base of the cliff, and Sam and Sonora splashed through. Sam looked toward the parking lot.

"You see Crick?"

"No, and I don't see Keaton either."

"Must have gone over the guardrail."

"Okay, Sam, you circle left, I'm going behind them that way."

Sam looked one more time for Crick. Nodded. "Go, girl."

Sonora straddled the railing, climbed over the hill to the brush. On her left was the Kentucky River. She could see Barleycorn's Floating Restaurant and knew that if she went the other way she'd find the remains of the Sundown Saloon.

There was grass underfoot, waist-high weeds. Her shoes were heavy with mud. The rain picked up, her clothes streamed water. She half-ran half-walked, moving down the path. Rounded a bend. And there they were, no more than three yards ahead. Just out of reach.

Sonora stood still for a moment, catching her breath. Her spine felt tingly, palms suddenly wet. It was almost absurd, the tiny blonde next to the large, broad-shouldered male.

In her mind's eye she saw the bloodstained shoe in Ashley Daniels's car, the fan of blood-soaked upholstery.

She raised her gun, aimed with the utmost care. Keaton was still too close, but he was pulling ahead. She waited till he was clear. Held her breath and fired.

Selma Yorke flinched and turned around, blond hair dark with rain. No hit.

"Police," Sonora said. "Selma Yorke, you are under arrest. Stand aside, Mr. Daniels. Move it, move now, drop that gun—"

"Sonora, she's got Ashley stashed out here in the woods. She's hurt, but she's still alive." Keaton held up a jacket, sun yellow around splotches of blood.

Selma looked at Sonora. "You found me."

That first time Sonora had seen her, there in the cemetery, it had been a letdown, how drearily normal Selma looked. Today, even with the short blond hair plastered with rainwater, she was oddly pretty—cheeks pink and flushed, an edgy air of energy and purpose. She met Sonora's eyes just for a moment, then looked away, gaze shifting like a lightning flash. Sonora had seen it twice before, this inability to focus and meet a gaze. Both times from someone on the verge of major breakdown.

"Put the gun down, Selma."

Selma cocked her head to one side. "You'uns could have shot me right in the back. How come you didn't?"

"I tried, I'm a bad shot, that's all."

Selma laughed, but Sonora registered the flicker of pain that came and went.

"Come on, Selma. Put it down, and we can go somewhere dry and warm and talk."

Selma shook her head. "This isn't about us, Detective. This is about me. Me and him." She put her gun to Keaton's head.

The nightmare, coming true. Sonora gritted her teeth. "Let it go, Selma. You don't have to do this."

"I do have to."

"No, you don't."

"I want to."

Sonora steadied her aim. "Out of the way, Keaton."

"Don't move," Selma told him.

Keaton looked at Sonora. "Look, if there's any chance—"

"Ashley's dead, Keaton. Her car's full of blood."

"You *know* she's dead?"

"I saw her body, now *move*. Go!"

"Girlfriend, you'uns are fibbing and you know it."

Keaton looked at Sonora and she knew, from the expression on his face, who he believed.

"Keaton, she's playing with you."

He shook his head. "I've got to see her. I want to see Ashley."

Selma looked at Sonora. "Want to?"

Golly gee, Mom, look what I did. Sonora knew better than to refuse.

"Come on, Detective. You first, then him and me. And you lose your gun now, or I'll shoot him right here." She put the muzzle of the gun at the hollow of Keaton's throat, and Sonora remembered kissing him there, and the way his arms felt when he pulled her close.

She blinked, set the gun on the side of the path. Wondered where the hell Sam was.

Selma motioned with her head. "That way. Toward the river."

Sonora turned her back and walked.

She waited for the gun to go off, another little game, but the sound of footsteps and heavy breathing let her know they were no more than a few feet behind. Up until now, all her energy had been focused on the chase, bringing Selma in. She would be grateful, now, if she could bring Keaton out alive.

She picked up the blood trail as they moved downhill, a rusty smear on a sapling. She imagined Ashley Daniels stumbling down the path, thought of the blood-soaked shoe in the car, the forced march through the rain. She wondered if there was the smallest possibility Keaton's wife was alive.

The mud caked on the hem of her jeans slowed her down.

Sonora smelled the river, the rain, realized that if she lived, she'd never be able to look at the muddy waters of the Kentucky without remembering. She saw the footprint out of the corner of one eye, a long smear where someone had fallen. Saw Ashley Daniels's black slingback pump lying on one side, caked with mud. Sonora turned and faced Selma.

"Where is she?"

Selma pushed hair out of her eyes. "Keep on going and I'll show you."

"I don't think so." Sonora pointed to the shoe. She heard Keaton's intake of breath, saw him surge toward the edge of the path.

"No." Selma had the gun up.

He'd never survive a shot that close, Sonora thought.

"She goes," Selma said.

Sonora moved to the edge of the path. Looked over her shoulder. Keaton was white, rain running down his cheeks. She was afraid to turn her back, afraid he'd be dead if she moved too far away.

Selma moved the gun. "Right down there."

There would have been more blood, Sonora decided, if not for the steady drum of rain. The ground sloped steeply, and she braced herself by hanging on to the thicket of trees. She could see Selma and Keaton when she turned her head, knew they were watching.

A patch of yellow caught her eye, sunny yellow showing behind a fallen tree. Sonora slid down the slope to look.

It was the feet that bothered her the most, the ripped stockings and torn flesh. She imagined Ashley Daniels, bleeding and afraid, stumbling through the woods to her death.

Her manicure was intact, she had not fought. Her white silk shirt was sodden, showing the outline of the lace demicup bra, pink flesh beneath. Her shirt was liberally stained, as if she'd had a lapful of blood.

She'd been shot once, in the stomach. Sonora looked at the black gaping wound, surprised that Ashley had lived as long and walked as far as she had. There were drag marks through the leaves. Ashley had likely collapsed on the path, losing the shoe, and Selma had dragged her a few feet into the woods—not far—hiding her behind the rotting tree.

And now Selma was marching them right past the body; to where? The river, no doubt.

Sonora went through the motions, touching the cold wet hand, the side of the neck, avoiding the wide-open violet eyes, the oddly grumpy look on Ashley Daniels's face, as if she had merely been inconvenienced rather than in exquisite pain and fear.

Sonora looked back up to Keaton and Selma. She could make a break and run. She knew it and so did Selma. Might even catch Selma—should be cops everywhere by now. But she'd never get Keaton out alive.

Sonora headed up the slope, saw Keaton watching her, a hungry look. She avoided his eyes, grimaced at Selma.

"Now what?"

"The river," Selma said. She pointed with the gun. "Let's go."

Sam would be close, Sonora thought. Crick, and uniforms, and reinforcements. Time was on her side.

"Okay, the river."

"Wait a minute."

Sonora and Selma looked at Keaton as if they'd forgotten he was there.

"Did you . . . what did—"

Sonora touched his arm. Selma flinched and moved in closer. Sonora kept her voice low and calm.

"It wasn't her, Keaton. She's down by the river, probably, like Selma says."

"She's over there," Selma said. Flatly. A dangerous tone in her voice.

Sonora swallowed, mouth so dry she wanted to stick her tongue out and catch a drop of rain. Keaton shook his head, eyes taking on a flat glaze that made Sonora reach for him. He twisted sideways, a fast graceful pivot, and grabbed Selma by the throat.

Sonora surged toward them, saw the frown on Selma's face screw into a mask of rage, knew she would be too late. The shot was deafening, and so close Sonora almost felt the impact.

There was a moment of quiet as they stood together, like a trio of close friends, Keaton and Sonora shoulder to shoulder, Selma small and clutching the gun, the ragged fringe of short wet bangs like spikes across her forehead.

Keaton did not fall or groan or even seem to be aware of the crimson blossom spreading across his chest. He kept his grip on Selma's throat.

Sonora felt rather than saw the gun come back up. She shoved Keaton sideways, and he let go of Selma and fell. Sonora landed hard on his chest, waiting for the bullet that she knew would come.

But it didn't. She felt Keaton's blood warm his shirt and hers, felt the swift hard beat of his heart.

"Get *away* from him."

Sonora turned her head sideways. Selma was still on her feet, legs apart, bottom lip caught beneath little white teeth.

"Out of the way, girlfriend. Bullet go right through you into him, no difference to me."

"I thought he was different, Selma."

"You'uns thought wrong, we both did. I need to keep looking, that's all. Now you got about thirty seconds to move."

Sonora hung tight to Keaton, warm, solid, and wet under her chest. "No."

"You'uns don't believe I'll shoot."

"Yeah, I believe it."

Selma looked at her. "So now what?"

"You're under arrest. You have the right to remain silent—"

They said Selma never smiled, and it came and went so quickly Sonora wasn't sure it was ever there. And just like that Selma was gone, running toward the river in the rain.

Sonora moved off Keaton, put a palm flat against the hole in his chest. The bleeding had stopped, the pressure of her chest against his cutting the flow. His face was white, lips purple.

He opened his eyes. "Why'd you stop me? I could . . . I could have had her."

"Keaton—"

"Don't touch me." He jerked suddenly, eyes fierce. "Did she suffer? My wife?"

"No," Sonora said.

"You always tell me lies, Sonora."

She left him, chest trickling blood in the mud and the rain. Later, when the nightmares came, she would dream of him there, chest rising slowly with each painful breath, yards away from Ashley's body.

Sonora ran down the path toward the river, wondering why Selma hadn't shot her when she'd had the chance.

Rain pelted her head, and the drenched jacket slapped her thighs. Her breath came hard. She ripped the jacket off as she ran, threw it down on the pathway, ran harder.

Sonora heard the gun go off just as she caught sight of the river, water swirling around Sam's and Selma's knees as they struggled for control. Sam fell backward, taking Selma with him, brown droplets spattering Sonora as she ran full tilt into the river.

Selma came up first, small blond head like a seal. She looked like a very little girl, wet, angry, and afraid. Sonora felt the shock of water, warmer than she'd expected, and she wrapped her arms around Selma's shoulders, thinking with surprise how small boned and fragile she felt.

"Sam!"

He surfaced just as Sonora called his name, still alive, strong, in one piece.

"Thank God," Sonora muttered.

Selma screamed and Sonora tightened her grip, but Selma bucked sideways and slipped away. Sonora pitched forward after her, missing and going under. She was back up in a second, coughing, rubbing her eyes.

"I got her," Sam said, and he pulled Selma up out of the river, one hand on her neck, the other a tight fist in her hair.

61

The basketball goal had not been in the budget but had proven to be a good investment. Sonora threw shot after shot. She was getting good. She played every time she saw Selma in her head. She played a lot.

Sometimes, late at night when she could not sleep, she wondered what would happen if she and Selma were merged into one—wondered which side would dominate, the good or the bad. Did she have enough good in her to balance Selma's bad? Was there a good part of Selma—or could there be? What would a good Selma be like?

Sonora thought of her brother, the hot charred remains of his little apartment in the saloon.

Nothing good in Selma Yorke.

So why hadn't Selma killed her that day in the rain? Killed her and gotten away?

The front door opened, and Tim and Heather came out onto the porch. They looked at each other, whispered something, and stood at the edge of the driveway, bundled up in their jackets and gloves.

Sonora wished she could make her mind go blank. She had not slept more than an hour or two a night since she'd brought Selma in. She lay in bed, wide-eyed, hour after hour. The only time she felt sleepy was when she was driving. Which was bad timing, any way you looked at it.

"Mommy?" Heather looked at Sonora, eyes serious behind the tiny gold-rimmed glasses. "Come in now, Mommy. It's cold."

"I'm playing." Sonora bounced the ball hard on the concrete.

Tim and Heather looked at each other, exchanged more whispers.

"Mom, want to watch *Witness*?"

"No, thanks."

"Want some chocolate?"

"You kids go ahead."

Tim frowned. "Can we play basketball with you, Mom?"

"Don't you have homework? Algebra, Tim?"

"We did our homework, made up our beds, and cleaned our rooms."

Sonora stopped and looked at them. Really looked. Doing their homework, making their beds, cleaning their rooms—that caught her attention. Offering her chocolate, her favorite movie. And something like a catch in their voices.

She had been looking at them and not seeing them for too many days in a row. There were times when it had to be like that—real-life moms with real-life jobs, and intervals where your attention and focus slipped away, and you told the kids to hang in there, let me catch this killer, then we'll get your school clothes, your new shoes, spend one day in the malls, and one at the movies or something fun.

But there were limits. And she realized, looking at them standing side by side, breath fogging the air, what babies they were. And how much she expected of them. Too much, maybe.

High time she got back to looking after them, instead of the other way around.

She should tell them she loved them, should tell them how proud she was of them both, but before the words came, Tim had snatched the ball.

"Mom, you're looking pitiful out here. If you want to shoot, do it like this."

The ball slid through the net, and Heather snatched it up and tossed it into the air. It went wild and rolled into the street. Sonora heard a car engine. Ran to the edge of the driveway.

The car came to a halt, and the driver motioned Sonora ahead. She hurried across the street, and the driver waited, motioned her back. Patient of him, she thought, and took a second look.

Keaton. He parked in front of the house and got out of the car.

The children watched from the driveway. They looked annoyed. One moment they'd had her attention, and now it was gone again.

Keep this short, Sonora thought. She bounced the ball on the sidewalk. "Good to see you up and around."

"You didn't come and visit me at the hospital," Keaton said.

He had lost weight, too much weight. His eyes held a hunted look that gave Sonora the panicky feeling that maybe time did not heal all wounds, that scars could run too deep. She wanted to touch him, brush the back of her hand on his freshly shaven cheeks.

Don't touch me, he had said. *You always tell me lies.*

Sonora kept the ball bouncing in a slow steady rhythm. She had called the hospital every day until he was out of danger, but saw no reason to bring it up.

"Let's walk a little," he said finally.

Sonora handed the basketball to her son. "Play with Heather, I'll be back in a minute."

Heather had her solemn look, chin down, and Sonora hesitated, then ran back and hugged her, whispering promises of the dinner they would cook, the fire they would build in the fireplace. It took a promise of Victoria's Secret bubble bath to bring the chin up and the smile out.

Sonora stood up, brushed Heather's hair out of her eyes, saw Keaton still and patient. She noticed a startling touch of gray in the hair at his temples.

He waited till she was beside him before he started walking. "I missed Ashley's funeral. Did you go?"

"Yes," Sonora said, trying not to remember.

"I'm glad. So, what's going to happen with her?"

They both knew who he meant.

"She'll plead insanity, and I think it'll fly. Then she'll be put in an institution for the criminally insane and periodically petition to leave. Which will never happen, hopefully. But she won't be executed."

He put a hand on her arm. "I wanted to thank you for saving my life, that day. And to tell you that you're a very good cop."

He bent down and kissed the top of her head. They walked back to the driveway and the children, who were staring wide-eyed and watchful.

Keaton snatched the ball from Tim and dribbled it up to Heather. She shook her head.

"I never have got a basket. I'm too little."

He lifted her high in the air beneath the net. "You just need a little extra height."

Heather threw the ball and it touched the rim, rolling around the edge. Sonora held her breath. The ball fell through the hoop.

"Swisher!" Heather said, waving a hand in the air.

62

S am put a cup of coffee on Sonora's desk. She said thanks but
didn't look up, intent on getting her lipstick straight.

"Why don't you call it quits, girl?"

Sonora glanced at Sam. He was glaring at her, rubbing the back
of his neck.

"I mean it, Sonora. We got her up one side and down the other.
We're putting files to bed every which of way, the casebook is a
beauty. We got more physical evidence . . . quit looking in the mirror and talk to me."

"Sam, we've had this conversation."

"You don't have to be the one talks to her, Sonora."

"She wants me."

"Who cares? You still feel like you owe her?"

"I do owe her."

"Sonora." He took hold of the mirror, but steadied it instead of
snatching it away. "Look, girl. Look at your eyes. Look at the shadows *underneath* your eyes. Now I talked to Crick, and he said all
you got to do is say the word."

Sonora looked into the mirror, remembering her first week
working homicide.

She'd been invited to a drunken pub crawl in honor of one
Burton Cortina, who was moving to Fraud and Forgery. He had
been kind to her, taking the time to make her feel welcome when
she was brand-new and shy.

They'd talked amiably and loosely, strangers who'd had too
much to drink and the comfortable knowledge that their paths

were unlikely to cross in the near future. They had both confessed homicide their highest ambition, and had a beer on it. Sonora had been unable to look at him without pity.

"You think I'm crazy, giving it up, don't you, slugger?"

Sonora shrugged.

"I know how you feel, probably better than you do yourself." He had glanced in the mirror behind the bar, then faced her with a dead look in his eyes that she'd seen on other cops, older cops. "All I can tell you, slugger, is that one day it gets to be enough."

That was all he'd said, but the words had stuck, hanging over her head like a threat.

"I'm okay, Sam."

"Yeah? And how's your ulcer?"

"Gone."

"Gone? No kidding?"

"No kidding." Sonora blew on the mirror, fogging her reflection. It was true. Since that day by the river, the anger she'd felt for who knew how long had drained away, giving her a centered, steady feeling. She didn't hate them anymore—not her dead husband, not Chas, not her father. Not Selma. The ulcer hadn't twinged since.

Sonora checked her watch. Almost time. She called home to check on the kids—in the middle of these long sessions with Selma Yorke, she needed to hear the voices of her children.

They were fighting over the last blueberry bagel. Sonora told them to split it—radical thought—and hung up. Checked her watch again. Grabbed her notes.

Gruber gave her a thumbs-up when she passed him in the hallway. She peered into the interview room. Selma was already there, sitting complaisantly beside her lawyer, Van Hoose. Van Hoose always managed to keep a poker face but was often pale and shaky by the end of each session. Sonora saw major counseling in his future before the year was out.

She studied Selma, as she always did, wondering if Dr. Fischer was right, if she'd been reaching out, going through some weird metamorphosis. Wondered about the anguished Selma in the phone calls. Wondered why a woman who could douse someone with gasoline and set them on fire wouldn't shoot her when she had the chance.

Sonora pushed through the door, startling the lawyer but not Selma, who sat quietly, hands on the table. She had cut her bangs again, which meant things were not going well. Her brown eyes were bloodshot, hands steady. She wore prison denims. She looked small.

"Hello, Selma." Sonora nodded at the lawyer, who said hello. She put a fresh tape in the machine, sat across from Selma. Tapped a pen on the edge of the table. "Selma, you want a Coke or something?"

"No."

Sonora made a note in her interrogation log. It was her habit to keep track of everything—time in, time out, every offer of refreshment, cigarettes, bathroom breaks. No rubber hose in Cincinnati.

"Let's talk about your brother today," Selma said.

Sonora pushed away from the table. "Let's not. Let's talk about the fire again, where your parents got killed."

Selma frowned. "We already talked about that."

"Did you do it, Selma? Did you set that fire?"

There was a tap on the door. Sonora got up, frowning. Gruber.

"Sorry. Phone call for the counselor, supposed to be urgent."

Sonora looked over her shoulder at Van Hoose.

"I'll take it. Only be a minute." He left the room like he was glad to go.

Sonora closed the door behind him. Turned off the tape recorder, looked at Selma. Bad seed? Anything good, anything salvageable? She was having long talks with Molliter about this, and neither one of them was happy.

Sonora sat down and leaned across the table. "Just you and me, Selma. Did you set that fire?"

"I got something for you." Selma reached into her pocket, and Sonora felt her heart skip. Selma slid a cassette across the table.

Sonora picked it up, read the label. Whale songs.

Sonora swallowed. "This what your parents sounded like, the night they died?"

Selma looked at the floor. "All of 'em sound like that. Stuart did."

Sonora felt the wash of tight, panicky breathlessness that came whenever she thought of her brother.

"Why didn't you kill me that day in the park?"

Selma looked up. This time there was no question, no mistake. Selma Yorke smiled, lips curving gently in a way that was eerie and sensuous.

And Sonora wondered who had who.